KATHRYN TROY

NIGHT OF STORMS AND SORROW

FROSTBITE BOOK THREE

NIGHT OF STORMS AND SORROW
Frostbite, Book 3

CITY OWL PRESS
www.cityowlpress.com

Cover Design by MiblArt. All stock photos licensed appropriately.

Edited by Tee Tate.

For information on subsidiary rights, please contact the publisher at info@cityowlpress.com.

Print Edition ISBN: 978-1-64898-572-0

Digital Edition ISBN: 978-1-64898-573-7

Printed in the United States of America

BOOKS BY KATHRYN TROY

Curse of the Amber

The Shadow of Theron

A Vision in Crimson

Dreams of Ice and Shadow

Night of Storms and Sorrows

PRAISE FOR KATHRYN TROY

"Exciting and engaging from the first page to the last, *The Shadow of Theron* is a high fantasy filled with romance, magic, and twists and turns that will keep the reader enthralled from beginning to end." — *Elayna R. Gallea, author of Tethered*

"Major Zorro vibes... excellent writing with gorgeous vocabulary." — *R.M. Krogman, author of The Keepers of Midgate*

"A vibrant, vivid world with a rich culture and complex religious system that draws the reader in... *The Shadow of Theron* is an exciting and riveting fantasy novel with an intriguing plot and well-developed characters that will keep the reader engaged until the end." — *Briar Boleyn, USA Today Bestselling author of Queen of Roses*

"Brimming with pulse-pounding adventure and sweet romance, this retelling of Zorro was such a joy to read." — *Olivia Wildenstein, author of House of Beating Wings*

"A wonderful book, fantastic action, a detailed and rich living world, and full of a passion you don't see too often in the genre. A can't miss!" — *Joshua C. Cook, author of Blood of a Fallen God*

"The heart of *Curse of the Amber* has the ability to steal the reader's breath and not return it until the very end. With the amount of details, as far as not only the story but also the glance into archeological procedures, the audience often feels they are living a different life rather than merely reading... There is a solid hook from the very start that no one is able to resist- pulling one in and giving them the ride of their lives." – *InD'tale Magazine*

To the First-Born Daughters:
"Beware; for I am fearless, and therefore powerful."
– Mary Shelley, Frankenstein

AUTHOR'S NOTE

This book is intended for a mature audience. It includes instances graphic violence, self-harm, suicidal thoughts and ideation, ambiguous consent, sexual assault and child abuse.

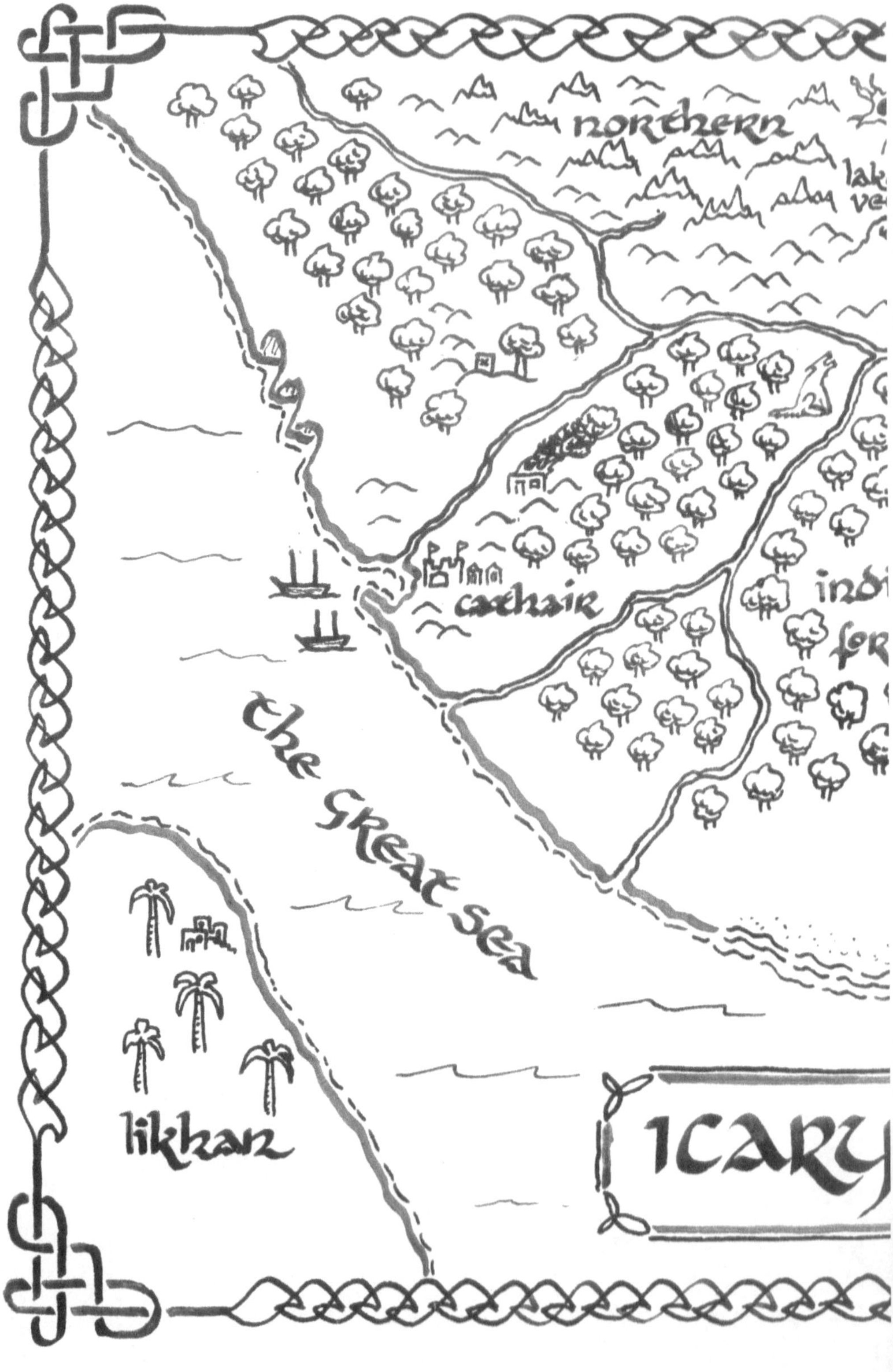

northern
lake ve
cathair
indi
for
the great sea
likhan
ICARY

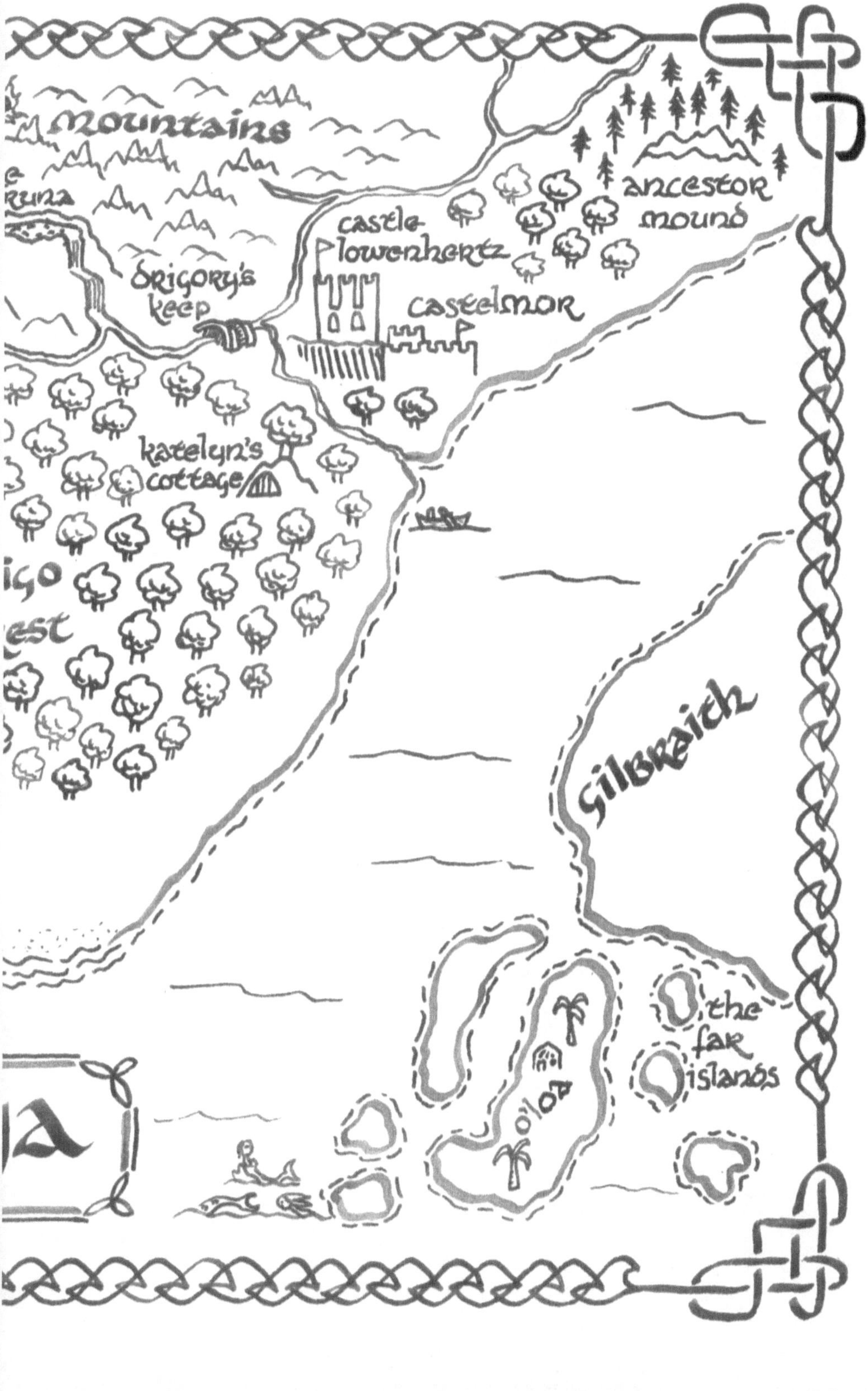
mountains
castle lowenhertz
ancestor mound
grigory's keep
castelmor
katelyn's cottage
gilbraith
the far islands

PROLOGUE

Haydee fled to the desert, carried on the shadows by an infernal wind that howled between the buildings of Likhan and out to the Burning Sands. She quit the shadows as night fell, collapsing onto a dune that slid under her weight until she reached a flattened area surrounded on all sides by wind-whipped mounds. Her breath was ragged, and she gasped for the clean air of the night. The smell of her own seared flesh filled her nostrils and invaded her lungs, choking her. She tentatively raised her fingers to her cheek, straining against unseen bonds to confirm what she already knew. The flaming fetters had ruined her face, and would not abate until they had dug down to the bone and turned her skull to ash. Her silk robes lay in scorched tatters. Haydee rolled onto her side and screamed, piercing the far-reaching silence. Countless grains of sand had entered the channels furrowed across her once-proud cheeks, nose, and chin as her face had touched the shifting ground. They bit into her wounds, multiplying her agony.

Haydee felt the last traces of life seep out of her skin, swirling and hovering in the night sky like midnight tentacles, hungry for their promised feast. She lay with her eyes turned skyward, and allowed her hatred to coil around her charred heart. Hatred for her parents. For Reza and Mehmnet, for Darien. For the Icaryan Queen. She felt the shadows snake and swirl around her limbs, pulling her apart. The sky shifted in its blackness, and she saw the night shudder with the darker shadows of the dead realm. At last, she could see both as they were, and would see neither evermore. She exhaled, welcoming the shadows until her flesh was devoured. Nothing remained, as though she'd never been there, had never *been* at all. The obsidian cloud thundered, charged with violence. With vengeance. The cloud spread outward, stretching and billowing until it became a thick blanket over the desert floor. The heavy storm rumbled above the sand, retracing a path that carved through the desert and back toward the pulsing rhythm of life—toward the city.

1

By the time Luca and Kate came down to breakfast, there wasn't much left on the table.

"Can I get some fresh eggs, please?" Kate asked as she took her customary seat. Luca set about picking over what was left of the bread and cured meat and assembled an array of jams in a little arc around himself.

She felt his eyes on him, knew what he was waiting for.

Her cheeks warmed at his expectant gaze. She cleared her throat and folded her hands in her lap. In the most subdued voice possible, she said, "So…we're getting married."

Cyrene's face brightened, her mouth opening wide to the shape of an "o." Before she could say anything, Allistair blurted, "Well I should hope so!"

"Aw shut up, will you." Kate's cheeks flushed a violent crimson.

Ted kicked him under the table. "What's the matter with you?"

"What?"

"Can't you see that they're happy?"

"It's wonderful news!" Cyrene chimed in.

"This isn't 'jolly old England,' ya dunce!" Ted cried. "If she's getting married it's because she *wants* to get married, yeah?"

"I just *said* that it was a good thing, didn't I?"

Ted threw his hands up in the air.

Kate hid her face in her hands. "Oh my god."

Luca watched this little drama unfold with a smile. He spread his palm across Kate's back and said, "It was a long time coming."

Kate emerged from behind her hands. Her smile was brilliant.

"See?" Ted insisted.

"Honestly, Allistair." Cyrene frowned.

"Right. Sorry. Couldn't be happier!" Allistair pasted on a smile that caused Kate to spit out the food she had just begun to chew.

"Oh, that's lovely," Allistair said.

"You're an idiot, you know?" she retorted.

"I have an inkling."

The smile Allistair wore as he rose from his chair was genuine. The rest of the people seated around the table followed suit, and Kate and Luca stood just in time for a round of congratulatory hugs.

"The eggs are going to be cold again by the time I get to eating them."

"Sit, sit," Ted urged. He rubbed his hands together greedily as he resumed his seat. "I've been waiting a long time to plan a wedding."

Kate put her fork down at that. "Oh, no."

Ted's face fell. "No, you can't!"

"I do not want some big, overblown wedding with people piled high as the rafters, partying until god knows when. You'll never get them all out!"

Ted flopped back into his seat, deflated. "You're no fun."

"I don't care."

Luca could see what was on her mind as she took a long drink of her tea. A big wedding would take time to plan. Time that would see her round in her wedding dress, or with a babe in her arms. The picture of herself she was conjuring in her head, in the most extravagant dress she would ever wear yet robbed of her figure, filled her with dread. Ted's abundant disappointment cut in on her thoughts.

"If not here, then *where?*"

"Why not the glen? I do live there, after all."

"But you live here too." Ted crossed his arms over his chest, inconsolable.

"Why don't *you* get married, then? Then you can do whatever you like."

"It's not fair! I've been waiting for so long—"

"And you're going to wait some more."

Luca stepped in before things got any more heated, folding Kate's fingers together with his own.

"I can't think of a single Icaryan who *wouldn't* be disappointed if they'd missed the marriage of their queen."

"That's right!" Ted barked, more animated now that he had found a ready ally. "Can you imagine the lot of them being told, 'sorry, you're not invited?'"

Luca felt Kate falter. The belly she pictured in her head swelled bigger and bigger, almost to bursting.

"What about…a large wedding…in the glen?"

Kate blinked.

"It wouldn't take you that long to plan, would it, Ted?"

Kate's nerves crackled between her shoulders. She wasn't accustomed to having to confront her vanity. But there it was.

And Luca was right there, eager to accommodate such a selfish wish. She couldn't help but smile and lean into him.

Ted caught on quickly. "No time at all."

Kate thought for a moment beyond her own desire.

"I need to go back to Likhan…"

"I know," Luca said. "And I'll go with you. But let's rest, just a little while, and do this one thing for ourselves."

For the first time that morning, Kate seemed to seriously consider it.

"We still have eight months, seven I suppose. That should be enough time to—"

Kate paused as she spied Luca's face. He had gone deathly pale. Her words had made him remember.

"Uh…"

"*What.*"

"You may not have seven months."

Kate blinked. "What do you mean?"

"A vampire is born much quicker than a human child."

"Oh!" Cyrene's hand flew to her mouth. Allistair put a quieting hand on her shoulder.

"How long?" Kate asked.

"But this child would be three-quarters human, so there's no telling—"

"How. Long?"

Luca's face contracted, bracing for her reaction. "Six months. Or maybe…three or four."

"But Kate, didn't Drigory say you were already—oomph!"

"Shut up, Al," Cyrene said.

"Excellent." Kate pursed her lips and took the news with subdued grace.

"It'll be fine," Luca cried, desperate for her to believe it. "You'll be fine."

I promise.

Kate took a deep breath and slowly let it out. "Right. Well. Ted?"

He sat upright. "Yes?"

"The glen. Two weeks. Can you do it?"

He opened his mouth, then shut it again, several times, like a fish out of water as he searched for the right words.

His sister was out of patience.

"Can you do it or not? If it's going to be slapped together, just tell me."

"It'll be perfect. I promise."

THE BANKED FIRE DREW KATE'S IMMEDIATE ATTENTION AS SHE AND LUCA retired to their chambers. Ash was all that remained of the spells Kate had fed to the flames the night before, but she soiled her hands sifting through it anyway. Just to be sure.

Luca didn't bother to dissuade her. He knew she wouldn't breathe easy until every last speck was swept away as she cleaned the hearth and went about setting a fresh fire. And anyway, he had other things on his mind. Things *he* had left unfinished.

"Before we leave for Likhan…"

"I haven't forgotten."

"I heard him, summoning everyone to the Ancestor's Mound. But he wasn't there. What do you think it means?"

Kate piled more wood into the hearth. She took her time before answering. I don't know. We'll check the cave in Cathair before we leave for Likhan. I promise."

That was all either of them could do for now.

"Come here," Luca said.

He settled next to her before the fresh fire, and stretched out his arms to envelop her in a warm embrace. This morning was cold, colder than he had witnessed since he'd come to Icarya. He wouldn't be surprised if it snowed again soon. She sat with her back half to him, giving him the chance to admire the glow on her cheeks, warmed by the fire, and the gold that flickered in her hair as the reflection of the flames danced through it. Sparks danced in her deliciously brown eyes that had, if only for a moment the day before, turned red.

It pleased him more than he thought it would to see her like that, her eyes filled with that familiar bloodlust. He wouldn't see it again for a long time, he knew, but they were agreed. He would turn her, in time. The thought of it made him flush with desire.

2

Darien stifled a yawn. It wouldn't do for him to appear disinterested, not after the esteemed family before him had taken such pains to present their daughter to him with all the pomp they could muster. But it was the third such visit he'd had in as many days, and he had not eaten. It was hard.

And the girl in question had yet to speak.

It was better, he supposed, than having to face yet another enraged widow demanding blood for the loss of her husband. Especially when he had no answer for them. Queen Kate—his aunt, he reminded himself again—had destroyed Haydee's shadowy minion and saved the city. But before that, she had cut the Hi'dinn in half. Literally. That was all some families cared about. He'd have to find some way to pacify them, he knew, but whenever he thought on it, his mind always drifted back to the raucous cheers of the newly freed, and he'd be confronted anew with the reality that his heart just wasn't in it.

The young man standing before him had stopped speaking; he stared openly at Darien, expecting an answer.

Darien blinked and tried to focus. He really needed to eat something.

The man's tone reminded him of nothing so much as the hawking shouts of the old slave market. It sickened him.

The young seht dodged the question, whatever it was, and directed his attention to the young woman bedecked in all her finery.

"What of her personal interests? How do you prefer to spend your time, Shiri?" Darien asked, directing his attention to the girl.

Shiri did not raise her gaze from the hands folded demurely in front of her as she answered.

"Whatever pleases you, Great Seht."

Merciful Tel. If any of them ever gave an original response to that question it would be a miracle.

A great noise erupted behind Darien's left shoulder, masked as a coughing fit. He knew that if he turned around for just one look at Alaric's face, he would lose it. He worked hard to school his expression. Laughter coiled in his jaw regardless.

"I do have other matters to attend to, but I will consider your suit."

Darien stood, keeping his smile in place as Shiri and her family gathered up their belongings, clearly put out to be leaving empty-handed.

He turned to Alaric just as soon as they were out of sight.

"Don't ever do that to me again."

Alaric hunched over and bowed his head, raising his voice an octave. But he just couldn't stop giggling. "Whatever you say, Great Seht. Your wish is my command, Seht."

Darien raked a hand through his hair, grateful that he no longer had to suppress his smile. "Tell me that's the last one."

"Your torture is to be prolonged into the afternoon. And two more have requested an audience tomorrow."

Darien groaned as they walked back to his private chambers, where his head housekeeper, Mavis, bless her soul, had a feast laid out and waiting.

"Why do you even agree to see them?" Alaric asked.

Darien chuffed and reached for a bowl of pistachios to his right. "It's bad enough most of the Houses are scrambling, and never wanted me as their seht to begin with. I should count myself lucky that there are even families willing to tie themselves more closely to my reign."

"They're going to expect you to choose one of them."

Darien swallowed the food in his mouth and replaced it with more just as quickly.

Alaric stared at him. "You can't be serious."

"Whyever not?" Darien asked.

"Because!"

"Because what?"

"Because you don't love any of them," Alaric said quietly.

"The woman I loved tried to murder me, and everyone else. She still might."

Alaric pressed his lips into a grim line. "She was not the first nor the last woman to tell a man what he wanted to hear."

"You still have to admit, my judgement proved particularly faulty on that front."

A witty retort was not immediately forthcoming. Darien didn't know quite what that might have been, but he was disappointed nevertheless when it didn't come.

He pressed on, voicing aloud what he'd been telling himself over and over again.

"I need something to pull Likhan back together. I already have the favor of the free."

Alaric's expression turned hard. "There's not a single man who has paraded his sister in front of you without an agenda of his own. The only reason they didn't charge into that area with the others and get themselves killed is because they believed they could make you an instrument of their profit. You'd be rewarding them for thinking exactly that."

The fact that Alaric was right did nothing to improve Darien's mood. He pinched the bridge of his nose, trying to banish the stress that had been collecting there all day. All week, if he were honest.

"What of your plans to use Icaryan light to bind the districts? That would erase the need for a marriage, wouldn't it?" Alaric asked.

"That's not entirely up to me, is it? Unless you've heard back?"

Again, Alaric was ominously silent.

"I wouldn't be the first seht to make a politically advantageous match."

"But you weren't supposed to be like the other sehts."

The retort cut deep. "What would you have me do?"

"Fill your bed, and often."

"I'm *not* going to do that." That Darien's own father did the same was a sore point, and went unspoken.

"Then find the one who'll give you the least grief," Alaric said.

"Like you, huh?"

"What do you know about my grief?"

"I'm as observant of you as you are of me," Darien replied.

"Hmmph." Alaric buried himself in his food, giving Darien a chance to look over the pile of correspondence Mavis had left just to the side of myriad spices and marmalades. The topmost of the pile, a neatly folded sheaf of clean white parchment, caught his eye. Removing the ribbon and unfolding it only confirmed it.

"Alaric."

"Hmm?"

"I'm sorry."

Alaric wiped his hands on his lap before taking the paper from Darien. His brow furrowed as he read the words on the page, inviting him to the wedding of…

"I thought…"

He turned the invitation over in his hand, trying to make sense of it. He was surprised to find a note, written in Kate's own hand, scrawled across the back.

I will understand.

Alaric shook his head and handed the paper back as he rose from his chair. "Darien, if you're lucky enough to find a girl who twists up your insides every time you see her, don't be fool enough to let her out of your arms."

The night was warm, but not humid, as amber stars winked on in a blanket of pink and purple twilight. A soft breeze meandered through the thick greenery adorning every space as Alaric headed straight to his room. He prowled about the space like a caged animal before finally kicking a heavy chair, turning it over on its side and causing it to splinter at the base. He dropped down onto the bed, his hands clenched into fists in front of his face. He couldn't fight the ache in his heart any longer, and let hot tears fall.

3

The room would not stop spinning. Kate struggled to keep her focus on Luca, staring into his eyes long enough to chase the symptoms away.

"Thank you." She exhaled, finally able to enjoy the crisp morning air without an attending bout of nausea.

Cyrene looked on in wonder as Kate's demeanor shifted from supreme discomfort to surprising calm.

"That's going to be mighty handy when this child comes."

"I've been dead before," Kate countered. "I think I can handle the pain."

"I was dead. Trust me, you're going to wish you were."

Kate paled. "Oh god."

Luca pressed a reassuring hand to the small of her back. "You won't feel a thing."

"That's really unfair. Can you do that for me too?" Cyrene asked.

"Excuse me?" Kate said.

Allistair scooted closer to his wife on the thin patch of linen they had laid out in the West garden. "Seems your little one is to have a playmate."

"Congratulations!" Ted shouted. "I should have had money on how little time *that* took."

Kate laughed. "And you would have lost."

"It's no good, this," Allistair said. "Two pregnant women in the house. I'm building a hut out here."

Cyrene's eyes bulged out of her head, her face turning a menacing shade of red.

Kate followed. "Now that you've had your fun, you think you can just send us off, like bare-breasted barbarians?!"

"It's for me, ya git!"

Ted finally allowed himself to exhale, now that he didn't have to prevent his brother's murder.

Allistair turned to Luca with his finger to his nose. "There's space for three."

"I'll stick with my bride, thank you."

"You say that now. Immortal, eh? We'll see."

KATE STRETCHED A LENGTH OF BONE-COLORED SILK ACROSS HER abdomen, and grimaced.

"It's not going to sit right. I'll look even rounder than I already am."

Taelus took a deep breath. The more fabrics Kate examined in the mirror and discarded, the harder it became to keep her calm. Her gaze roamed over the colors and patterns scattered across her bed, spilling out of countless trunks that the tailor had hauled into her chamber.

"Your measurements are exactly the same as they've always been."

She squinted at him as he held the tape up for her to see for herself, then turned her attention back to her reflection, stripped down to a thin shift and still feeling like her skin was being stretched to its limit.

Just sore, she reminded herself. *Normal.* But that didn't make her feel any better about having to choose the most important garment of her life in her present condition.

"I just...I'm only doing it once, you know? I want it to be...perfect? Memorable," she corrected. One day, she would live forever, like Luca.

She wondered how much of her memory would fade, how much of her eternal lifespan she would be able to recall with any meaning. She didn't want to forget this.

A luminous bit of lace caught her eye. She bent down to pull it out and get a closer look, and found not a bolt of raw material, but a gown of gleaming ivory. Hand-crafted lace crept up the length of the skirt, a forest of flowers in sunshine gold. The creamy, crystalline tones of the dress seemed made for her as she let the fabric glide across her fingers, a perfect accompaniment to her pale skin and vibrant red hair. Shimmering bits of glass winked at her as the dress moved, sewn on with unicorn silk, bestowing the gown an ethereal yet earthly quality—a unicorn's secret beauty.

Struck speechless at first sight, Kate finally regained the sense to ask.

"Whose dress is this?"

"Yours, my dear."

Kate's head reared back in disbelief. "I've only just gotten engaged, how could it—"

Taelus held up a hand. "I began on the very day you returned home with your young man in tow. I took one look at your eyes and saw such a light, such a sparkle there. From that moment, I knew this day would come, and took it upon myself to capture that sparkle for you. It is fitting, no, for a queen of the forest? And look," he said, slipping it on over her head, "the fit is still perfect."

Kate's heart pounded in her chest, and she feared she would ruin the gown with her tears.

"Taelus…"

"I have been waiting a long time to make something like this for you. To see you in it gives me great joy."

"Wow."

Kate turned to see her brothers standing in the doorway.

"I knew you were pretty," Ted said, "but this is…this is something else."

They both stepped into the room, with Allistair holding a large box in blue velvet in his hands.

Ted nudged his brother, who cleared his throat. "About the

ceremony…we have a gift for you too. What you and Luca do…Ted and I can't do those things. We'll do everything we've always done to help you, and more, but Icaryans should know who to look to in their ultimate need. We've talked about this, and discussed it with Cyrene and Kaspar too, and we've made a decision."

Allistair opened the box to reveal a crown, a gold and silver wreath of flowering branches studded with gems, forged from the metals of their old ones.

"A new crown for a new king," he said. "This was always meant to be your throne. You don't need us anymore."

Kate opened her mouth to protest, but Allistair didn't give her the chance. "There should be a clear seat of power. You. Your husband. Your child."

"But what about Kaspar?"

"He can still be prince if you wish, and the same way we helped each other, he and your child may one day benefit from each other's counsel. How it plays out in the end will be their choice to make."

She took the crown from them, feeling the weight of it in her hands. "Thank you."

"Luca. Please, come in."

When Allistair answered the knock on his door, he was surprised to find his brother-in-law to-be on the other side of it. "I really am so happy you've found each other. She couldn't have chosen a better man."

Luca dipped his head in quiet thanks, uncomfortable with all the recent praise. Allistair was the latest in a long line of Icaryans expressing their gratitude for saving their lives, and the life of their queen.

"What can I do for you?" Allistair asked as he gestured toward an oversized chair, upholstered in chocolate-colored leather.

"I was hoping to do something special for Kate, something she won't expect."

"What did you have in mind?"

"What do you know of Mozart?"

Allistair's eyebrows rose to his hairline.

"She hums it frequently, but...I thought perhaps if you were familiar with it, you could explain it better to the musicians than I could."

Allistair raised one finger in the air as a thought came into his head. "I'll do you one better." He rose from his seat and crossed over to a work desk on the far side of the room, rummaging through shelf after shelf until he found what he wanted.

"Here. It's sheet music. I have no idea how it got here. I have a habit of collecting anything of Earth history that I think is worth preserving. It will sound more Icaryan, though, the instruments being different."

A blending of two worlds.

"She'll really like that," Luca said.

~

As the flurry of excitement buzzed through Castelmor, Kate and Luca set out for her cottage in the woods. When the impending celebration reached even there, as the clearing underwent a transformation worthy of a grand wedding, they retreated further into the forest, and found a happy serenity in each other's arms, three hearts beating in tandem.

4

Alaric moved swift and silent under the night sky's starry expanse, past the prim rows and arcs of the Council district toward the winding, pathless clusters that the free folk had erected almost overnight in their exodus from the Great Houses. It was harder for him to keep his footing on the makeshift roofs and broad lengths of coarse fabric protecting the families beneath from the elements, but the tight twists and turnabouts below defied reason, and it was impossible for him to navigate on the ground. From above, he had the advantage.

So long as he didn't shift his weight to the wrong place and crash through someone's ceiling.

The constant balancing act kept him focused, alert to the tensing of every muscle, his piercing gaze hunting for any possible perch or precarious place, his ears pricked to every conversation taking place beneath him as the quarter of the city nearest the desert came alive. It was a mercy that wiped his mind clean of everything else. Up here, his only thought was on the grand design of the Free District that at least he could see, if not understand. And once he had his quarry in his sights, he would not let him go again.

It was deep into the night when he finally laid eyes on him. The stall keeper selling his target a length of chain didn't seem bothered in the least that his customer kept his face hidden behind a dark hood the color of midnight. Though from this angle, it was impossible to tell whether the salesman could clearly see him or not.

Alaric inched closer across the rooftops, careful not to shake any boards loose and herald his presence as the haggling continued. The wind kicked up something fierce, forcing Alaric to slow his steps and tighten his grip. He was just close enough to see the man robed in shadow take a sharp left around a bend before ascending to the upper level of a structure, accessible only by sand dune.

Alaric darted across a clothesline as he watched the figure enter through one open window and exit another, effecting a sharp right turn that brought them out to a line of food stalls.

The smoke wafted up, searing his eyes. His chest shuddered as he contained a cough, causing the pillar he was balanced on to sway at a dangerous angle. He nearly plummeted, and almost lost track of the hooded man again. He didn't know if the convoluted path the figure snaked through the night was just the nature of the district, or if it had been done deliberately for his benefit.

It wasn't Haydee. Of that, and that alone, Alaric was sure.

Alaric's prey didn't leave the food market. Rather, he passed *through* it, disappearing beneath the multicolored patchwork of the canvas canopy. Alaric cursed, and skipped across the wooden tentpoles in a mad dash to reach the end first and see which way the hooded man headed next.

Did he know he was being followed? Alaric was always so careful; he'd never had a problem catching up with his marks.

Then again, he'd never had to chase them across a ramshackle skyline.

This person knew where he was going, and disrupted nothing as he moved in and out of private spaces at will. No one from the Houses could accomplish that. There was a wolf among the free folk. And it was Alaric's job to put him down before he even caught sight of the seht.

The cloaked figure emerged from the farthest side of the market, headed west. He wasn't running, but he moved very much like a man in a hurry. There was something about him, something in his stature and the way he moved, that was so very familiar. Alaric couldn't put his finger on it.

Alaric ignored a splinter gnawing into his palm as he gripped a wooden beam and lunged at it with all his weight. It bowed in the middle, but didn't crack as it swung from leaning against one building to the next. It clattered against the thin metal roof of the shorter, squat home, startling the people inside. But it didn't matter now. The midnight hood was gone. Again.

"Mother..."

Alaric punched the base of the post as he slid down to the ground, bested again.

This was a mistake he could not afford to make. Like it or not, he would have to tell Darien. That he had enemies here, among those he had set free. The young seht already had enough on his shoulders.

Alaric grimaced, and shook off his fury. He would fix this. And when he did catch up to him—because he *would* catch up to him—he would not be at all surprised to find someone he'd known all along.

5

The gentle rain of the previous night mixed with the early morning sunshine made the glen sparkle. Glowing paper lanterns turned the delicate petals of cascading wildflowers deep and vibrant. At the edge of the grass line bordering the forest, a pair of small tents in soft white had been erected to house the bride and groom. Standing tall between them was a larger structure, more ornate, intended for the wedding night.

Luca exited his tent, adjusting the lapels of his coat, a finely tailored garment of darkest night embroidered with gold, before crossing over to where Kate was smoothing out the front of her dress.

She caught sight of him in the mirror and smiled.

He came closer, wrapping his arms around her waist, his slender fingers mindful of all the crystals and adornments held so delicately in their place.

"I never want to forget this moment."

Kate breathed deep, and simply existed in his arms.

The ceremony began with music, an old Icaryan love song, for the goddess and the object of her affection. It was customary for the groom to bow upon meeting his wife before those gathered. Luca chose to kneel, his fine clothes touching the ground as Kate smiled down at him. It was not often that she blushed, and Luca relished every opportunity to bring her feelings rushing to her cheeks. Their eyes never strayed from each other as he stood, taking her hands in his own as Alaric bound them together and spoke the solemn words over them. Their answers came in the silence between them, vows made soul to soul. They donned their rings, two lustrous dark bands cut from the same fallen sliver of the elder moon.

When Luca thought the ceremony was just about over, Kate glanced at her brother, who produced a wreath of woven metal. As Luca dipped his neck so she could place it on his head, the whole of Icarya fell to its knees. He was shocked. Overwhelmed. Outright terrified. He stared with rounded eyes as the corner of Kate's mouth quirked mischievously upward.

I know exactly how you feel.

Allistair's booming voice cut through the thick quiet. "It is my pleasure to present to you, your queen and king! Your Highness, you may kiss your bride."

The glen erupted in outbursts of joy as Luca swept the queen off her feet. As he did, the first bars of Mozart's "Divertimento" announced themselves with great gusto. Luca beamed as the light of recognition shone upon his wife's face.

"You see. I told you you wanted this."

"Perhaps I did," Kate said, squeezing his arm as they stepped into the middle of the great revelry already in the making.

Philip and Cara were among the first to congratulate them. Their young son Cirrus didn't think twice about nuzzling Kate's belly. She ruffled the bit of glossy white mane tucked behind his ears.

"You two are going to be the best of friends."

Julian was next in line, and nearly shoved the young pegasus aside. "How am I supposed to top this?" He gesticulated at Lilla, dressed in a modest frock of petal pink. "Just look how big her eyes are!"

Kate shrugged. "You could always use the castle."

Lilla's expression grew deathly serious. "Don't joke."

"I'm not. Talk to Ted. He'll be thrilled."

DARIEN WAS NEXT IN LINE TO CONGRATULATE THE NEWLYWEDS BUT turned at a timid tap on his left shoulder. He turned to see his father behind him. For a moment, he forgot to breathe. He'd spoken to him before, of course, on *many* occasions, but none like today. There was no more pretending, for either of them.

Darien didn't know what to say. Before he could come to his senses and think of something, Ted enveloped him in a tight embrace. Darien hugged him back, and finally remembered to exhale.

"I stayed away for your safety," Ted said, pulling apart to place a hand on his son's cheek.

"I don't know what to call you," Darien said.

"Theodore will do," Kate interrupted. "It's not a good idea that anyone else know. At least, not yet."

Darien nodded. "Things are off to a good start, if a little shaky."

"You'll have the hardest time with the families whose fathers I've cut down," Kate said.

She'd hit it right on the head.

"So far there's no outward hostility," he answered.

"*That's* not encouraging," Luca said.

Darien blushed. "No, but we are keeping an eye on things."

LUCA SENSED THE SHIFT IN HER MOOD AS SHE NODDED THOUGHTFULLY, withholding information from

Darien.

"ALARIC SENDS HIS REGRETS," DARIEN SAID, BY WAY OF CHANGING THE subject.

Kate didn't nod in acknowledgement, but merely blinked.

Luca pressed a thought across to her. *We agreed not to invite him.*

You agreed. He's an Icaryan and I'm his queen.

Luca wasn't satisfied. He was anything but.

Kate took a deep breath. *I knew he wouldn't come, but the gesture was deserved.*

"What about Haydee?" she asked, coming back to the conversation.

"There's been no sign of her. No one saw where she went to," Darien answered.

"She didn't go back to where she came from. I checked. I want to gather some more information before I come back, but we *will* come soon. If anything happens in the meantime, Alaric knows how to reach me," Kate said.

"This is a celebration," Ted cut in. "No more talk of serious things."

That reminded Darien. "Yes, I almost forgot. I'd like to set a more positive tone in the city for our new alliance, and maybe start laying down some exchanges. I thought we might start with a festival. Kaimar is coming with the next moons. It's a time of crossroads, an opportunity to feed the dearly departed and ward off lingering spirits."

"That sounds like All Hallow's Eve," Kate said.

Ted squinted and scratched the back of his neck. "Why do I know that?"

"When we were children, we had a holiday like that. It included a fair amount of food, and a masquerade."

"Ooh. I could do that," Ted said.

"Oh, good!" Darien exclaimed. He and Ted walked off to settle the details between them.

KATE DANCED THE NIGHT AWAY WITH HER HUSBAND, BROTHERS, AND nephew, but something nagged her insides, something Kate was hiding from herself. Even surrounded by her joy, Luca knew it was there as her eyes scanned the throngs, growing stronger as the night waned.

As the last merrymaker stumbled away, Kate and Luca settled into their bridal tent. Plush, jewel-toned pillows were piled high in every corner, accenting the pristine white bed linens that made the center of the room look like a cloud at sunset.

Luca took off his crown, and hers, and laid them aside for the night. "I can see why you don't wear this all the time." But it was exquisite, and crafted with care. Luca stood admiring the symbol of his new status when he heard an exulted gasp from the other side of the tent. He turned and saw Kate looking down at a small square card of clean white paper in her hand. He crossed the space to peer over her shoulder at the neat, pretty lettering.

You looked beautiful today. I owe you a dance. William.

"William..."

The name sounded with wonder on her lips. Replacing the card on the table, she picked up the silver brooch that lay next to it, fashioned into a Celtic knot. She turned it over in her hands, her fingertips roving slowly over the smooth, intricate design. Something about its curves reminded her of her medallion, the one she had destroyed and would never get back.

Luca's fingers grazed her own as he took it from her grasp, replaced it on the table, and wrapped his hand around her waist.

"My bride. You're everything I ever wanted."

His kiss was deep and demanding, imprinting itself on Kate's brain. She tucked her hands under his coat, wandering up to his shoulders as she lifted it off his frame. His lips were hot on her neck, the top of her breasts, and she let her hands rove, clasping his hair and removing the remaining adornments and jewels surrounding them like a curtain of night. Luca pushed down the delicate sleeves of her dress, baring Kate's shoulders. As he turned her around to unlace the back of her gown, she kept her arm bowed to clasp his hair. Once her gown was undone, Luca's hands were free to roam, over her breasts, between her legs. Kate crumpled in his embrace. He lifted her onto the bed and removed his shirt. The grazing of skin on skin was hot and demanding. Her thighs bucked him, urging his pants to come off. Luca dropped to the floor, lifting a leg in his arms as he leapt upon her and consummated their marriage.

As their passion intensified and Kate's screams grew louder, her mouth lay open. She felt a new, deeper hunger overtake her. She clawed at him, begging for more. More of his hands and mouth on her skin, more of his body melding to hers. When her hunger honed itself to a point, she became heedless of all thought and acted purely out of lust. Out of thirst. She flipped him over, pushing up against his chest with surprising strength and speed. Luca's eyes widened at the sight of her, and at the red lust glowing from her deep brown irises like a blood moon. His desire became almost too painful to bear. Shuddering, he pulled her face close to his and tipped back his head, drunk with want, offering himself up to her. She bit him hard in the throat. He cried out at the sweet release of his skin opening as Kate drew the blood into her mouth. His breath grew ragged as she fed deliriously, and he grew languid with an ecstasy beyond anything they had yet shared. His skin prickled with pleasure at her every breath, her frenzy like a contagion. Their bond grew stronger, thicker, tighter. Their existence merged. His mouth sought hers, sucking on the raw sweetness he found there. He went on the attack, rolling her over again in a fit of violent lust, and they rutted like crazed beasts, succumbing to the demands of their flesh, tearing and lapping, mindless to everything but each other.

~

THE THREAT OF WINTER WAS REAL AS A MORNING WIND SLIPPED OFF THE mountains, creeping its way along the grass and into the bridal bed. Luca inched closer to his bride, and with a gentle hand swept a curl from her peacefully resting face. She opened her eyes slowly, her skin tingling to life at the warmth of Luca's hand on her back.

He smiled softly at her, almost awkward in the wake of their unexpectedly brutal wedding night. Kate blushed as he brushed his knuckles against her cheek, and she pressed herself closer to him, laying her head upon his chest. The way his slender fingers wove their way through her crimson tendrils brought her close to purring.

Nothing needed saying. Their shyness melted away in their embrace, their vulnerability snuggled safely in their affection. What had passed, neither regretted. They lay together for a long time, man and wife, savoring the blossoming new nature of their union. Nothing had ever felt so right.

When their hunger demanded that they rise, Luca pulled on his shirt and coat, reaching for the stone jug of water on the far table. The buttery smell of fresh, warm bread caught his attention. He opened the flaps of the tent to find an array of covered dishes bearing breakfast for the newlyweds. Luca carried the trays into the tent as Kate wrapped the cover from the bed around herself to fight off a chill.

"This is your brother's doing, I imagine," Luca said, eyeing the soft, sweet cheese greedily as he laid it thickly on warm bread.

"That was thoughtful," Kate replied, angling for the plump grapes and the thin slices of salted, cured meat. The fat melted on her tongue, and she cooed as she filled her belly.

"I wish I could take you away someplace," Luca said, brewing a pot of tea and placing a sweetened cup in Kate's lap. "I've heard Gilbraith is beautiful. Or we could go back to O'loa. It might be an ideal spot to have a newborn," he said, settling into his thoughts. "It would give us time together, to get to know each other, before the masses swoop in."

"We still have time enough for that. Our best chance at some peace is having things in Likhan better settled before then."

"Will we leave right away?" Luca asked.

Kate shook her head. "Drigory's collection may not reveal much, but any intelligence is better than nothing. Today, though," she smiled, curling into his arms, "today is ours."

They spent it quietly, lounging, napping, and making love in pursuit of a peace that would hold them to their purpose in the dark days to come.

The following morning, Kate affixed her scarf across her chest, over her blue traveling dress. She moved with deliberate slowness, reluctant to leave these blissful times behind. She caught Luca's wistful reflection in the mirror and turned to him. A sad smile curled at the right corner of his mouth as he pulled his wife to him, caressing her cheek. His voice, when it came, was strained with emotion.

"I'll never forget how you looked in that dress."

6

Kate wasted no time voicing her displeasure when they arrived at the troll's underwater abode at the base of the Northern Mountains.

"Your potions aren't as effective as they used to be."

"Aren't they? It only cures *unwanted* conditions," he retorted.

Kate blushed and pursed her lips.

Drigory harumphed.

Kate was not at all happy to be there, and the feeling seemed to be mutual. He had the pertinent books stacked neatly on the table in preparation for their arrival, presumably to hasten their exit. Kate held her tongue as they leafed through the small stack, but her wrath grew palpable as they worked through the texts. There were small tidbits of information about the nature of shadow magic, but nothing more. Not how to overcome it.

"It's an indelible part of the world," Drigory said, reading the frustration plain on her face. "You can't erase all shadow. Shadow magic practitioners manipulate that other world, striving to exist only in its in-between spaces.

"I've been to the shadow realm before," Luca said. "It's like a negative of the world. Empty expanses with certain places anchored to worldly shadows. Wandering in it is like falling into a bottomless puddle."

"Have you ever killed a shadow creature?" Kate asked.

"Yes. But not one that had bent the shadows to her will."

Kate considered. "Alaric said she fled when I bound her beast and lit it on fire. I don't know if that would have been enough."

"Your own fire?" Drigory asked, his interest piqued.

Kate nodded.

"Given the strength of your abilities, I'd say it's enough," he replied.

"I'm done with that," Kate said.

Drigory looked at her. Not directly—he seemed to focus on something she couldn't see. Whenever he looked at her like that, which was all the time, it infuriated her.

"Forgive me if I'm not convinced," he scoffed.

Her rage expanded, stretching the magical aura flaring at the edge of Kate's skin that always held Drigory's attention. The book in her hand turned to cinders.

"I said I'm done!" she cried.

Kate and Luca were both startled by the sudden immolation. When her terror washed over him, Luca knew Kate hadn't done it voluntarily.

Drigory only sneered. "But is it done with you?"

Kate leaned back in her chair, allowing her husband's soothing influence at her back to cool her ire.

"Where are they?" she asked.

She and the troll stared hard at each other for a long time. But Drigory kept his silence. Luca felt Kate push her pain and disappointment away to the depths of her gut as she stood to go without another word. Once out of Drigory's sight, Kate grabbed Luca's hand and spirited them away, becoming as insubstantial as the air, carrying them on the wind back to her cottage on the opposite side of the river. The sky blushed purple at the coming of night.

Luca staggered as his feet touched solid ground again, or rather, as his feet once again fell solid upon the earth. His head spun.

"That was very strange." He rubbed his brow and tried to get his bearings.

"What if he's right?" she asked.

Luca waited, knowing there was more on the tip of her tongue.

"If I don't know what's wrong with me, how can I control it, or chase it away?"

An abandoned dhampir left by his parents to his own devices, Luca had felt the helplessness that now crept into Kate's heart many, many times.

He took her hand in his, and sat them both down on the grassy ridge before their home that led downward to the small rushing stream, watching the fading sunlight dance on its surface.

"I wasted a lot of time fighting the truth of my nature," Luca stated, his voice, soft as velvet. "Only when I accepted what I am was I able to be my fullest self. I am what I am. And it isn't wrong. *You* taught me that."

He felt her soul glow warm at his kind words, acknowledging that he had spoken true.

"What if it hurts the baby?" she whispered.

Luca unfolded his fingers from Kate's and caressed her belly, feeling a small curve beginning to take hold there. He felt his child's heartbeat strong against his fingertips.

"She's as fine today as she was the day she was conceived. You've shown quite a bit of your nature since then."

Kate thought about all she had done to cage and destroy the shadow demon that had threatened to eclipse Likhan. "I don't know which had more effect…my blood magic or me," she said.

"We'll find the answers. Together."

Kate nodded, her downcast eyes glistening. "Thank you."

He patted her leg, kissing her cheek as he rose to his feet.

"Rest. I'll find dinner."

Instead of heading toward the stream, he turned his steps to the forest behind them, taking Kate's bowstring and her quiver of arrows. Luca took his time stalking the forest, moving between the trees, savoring the quiet. He was as silent as a shadow himself, shrouding his presence on the dark side of a tree, causing his footfalls to make not a sound on the brittle leaves blanketing the forest floor. A sizable stag came into his sights. With the patient endurance of the best hunters, he strung the bow, his eyes ever on his prey. He felled the beast in a single release, and carried it back to the cottage slung over his shoulders.

Kate's eyes went wide at the sight as Luca laid his catch at her feet.

"Fish would have been fine."

"My appetite is for something stronger than fish tonight. Especially in this weather." He knelt by the fire Kate had built in his absence, warming his hands. "I trust you'll find something to do with it all?"

As the indigo night settled around them, the cottage exuded a dozen smells of venison—smoked, salted, hanging from the roof, tightly wrapped and stored cold, dried, marinated, and lastly, grilled, with two sumptuous steaks for their twilit meal. As their repast began, Kate let out a mock whine.

"What is it?" Luca asked.

"I just thought how good this would be with garlic—and the idea repulsed me."

Luca smirked, finding her misfortune endearing.

"But I love garlic."

"Not anymore you don't."

"But it's so good for you…what a bum deal."

Luca laughed into his food. "You'll live."

7

William paced the room. He was tired of repeating himself, but there was nothing else for it. He couldn't fathom why what he had been saying over and over again wasn't having the desired effect.

"She's my daughter, godammit!"

"And what does that solve?" Drigory countered. "How does that help us in any way?"

William looked to his mother, who remained silent. She had been silent for the last half-hour. It was infuriating.

"Ye canna keep her from me. Her mother did, and I'll be damned if I continue to let ye keep me away. She *needs* us. Why shouldn't we go to her?"

Drigory repeated *himself* for the umpteenth time. He looked none the happier for it either.

"We mustn't interfere!"

William slammed the palm of his hand against the nearest bookshelf. "That's not good enough! Not anymore. Tell me *why*."

There was no answer. Not from Drigory. Not from his mother. William threw his hands up in the air and stormed out. Drigory gripped the arms of his chair and got to his feet. Meryn hadn't so much as twitched.

"Aren't you going to stop him?" Drigory asked.

"I couldn't stop him if I tried." Her voice sounded tired, resigned. But Drigory sensed something else there, and it irritated him.

"You don't *want* to stop him."

"No. I don't." Meryn leaned back into her chair and clasped the pendant that always hung at her neck. "If you'd tried to keep me from my son, you couldn't stop me either."

8

Icarya is yours, my golden one. When you're grown, you must take it.

Darien shook the memory of his mother free as Alaric knocked the dagger out of his hand with a resounding clatter.

Alaric ground his teeth. "Are you even *trying* to pay attention?"

"Sorry."

He picked it up and readied himself again. But still his thoughts were elsewhere. This time, he wondered about his father—what he thought of him, what he thought of what he was trying to accomplish with the Hi'dinn. What was left of it, anyway.

Alaric landed a swift kick to his wrist, and down went the dagger. Again.

"You can do better than this," Alaric insisted.

"My muscles are tired, and all I'm trying to do is hold *on* to the thing. Can we try something else?"

"If your muscles are hurting, that means they're working. Tell me when it *doesn't* hurt. Then we'll talk."

Darien had heard it already a hundred times. This time it grated.

"I suppose if someone should put *their* dagger to my throat as I sleep, I should say to him, 'Hold sir! I have a serious dagger in my robes, but I don't know how to use it. Come back in a moon's time, then we'll see what's what?'"

Alaric's eyebrows rose. "You're in a fine mood, aren't you?"

"Don't test me..."

DARIEN WAS RIGHT, OBVIOUSLY. ALARIC KNEW THAT. HE WANTED TO teach him correctly, to protect him from the dangers banging down the door. Dangers like the ones who had taken his mother and his adoptive father from him. Dangers like Alaric. But time was short. And he couldn't begin to make up for all that Darien had suffered at his hands if someone was to murder him.

"Alright. Then stop me," Alaric said.

"What?"

Alaric took the dagger from Darien's hands and pointed it at him. "Take it from me." He took a step forward.

Darien threw up his hands in front of him and stepped back. "How do you suggest I do that?"

"You've seen me take it from you a hundred times, in a hundred different ways. Now shut up and stop me."

Alaric quickened his pace. When Darien retreated, Alaric made up the ground between them easily. The wide-eyed look in the seht's eyes made him sick to his stomach, but forward he pressed. When Darien's back hit the wall, his expression shifted, his jaw set in a firm line.

He gripped Alaric's wrist with both hands, shoving the knife aside but without dislodging it from Alaric's grip. Alaric corrected his stance immediately, the business end of the weapon at Darien's throat.

"Try again."

Darien pushed harder this time, but Alaric held firm. A surprise punch to the gut forced him to step backward, and Darien earned himself more room to move. He went underhanded this time, but Alaric twisted to the side. Darien switched tactics and grabbed him by the wrist, turning inward on Alaric and pressing his back against him.

"Step back!" Alaric shouted.

But Darien didn't need the reminder. He dug in and hurled Alaric over his shoulder with enough speed that Alaric's head made a resounding crack as it hit the tile floor.

"Argh. My back."

"I'm sorry! I'm sorry! Are you okay?"

"Peachy." Alaric groaned and wiggled the fingers of his right hand. They were empty, the dagger lying a few inches away.

"I did it!" Darien cried.

"Next time, could you 'do it' outside, on something soft?"

Darien smiled and extended his hand. "*Are* you okay?"

"I'm fine. I think I'll just stay here for a while." Alaric lay sprawled along the floor and let his eyes droop.

"Thank you."

Alaric's eyes snapped open.

"You know, for—"

"Don't."

Darien furrowed his brow at Alaric's sudden sharp tone, but was distracted just as quickly as his father's arrival was announced. He looked again at Alaric, still on the floor.

"Go."

Darien welcomed the distraction of planning the festival in conjunction with Ted. His father's enthusiasm was contagious as they squared how to knit their cultures together. When a lull came over the conversation, Darien stepped tentatively into the gap.

"Mother always spoke highly of you."

Ted rubbed the back of his neck, which made Darien question whether he'd just made a huge mistake. Before he could take it back, Ted spoke.

"Your mother was…she was the most beautiful woman that I ever saw. I would have given her anything, and I would have given anything to have the two of you with me. I've never met another like her, no matter how hard I try." The corner of his mouth quirked upward, but his eyes were full of regret.

Darien didn't know what to say. He swallowed hard.

"I heard about you and Haydee, before all this."

This is something Darien did not, had not talked about with anyone. Even Alaric. But somehow, with his wounded rake of a father standing before him, he couldn't hold it in any longer.

"All my life, I loved her, wanted nothing more than to be with her, and make it so that no one would ever have to go through what she did ever again. And now—"

An incredulous laugh escaped him like a gasp for breath. "I never knew her at all. I've lost my center."

With a hand on his shoulder, Ted led him to the far side of the balcony that looked out over the shanty towns.

"See them? You gave them back their lives. Their *children's* lives. Let them be your center."

He was right, of course, but it was exactly what Darien needed to hear. "I'm glad you're here," he said.

"I wouldn't want to be anywhere else. You're a precious commodity now—an unwed seht. Have you received any offers?"

Darien let out a bark. "Droves of them."

"And?"

"Their families tell me of themselves, of what benefit they could be to me. They say nothing of the daughters they would have me bind myself to."

"That's to be expected."

"I don't know what to do. Any choice will surely cause insult to another. And *none* of them feel right."

"There's your answer then, isn't it?"

~

GOT YOU.

Alaric leapt down from his rooftop perch, primed to follow the path leading deeper into the free market and paying no heed to the darkened curtain casually blowing in the wind. But this time he knew better.

He grabbed his hidden target hard on the shoulder and spun him round and aimed his knife at his gut. The moment he caught sight of his quarry's face, he retracted it just as quickly. Alaric smiled wide to set his eyes upon the hidden threat to Likhan that he had been after for weeks, the man—*woman*—he'd been tracking all this time.

"Don't I know you from someplace?"

Christine was prettier in the flesh. The violet of her eyes was more vibrant, the dark curls of her hair lustrous to the point of radiance. He was surprised, but not at all pleasantly, as she took his stunned reaction as an opportunity to slam the flat of her palm against his solar plexus and knock him back a step. She dodged to the side to attempt her escape, but it wasn't nearly enough.

"Oh no." He caught the shadowy fabric that had allowed her to evade him for so long between his fingers and tugged hard, bringing her squarely back to where she'd been a moment before: trapped between the solid walls of muscles that were his arms. The back of her head thudded against the stone building for good measure.

"Let go," she growled. Her eyes flared at him, but she was clever enough not to cause a ruckus.

"We're just getting acquainted," he replied. His tone was casual, but it dripped with hidden malice.

"I know who you are," she snarled, "and I don't need your help."

Alaric pressed more firmly against the wall, caging her with his body.

"She know you're here?"

"Don't be stupid. She sent me."

That stung. "She didn't tell me."

"Why the hell should she?"

Alaric's eyebrows rose into his hairline. "I don't know. Maybe so I could stop wasting my time chasing your tail and focus on something that's *actually* important?"

She sneered. "You couldn't catch me."

"And yet, here we are."

Alaric's grin widened as his barb struck home.

"So, what is it that you don't need my help with?"

Christine turned away and tried to shove him aside. It was about as useful as trying to push a mountain out of the way.

He tsked. "Not until you tell me what you've been up to."

"Fine. Dammit. But I can't do that just standing here."

"Temper, temper. Alright darlin'. Lead the way."

He flashed a toothy grin at the sight of her irritation at his endearment, and followed her through the market as she visited the stalls in a random pattern, carrying on what seemed like small, useless chatter with the stall keepers, except at every stall, she exchanged whatever she held in her hands—a bouquet of herbs, a pouch of dried beans, a cloven hoof transformed into a charm, and as they went, Alaric realized they had moved beyond the busy market, much deeper into the newly erected freed town than he had ever been.

He remained quiet but alert, watching Christine's every signal and gesture as they wove their way through the residential streets, where even these buildings were abuzz with conversation and activity in defiance of the late hour. Every face they encountered seemed to recognize her. They gave Alaric the side-eye, but he simply smiled and said nothing as they passed deeper and deeper into the neighborhood, coming so close to the edge of the desert that the sand from the dunes whispered through the open doorways whenever there was a breeze.

A tall, wiry man, all bone and sinew, greeted them at the end of a line of houses, offering them a drink from a clay jug in exchange for a small scrap of linen dyed purple with a crescent moon no larger than a fingernail embroidered into the corner.

"All is well tonight," he said, taking the jug back from Christine after she had her fill. "We watch and wait for the return of the seht's champion."

Christine nodded. "She arrives with the dawn, and will lie in wait where the watchman faces the sea."

The nameless man nodded and slaked his own thirst from the clay jug before returning his attention to the basket that lay half woven between his feet.

Christine turned and left him to his craft, going back through the streets a different way than they had come, with Alaric following behind.

"What was that?" he asked.

Christine ignored him.

"Seriously?"

She let out an exasperated sigh, like it was *her* secrets she was about to spill. "Before Darien became the seht, it was necessary for the enslaved from different Houses to communicate with each other in secret. It was vital that news essential to the community be untraceable by their masters."

Alaric jerked his head behind them. "That's what we just saw?"

Christine nodded. "The Unbroken Chain. Now, with an urgent sense of purpose."

"To monitor any threats to the seht."

"You're not as stupid as you look."

Alaric ignored the jibe. "How did *you* find a way in? And what's this got to do with our queen?"

"That's her business."

"You said you knew me. Why didn't I know about you?" he asked.

"I already said I don't need your help."

"I don't remember offering it."

"Good."

"What crawled up your backside?" A wicked grin spread across Alaric's lips. "Not used to being caught so easily?"

"It *wasn't* easy," Christine snapped back. "It took days."

So she *had* deliberately evaded him. "That's right. Only days."

She ground her teeth in frustration.

So, it irked her. Good. Fair payback for stringing him along all that time, from distracting him from the real threat. He expected another sharp retort, but she flitted to the right down an alley, one so well camouflaged that he never would have known it was there if he hadn't just seen Christine walk through it. He had no reason to follow.

Alaric wound his way slowly through the city and back to Darien, mapping out everything he could remember in his head about the winding network Christine had revealed to him along the way.

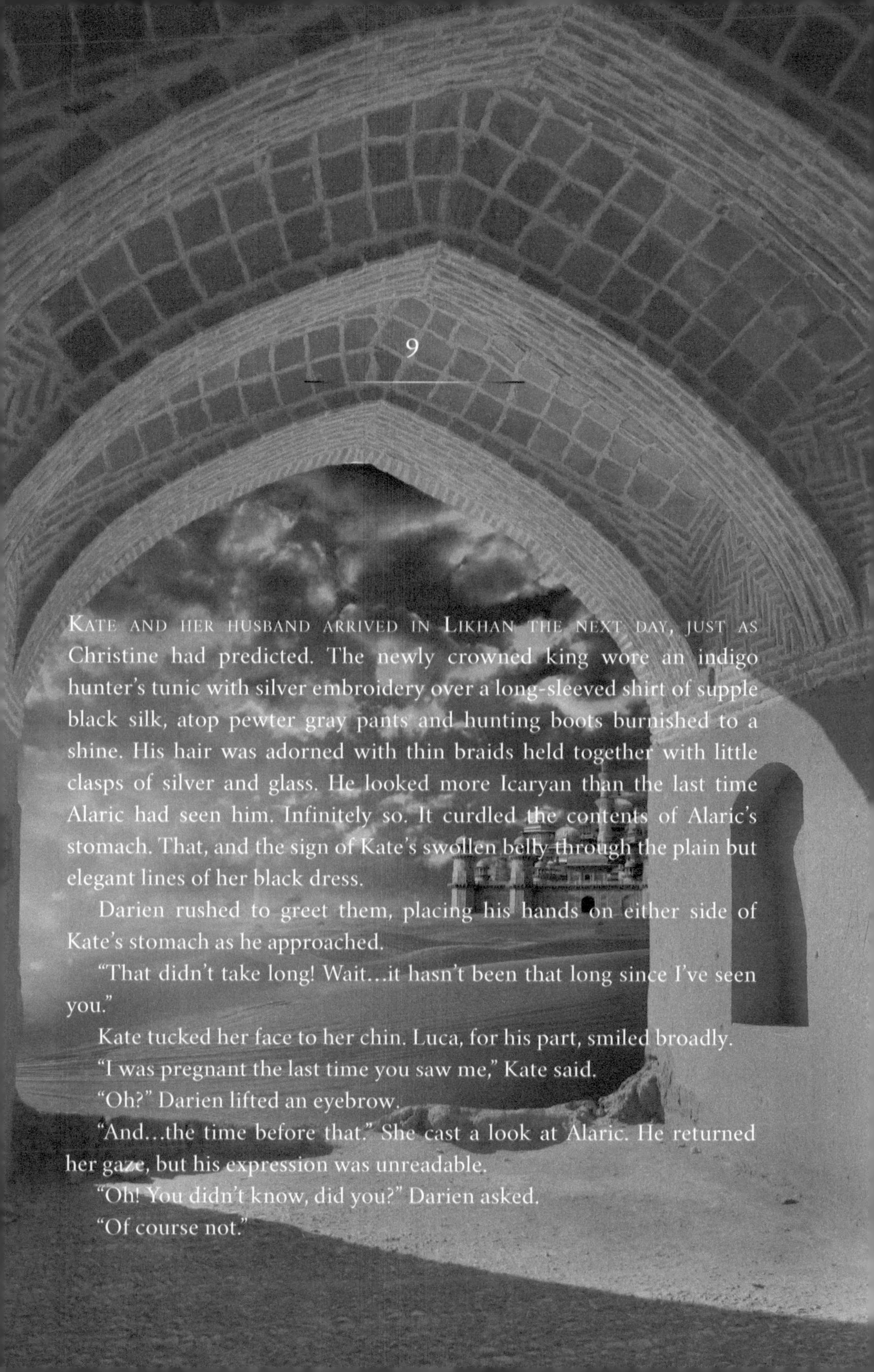

9

Kate and her husband arrived in Likhan the next day, just as Christine had predicted. The newly crowned king wore an indigo hunter's tunic with silver embroidery over a long-sleeved shirt of supple black silk, atop pewter gray pants and hunting boots burnished to a shine. His hair was adorned with thin braids held together with little clasps of silver and glass. He looked more Icaryan than the last time Alaric had seen him. Infinitely so. It curdled the contents of Alaric's stomach. That, and the sign of Kate's swollen belly through the plain but elegant lines of her black dress.

Darien rushed to greet them, placing his hands on either side of Kate's stomach as he approached.

"That didn't take long! Wait…it hasn't been that long since I've seen you."

Kate tucked her face to her chin. Luca, for his part, smiled broadly.

"I was pregnant the last time you saw me," Kate said.

"Oh?" Darien lifted an eyebrow.

"And…the time before that." She cast a look at Alaric. He returned her gaze, but his expression was unreadable.

"Oh! You didn't know, did you?" Darien asked.

"Of course not."

Luca scoffed. "Like that would have stopped you."

She returned her husband's wry smile. It was sickening.

Darien spared Alaric a look, and tried to keep the mood light in the face of his murderous stare. "There have been no new incidents since you've left." He turned then to Luca. "It's your first visit to Likhan, isn't it? Would you like a tour? Perhaps the garden first?"

Luca sent a questioning glance to Kate, who took a deep breath, and said, "Later. First, we need to go to the bazaar. Make sure all the remaining heads of the Houses are there."

Darien's tone shifted. "I don't think that's a good idea."

KATE DIDN'T SAY A WORD. SHE JUST CONTINUED TO STARE AT HER NEPHEW until he relented and led them to a small bazaar, smaller than the one at the city center, which catered solely to the wealthy. A great crowd of onlookers had already gathered. Luca pulled Kate's crown from the inner recesses of his robe, placed it atop her hair, and kissed her forehead.

Be careful.

She smiled softly at him and turned to watch the widows and sons of the men she had killed come forward. The crowds parted, allowing them passage to the center with ease. Kate smiled to herself. Every afflicted family was there; their reputations and social standing wouldn't allow them to be elsewhere. She took two steps toward Darien. He was flanked by Ted and Alaric, who looked equally confused as to what they were all doing there. Kate spoke so quietly that only they could hear.

"Whatever happens, don't interfere."

Darien blanched as realization dawned on him. He opened his mouth, but she did not let him speak.

"Don't stop them, do you hear? No matter what. It is necessary."

Ted frowned. "Kate?"

"It'll be alright, Teddy. I promise." She turned her back to them and took up her place several paces in front of Darien. Behind his back, Alaric pulled Ted by the shoulder, allowing the seht to stand tall, alone.

"Will someone tell me what the hell is going on?" Ted growled under his breath.

Alaric gave his answer reluctantly. "The blood law."

"The what?"

Both men were silenced when Kate addressed the crowd in a clear, loud voice.

"When Darien challenged his uncle and ascended to the seat of the Seht, he named me as his champion. I was willing to serve, as a demonstration of Icarya's desire to improve our relationship to our mutual benefit." She looked to Darien then back to the crowd again. "He did not, however, give me the authority to rob Likhan of its respected leaders. He mourns their loss with you, and has set me before you. Their blood is on my hands, and mine alone." She folded back the sleeves of her dress, baring her arms, and laid them out on the stack of wooden crates piled in front of her. "Exact your toll."

There was a general rustling, but none of the families lining the border of the crowd moved. At first. Then, a crone with a hard face, in full mourning white from head to toe, stepped forward. Her gray hair was pulled tightly back against her face, sharpening her scowl.

"It is not my place to lay hands on a queen. Even though she be not *my* queen."

"I have made myself an agent of your seht, and so I make this offer," Kate replied.

The women stared hard at each other.

"What do you get out of this?" the woman asked.

Kate didn't respond, but the woman's hatred was too great. She was goaded by Kate's wicked smile, and pulled a curved dagger from her robes. Kate didn't so much as blink. This infuriated the widow, who slashed a long line against Kate's left forearm, spilling blood all over her white clothes, the ground, and into the sand. She spat on Kate.

Kate remained seated, but breathing hard. Luca, barely a step behind her, brought his hand to her shoulder, and slipped his fingers under her collar to the skin beneath.

Ted and Alaric averted their eyes, but Darien looked on, absolutely refused to turn away. He nearly ground his teeth to dust to stop the flow of guilty tears.

One after another, they came, slashing Kate's arms to ribbons. One young man brought not a dagger, but a spear into the circle, and pierced her right hand. He succeeded in wrenching a groan from her as the bones in her palm cracked and splintered, and blood gushed from the wound as he ripped the spear away. Kate's blood fell faster than the sand could drink, and puddled at her feet. Her arms grew slippery, slick in a pool of their own gore.

Luca's expression was hard as granite. His eyes were reduced to slits as he etched the face of every person who assaulted his wife into his memory.

Kate tried and failed to curl the fingers of her right hand, and could only shudder as her breathing grew labored, the heat bearing down on her from above, her vision swimming from the loss of blood. She wavered in her seat, and tried to inhale. She had not much flesh left to give, and the last few struggled to make fresh marks, cutting only deeper into open wounds. But beneath it all, Luca's touch worked to undo the damage, weaving muscle and sinew back together again.

Two brothers and their mother approached, one son on either side of her. Kate braced herself as they flanked her. Their mother stood before her, silver hair flowing past her shoulders. She leaned forward on a wooden cane, peering into Kate's eyes.

"You took the father of my children from this world."

The brothers looked at each other over Kate's head, then they looked at her. They each put a gentle hand on her shoulder. The woman took Kate's head in her hands, knelt before her, and kissed both cheeks.

A small child, no more than six, approached slowly. His face as he came closer was as pale as Kate's, his eyes as full as the elder moon at the unadulterated sight of violence. He looked at her, scared and sad. A minute blade trembled in his tiny hands. Shaking, she smiled at him, and mustered enough of herself.

"It's all right," she whispered.

The child looked back and forth between her and his father. His eyes glistened.

"I'm sorry," he whispered back.

Luca felt Kate's skin flash cold under his fingertips. It startled him, but it was gone just as quickly. She was fighting it.

The boy made a small, superficial cut on her cheek beneath her left eye. Blood trickled, augmented by her tears as the boy left her, head down, and returned to his father's side. She looked up at the man, who placed his hand on his son's head as he raised a crossbow with the other.

Darien set his stare fast on the arrow wielder, his jaw working furiously.

Kate felt Luca start beside her. His rage and anguish choked her, robbed her of words. She stayed him as the man released an arrow, piercing her in the right shoulder. The bolt knocked her back, sending her head crashing against Luca's arm. Blood spilled anew. She reached up with a trembling hand, and snapped the shaft of the arrow lodged beneath her shoulder blade with her ruined hand.

~

LUCA'S MOOD TURNED BLACK, AND THE SKIES WITH IT. THUNDER threatened. In a place that had never seen more than a few drops of water fall from the sky each year, it was no wonder that a great number of the crowd scattered at the ominous gathering of storm clouds, and the high shriek of winds that whipped and lashed sand in every direction. Luca's eyes blazed at the archer with a crimson fury that did not abate, but turned the dark man's skin several shades whiter. The only thing that stopped his rage from boiling over was Kate's soft voice in his ear.

"Let me up."

Luca unhanded her and released his grip on the winds.

She used just her legs, the only limbs with any power left to them, and stood to face the seht.

THE VOICE OF HIS FATHER CAME UNBIDDEN IN DARIEN'S EAR.

"Nice traditions you have here. A pregnant woman sliced to a bloody mess. I see things haven't changed much since last I spent time in Likhan."

Darien pressed his eyes shut as Ted stomped away.

AS KATE GOT TO HER FEET, THERE WAS A RUSTLING TOWARD THE BACK OF the crowd. People craned their necks to see the source of the voice that rang out over the silence.

"Can a mighty oak be felled with cuts and bruises, knives and arrows? No! Its roots are ancient, and strong, and it stands firm."

Kate locked her knees in place, willing them not to buckle. The voice from the crowd, flickering in and out of Kate's vision in a flash of indigo, continued.

"Its branches, though they bleed, run with life, its shade gives freedom!"

The free folk at the edges of the crowd echoed her with booming attestations and protests at the violence against their champion.

"That tree you *cannot* cut down. For that is *not* a tree. That is the Grand Forest, the heart of us all."

Christine emerged from the swell and cheers and kneeled in the center of the circle.

"Hail, my queen."

DARIEN OPENED HIS EYES AGAIN AS KATE CALLED TO HIM FROM THE circle, blood streaming, her arms spread wide in front of her.

"Great and Merciful Seht, are you satisfied?"

His irises were like chips of ice.

"The blood debt to the Great Houses is paid. You are all witness to it. Remember well the men who fell to my champion, High Queen of Icarya, Empress of the Lone Islands, and Ruler of the Grand Forest, for their treason in refusing to accept my succession. The old Likhan dies with them. I am your seht, and I call on you to come before me in the morning to swear your loyalty and secure your place in our new city. From this day forward, any who raise a hand to strike at our newly freed brothers and sisters, their children, or our Icaryan friends and their agents, who have given of themselves today though they were *not* bound by Likhanni law, that hand shall be forfeit. Along with their wealth, their lands, and their lives."

From the back of the crowd, the woman who had cut Kate first cursed herself for a fool.

Kate stood all the taller, her triumphant grin mirrored in Darien's eyes. She nodded at him imperceptibly, relieved he had seized the opportunity she had given him.

Alaric noted her cold, calculating countenance, her iron will unnerved by the blood that flowed, and saw his queen.

Darien departed from the square. Those who remained took that as their cue and scattered.

LUCA TOOK THE HEAVY CAPE OFF HIS SHOULDERS AND WRAPPED KATELYN up in it, carrying her away behind Darien. Alaric followed, and their procession made its way back to the Seht's palace. Luca pulled the fabric tighter around her as he walked, cradling her neck in the crook of his elbow.

It's almost over, love. I've got you.

She groaned and sank into his arms.

Around the first bend of the square, Luca was stopped by a middle-aged woman, her dark brown skin smeared with sand that glimmered in the oppressive heat of the sun.

"Please, Highness," she begged, her head down and her hands up, "please accept this from my mother, my sister, and me. It is made from the smokethorn's bark, and will ease the queen's pain." Tears shone on the woman's downcast face.

"Thank you," Kate murmured, taking the aged leather pouch from the woman with her good hand and placing it on the curve of her stomach. The woman bowed lower and withdrew backwards from whence she came. The path back to Darien's palace was choked with throngs of citizens offering healing powders, balms, salves, and elixirs, giving all they could to aid the recovery of the woman who had punished their masters, secured their freedom, and protected their city from the shadowy terror that reigned over the plaza and terrorized them still in their dreams.

Once inside the palace walls, Darien barked furious orders at his staff to bring him clean bandages and hot water as Luca eased Kate into a chair. She sat remarkably upright.

Darien turned his wrath on her. "The next time you want to cut yourself to ribbons in *my* bazaar, you better damn well clear it with me first!"

Ted turned a scalding gaze at him, but bit his tongue. He knelt beside his sister and stroked the hair from her sweat-laden forehead.

"By the gods, Kate. What were you thinking?"

Darien grabbed bandages from a servant who scurried past him, but before he could approach, Luca took the bandages and bowl of water from him without a word. Setting everything aside, he slipped his hands down the front of her dress and behind, taking firm hold of the arrowhead protruding from her back.

"What are you doing?!" Darien asked.

Luca ignored him. "Ready?" he asked Kate.

"Go," she grunted. He removed the shaft swiftly and pressed his hands to either side of the wound as blood spurted out. She laid her head on his chest as he willed her flesh to close. Her arms were nearly healed on their own; he concentrated his efforts on her hand, stitching the bones back together correctly.

The alarm of those watching shifted to shock, then calm, as they saw for themselves that it really *would* be alright.

But Kate's demeanor was far from calm. Her eyes flashed with latent malice, and Luca felt her skin again wax cold as they peppered her with questions. "I've taken worse lickings," she said in a voice filled with gravel. "And given worse too." She laughed and bared her teeth. "At Telmar, at Sauraum. At Vehlen."

Luca stared hard into her eyes, willing her to stay focused, and not lose herself to the dark memories that crept along her veins like ice.

You didn't mean to do those things.

"Oh indeed I did," she answered aloud. But he heard the swagger in her voice falter, and he pressed her.

That's not who you are. Look at me, Katelyn. Stay with me.

She complied, holding his gaze until her muscles shuddered and she crumpled in his arms. Brow furrowed, she murmured against the curve of his chin.

"Where...what did I—"

Shh. It's over now. I'm here. I'm here.

She blinked, and nodded as the days slid back into place in her mind. Her heart raced at the thought of how far she'd nearly gone, if only in her mind, but Luca quashed those fears before they took hold.

He scooped her up again, leaving the bloodied rags behind, and carried Kate off to rest.

Ted, Alaric, and Darien shared awkward glances as the royal couple left them by themselves. Darien's servants made quick work of clearing away the gore.

Christine came into the room unannounced and set herself before the seht.

"We've met before," Darien replied, "or so I thought."

She raised an eyebrow. "Beg pardon?"

"Oh, did I forget to mention that?" Alaric stepped in. The look on his face was one of absolute glee. "You see, I've been here for a while, but not always as myself."

Christine was unamused by Alaric's cryptic tone, which only deepened his smile. "I required a disguise, and our good queen was kind enough to provide me with a body to hide in."

Her face turned a shade of red the likes of which Alaric had never seen. It was positively delightful. He inched closer, his knowing voice draped in velvet.

"As Seht Darien said: We've met before."

Christine's fists were balled tight as sledgehammers. She shook so violently, she was liable to chip a tooth.

"Don't forget to breathe, now."

She had. Christine had indeed forgotten to breathe as fury raged across every inch of her skin. Ripping his head off wouldn't get her anywhere. But it would be damned satisfying, and it was all she seemed to want to do.

She swallowed it and remembered why she had come.

"Let's go," she barked at him.

"Go?"

"We have work to do."

~

The energy in the Great Quarter of the bazaar was subdued.

"Guess people don't like the sight of blood when they're bargaining over their fancy baubles," Alaric observed. "I'm surprised they didn't close up shop altogether."

"Come on."

Christine pushed him forward to the spot where the sand was saturated to a dark red paste and shoved an unmarked clay jar into his hand.

"Not so rough," Alaric chided, though the smirk never left his mouth. "What are we supposed to be doing?"

Christine didn't answer him. She simply knelt before Kate's spilled blood and began scooping it into a jar of her own with a wide paper fan. She tossed a similar fan on the ground next to her as Alaric joined her.

"*Left* hand," she snarled, "and don't leave any behind."

"Are you always this pleasant?" Alaric was in earnest now, the mirth gone from his face. She didn't answer him, didn't even look up, but continued to collect the queen's blood as if he wasn't there.

Something else is eating at her, Alaric thought as he watched and mimicked her broad, circular swipes at the ground that urged the blood-stained sand into her jar. When they had gotten the last bit up and sealed the vessels shut, Christine snatched away the jar in his hands before he even opened his mouth to ask a question. Alaric wondered why she'd even bothered bringing him along at all. He wanted to shrug it off, but if he knew Kate, he knew that there was nothing she ever did without a reason.

AT DINNER, ALARIC ENDED UP SEATED ON KATE'S LEFT SIDE, BUT IT DIDN'T feel right to ask her all the questions he had on his mind. Not when all he could think of was all that had come before. And all that would never come to pass. There was a long silence between them before he murmured:

"Congratulations. It seems you've found all you've been looking for."

"Thank you. I'm sorry you have not."

"All will be ready for the festival tomorrow," Darien said. "At least, I think it will." He looked to Mavis, who peered over his head to glance at Kate before answering in the affirmative. "I don't mean to complain, but I can't see what's taking so long. I requested a simple costume."

"Simple does not always mean quick. All the same, everything will be done in time," Mavis answered.

The flow of the conversation was enough to shift Alaric's focus in a more pressing direction. "I have some things to report," he said to Kate.

"Another night's worth of spying won't hurt." She turned her head away from him and said, "See me in the morning."

He leaned back in his chair and pressed his lips into a thin line. He did not speak again.

~

LUCA JOINED KATE ON THE BALCONY OF THEIR ROOM AS THE STARS flickered on across the desert sky.

He settled into the wide-thatched wicker chair that Kate occupied, cradling her between his legs as he brushed her hair in long, soothing strokes. He sang as he worked, rebraiding small sections of her hair as he smoothed away the day.

Kate leaned into him, letting his sweet, low voice soak into her very marrow.

"You've missed your calling."

"I only sing for you," he said. After a period of quiet, Luca spoke again. "You need to leave him alone, Katelyn."

"I know. I just…I've been where he is now. I wouldn't wish it on anybody."

Luca sighed. "If I wasn't here, if we'd never met and he'd come back into your life again, would you have gone to him?"

There was a long silence before she answered.

"No. Alaric is all chaos. He's what I see when I look in the mirror. He reminds me: of who I used to be. Of who I thought I had to be. You bring me peace."

Luca chuckled. "*I* bring you peace? You can say that, after all we've been through?"

"Wherever we go, *you're* my home."

"There's a charm about you, Kate. People are drawn to you. Push him away. Be cruel if you have to. Let him let you go, so he can get on with his life. It's the best thing you can do for him."

"You're right," she groaned. "I know you're right."

"Now. You have more important things to worry about. I haven't made love to my wife in…hours."

Her hair brushed to a glossy shine, Luca was ready to muss it up. He withdrew his slender fingers from her hair and found purchase in the weight of her breasts, delighting in the audible uptick in her heartbeat.

She laughed as he swept her up and carried her to the bed.

In the balcony above theirs, Alaric sat with a face of stone. Not a single muscle betrayed the anguish roiling his gut.

10

Unable to stay in his room and endure the sounds of sex above him, Alaric went out into the city. But even there, he could find no peace. He couldn't focus his disordered thoughts; he couldn't even see straight. He barreled headlong into a brothel as if it were a matter of life and death.

"Bring me a redhead. And be quick about it!" He wasted no time when she came, undoing his fly in a matter of seconds.

"On your knees."

The ale was sour and cheap. Alaric imbibed as much of it as he could, as quickly as he could. When his hand was empty, waiting for his next refill, he grabbed the throat of the woman who had his cock in her mouth and squeezed.

She pulled away from him as he choked her and tried to shove him by the hips. He snarled at her and tossed her to the floor.

"Enough," he snarled.

"You still have to pay!"

He threw his coins at her and stumbled out into the alley, fumbling with his britches.

"Get your head back on straight?"

Christine was leaning against the wall facing the squalid establishment, her arms crossed.

"Step off."

She shoved him hard into the wall when he tried to pass her by. "We don't have time for this shit."

His bleary gaze burned through her. She scoffed, looking more annoyed than Alaric thought she should.

"That's what she does. She lets you get close, then pushes you away. Get over it."

She pulled him through the streets and turned abruptly into a hidden alley. It was so well camouflaged by the winding pathway that you wouldn't know it was there unless you were looking for it. The only difference was the façade on one of the buildings was slightly askew from the ones before and after it. It gave the intersection the appearance of a solid lane, with nowhere to turn except into the wall.

"You're not like I thought," Alaric said as the fresh air helped to clear his mind.

"I don't know what she told you about me, but I don't just blush and spread my legs for every pretty face. The outward charms may have been yours, but I was drawn to the person *beneath* them."

He'd missed a step.

"What do you mean?" he asked.

Despite her curt declaration, Christine did blush just then. "She *didn't* tell you..."

"Tell me what?"

Christine wasn't about to enlighten him. He had to put it together himself. He knew almost nothing about Christine's relationship with Kate, except that she met Christine disguised. Disguised...as...

"It was *me*?"

Christine looked away. Her pace quickened.

"She met you, flirted with you, made you blush—just like you're doing now—looking like me."

He was flattered. But something about it wasn't sitting quite right.

"What do you mean, you were drawn to the person underneath?"

"I'm...attracted to men *and* women."

"That's sexy."

"Is that *all* you think about?"

"Pretty much…"

They kept walking, deeper into one of the free neighborhoods, once again traveling farther than he'd ever gone on his own.

In a tone as sweet as rotten lemons, Christine asked, "Have you met His Royal Highness?"

"Oh, he's a real treat."

Their eyes met. For the first time, they smiled at each other, and laughed. Alaric noticed the torchlight sparkling in her eyes.

When they finally arrived at their destination, Kate and Luca were already there.

They were seated at a long table, already having pushed aside a smattering of marked porcelain tiles, printed cards, Likhanni coins, and betting slips. Laid out on the table instead were a handful of costumes, all hooded in a glittering blue intended to represent a naiad, ready to be distributed. Darien's head housekeeper stood ready to distribute the copies to every link in Likhan's Unbroken Chain.

"*Everyone* will see the seht wearing this in the plaza during the day," Kate explained. "We will use that to keep him safe at night. Christine, you'll be with Darien."

She nodded.

"Why not me?" Alaric demanded. "I've been at Darien's side all this time."

"Exactly. People will expect you to be with him."

Another thought struck him. "Why isn't Darien here?"

Kate didn't answer.

"I don't like this. He should know," Alaric said.

Kate cocked her head. "You like him."

Alaric shrugged. "Am I not supposed to?"

Christine interrupted. "It will be easier for me if he does know."

"Alright. Tell him what you must then."

Christine gave the replicated costume a once-over. "This doesn't look anything like a water nymph."

Kate let out an exasperated sigh. "He's fucking Likhanni, Chris. He's *not* going to notice."

She shrugged. "Just sayin'."

An expected knock came at the back door. Luca opened it to a wide array of merchants, tradesmen, and lesser servants who had removed themselves to the free quarter.

Kate rose to greet them. Christine nodded to each link in the chain as they entered, and they returned the gesture. Some gasped in awe as they beheld Kate's arms, unbound and unharmed, mere hours after her brutal ordeal. But their sense of decorum stopped them from staring or asking questions. They simply accepted the impossible.

"My representative Christine Del Mar has invited you here tonight to aid in the protection of your seht in his hour of need, and to secure his position in this city." Among them, a craftsman by his attire, stepped forward. "We owe the Great, Merciful Seht our freedom and our lives. We are ready to give them to protect him."

"Likhan and Icarya thank you for your loyalty and your bravery. There is compensation enough for you there," Kate said, indicating a row of chests lining the left wall.

The merchant spread his hands open before her. "We will accept no payment. It is an honor to serve the Great and Merciful Seht."

All who were gathered nodded and murmured in agreement.

Kate smiled widely. "I suspected as much, and I thank you." She walked over to the row of chests and opened them, revealing weapons, clothing, and food. "Then take the things you will need for the coming night, and enough to feed your families' bellies."

The people readily accepted the sheathed daggers and crossbows, swords and Icaryan torchlights. As they gathered their goods and their disguises, Luca gave quick pointers on how to roam the city with the intent to obscure their trails, how to double-back and become the tracker, how to defend themselves against surprise attacks and to keep their faces hidden.

The swords across *his* back commanded immediate respect. They asked questions and had him correct their stances and their grip on their newly acquired weapons. He pointed out kill spots between the ribs, in the thigh, and at the collarbone. He warned that they should be used as a last resort. When they all seemed satisfied and confident, Kate spoke with parting words.

"Any men we put down will fall on the seht's shoulders, and may cause him more strife in the days to come. I appreciate your anger at those who oppose your seht and oppose your liberty, but I *urge* you to show restraint. Let the justice of your Great and Merciful Seht be their punishment."

Our homes will be open to you, and provide any shelter or protection the Seht may require of us. We will not fail our seht, Great and Merciful as he is!"

Kate bowed her head. "Go quiet and careful now. You may be watched at this hour."

Her warning was unnecessary, as those of the Unbroken Chain knew all too well how to cross the city unnoticed. A trio assumed the look of two friends dragging a drunken third home. Others relied on similar ruses, and carried with them sacks heavy with fresh milk, pouches of grain, salt, healing balms, sachets of tea brewed to ease hunger, or pain or illnesses of the mind, smoked venison, and fresh apples.

As the Icaryans were left alone, Christine gave Kate her due. "Clever move."

"Hmm?"

"You knew they wouldn't take coin, so you gave them food."

Kate smiled. "When in Rome…"

"Huh?"

"When in Rome…do as the Romans do."

Christine pressed her hands to her hips. "Is that another one of your quaint little Earth sayings?"

"There's nothing quaint about it. Understanding local customs is the key to good relations. You have to ask a Likhanni twice before they will accept a gift, and food is never refused as a general rule. It is observed as wasteful, disrespectful even. 'When in Rome…" she repeated. "Though Earth humans are by and large a bunch of arseholes, there's one thing you can't take away from them. They are surprisingly ingenious. And they are masters of war."

"Hmm."

Kate turned to Luca at his subtle reaction.

"Am I wrong?" she asked.

"No. I just never thought about it that way before."

"I *am* smart, but not every good idea I have is mine alone." She turned to Christine and grinned. "I stand on the shoulders of giants."

Christine rolled her eyes. "Gods that's annoying. Are you ever going to run out of them?"

"I haven't yet."

Alaric cut in. "This is all very illuminating, but those people did not look menacing. A few minutes' instruction by your husband is not enough to make them warriors. Why not bring in your own men?"

Kate shook her head firmly. "*They* are the future of Likhan. They must take their fate into their own hands, and we must be careful not to overshadow Darien. We are here because he needs our help. He must not always. They may not be soldiers, but they're something better. They are *survivors*. They are the once-enslaved, who endured the horrors of their lives long enough to see their freedom. Never underestimate the stores of strength buried there."

Alaric conceded the point. He noticed then that only Kate and Luca were left without decoy costumes.

"What are you going to do?" he asked.

Kate's expression turned grave. "Likhan has more than civil unrest to worry about."

"Haydee?"

"I don't know."

"But you feel it?"

Kate nodded. Alaric nodded back.

"That's good enough for me."

11

Darien adorned his costume with rings of lapis lazuli and blue opals to add that iridescent glow he thought was missing. He donned the heavy golden chain of the seht as he made his way to the throne room, where the most prominent families of Likhan had already assembled. At least, most of them had.

The widow and two brothers who had not laid a hand on his aunt in anger he heard first, followed by those who had already offered their daughters in marriage and had not been seen anywhere near the goings-on at the bazaar. There were other families without daughters to offer but who appeared equally sincere, and those whose grinding of teeth was audible as they swore their allegiance. Among the last bunch, the crone who had struck first was prominent. Her family and the man who had come bearing a crossbow were the last to arrive, not seeing another choice.

Their open hostility to his reign formed a palpable anger in his chest.

"I do not accept your pledge. You are struck off. I want you out of Likhan by nightfall."

Their pride now turned to fear. Darien smiled broadly as they pleaded.

"Where will we go?"

"The desert is wide. There is space enough there for your ilk." His lips quirked in wry pleasure. "You could always try your luck in Icarya. I hear that food and work are abundant there."

He rose, not leaving any room for debate. When he turned to leave, he was surprised to find his father looking on.

"I thought you'd left."

Ted shook his head. "I was angry yesterday."

"You had every right to be."

Ted dipped his chin. "Still. You need to do what *you* think feels right. I'm in no position to tell you otherwise."

There was an awkward beat, after which Ted said, "But, if I thought you'd done something *really* thick-headed, I suppose I'd tell you. If my opinion is welcome."

Darien clasped his hands. "It is."

Ted squeezed him back. "I've wanted this…for a very long time."

That was all Darien needed to hear. All he had ever hoped to hear.

"I've still got to get ready. I'll see you later?" Ted asked.

"You will," Darien answered, and quickly left the complex to join Alaric and Christine as the day dawned and the holiday began in earnest. They toured the central plaza, examining all the stalls selling Icaryan foodstuffs, both fresh and prepared, freedmen selling their home-woven tapestries and hand-crafted jewelry, and elaborately embellished cups, bowls, mirrors, and the like from the Merchant Quarter. Along the way they studied people's faces, locating all persons of interest. At the top of that list were those whom Darien had banished just that morning. After breaking away from their little group to take a gander over at the Noble District, Christine confirmed that they *looked* to be moving out.

~

She conversed with Darien normally. But Alaric—she wouldn't look him in the face. Whenever he spoke to her or asked her a question, he got only a curt, one-word response. If she ever caught him looking at her, or heaven forbid *smiling* at her, she scowled and quickly turned her face away.

"Let's not let the fact that I've seen you naked affect us working together."

He'd said it close to her ear, rather than announcing it to the whole city, but nevertheless—her cheeks turned a brilliant shade of crimson. Her eyes shot daggers at him that gave his heart a little flutter.

Then she rallied and spat back, "I'm surprised you give a shit. You have had the pleasure of our illustrious queen's company, have you not?"

That gave Alaric a start. Before he could even stop himself, the words were out of his mouth. "I wasn't complaining."

Her pace slowed, and the fire in her face cooled some.

And just like that, Alaric's impulse to needle her evaporated.

DARIEN STOPPED TO ENJOY THE MUSIC BEING PLAYED IN THE VERY CENTER of the plaza, traditional songs meant to pull lingering spirits in and direct them safely away from the living and out into the desert. His attention was drawn to the girl playing the harp while she sang. Her delicate fingers strummed the strings with grace and precision. He became quickly enchanted by her hands and her sweet, sad melody, full of devotion.

Their eyes met as the song ended. He joined the applause, nodding in her direction. She blushed and bowed her head. As the musicians dispersed, Darien approached to thank them personally. He sought out the harpist. She was not easy to find amid the bright flowing costumes of the dancers, but her attempt to make herself invisible was hampered by her oversized instrument, which he spotted seemingly floating away of its own accord. She finally stopped trying to escape when he greeted her.

"Blessed Kai-Mar."

She kept her neck bent in a deep bow as she replied in kind.

"Greetings, My Seht. A Blessed Holiday to you." Darien pressed the tips of his fingers under her chin. He barely touched her as he lifted her face to his and found dark round eyes, a delicate nose, and soft, welcoming lips. Gleaming raven hair framed her face, her skin a rich, heady caramel. He withdrew his hand as she looked up at him, though her trembling still reverberated on his fingertips.

"You played exquisitely."

She dipped her head again in gratitude and took the opportunity to shield her eyes from his gaze.

"I've seen you before, haven't I? At my uncle's sending."

"Yes, My Seht. I've played for some years now."

"Where did you learn to play with such passion?"

The girl seemed unsure how to answer.

"You seemed transported by your music," Darien offered. "I watched you play, heard the timbre of your voice. It was quite moving."

She dipped her head again, further this time. "I am honored to have pleased you, My Seht."

Darien heard himself called away by Alaric and Christine, who had hung back as he mingled with the performers. He made a respectful bow.

"Thank you for the superb music. Enjoy the festival."

Alaric was smirking when Darien returned to his side. "See something you liked?"

"Do you have nothing else to do, Alaric, that you need to watch my every move?" Despite himself, Darien was smiling.

"Not today."

~

KATE ASSESSED HER REFLECTION IN THE MIRROR. HER SKIN WAS PAINTED the shimmering gold of Icarya's forest god. Hundreds of jewel-encrusted leaves hugged her curves in a bodysuit that left her arms and legs bare, save for the soft brown leather boots that reached up to her thighs. Bits of gold and copper were woven into the braids of her hair. Poking out from her crown was a pair of antlers.

Luca appeared as a raven. He wore a feathered cowl around his shoulders and had applied a thick band of black grease paint across his eyes that came to a sharp point at the bridge of his nose. The knuckles of his gloves were armed with silver talons.

Her skin prickled as Luca pressed his fingertips to her shoulders.

"I can't shake this terrible feeling," she said. "It's just me I suppose. Thinking every little thing is a sign of danger ahead." She tried to take a deep breath and uncrossed her arms. "I've never felt so paranoid."

"No. I feel it too."

As NIGHT FELL, PAPER LANTERNS IN BRIGHT REDS, YELLOWS, AND PURPLES were lit, strung up from the columns of buildings and across the top of alleyways all throughout the city. The festivities coalesced around the Hi'dinn Council House, flowing out onto the steps and into the garden. Lush fabrics and pillows in blues and greens were strewn about on the tile floor everywhere people might sit as they all ate communally from large dishes. Likhanni of all classes were forced to mingle as they attempted to get close to where Darien and his coterie were seated. He, along with his father, his aunt, her husband, and her two agents dug in to the feast. Kate filled her plate with what the free folk had brought: slivered nuts and fermented desert fruit.

"Will you not have some of the more festive foods?" Darien asked.

"These *are* festive," she replied coolly.

"But—"

"I live in a tree, remember? I prefer simple fare."

For their part, the free folk and the nobles gravitated toward fresh produce from Icarya. Icaryans had also brought with them two sides of venison, a suckling pig with apples and mushrooms, and fresh-baked pastries by the crateful. Likhanni were so used to everything being stewed after having been dried or cured to preserve their foodstuffs in lean times. Very few plants grew in Likhan, and even fewer of them were edible.

All around him, Darien overheard conversations that filled him with hope. Servants who worked in good homes recommended their relatives, becoming united under caring and considerate households.

Women from different quarters complimented each other's food and shared recipes.

The brothers of House Solimani were extra generous. All the bigger houses were, as a demonstration of their devotion to the seht and his new vision for the city. Those who had, and those who had not, had given all they could spare. They feasted together for hours, sating themselves on food, drink, and a renewed sense of hope.

Gideon drew huge crowds of people. Many Likhanni had never seen a gryphon before. They gasped in awe at his impressive wingspan. Ted made the introductions.

"Gideon, this is Seht Darien of Likhan."

"Pleased to make your acquaintance," the gryphon answered.

"The pleasure is entirely mine." Darien's eyes went round as a child's, his smile stretched from ear to ear. Ted remembered that feeling well—the sense of wonder that accompanied meeting a creature you'd only ever heard about in stories for the very first time. He smiled.

The Icaryans that had made the journey to Likhan brought music of their own, along with their more raucous definition of revelry. They played and sang and drank a bit too loud, a bit too rough, their frolicking and frivolity just…*more*…than the "civilized" Likhanni were accustomed to. Kate gleamed with pride.

"We don't stand much on ceremony," she said.

Kate moved to the center of the room and stretched out her arms, calling Icarya to her in that age-old way. They danced and leaped around each other in wild circles, the way creatures and men have moved to music since the beginning of time, drawn only by instinct and nature. With her husband looking on, her heart swelled.

I have everything I've ever wanted in this moment.

When the dance was done, Kate caught up with Hercules.

"You're looking well," she said. "Wife keeping your belly full?"

"It's all muscle! I feel better than I have in over a century. Keeping her belly full too!" he laughed.

"Oh my! We'll have a gaggle of littles running around by this time next year. Won't that be nice?" Corbin climbed up Kate's back, sporting a bright blue feather twice the size of his entire body tucked behind his ear.

"I've stacked the deck, as you've asked," he said.

She lowered her voice, then said to Hercules, "Keep your eyes peeled tonight."

"I always do."

THE EARTHY SOUNDS OF ICARYAN WIND AND STRING INSTRUMENTS harmonized with those of the Likhanni musicians deep into the night. The Likhanni players were dressed in brightly colored flowing robes that made them look ethereal. They were not costumed, not exactly, but they blended in with the festivities well enough.

The harpist was positioned next to a faun, who played a much smaller set of strings, his instrument tucked beneath his chin. She complimented his playing during a break.

"I couldn't tell if you were listening. You seemed so distracted," he replied.

Arjuna turned back to the man who had occupied her thoughts all morning, admiring his costume and how the bright blue flares of his costume dress complemented his lithe figure, how the sweeps of glittering silver and blue accentuated his sleek brow and sculpted cheeks.

"This morning, the seht greeted me. *Me*. He told me my music moved him." She shook her head. It had all seemed so impossible, like being inside a dream. She turned again to the faun beside her.

"Your melody is so elegant, so graceful."

"It's improvisational. Whatever feels right. Shall we try it?" the faun asked.

The girl hesitated. "I am not Icaryan," she said, almost sadly. "Likhanni music values form above all else. The most beautiful music is beautiful for its flawless execution."

"And yet, he complimented your passion, did he not? Your music's emotional power?"

She smiled at the memory of it. "He did."

Torrence settled a wreath of leaves and white winter berries upon her head. "Now. Let's play for him."

Arjuna began again, letting the faun take the lead. Soon enough, she lost herself in the music, as she always did. She was grateful for the power her music held over her, its ability to erase her fears, the stress of her homelife, and her burning, forbidden love for the gentle and generous Hi'dinn Councilman who was now Seht. She gave herself over to a joyous melody, thinking only of the faun's music, paired with her strings as effortlessly as one is with their own breath. The pair poured all of themselves into their playing. When there was nothing left to say between them, the melody softened until its whisper echoed off the marble walls only in memory. Several silent notes passed before they were buffeted with the deafening roar of applause. Arjuna's face grew hot, and her chest pounded beneath her dress as she saw the seht. His smile was bright and gleaming, and meant only for her.

FOLLOWING THE MEAL, THE REVELERS DISPERSED THROUGH THE STREETS. The spirits were about and needed to be chased out into the desert with their merrymaking. The departed were all mourned and honored properly, but the younger moon crossing the path of the elder drew them close, and they needed to be reminded that the time for separating from their families had already come and gone.

Darien thanked everyone for their outpouring of goodwill as people left the Council House in droves.

"Let us go out in a great show of our solidarity, our new hope and pride, and let those ghosts still bound to this world be gone from our shadow."

He descended the steps with Christine at his side. Alaric ascended to the rooftops unseen. Should they run into any trouble, he was the ace up her sleeve.

KATE AND LUCA EXITED THE COUNCIL HOUSE FROM ANOTHER DIRECTION. But before Kate walked too far away from him, Luca snatched her by the arm and pressed her up against a marble column, his voice a soft murmur against her throat.

"I may not get the chance later."

He knew better than anyone that Kate was feeling insecure about her changing body—her growing belly. It was utter nonsense, and it all melted away as he hiked up her thighs and filled her. He ached for the taste of her blood on his tongue, but he stopped just short of that. They both needed their strength. It turned their lovemaking all the more fervent, and he clawed at her thigh as he ground into her.

~

KATE COULDN'T STOP STARING AT HER HUSBAND. HE LOOKED ABSOLUTELY beautiful as the raven. His dark beauty, his true self, though costumed, felt like a reflection of the life that had taken root in her soul. Their child nestled snugly in her belly proved no obstacle to him, and she forgot to worry about everything that was fading—her youth, her humanity. She felt beautiful in his arms.

When they had stolen all the time together they could, Kate and Luca split up, following their senses toward those points where the impulse of danger felt strongest. The feeling surged as the night grew long. Kate wanted so badly to exert control over whatever was going to happen before the public became aware of it. The first national holiday presided over by Darien was important to his position in the city. A general panic or widespread attack would spell disaster.

12

For all her preparation and good intentions, Kate could not contain the dark thing that took hold of Likhan. The shadow did not manifest as a solid beast, but as something sprawling, extending its fingers outward and billowing its way through the meandering avenues of the city. From the far ends of Likhan, she and Luca sought out the core of the sorcery, hoping to find Haydee there and stamp her out before she could do any more damage. But if there was some sentience at the heart of the shadow, it was beyond their ken.

The night fog spread itself across Likhan like a cancer. Congealed creatures arose from concentrated patches, smaller in stature than the hound Kate had fought last, but equally dangerous. They scattered through the streets in great leaps and bounds, the billowing of darkness like the flapping of wings. In places where shadow gathered, the line between Likhan and the shadow realm was stretched thin. People walking into the darkness in one lane came out another, defying every law of physics. Some did not come back at all.

~

"How you have forgotten me."

Darien spun at the sound of Haydee's voice echoing through the night air. But she was nowhere to be seen. *Nothing* was—the entire city was besieged by darkness.

"Christine? Alaric?" He turned his head quickly every which way, but he was alone, and nowhere near where he had just been not a moment before.

Haydee's voice called to him again, more plaintive this time. But clear was the menace that lurked beneath. He turned away from it, as much as he could turn away from a sound that seemed to call out to him from nowhere and everywhere all at once. He ran. It was all he could do to escape the voice calling out to him. The city rotated and shifted around him as the natural order of space and time crumbled. The street lay empty before him in a gaping expanse. Panic rose in his throat. He ran in whatever direction opened before him, to get away from the accusations of disloyalty and betrayal battering him on every side.

SHOUTS DREW CHRISTINE'S ATTENTION AWAY FROM DARIEN. SHE thought she had lost the last of their tails some time ago, with Darien none the wiser, of course. Had she miscounted? No one had been following them for the last half hour, she was sure of it. And she didn't see anything now that suggested anything different. It was no more than a second before she turned her head back in Darien's direction, only to find him gone.

"Shit."

She chose a direction and made to take one step forward, but Alaric dropped from the sky and trapped her arm in a vise before she could.

"You didn't lose him. He just...disappeared."

Worry was etched deep into his face as he swept his gaze in every direction, just as she had done a moment before.

"What do you mean, he *disappeared*? He was standing right there!"

"I saw him dissolve into darkness right next to you. We'll find him," he said, yanking harder on her wrist as she tried to escape, "but I'm not gonna lose you too."

They were reluctant to stray too far from where they'd last seen the seht—but every street and alleyway was deserted as far as the eye could see. Screams rose up across Likhan, bouncing off the stone walls of shops and homes and wooden doors slammed shut and windows were shuttered tight.

Out of the darkness, a pair of glowing red eyes appeared. Christine stepped back.

"Alaric..."

"I see it."

He drew his sword, but was too slow. The shadow was already upon them. But *this* shadow was a face they knew. He stopped just ahead of them and raised an eyebrow.

"Where is your charge?" Luca asked.

It took a moment for either of them to answer.

"Gone. Disappeared right next to us," Christine said.

"Were you following us too?" Alaric finally asked. He was still trying to catch his breath from the shock of Luca's sudden appearance—and his altered countenance.

"I was following the shadows," Luca said. "Now they're gone again."

"*With* Darien," Christine said.

"Stay close to me."

Luca walked past them without another word. They had no choice but to follow. They exchanged silent expressions of incredulity as they watched the shadows part and shrink back in fear before Luca. Any creature caught foolishly scampering about his feet fell to the ground in two halves, pooling at their ankles before dissolving. Neither one of them ever saw his sword move. They were nearly smothered by a vicious aura, swollen with an iron authority, that seeped out of him like a miasma. Christine and Alaric cowered at his back.

After winding through a fair bit of the city, Luca pointed his nose in the direction of the desert.

"I can't keep you with me anymore. I must move faster, and I can't do that with you behind me."

"I can help," Christine insisted.

"So can I." Alaric was not to be outdone.

"No, you can't. To walk in *these* shadows is to invite death. Stay too long, and you'll lose your life to it."

"What about *you*?" Christine asked.

"I'm already dead."

Alaric didn't even try to wrap his head around that.

"What should we do then?" Christine asked.

"Stay in the light, as close to it as you can."

LUCA LEFT THEM AS ABRUPTLY AS HE HAD COME AND FOCUSED HIS thoughts on Kate.

Darien has been taken. I'm going after him, into the desert.

I'll meet you at the edge of town.

No, Luca replied, his thoughts stern and full of worry. *If you do, you'll miscarry.*

There was a beat where nothing needed saying. They both knew what the other was thinking.

Do it, Kate said.

Luca slipped into her mind, soaking into her thoughts ever so gently, and set in place a command, one that would stop her from going after him and would keep her and the baby safe. She knew she couldn't trust herself not to risk it.

Stay in the light, he warned.

I make my own light.

Be careful, my love. I'll be back soon.

HERCULES HAD FIGURED OUT PRETTY QUICKLY TO STAY OUT OF THE darkest wisps of the shadows. Seeing as he wasn't familiar with Likhan's layout, he didn't mind being lost one jot. He rampaged through the streets like a bull, killing any monsters unfortunate enough to land in his path. The determination of his grip made up for the shifting, intangible nature of the beasts as he caught them by their spindly legs and dashed them against the sharp corners of buildings and marbled pillars of the Council House. After knocking the nuisances about for the better part of the night, he spied yet another screeching monstrosity, this one on fire. It seemed to be rolling itself on the ground to snuff out the flame, but it was no use. It was reduced to a pile of ash by the time it collapsed at his feet. Kate emerged from behind it, setting the avenue aglow as she approached.

"Not to say I'm not enjoying myself, but they just keep coming," he said.

"We have to beat them back, at least until sunrise," Kate said.

Together they blazed a path back to the Council House. It was pandemonium. People huddled in groups, crushing each other in a frenzied race away from the stone columns as shadows formed at their base and caused some to give way. Hercules caught one just before it crushed another family and laid it roughly on its side. People who fell into the shadows came back out again in a distant corner of the room. Some in pieces. Families gripped each other for dear life to stop from being spirited away, but the sorcery that pulled on them was too much to overcome.

Kate spun in every direction, not knowing which way to turn. She upset platters and pillows, adding to the chaos of the hastily abandoned feast as terror had taken hold.

"What are you looking for?" Hercules asked.

"A vector! I need..."

Kate's voice trailed off as she resumed her frantic search until, finally, she found something she could use. She grabbed the jug of wine at her feet and tossed it at the nearest column. A fresh wave of crise rose up at the sound of pottery shattering.

"Are there any more?!" Kate bellowed to the crowd, enlisting them to her cause.

"Here!" Torrence cried, and dashed his findings against the wall as his queen had done.

When the white-washed walls were soaked in wine the color of blood, Katelyn pressed her palms to them and set the Council House ablaze.

The screams of the Likhanni reached a fever pitch.

"Please, please don't run!" Kate urged. "It won't burn. It's only me."

THE LOT OF THEM LOOKED READY TO BOLT LIKE A STAMPEDE OF elephants. Corbin knew what he had to do.

He scaled the nearest column as fast as his legs could carry him and raced headfirst into the flames.

"See? There's no heat! It's only light. You're safe here!"

His small voice echoed across the marble, over the heads of the terrified. For the first time in what felt like ages, the Council House grew quiet.

They watched with gaping mouths as the blaze licked along the walls, encircling them in a ring of fire. Its light shined on their faces and pushed the darkest of the shadows back into the deepest recesses of the rubble. With a collective sigh of relief, the Great Hall of the Council House was secured. Men and women embraced each other and slowly moved to clear away the debris and find a place in the center of the circle to rest.

HERCULES KEPT HIS GAZE SQUARELY ON THE SOURCE OF THE FLAMES.

"Kate..."

"I'm okay. I'm okay." With a shuddering breath, she removed her hands from the wall. The fire raged on, no longer needing to be fed.

With a dazed expression, she moved away from the wall and toward the stairs leading back out into the city.

Hercules grabbed her by the arm. "Where in Tartarus are you going?!"

"There are still people out there. I have to clear a path."

Lower, he said, "You can't save them all."

"I have to try."

13

Alaric and Christine scurried along the edges of alleyways and street corners looking for shelter, but the shadowy grip on the city kept moving and shifting, and they were forced to move and shift with it. They stopped to catch their breath under a cluster of paper lanterns, but each of them knew without saying anything that their respite wouldn't last long. The strings holding the lanterns above their heads had snapped on one end, leaving them swaying off the side of an abandoned home. They blew wildly in the wind that funneled its way through the city like a low-lying tornado, spreading the darkness. Alaric released his grip on his knees and pulled Christine close to him, pressing her face to his chest and cradling the back of her head against the raging wind that battered their cheeks with a brace of desert sand.

His heart was thundering so loudly in his chest that Christine could hear it through the layers of his vest, dyed in the golden brown of a lion. It suited him. He pressed her face deep into his chest, nearly smothering her with the heady scent of the night's exertions. She was too tired, and too relieved to be shielded from the onslaught of the sandstorm to push back. So why was she so angry?

She struggled against him, and against the feelings that churned her gut but that she could give neither name nor voice to. But Alaric squeezed her all the harder.

He growled. "Stop fighting me." His voice was ragged and his chest heaved. They weren't going to be able to keep this up much longer.

Christine craned her neck so that, rather than her face being flush against his chest (really, she barely came above his abdomen), she was staring up at him. It was a long way up, but she found him craning his neck in the opposite direction, staring down at her.

"There's nowhere to run."

In answer, Alaric tightened his grip even more. She didn't think it was possible, but he nearly squeezed the life out of her as he rolled them both to his right, away from the corner of the building just as its edges became ashen and dissolved. He pressed her hard against the part of the stone that remained solid, at least for the moment.

"Should we try to find Luca?" she panted.

"Mr. Dead But Not Dead? No thank you."

"We were safe with him, at least. He could fight...whatever this is."

Alaric stretched his neck up, but there was nothing but shadow and sand in every direction. He shook his head and tucked it back down again.

"Wherever he is, he's gone now."

"It's just as well, I guess. He wasn't the best of company."

The corner of Alaric's mouth twitched a fraction, but the rest of his expression didn't follow suit.

A horrendous screeching sounded nearby.

"What now?"

ALARIC TURNED IN THE DIRECTION OF THE NOISE. IT HAD GONE QUIET again, and he squinted to see, but there was nothing there. With his luck, whatever had made that sound was coming their way, fast. He had no idea what to do about it. He'd shoved away the sinking feeling that, like the building that was disappearing at their backs, Darien would never be seen again. Focusing on Christine, making sure that *she* didn't vanish too, had kept those thoughts away. But now there was nowhere left to hide.

Again, he heard that hideous wailing, and again his corded muscles tensed as he searched frantically for the source of the sound that split the night.

What he saw made his heart leap into his throat.

"Come on!"

"Alaric, stop! It's too dangerous!"

As if he didn't know. At any moment, a dark cloud could gather and gulp them down faster than he could blink. He sprinted across the cobblestones, holding on to Christine's hand for dear life as he dragged her as fast as he could toward the ball of light he had seen flash when a shadow demon had met its fiery end. Through the ever-shifting hellscape, he raced like a madman to the one thing that remained steady.

~

KATE DUG DEEP, DIVIDING HER THOUGHTS SO SHE COULD FILL EVERY street with flame without becoming flame herself. The further her fire spread, the harder it became to remain conscious and solid. She had to walk deeper into the city in order to reach its furthest environs. She was more than a mile into the heart of Likhan when she had to stop and remind herself to breathe. The cool stone of the alley felt so refreshing against her back. She was depleted, but there was still so much more left to go. Her thoughts slipped from her control and began to wander as she crouched on the ground, using only the smallest measure of energy to reach each swaying lantern and keep it burning, slowly inching her way forward to the free towns and the open desert beyond. When she stretched her neck up to the sky for a gulp of fresh air, all she could see was on fire. Her mind shifted; she saw not the adobe homes of Likhan, but the spired domes of Vehlen. With great difficulty she shut her eyes to it. But it only allowed the screams of the dying to come roaring back to her. A stiff breeze whirled around her, and she thought of the little boy, the nameless innocent begging for help, splintered and cracked into icy rubble at her feet. She rubbed her stomach and tried to cry. But every inch of her was on fire, and tears would not fall.

She craved water with a thirst so deep and so profound in a way she had never done before. Paralyzed by ice, fire, and an unquenchable thirst, she wrapped her arms around herself and wailed at the chaos surrounding her. All semblance of control was lost from her until, without any forewarning, an unbearable pain seized her left hand. She shrieked and grasped for it, as if she expected not to find it there. She tested her fingers. They moved, stiffly, tingling with numbness. Its cause was unknown, but the pain shocked her back into focus. She put the faces of all she loved and images of her forest haven to the forefront of her mind and picked herself up off the ground.

She was barely cognizant when Alaric and Christine came careening around the corner. She kept mumbling to herself, over and over again: "I didn't mean to kill him. He was just a little boy." With arms outstretched, they rushed to her. She had just enough sense to shrink back.

"Don't touch me!"

14

Darien fled deeper and deeper into the unknown, trying to escape Haydee's voice. More than once, he considered giving in to her taunts, to fire off a few barbs of his own, but he was fearful of alerting her to where he was, if she didn't know already. Her pain was palpable in his ears, but he found that his own anger at her betrayal was equal to hers, and coupled with loathing. But that last was directed at himself. He was keenly aware of his inability to fight his mortal enemies, let alone a force like this. The city he was sworn to protect was sinking into madness. And he could do nothing. He couldn't stand and fight. All he could do was run. No matter where he turned, there were monsters. Once such a beast faced him now, coming up from between the stones before his very feet. Every muscle in his body pulled tight to attention. The memory of Kate wounding the gargantuan hound in the square flooded his memory. He recalled what he had observed then—it was all in the timing. His mind quivering but his legs solid, he stood his ground. When it leapt for him he ducked, and it sailed clean over his head as he ripped a deep tear along its underbelly with his dagger. Its momentum hit the wall in a pile of ash and dissipated like a spent storm cloud.

There was not time for a sense of triumph to wash over him, as countless hordes screeched and squealed in the not-too-far distance. He may have bested one. But he could not conquer them all. He backed himself into a corner, using the halo of light from a column of paper lanterns as his shield. He could feel more than see them as they encircled him, coming closer and closer to the rim of light. It would not be enough to keep them at bay.

The first to break away from the pack leapt onto the roof and snuffed the lanterns out from above. Darien sprinted to his right. The beast lunged for him. It missed his head, but an errant talon caught him by the thumb, ripping open the top of his finger. Darien clutched the bleeding digit to his chest as he ran, not sure where to run. He feared he would run headlong into a sheer wall of darkness when a door opened behind him, and he was yanked into a ball of light that cascaded into the street.

His rescuer slammed the door closed again as soon as she had pulled him across the threshold and hastily rebarred it with a heavy wooden beam. When the threat had passed, they turned and faced each other.

"You!"

"Are you alright, My Seht?" Arjuna asked.

"What are you doing here?" he asked in reply, still stunned.

"I live here, Great Seht."

She pointed all around the room to the Icaryan lanterns that poured light into the space and beyond the shuttered windows in thin shafts. "The shadow does not venture close here."

She bowed until her gaze tracked Darien's bloodied finger.

"Oh!" She gathered his hands in her own and drew him farther into the space. It was not a shanty house, but it was humble, with only two rooms—the one they were in, in which all the eating, cooking, working, and selling took place, and the one above, reserved for sleeping. She sat Darien down and scurried to the opposite side of the room for a jug of water, pouring a small amount of its contents into a stone bowl. She returned with the bowl and clean linens from a small hidden cupboard.

"I'm supposed to be taking care of you," he murmured. Despite the marked difference in their stations, he found it impossible just then to meet her eyes. His insecurities had never felt so raw, so exposed.

"You *have* taken care of us. Of me. I would have been sold on the market day next if not for you. Please," she offered, "let me care for you tonight."

Without waiting for an answer, she laid a thin, course linen over her lap and laid his hand on her knee as she sat facing him. With her left hand, she turned one of the lamps away from the windows and toward them. She dabbed at his thumb gingerly. It was a small tear, but deep. Before going further, she tied off the joint with a scrap of ribbon off the table to stop the flow of blood so she might see the wound properly.

"Thank you." Darien's voice was quiet and small. He had heard of such things happening, of poorer merchants in bad straits selling off their daughters, if their faces would bring in a tidy sale.

"Is your father doing so poorly as that?" he asked.

"My mother is very ill, and confined to her bed," she said, gesturing upwards. "I help my father as much as I can, but…" She shrugged. "We can no longer afford assistants, and the larger weavings take much longer to complete." Arjuna pulled a sewing needle through the fire as she spoke, and pressed bits of a poultice into the cut with her finger. She gestured to the other jug she had carried over to the table. "It's bitter, but it will dull the pain."

Darien swallowed the concoction down quickly, then allowed his gaze to roam the space. He saw tapestries hanging everywhere. The imported lamplight that most assuredly had been purchased to allow long nights at the loom illuminated their fine details.

"He would have sold you to the highest bidder, and yet you help him?" he asked, his indignation rising.

"He is my father. It is harder to break *those* bonds."

He grunted in acknowledgement. "They're exquisite."

She dipped her head ever so slightly, concentrating on the work before her. "You are welcome to any that might please you, Great Seht."

He smiled at her, but she was so caught up in what she was doing that she missed it.

"Darien."

"Seht?" She looked up at last.

"I would prefer that you call me Darien," he said softly.

"I would never ask for such an honor."

"You didn't."

The heat that rose to her face, reflected in the soft flow of the lamplight, brought a smile to Darien's lips.

"May I have the honor of your name?" Darien asked.

"Arjuna, My—" she corrected herself, and repeated, "my name is Arjuna."

He nodded. "It suits you."

"In what way?"

"It's lovely."

Great care was dedicated to the mending of his hand. Arjuna pulled a fine needle through his skin in small, close stitches as shadows blasted past the windows, shuddering the shutters like a sandstorm, only without the sand. It was the night that raged over them, threatening to swallow Likhan whole.

Darien watched her as she worked, enchanted by her slender, agile fingers, their painstaking effort, and all they had proved capable of: beauty, passion, and tenderness.

She closed his flesh to a nearly invisible seam, cut the thread with her teeth, and began to bandage the offended digit.

"It will not heal stiff," she said confidently. "You will be able to use it as you did before."

She prepared to clean her tools. He separated his hand from hers to raise her chin, challenging her to look into his eyes. He saw an eager fear there that mirrored itself in his own heart.

"Thank you, Arjuna," he whispered.

"It is my honor." She smiled brightly at him, and he tucked an errant tress behind her ear.

Something deep in his chest flickered to life.

A loud banging at the door shattered the quiet.

Alaric's voice vibrated through the shutters. "Let us in!"

"Alaric?!" Darien leapt to his feet. Arjuna rushed to the door to unbar it, with Darien quickly at her side. Alaric and Chrisine burst into the room as soon as the way was opened.

"How did you find me?" Darien asked as they both clutched at their knees, struggling to catch their breath.

"Sheer accident," Alaric wheezed. "We saw your light." He pointed to the lantern facing the window, but dropped his arm down just as quickly. He looked like the effort might make him fall over.

Christine found her voice, and said, "Come, Seht, you'll be safe at the Council House. The queen has made it safe."

Darien turned to Arjuna. "Come with us."

"I can't. My mother—" She looked upward, and they heard the shifting of bedclothes on the thin pallet of straw above. "I can't leave her here alone."

Darien stepped closer to her. "I can't just leave you here, to be swallowed up by shadows."

"*Go*, My Seht. You must."

Alaric laid an impatient hand on Darien's forearm.

The seht took Arjuna's hands, kissed the knuckles of her fingers, and pressed them to his forehead in a sign of deep gratitude. Her breath caught in her throat.

"I'll be back for you. I promise. Keep yourself safe."

Darien was surprised to find his aunt leaning casually against the wall when he stepped outside. He was even more surprised by the flame that engulfed her entire body, but seemed not to singe even the tips of her hair. When he blinked, he thought he saw shards of ice flicker across her skin, rather than the flames, but they were gone just as quickly again. He made to approach her, but both Alaric and Christine took hold of either side of him.

"Keep your distance please," Christine warned. "And," a little lower, she added, "talking to her is useless. She's in one of her special moods."

Kate's expression oscillated between blank and a bored, impatient malice. "Chris, if we get through this night before I slit your throat, it will be a miracle."

"See?" Christine said.

"What's wrong with her?" Darien asked.

"She's just confused. Her mind is in too many places at once."

"I'm sure she doesn't mean it," Alaric said, more to Christine than to Darien.

"Sure she does. Now, Your Magnificence—"

"I hate it when you call me that," Kate interrupted.

Christine gave a wry smile. "Yes. Yes you do."

Kate smiled weakly. She was in there, somewhere, still at the helm.

"Which way?" Christine asked.

~

KATE STARED AT THE SKY, THE BLANK EXPRESSION RETURNED. SHE struggled to put her mind back together, now spread so thin that fire and ice were deadlocked, and Kate's will stuck between them, ever shrinking.

~

CHRISTINE PRESSED HER. "WHICH WAY, KATE? *WHICH WAY*?"

After a few seconds when she did nothing but let her right hand twitch, she pointed absently in an easterly direction. She led her party through winding streets, staying in places already blazing with her fire and holding steady, and avoiding streets so dark that they disappeared like so much vapor.

At one point, Alaric happened to look down.

"Holy fuck! Kate where's your hand?"

She raised what to him had looked like only flames a moment ago. Her hand was, in fact, there, but perhaps less tangible than the rest of her.

"I noticed it too," she answered, spreading and stretching her fingers before her eyes. "I don't know what's wrong with it."

The alley ahead of them grew tight. They all felt it as if they were squeezed into an impossible choice: step into Kate, or into darkness. Kate was aware as well, and paused at an intersection, letting the darkness creep closer and closer to them. She called the flames burning across the city to herself. The world turned frighteningly dark as with a great intake of breath, the aura surrounding her grew black before she pushed the fire out again, blasting through the streets and evaporating the creatures before moving on. A low flame rekindled itself around her, and the places where she'd already lit a fire licked back to life.

They were nearly to the Council House when a bigger shape gathered before them. It took on Kate's shape, her face, with eyes furling clouds of ash. A colorless, immolated reflection of Kate blocked the path forward, starting straight at her in dark challenge.

Kate's expression hardened, and she bit out a sinister laugh.

"I've been wanting to kill *you* for a while now. Hold this for me, will you?" Without taking her eyes off the mimic, she shot her blaze outward, catching Darien square in the chest. As soon as her fire had left her, an intense cold took its place. The tips of her fingers turned blue. She curled them like talons. Instead of taxing her further, the fight brought her focus. Once she struck at her opponent and found the right rhythm, she didn't let up.

~

Fire caught Darien hard around the throat like a garrote. He fought to free himself from its molten grip, but he only managed a wet sound that emanated from the back of his tongue as the flames strangled him.

Alaric and Christine fared no better, but it was he who had become the source of the fire, and he who could not concentrate enough to put two thoughts together, let alone douse the inferno that engulfed them.

Somewhere in the recesses of his mind, his aunt's voice echoed.

Think of the mother who was stolen from you. Think of your uncle, who tried to kill you. Think of Haydee.

With every word, every memory invoked by the names on his aunt's lips, his sense of loss, his weakness, his sense of inadequacy grew. Frustration turned to rage. Something flickered on inside of him, and the fire flared more brightly, singeing the monster beckoning at his heels. He could feel the edges of the fire now, see it in his mind's eye. Darien pressed his eyes closed, concentrated, and enveloped them in a white-hot ball of light. At last, he could breathe.

THE SHADOW DIMINISHED IN SIZE WITH EVERY BLOW. IT MADE JABS FOR Kate's stomach, but she dodged it, spinning the creature around and twisting its head off its neck with her bare hands. It crumbled and dissolved like volcanic ash and drifted away. The ice on Kate's fingertips fizzled out into nothing.

For a moment, everything was silent. The air was cool and clean, and Kate drew it into her lungs in great heaves. The respite only lasted a minute. Bracing herself, she stretched out her fingers and called her fire back to herself. It hopped back into her right hand and up her shoulder. The flames turned blue and settled into the invisible border between her skin and a freezing mist that clouded around her as ice met fire. Within the span of a breath, she was ablaze again.

DARIEN FELT THE FLAME SUCKED OUT OF HIM AS IF IT WAS HIS VERY LIFE that was being ripped away. He drew in a shuddering breath as the last of its heat left him. But something somewhere, that he couldn't name if he tried, stayed on. Something had been left inside of him—something that might have always been there.

WITHOUT FURTHER CONVERSATION, THEY FINALLY ARRIVED AT THE Council House. Hercules was taken aback when he met them.

"You look wiped out," he told Kate.

She didn't respond, only tilted her head from side to side in acknowledgement.

"Kate. You've done all you can, but you need to stop now." He lowered his voice. "If the sun was *going* to come up, it would have been high in the sky by now. You can't keep this up forever."

"I hate to agree with him," Alaric chimed in, "but you don't look so good."

Kate closed her eyes. She let out a sad, hopeless laugh, but still, she did not answer.

"Come on, Kate. It's enough." Christine pressed.

Darien weighed in. "Please Katelyn. I can't ask you to sacrifice yourself, and with no end to this darkness in sight. You can stop now."

Kate shook her head. "I have been *trying* to put it out for the last hour."

Their eyes widened.. Kate swallowed and licked her lips.

"Isn't there anything left to drink around here?"

Alaric's eyebrows shot up to his hairline. "Grab all the water you can. Now!"

Everyone around him complied, not knowing why but understanding that the urgency that had flooded his voice was not without reason. They brought enough water to draw the queen at least two baths, if not three. Alaric wasted no time in dumping the first bucket handed to him over Kate's head. She screamed from sheer shock.

"Stop!" Christine cried. But he wouldn't. He unleashed torrent after torrent upon her until, at last, her fire went out.

~

KATE OPENED HER MOUTH, TAKING IN AS MUCH AS SHE COULD. WATER cascaded all around her. She felt drowned inside and out—and it was an utter relief. Her knees buckled, suddenly unable to bear her weight. She slid to the floor, melting into the golden puddle that had collected around her as the paint was washed from her skin. Curled in on herself, she looked like a wounded creature of the forest, her godliness spilled out all around her. After several heavy breaths, she sat up and coughed, expelling the excess fluid from her throat.

~

LIKHANNI AND ICARYANS ALIKE STARED IN AWE AS SHE LAY COLLAPSED ON the floor. Her outpouring of power, of herself, had been for their protection. The Council House filled with whispers of thanks, and words usually spoken not to a queen, but a god.

Alaric crouched in front of her. "Kate?"

She smiled and gripped his shoulder.

Christine let out a sigh of relief and wrapped her cloak around her drenched and dripping queen.

"I'm sorry," Kate murmured, "sorry for…for…"

Christine shrugged it off. "You weren't quite yourself, were you?"

"I'd never hurt you. I never meant to hurt you."

Christine did not reply.

Kate saw the question in their eyes. Who was the boy, the one she didn't mean to kill. She didn't answer them. She didn't *want* to answer them. She wanted to banish him again to the back of her mind. She pulled Christine's midnight cloak closer to herself, seeking to blot out her internal cold.

Kate craned her neck upward and called out weakly, "Corbin? Corbin!"

He hopped onto her chest. "Your Majesty. Are you alright?" He nuzzled her. She returned the affection by scratching behind his ear. "Corbin, I need you to do something for me. Christine, can you get my satchel from my room, please?"

Christine hurried off, and Kate turned her attention back to her general.

"Go to Castelmor. Tell Allistair that I need electric torches," she said, enunciating her words carefully.

Corbin's whiskers twitched. "What?"

"Ee-leck-trick torches. He will understand. Tell him they need to be small but powerful. Tell him the situation is dire."

"How many?"

"One hundred at the least. A thousand would be better. *Five* thousand if I could snap my fingers."

Corbin nodded. "Ee-leg-trick torches?"

"That's right. Here," she said, taking the satchel from Christine as she returned. "This will get you there." She pulled out a small vial of a clear, viscous fluid. On its label was scrawled the word *Messenger*..

"Alaric, give him enough for the trip home?" Kate asked.

Alaric took the vial from her and prepared to apply the spell on the scruff of Corbin's neck.

"What are you doing?" Corbin asked.

"You'll see," Alaric said.

"I don't care for this situation, you know, with your knife at my back."

"You may care for it even less in a moment."

Corbin began to grow as the spell made contact with his skin. His dark coat was replaced with brown and white speckled feathers. His sharp nose hardened into a beak, his eyes grew larger and farther apart. He hopped around, getting a feel for walking on two legs and flapping the broad wings of a screech owl.

"I say, I think I could get used to this!" he said. "The prey becomes the predator, eh?"

Kate smirked. "I thought you'd like that."

He took flight without incident and was quickly on his way.

"Is there anything else you need?" Alaric asked Kate. "Food?"

"*Yes.* Please. I'll need every morsel you can find." Her turn of phrase confused him, but he resigned himself to it as he piled heaps of food onto a large platter.

Darien followed him, adding to his load. Alaric glanced at him sideways and saw him working his jaw, though no sound had come out.

"You look worried," Alaric said.

"Of *course* I'm worried."

"She's doing everything she can." Alaric sighed heavily, compelled to give credit where it was due. "So is Luca."

"I know," Darien said. "I hope it'll be enough."

"It's never *not* been before."

"Alaric…I'm worried about Arjuna."

"Who?"

"*Arjuna*, the musician from this morning, the one with a house full of lanterns. I can't stop thinking about her."

"With a face like that, who could blame you?"

"It's more than that. She was very tender with me, and…"

Alaric waited for his friend to get to it.

"Her mother is confined to her bed, and she won't leave her. But I don't like the thought of her out there alone. And I have to stay here, put on a brave face."

"Want me to go get her?"

"Would you please? I know it's a dangerous thing I ask, but—"

"I'll manage."

"Thank you, Alaric, I'm in your debt."

Alaric's face sobered. "You don't owe me anything." He whistled to Christine on his way out the door. "Going to get a damsel in distress. You comin'?"

"Do you remember the way?" Christine asked.

"Go. I'll guide you," Kate offered.

"You're not going anywhere," Alaric retorted.

Kate sent him a withering look, then gestured past him to where the ring of fire encircling the Council House had opened up. Some of the light from outside flickered brighter until a clear path came into view. Alaric turned back to her, seeing the exhaustion reflected in her eyes.

"Go quickly."

She grabbed Christine by the wrist as she passed. "Be nice," she said under her breath.

Christine merely snorted. But her discomfort was unmistakable.

"He might surprise you."

Hercules sat down next to Kate and shooed the others away. "Go on. I'll keep an eye on things here while Her Highness recovers her strength."

Without thinking too hard on it, she closed the ring of light behind them, and kept her mind closed to the fire as she set about eating. She'd made some headway before Hercules prodded her.

"Feeling better?"

"Not quite," she said. "Where is my husband?"

15

Darkness blew across the barren waste like a sandstorm. Luca pulled up his cape to cover his eyes and mouth as the line between the desert and the realm of shadow melted and dissolved. He had long ago shut his mind off from Kate, the moment his feet left the city's limit and touched upon sand. She would not suffer the ill effects that plagued him now, the slow but sure draining of life. But knowing she was safe from this singular threat did little to quiet his worry over every other challenge she faced, and how he was at a loss as to how to help her manage the magic that consumed her. The fear of her being overwhelmed by her own nature hastened his steps all the more.

A phantom whisked across the sands, a shadow among the shadows, running headlong to the darkest places. He gave chase until he came to an outcropping of jagged rocks. He breached the summit and tried to pinpoint his quarry. He saw nothing off in the distance, rather, he felt a power furrowing beneath his feet. He quit his perch and descended the cavernous bowels of the steppes. The deeper he went, the more there was a total absence of light. He could hear Haydee's minions squealing, scrabbling over each other to get away from him. He flew past them without a thought, traveling down, down, into the depths of a pit he couldn't see to the bottom of. A wider tunnel opened before him, but before he could traverse it, he realized his prey had doubled back. He swung his blade swiftly behind him, but he aimed too high for Haydee's diminutive figure. His blade managed only to cut the darkness above her head.

For all his superhuman speed, he could not strike a fatal blow, as the demoness kept forming and reforming herself, retreating into vapor whenever his sword came too near. He tried to mimic her movements, but the sword that would end her could not do the same, and it hindered him. After another swipe at the air, she wrapped all her force around his left hand, squeezing so hard that his hand severed at the wrist. He didn't so much as flinch but moved quickly to finish her. He severed both her legs just as he felt the sensation go out of his hand and she toppled to the ground. He aimed his sword at her chest, but she let out a scream like the howling of wind and slipped away on a gale that carried her west.

He tore apart his robe and wrapped his left arm to stop the bleeding and the fast flowing of life out from the open wound. That done, he was ready to pursue her again. But as he looked in Haydee's direction, he stopped.

Far in the distance, the lights of Castelmor dimmed and flickered, giving way to shadows. As he stood debating, Haydee's dark creatures crept closer to Icarya, but it did nothing to weaken the ones surrounding him. They ventured closer to lap up the blood spilling from his missing limb. He gave them a good thrashing, then raced, panting, back to the city at the edge of the desert.

~

ALARIC AND CHRISTINE HURRIED FROM ONE FADING LANTERN TO THE next. As Likhan shifted on its axis, so did the path that Kate—or at least, some part of Kate—illuminated before them. They were deep into the city now. The Council House was far from view, and there was no end to the darkness in sight as they waited for a light to guide them onward. Christine inched her way forward to peer into the next alley, but Alaric pulled her back.

"Let go of my hand. I'm not a child," she spat.

He ignored her, as he had all the dozens of times she'd tried to wrench free of his grip. He made it so that she was always aware of him, whether she wanted to be or not. Kate's admonishment rang in her ear. But she knew they had been together, knew Alaric had fallen hard for their queen. Even harder than she had, it seemed. The thought of Kate passing him to her, or she to him, made her insides roil. Her thoughts bubbled over, too big for her to hold in.

"I won't be your consolation prize."

Alaric raised a half-curious, half-irritated eyebrow. "A consolation prize for what?"

"Not *what*," she answered. "Who. I'm a poor substitute."

He still had no idea what she was talking about. And why should he, when her thoughts made so little sense even to herself?

"*Kate*," she hissed.

"I wasn't thinking about her."

The scowl on Christine's face softened.

Alaric's lids lowered, his gaze concentrating hard on her mouth. A light flared to life ahead of them, but Alaric didn't move. He pressed his hand flat against the wall, boxing her in again.

~

Bad idea.

He'd hurt enough women in his life. He didn't need to add any more.

~

Christine saw the want in his eyes.

"It's too dangerous," she said.

"You have no idea."

She thought he would keep pressing, craning his neck all the way down until their mouths finally met, but he stepped back instead, causing her to stumble.

"Can we go now?" Alaric said. "You shouldn't let my pretty face distract you." He replaced the hard set of his jaw with a broad smile.

Christine's scowl returned with a vengeance. "Don't let me keep you."

They moved on to the next light, then the next. They didn't speak, but all the same, Alaric retained his grip on her hand.

"ARJUNA?"

Alaric and Christine finally arrived at the only light in Likhan not kept burning by Kate.

"Yes? Is the seht safe?" she asked.

"Yes," Christine answered.

Arjuna raised a hand to her chest in relief.

"He is concerned for your safety and asked that we bring you and your mother to the Council House without delay," Christine said.

Arjuna looked down at her hands. "That's very kind of him. He shouldn't concern himself with a humble servant like me."

"Seht Darien concerns himself with all his subjects," Christine answered.

Arjuna's face fell. "Yes, he does. Very much so."

Alaric corrected Christine. "You, more than most."

Arjuna perked up again. "Sire?"

"He didn't send us out here for the populace. He sent us here for you." He quirked the corner of his lips upward in a rueful smile.

Arjuna's cheeks warmed.

"Come on, then. Where's Mum?"

"She's resting now." Arjuna walked past Alaric and led them upstairs to where her mother lay prone. She turned and lifted her head in the direction of her daughter.

"What's wrong with her?" Christine asked.

"She can't feel anything past her waist."

"So she won't mind if I sling her over my shoulder, then?" Alaric loped toward her.

"Alaric!" Christine cried.

"There's plenty of space to lie down and be comfortable when we get there. If we take the bed, *both* our hands are tied."

Outraged or not, Christine understood the danger that posed. She appreciated his pragmatism. Though gruff and coarse, he had a kind smile as he first put a blanket over his shoulder, then the woman.

"Ok. Anything else you'd like to take with you?" he asked.

Arjuna looked around, then unfixed the Icaryan lamp from its mooring.

"*Good* idea," Christine said.

"Brilliant," Alaric said. "Now let's get the hell out of here! Sorry, Mum." He put his hand on her bottom to settle her weight more firmly on his shoulder.

"I'm not," the woman quipped.

Alaric barked in laughter. Arjuna pressed her hands to her cheeks to cool her embarrassment. "Maman!"

They made their way back to the Council House with all haste.

16

Trying to keep track of every Likhanni that had gone missing was a daunting, nearly impossible task. But it had to be done. And Darien needed to do it himself. One young woman was most insistent in helping him. He couldn't remember her name; she had been presented to him in the endless parade of potential brides from powerful families. She didn't speak. At least, not directly to him. She directed her kind and caring words to those she comforted, bringing food to the hungry and tending to the injured. When Darien himself became weary and needed to rest, he thanked her.

"You've been very helpful," he said.

The girl nodded, and looked up at him through lush, veiled eyelids.

"That's what binding with a powerful family can do. I can be of great help to you."

He appreciated her candor, at least. But he needed time away from her, time to think. So he nodded and turned to walk where he knew she would not follow, and took a seat beside his aunt, who seemed to be slowly but surely eating her weight in leftovers.

"Luca's still not back?" he asked.

Kate shot him a subtle, annoyed look for stating the obvious.

He shifted in his place, searching for a delicate way to broach the subject. "With Luca gone—"

"He's *not* gone. He's just not back yet."

Hercules saw the young seht's struggle, and tried to cut in. "Even so, he's just one man. You're exhausted. We need to do more to get at the heart of the problem."

"I'm not entirely pleased with this situation," Darien said. "With Icaryans doing all the heavy lifting, I mean. Don't think I'm ungrateful! Gods, don't ever think that. But Likhan needs to do more to protect itself. *I* need to do more."

"Agreed," Kate said. "We don't want anyone getting the impression that you take orders from me."

"All the same, what *can* you do, against a thing like that?" Hercules asked, gesturing to the unabating darkness outside.

Darien had anticipated this question, and had come to the conversation prepared. "There's a story, a very old story, about an ancient treasure, one used to call for aid in a time of great need."

"The Telmerien horn," Kate supplied.

"Yes."

"The what?" Hercules asked.

"It's a horn, carved from bone and enchanted by the Great Magician."

"*Icarya's* Great Magician?"

"The whole *world* is Icarya. At least, in the beginning of our world, it was. Icarya as *you* know it is only its center. It is said that the horn was crafted right before the Great Magician disappeared. It was his last gift to this world, if it should ever need him.

"In the version I am familiar with, blowing the horn would summon the help you most require. Great Magician or no, it couldn't hurt, except..."

Kate's voice trailed off in a way that Hercules knew well. The sudden dip in her voice made him wary.

"Well?" he demanded, cutting right to the chase.

"The horn has been lost for thousands of years," Darien said. "It had come into the hands of a man named Laiuis, how I don't know, and he dropped it while crossing the desert during a great sandstorm."

"Not very smart of him," Hercules interrupted.

"Sometimes the sands come upon you without the slightest warning," Darien replied.

"Like now," Kate said.

"He didn't want to leave it behind, so he camped there until the storm passed," Darien went on.

"But it could have been *anywhere,* with all that sand and wind," Hercules said.

"Exactly. People came from all over to help. Laiuis, along with those who came to his aid founded the city of Likhan. The knowledge of where he had been when it fell from his hands before being swallowed up by sand was passed to his descendants, but even that has been lost with time."

Kate inclined her head toward Hercules, closed her eyes, and tried to remember.

"From the place where the sun meets your gaze, chase its rays until it is caught between the tower and the sea."

Darien's eyes grew round. "*Where* did you hear that?"

"Trap it in your gaze, until it sends out sentinels to guide your way. But don't be fooled. It will summon a beast of stone to devour you, and devour it must, for in its maw lies what your heart seeks."

Hercules scratched the back of his head. "Any idea what that all is supposed to mean?"

Kate took a moment to orient herself, then pointed in a southwesterly direction. "Go that way."

"That's it?"

"I can write the rest down, if you like," Kate said.

"Wait a minute!" Darien interjected. "I thought we already settled that I needed to do more."

"You cannot do *this*," Kate said in a flat tone.

"Why not? I can follow clues just as well as him."

Hercules raised an eyebrow.

"You're mortal," Kate answered simply, raising her eyes to her old friend.

~

SHE SEEMED TO LOOK PAST HERCULES, OR RATHER, *THROUGH* HIM, THE WAY she did sometimes. She wasn't even looking at him, really, but something else. Something only she could see. He knew better than to question her. It had never unsettled him the way it did now. He shook it off as he got to his feet.

Kate grabbed at his arm. "Hercules." She squeezed his biceps as uncertainty clouded her expression. "Be very careful, about what you wish for."

~

HE DIDN'T UNDERSTAND KATE'S WARNING. BUT HE HAD NO DOUBTS whatever that, when the time was upon him, he would.

~

AS HERCULES LEFT THE COUNCIL HOUSE, ALARIC AND CHRISTINE WERE just arriving, with Arjuna and her mother in tow. Alaric's face had darkened two shades from the exertion, and he moved quickly to claim the nearest free space on the floor as Christine and Arjuna scurried about his feet preparing a soft place for Arjuna's mother to stretch out.

Darien rushed to their side. His eyes met Arjuna's. He was on the brink of embracing her, his chest heaving with relief. But Arjuna's gaze fell quickly from his, a sharp reminder than he was surrounded by suitors and their families. He checked his emotions out of respect. His relief settled into sadness. He greeted them warmly.

"Arjuna. I'm glad to see you and your mother are safe."

"It is…overly generous to concern yourself with us, My Seht."

His title issued from her lips opened a deep chasm in his chest, an unfathomable ache.

Arjuna's attention pivoted to her mother as she proceeded to cough violently.

"What ails her?" Darien asked.

"Stiff muscles. It began in her fingers, from too many hours at the loom. Soon, her knees were so brittle that she could no longer stand, or even sit. But forever prone, her lungs are…no longer strong." Arjuna looked down at her hands, clasped together for support.

"Is something else troubling you?" he asked. The mother's illness was a long-suffered one, Darien knew. But it was not the cause of the creases of worry across Arjuna's face now.

"My father never came home," she said.

Darien stretched his neck and scanned the crown. "He's not here?"

"No." She resorted to wringing her hands, but that did not chase her cares away. Darien stilled their nervous tension by laying his hand gently over hers.

She startled at his touch, then turned his hand over to examine his bandaged thumb.

"Does it pain you much?" she asked.

"No."

The warmth of their contact lingered as their fingers brushed against each other. Darien spoke first. "It's too early to say whether your father will return, but…Arjuna, you can rely on me. I'd not see you languish under any hardships."

"You are generous and merciful, Darien." She said his name with a smile, one that faded as she peered over her shoulder and caught sight of the woman approaching them at a brisk pace and reality came crashing down. "You have many responsibilities to the people of Likhan —not to me."

Darien was confused by her reply, by the withdrawal of her hand, until the girl who had helped him earlier, the one whose name had *still* not come to mind, kneeled beside them and asked after Arjuna's mother. She had asked her question in the same kind manner as she had before, but the sheer sound of her as she knelt, sending all her jewelry clattering against her wrists and her neck, cut the stark difference between the two women's stations. The jewels in her hair alone were worth more than Arjuna's family likely made in a year. Darien looked behind her and sought out her parents. They turned inward as he glanced in their direction. No doubt they had sent their daughter to Darien at the first sign of competition. He smiled at that, for he knew—it was already too late. He smiled politely at the girl, then spoke to Arjuna again.

"If you need anything, please come to me."

Both women bowed their heads as Darien took his leave.

"He's a good man, taking care of all Likhan's children," the woman said, staring after him. Arjuna mumbled her agreement.

"I shall be very proud to see such traits in my husband."

The young woman's words hit their mark, and lodged themselves deep in Arjuna's chest. It should come as no surprise, she knew, but still, she could not dislodge the barb from her treacherous heart, which had allowed her to hope.

Kate answered Darien's question before he even had a chance to ask it.

"Hercules will succeed."

"But what if he doesn't? What will we do?" Darien asked.

"He will."

"I still don't understand why you sent him. You're in no condition to defend us right now."

"I will if I have to. What we need now is something only *he* can summon. For my part, I prefer not to move until Luca returns, or until Haydee forces my hand. That's not why you came over, though." She smiled wryly at him.

Darien, for his part, was embarrassed by her forwardness. "As a queen and a newlywed, I was hoping for a bit of advice."

Kate patted the cushion beside her in invitation. "I'm hardly in a position to tell you what to do."

"But where do you draw the line between your private and public life?"

"What line? There's a *line*? Nobody told *me* about a fucking line!" she retorted.

To her right, Alaric and Christine chuckled.

Darien was not amused. "I *loved* Haydee. With all my heart and soul. And now..." he paused and looked to the darkness beyond. "I never knew her at all."

"That's not your fault, Darien," Kate replied.

"Isn't it?"

"How could anyone have expected something like this?" Alaric asked.

"I don't want to marry a woman I might not *ever* truly know, one who only cares for my position. But I fear that an unexpected choice might further erode the people's view of me."

It was Christine's turn to laugh. "Forgive me, but isn't that how you came to power in the first place? Doing the unexpected?"

Darien's cheeks flushed hot with indignation. "I did what I felt I had to. So all of Likhan could have a future, not just a handful of the cruel and wealthy. If not for that, you wouldn't be here and the whole city would have been swallowed up already. I *know* I did the right thing."

Kate smiled at him, gentling his ire with a soft voice.

"You've come to power as a man full of compassion for all his people, regardless of their station, so they might be free to seek out their own happiness. Don't you deserve the same?"

Darien paused. "You make it sound so simple when you put it like that."

"Oh dear. Nothing is ever simple," Kate said.

"It's a powerful move, what you're considering," Alaric said. "But not a wrong move, I don't think. There *are* other ways to build alliances with the houses. Ones that could limit the competition between them."

"Choosing a bride from among them may only stoke the flames," Christine added.

"Yes, I'd already considered that," Darien said. "Still."

"It's *your* life, Darien. You need to decide how to live it. And whom you want to live it with," Kate said.

Their advice did little to ease the tension coiling at Darien's back. "All this is hypothetical, I suppose. I don't profess to know the heart of the lady in question, and we certainly have greater—"

Kate closed her eyes and groaned, curling up on herself.

"Kate?" Darien ventured.

THEIR EYES WENT WIDE AS THEY TRIED TO GET HER ATTENTION. BUT THEIR cries were so much chatter, when such a strong preternatural sense was calling to her blood in sharp, insistent tones. She stood as the furthest corner of the Council House darkened. The only thing visible in the mist was a pair of glowing red eyes.

Luca stepped out of the billowing shadows with such swift, deliberate steps, that he knocked Kate off her feet. He took firm hold of her neck in his right hand, and with fully bared teeth clamped down hard on her throat.

Screams once again filled the Council House, first at the fright posed by the invading shadow, then at the sight of Luca feasting on Icarya's queen. The trio that had surrounded her rushed forward to pull him off her. But beneath him, she stretched out a hand to stay them, rooting them in place.

Lust rose inside her until it reached riotous proportions. The only thing holding her back was the command that echoed in her head.

I cannot feed you now. I am drained of my strength. I'm sorry. I'm sorry. All I am will be yours, I promise.

When Luca's mouth finally parted from her neck, he glared into her bloodthirsty eyes, willing her hunger to subside. Then he crumpled against the wall. His breath came in short, heavy gasps. His fangs slowly receded.

Kate rose at last, just enough to lay her hand on his chest. He cradled her head with his right hand.

Alaric, Christine, and Darien encircled them, frozen in shock. They approached the couple warily, stopping short as Luca opened his eyes, revealing a crystal blue.

Darien was the first to speak. "Are you…are you alright?"

Luca licked his lips and nodded. "I'm sorry if I scared you. I just…I just need…"

Kate felt shame burn like a hot flame inside him. He'd never dreamed of doing something so private, so *intimate,* in full view of so many. He felt raw and exposed and feared he had exposed her too. Tainted her, somehow, with such a public act. Only with great effort was she able to reassure him, to soothe his nerves enough to slow down his racing heart. She moved to clasp his hands in hers. Alarm bells ran in her head as she realized his left arm was tucked inside his shirt and out of view. She wrangled it free despite his efforts to hide it, and screamed.

Luca shoved his mutilated arm back into the folds of his clothes before she could inspect the wound further.

"Don't make such a fuss. It'll be back in a few hours."

She stared at him, mouth agape. There were no words.

"I promise, I promise," he said, pulling her head to him again. "Here." He gestured with his chin toward a knot tied into his clothes. "I saved the important part."

She undid the knot. Into her hands fell his wedding ring. She laughed, a sweet, tear-filled laugh, and pressed her mouth to his, mindless once more of anyone and everyone who looked on.

~

When his breathing returned to normal and the others once again felt comfortable enough to sit, Luca related his encounter with Haydee. "I wounded her, but not mortally. When she ran, I would have gone after her, but…" He turned to Kate. "I may not have been able to find my way back." He had suffered too much from the loss of his hand, and would have died in the desert. The delay before he rose again had been too great a risk.

Kate nodded in understanding.

It made him wince to deliver his gravest news.

"She's splitting her efforts. On the horizon, I saw darkness heading northeast."

"She's heading for Icarya?" Alaric cried.

Kate turned white, then green. She clutched at her stomach.

Luca worked quickly to reassure her, to undo the worst effects of his failure. "She *won't* escape me again. But even I can't be in two places at once."

A terrible thought took shape in Kate's mind. She raised her eyebrow, and looked to Luca.

His reaction was explosive. "No. No. No!"

"He would be on a very tight leash," she replied.

Luca laughed. "If you think that would work, you're insane."

"That's what everybody says."

"Uh…what are you talking about?" Alaric asked.

Christine elbowed him. "Don't you know when to keep your mouth shut?"

"Tell me another way then," Kate said. A calm determination washed over her countenance. Her mind was already made up. And Luca knew it. His blood boiled, and he howled, having no alternative to offer her.

"How do you know he will even agree?"

"Because," Kate answered, "we'll give him what he wants."

17

Hercules could see how the horn he was after had gotten lost in the first place. He could barely see his hand in front of his face as he tried to protect his eyelids from the onslaught of sand. He'd walked a straight line from where Kate had pointed to the first stone sentinel, an obelisk with a fancy carved headdress obscuring the eyes of something with a beak. Fair enough. But going from one sentinel to the next—that was the hard part. He remembered to head in the *opposite* direction from where the totem pointed, but the storm did its utter best to blow him off his course. Between the darkness and the sheer distance, he only knew he hadn't gone awry when he crashed into yet *another* horned statue. He might wander in the desert forever without ever having realized that he had missed his mark.

Hercules found his way to three such markers, having no idea how many there were. As an expert in monster-hunting, he rightfully assumed that when he came upon a gorgon wrought in stone, he would know it.

Scaling the monolith to survey the land, and possibly spy his next target, was hopeless. But he tried it anyway. Seeing nothing more high above the sands than he did below, he slid back down, but his lion's head hood snagged on a jagged piece of rock. He realized too late, and it caused a wicked tear. The damage was far beyond repair.

He cradled the butchered mane in his arms like a wounded cub and stroked its mangy fur.

"You've seen better days. So have I."

The thought stung in the corner of his eyes as he placed a kiss upon its head, then laid it to rest in the sand. The desert swallowed it up in a moment. Then it was gone.

Hercules rose heavily to his feet and continued on.

He cried out suddenly when the sand shifted beneath his feet and he was sucked under. But his descent was brief, and he landed in a depression etched out of a cool, slick stone.

It was even darker in the cavern, if that was possible. Once his eyes adjusted and he wiped the debris out of them, he spied a bleary blue green light being cast faintly against the wall in front of him. He turned, but could not find the source. In long, sweeping strides, Hercules tried to map the terrain with his feet, feeling for a bit of wood, or a bone, anything that might serve as a torch so maybe at least once on this gods-forsaken errand he could see where in Tartarus he was going. But in his vast experience in such dire situations, he never got what he wanted. And, as usual, he didn't need it. For the gaping space into which he had fallen vibrated, buzzing with a power the likes of which he had not felt in a long time—the power of a god.

His sight was unnecessary to the finding of the thing that sent his every muscle humming. Hercules knelt, and without seeing picked up the horn that had been dropped in the worst possible place. He brushed his fingers over the symbols etched deep into the bone, not understanding, but rather, *feeling* their strength. As he turned the Telmerien horn over in his hands, a sinister, silent thought slipped into his head, about the kind of help that might come, the kind *he* might summon. He tried to bury it as quickly as it came, but the image that had flashed across the back of his eyelids resounded over and over again, until the very walls seemed to shake with its force.

Hercules. Be careful what you wish for.

His emotions swirled about him—hesitation, fear, rage, the thought of the havoc he might wreak on Likhan. On Icarya. On his family. On himself. Somewhere in the mix was the sentiment that he had abandoned long ago as a boy—that of wanting his family with him. The desire to *not* be struck out, bound to Earth for what he could do. He felt again the first sign of his strength as if it were new, followed swiftly by pain. He remembered the first time his family died. His brain was flooded with images of the suffering in Likhan, and of what he was willing to sacrifice. He wished he had belonged, that he could call on them for help. He wished they had been to him, and to the world, all they could have been. Despite the pain, he missed his family. Missed a sense of belonging, even to them. And, not all of them were cruel. He had killed them all in revenge, but maybe not all of them deserved it. He had killed a part of himself too, that day.

Moving as if on their own, the muscles in his arm raised his hand and brought the horn to his lips. He blew with all the force his lungs could muster.

~

THE HORN'S CALL REVERBERATED AGAINST THE WALLS. IT ESCAPED OUT through the ceiling and raced across Likhan on the wind, reaching the ears of those huddled in the Council House, who lifted their heads in hope.

~

KATE WHISPERED UNDER HER BREATH. "GODS HELP US."

"What *is* it?" Darien insisted. He could not convince her to tell of what she saw without seeing. As with everything else in his life, he was in the dark. He knew how powerful Kate was. So the uncertain look on her face, bordering on panic, frightened him.

"Tell me, *please*. What is it that only he can summon?"

"The sun."

~

After the horn's call stopped echoing, when it was only a distant memory in his ear, Hercules found himself still alone. He looked around, behind—there were no secret tunnels or chambers for something to hide in. There was nothing. Confused, frustrated, and relieved—the disappointment, small and sharp in his chest that he refused to acknowledge—Hercules climbed out of the earthen maw and reemerged on an outcropping high above the desert. The storm had lulled. At least, it seemed that way from where he stood.

He felt a preternatural warmth upon his back, a glow from behind that cast him in a long shadow. The dark sands grew lighter as they blew furiously on all sides of him, whipping his hair in front of his eyes. He spun around, and the barrage of sand ceased. The light was so bright it was blinding. The blazing orb took shape, forming a familiar chin, nose, and golden curls in robes that shone. Slender fingers were as sunbeams, dimming only slightly as they took on a more solid aspect.

Hercules stood rooted to the spot as the sun smiled, opened its mouth, and greeted him.

"Hello, Brother."

18

The cave at the edge of Cathair's coast was desolate and cold. The markings Kate had made into the sand and rocks at its base, to chain the demon within, were washed away. Luca spied a dark shrunken shadow within the icy formation at the back of the cave. It appeared to be in stasis.

Luca hated what he was about to do. But he knew he had no choice. Melting the ice with water from the tide by the bucketful, slowly the shadow became a reality. It collapsed on the floor in a gravelly puddle. The much-reduced vampire lord made no noise, no movement but to shiver.

Dracula's skin was so clammy and pale he was almost translucent. The corners of Luca's mouth curled downward in a grimace. He tossed a leather skin on the floor. Its contents spilled onto the ground of the cave, mingling with the puddle. Dracula scrabbled toward the crimson puddle and pressed his tongue hungrily to the ground. Gravel mixed in with the blood, muddying up his face. At the first taste, the vampire drew back, his face distorted into a snarl.

"This is pig's blood!"

Luca blinked in an effort to keep his cool. His voice spewed forth like venom. "It's more than you deserve."

THE STENCH OF THE BLOOD CURDLED IN DRACULA'S NOSE. HE GROWLED, but he was too deliriously thirsty to care. He lapped it up greedily until there was nothing left on the cave floor but mud. The instant effect the blood had on his brain was dizzying. His mind was an utter mess. Essential questions formed too late as he felt a cold blade pressed hard against the back of his neck. He tried to stop himself from quivering, to regain a sense of dignity, but he was not fully thawed, so his efforts were useless.

"You released me, only to kill me?" He did not move his neck, but only stared at the ground beneath him.

Luca's grip clenched around the handle of his blade. His teeth ground together. Memories of all his father had done, and all he threatened to do, screeched and howled in his ears. He swallowed all of it, everything, back down.

"My Queen requires you."

Dracula said nothing, his mind stitching itself back together as feeling and warmth slowly crept back into his limbs. He twisted to gaze up at his son and spied a thick metal band around Luca's left ring finger.

"There is a threat to Icarya, a threat you and I are suited to face."

Luca stopped short of asking for his father's help. The words stuck in his throat like daggers. Dracula couldn't but feel his son's pride as his own. Once he'd found a thought he was comfortable with, Luca continued.

"In return, you'll be granted the oblivion you seek."

Dracula made to rise to his feet, but his son's blade never relieved the insistent pressure on his skin. He studied his son's face. Just how much this conversation grated on him was written plain. He didn't want to do this.

"And if I refuse?"

Luca's lips drew even tighter together before he spoke. "You go back to the way I found you."

Dracula raised an unconvinced eyebrow, until Luca reassured him.

"She's just outside."

Dracula had no doubt that the copy he'd made of the queen had only a fraction of the power of the original. He considered silently, but Luca continued.

"You'll be guarded at all times—"

"By you?"

"That would defeat the purpose."

Dracula absorbed the meaning behind his son's words. Luca's offer seemed straightforward, but every ounce of his existence knew better. Still, he was sufficiently intrigued, and his options were nil.

"Fine." He managed a nonchalant smile, but Luca was not to be rattled on this day. Nothing his father said or did shook the hardness from his face.

"Before we begin—"

Dracula smiled. "Now we get to it."

"You must pay for your crimes." Luca threw a rag in his direction. "Clean yourself up."

Dracula was amused. What punishment could Kate mete out that would not undermine her own purposes? Such a farce, seemingly for the sake of justice.

When Dracula's face was rid of the muck, Luca ripped the rag out of his hands with what his father thought was an unnecessary degree of force, gripped his shoulder, and spun him about, and made him face the mouth of the cave and the markings that still pulsed threads of potency through his shrunken veins. Luca felt Dracula's legs stiffen where they stood, but pushed him forward.

"Move."

Dracula had no room to disobey, and cursed under his breath despite his best efforts to remain aloof from this charade that he only half-heartedly appreciated. As he crossed the cave exit to the beachhead, a thunderous clap resounded in his head; the whole world flashed white. At last, Dracula thought, his wrathful god had come to smite him. But as a stiff breeze howled through his ears and pierced his soaked garments down to his very bones, he realized, crushed, that it was just a dream.

He blinked in the harsh winter sunlight as the shore came into focus.

His view of the sea was barred by throngs of people, standing in silent judgement. All of Cathair had turned out for the event, it seemed. The burly herbalist, bereft of his daughter, and a young woman whose face Dracula only remembered through the shared reminiscences of Rene, stood at the vanguard. From the corner of his right eye, he spied Katelyn, in long black robes that flapped somberly in the wind, the thick rustling of the heavy fabric as like a drum beating out the terse seconds before his punishment.

The point of Luca's sword pushed him toward Katelyn, who stood with her hands folded in front of her. As he suspected, her finger was adorned with a ring resembling the one that his son wore. A pair.

Kate's voice cut through his musings.

"You are accused of murdering Carla, daughter of Nestor, and Rene, Captain of the *Demeter*, wife to Chrysta, and father of Jace and Michel. What say you to these charges?"

Her face was as stone. Dracula looked back to Luca. His expression was unchanged. The vampire lord hung his head in an attempt to stifle a laugh. As if he had a choice. In truth, the charade was beginning to chafe. He stared at the sky, training his eyes above the heads of those who waited in silence for their queen's justice. In a clear, unwavering voice he replied: "Guilty."

Not a soul moved, for not a soul expected anything different. Katelyn moved from her place and stood to face him. Her eyes were inscrutable. In a voice intended only for father and son, she said, "The ultimate punishment, for the ultimate crime."

Only when she moved to Luca's side did he remove his blade from Dracula's throat. It was replaced by Kate's fierce grip on his neck. A shudder ran through him. Her touch pushed alternating currents of fire and ice through him, a power that couldn't decide what it wanted to be. It eroded his nonchalance as quickly as it had come and left him positively disturbed. The weakening restraint he felt slipping through the barrier between their skin filled him with a dread he had never known.

"On your knees."

His mind scattered, a chaos of troubling, disintegrating thoughts, destabilized by the incoherent force that begged to flood him. He swallowed hard and stood his ground. He felt a swift crack at the back of his knees that sent him prostrate. Dracula inhaled a sharp, ragged breath as Kate's grip around his throat tightened and her rage was let loose.

It chose fire. In a moment, the flames caught, biting into his skin, his hair, his eyes. Organs melted, bones dried and grew brittle. Thought left him, replaced by nothing but inchoate suffering.

And still Kate clutched his neck, her arm trembling as her limbs grew numb at the outpouring of power. It was taking more of herself than she anticipated, but any iota of doubt or fear pushed her fire into the shell at her feet all the harder in a relentless immolation.

The wind became heavy with the smell of charred flesh, and laid itself thickly over those gathered like a pregnant storm cloud. The crowd began to squirm. Some turned their heads. Others simply closed their eyes.

But there Dracula knelt, and so Kate's hand on his neck remained, until a gruff voice split the silence.

"ENOUGH!"

Kate's gaze peeled away from her purpose and lifted toward the affected onlookers.

Nestor took a small step forward, his mouth set in a grim line. His voice was hard and short when it came again.

"It's enough," he said. Then he turned his gaze to the sand and walked north along the beach, toward home.

With tears in her eyes, Chrysta nodded in assent, and followed.

As the remainder of Cathair dispersed, the thing Kate had clutched in her iron grip crumbled to dust. It spilled between her fingers, floated lifelessly into the air, carried by the wind above the cliffs, arcing a wide circle above them, and finally, back down into the sea. Kate and Luca stood alone.

That might have been the end of it. After a pregnant pause, Luca asked quietly, "Are you sure you want to do this?"

"How can we know?" Kate asked, her voice subdued. She was mindful, ever mindful, of Luca and how this day affected him, and might forever after. She kept her head slightly bent, and folded her hands again when she was sure they were clean.

"I won't force it."

Luca took a long while to consider. The thing he had wanted for so long, the aim that had driven him headlong into bloody peril for millennia, was accomplished. He wasn't relieved, for a dire choice still loomed before him. He didn't feel anger, or pain, or fear, or loss—he felt nothing. Hercules's words rang in his ears, speaking of a day like this one, that now seemed such a very long time ago.

"It changed nothing."

Luca was as he had always been. He wasn't more or less of a vampire with his father's ashes scattered, wasn't more or less of a man. Hadn't he been warned? Hadn't Hercules tried to explain? He'd have spent the time with his family, he'd said. Every moment Luca spent now was a moment wasted. He had a wife, a child on the way, and a kingdom to protect. And he would—at all costs.

Luca closed his eyes and cleared his mind. He stretched out his senses, searching for the tail end of the wind as it crawled across the surface of the sea. The sky darkened as he pulled, summoning the winds to him in great, galloping gales. Kate's hair whipped around her face. She shielded her eyes as the air swirled about her and Luca, carrying with it the fragments that had once made a legend. The gathering ashes funneled like a tornado into a plain porcelain jar laid at Luca's feet. Just as abruptly as the skies had been stirred, its troubled whisperings ceased, and Luca stoppered the jar swiftly and retrieved it from the ground.

Kate wrapped a tentative arm around his middle, unsure of herself until he turned his head in her direction and laid a kiss on her temple. Kate pricked up her nose. The terrible winds had cleansed the air of ash and the lingering smell of burnt flesh. In its absence was a cool, clean scent, one that drifted down from the top of the sky. It produced a singular sensation that Kate could always detect at the onset of winter.

"Snow is coming," she said, rubbing her growing stomach to soothe the chill on the edge of her clothes. "How long will it take, do you think?"

"Three days. Four, at most," Luca replied. As he put his arm around her back to guide her down the uneven, craggy terrain, her worry slipped through him in thickening threads. Worry over whether they had four days.

19

"You're not here. You can't be here—you're dead." Hercules didn't believe his eyes. He absolutely *refused*.

"Oh, Hercules. Whoever heard of a god who really died? Besides, you called me. I certainly didn't imagine it. We're here to help you."

"We?"

"Call me a representative, if you will. One deemed more acceptable than the others."

"Why would you help me?" Hercules asked.

"We bear you no malice. What you did was but part of the natural order. Did not Father kill Chronos, and he the Titans before him? Whether you like it or not, your actions are those of a god. You *belong* with us. You should hear him go on and on…he was never prouder of you than he was on that day."

"You murdered my family!" Hercules cried.

"*I* didn't do that."

Apollo drifted down the rockface, leaving Hercules scrambling after him. The sun god glowed, revealing the way like a ball of light.

Hercules caught up and strangled him. He felt his brother's power, and his fear, between his fingers.

"The only reason—the *only* reason you're here is to help these people. Have you no compassion, no care for people like my wife, who worshipped you, sacrificed for you, to gain your protection?"

"It was not my concern," Apollo replied.

"Then *whose* was it?!" Hercules roared.

Apollo sneered. "Do you prefer your new god?"

Hercules's brow furrowed in deep lines across his forehead.

"The Queen of the Forest, who does not know what she is?" Apollo supplied.

"She gave me everything I ever hoped for out of you. I would follow her to the ends of the world, and further still."

"Further from *me*?" A wicked grin crept up the god's lips.

In that moment, Hercules was unsure if he was talking to his brother or his father. He had seen this trick before, got the distinct impression that Apollo wasn't walking alongside him at all.

Their argument continued all the way up to the steps of the Council House. They were greeted with cheers of jubilation at the arrival of such brilliant light, but Hercules wouldn't let it go.

"People are born, they die. Cities rise and fall. *Why* should I help them?" Apollo asked.

"Why are you here then?" Hercules said.

"I came to help *you*."

"To help me help *them*." This ridiculous game of semantics made Hercules's blood boil, and he doubted it would make any difference at all to the people whose lives hung in the balance of his brother's whim. It was infuriating. Apollo had always had an unusual softness toward mankind, unlike the other gods. It was why the two brothers had never had any serious quarrels. But right now, with Apollo maintaining an aloof demeanor at odds with his own nature, Hercules was ready to knock his block off.

Apollo remained cool but implacable. "I have no affinity or connection to these people. They don't look up at the sky each morning with supplications on their lips. They do not bring offerings or build temples to the God of the Sun. They are strangers to me and I to them. And now, they are fallen prey to shadows. Seems a fitting punishment."

Incredulous, Hercules's voice turned caustic. "So, dying in an unending night is what they deserve for their ignorance?"

"If you like."

Hercules had had enough. "This was a mistake. You shouldn't be here."

Apollo tried not to let it show, but it was impossible to miss how the light flared around him at his brother's comment. "What would you have done then?" he asked. "Begged and pleaded with the Forest Queen to shield you? Does the son of Zeus need such protection?"

Hercules got up close, nearly nose to nose, and ground out his reply. "She would give her life, her *soul,* to shield these people, *her* people from harm, and she will give of herself until there is nothing left. Never *once* has she demanded a single head be bowed, never once demanded sacrifices at any altar. It is *beneath* her."

Apollo frowned at the rebuke, dimmed just enough to see. "That may be so," he said. "But mark me, dear brother. Somewhere, hidden deep inside your beloved queen, there *is* a god."

20

A pile of ash lay poured out onto a thin bed. By nightfall, the ground outside was covered in a pristine white powder that glistened in the moonlight. Snow continued to fall into the small hours of the morning, gently advancing its climb up the side of a nondescript hill, stretching to reach the accumulation sloping down from a cleft at the top of the mound on account of its own weight. Its only obstacle was the steam furling upward through a crack in the hill, reinforced in stone, which covered the snow in a slick sheen.

When the sun sent its first rays of the day out onto the desolate field beyond the hill, the ash on the bed had taken on the distinct impression of a person, having shifted imperceptibly but steadfastly through the night. By the second night, a shape with defined eyes occupied the bed.

~

The unending heat was gone. He was not cold, not warm. He was only aware that the fire that ravaged his soul, the eternal hellfire, raged no more. Darkness surrounded him. It was thick and opaque—a void. He held no concept of time of day, or how much time had passed. He had no sense of himself—he couldn't feel his fingers or toes.

Somewhere in the back of his mind, something buzzed. But it was quiet, and far away. It was meaningless, but it was all there was, so he reached for it. His curiosity was awakened by the inconstant humming, now closer to being a solid thought, now further away than another man's dream. It came in quick, sharp successions, with no pattern or order. Then there was silence, long stretches of nothingness that pulled him under. When the vibrations came again, they were weighty, and carried with them impressions of things unseen. The lid of a copper kettle opened, closed, and opened again. The scrape of a stone spoon against a bowl. The rustling of bedclothes. The snapping and hissing of a fire. That frightened him, but still he could not move, had no limbs with which *to* move. Yet the fire did not come any closer, its heat kept at a distance. Ever mindful of the heat, alert for even the slightest movement toward him, he was surprised when a chill prickled through him. Through an instinct that was obliterated but now reformed, he twitched. He sent his mind out, seeking some sign of the edges of his feet, his shoulders. They were there, but he did not yet have possession of them.

Before his disappointment fully formed, the vibrations returned. Their source this time was a soft yet masculine voice.

"He's not entirely sure his brother *is* his brother." Another voice, higher, replied.

"Have the lanterns arrived?"

"A thousand of them. They are slowly retaking the circle. He isn't saying it exactly, but he seems concerned. The god is proving unpredictable, and a dangerous distraction."

The sound of his son's voice flitted away, then, after a time, began again.

"We should move his family."

"Send a sparrow."

~

"Likhan is still without the sun. No one else has gone missing, but no one else has returned."

The woman's reply was strained, but insistent. "And yet Icarya remains untouched. Are you *sure* of what you saw?"

"I'm sure."

"GODDAMN HIM!"

The outcry was swiftly followed by a crash. A leather-bound book collided with wood and clay, or possibly porcelain. Aged pages snapped crisply as they fell into place, one behind the other at gravity's command as the book closed itself against the floor.

"There's nothing here that I didn't know before! The fate of the world hangs by a thread, and he's playing games with me!"

The deep voice was calm in contrast to Kate's ire.

"Maybe that's all he has."

"The hell it is! This is Drigory's way of saying he disapproves."

"Isn't there anyone else then? Anyone who would know how to combat this more effectively?"

The answer was solemn, and fraught with fear.

KATE SIGHED. "HOW DO I BRING BACK THE SUN?"

She sat on the edge of the bed, a makeshift pallet of straw covered by heavy, soft blankets. She rubbed her thighs, sore from carrying the extra weight in her belly in their cramped hideaway where she and Luca waited impatiently for *another* unpredictable, yet formidable ally to reawaken. The wind whistled outside, lifting the uppermost snowflakes off the ground for a final dance before settling them down again.

Luca sat beside her and rubbed her back to reassure her.

"She fears us. She has been slow to act because of that fear."

"She is cunning," Kate countered. "When she is ready, she will strike swiftly."

"She *will* fall, my love. Be sure of that."

"Before or after she swallows the rest of the world up in darkness?" She sighed again.

Luca's hand traveled up her back to her auburn waves tucked at the back of her neck. He loosened her curls, darkened now by the colder, shorter days, and wrapped them around his slender fingers, pulling his wife closer and kissing her cheek.

The churning of Kate's stomach settled at the warm confidence he exuded, and she turned her head toward him, falling deep into his kisses. Her hand crept up Luca's thigh, but he tensed as she drew near. She sensed his hesitation, his uncertainty with his father, dead as he might be, lying mere feet from them.

She separated her lips from his with a smile and led him outside by the hand. Their breath puffed clouds laden with want as they stepped into the deepening evening. The snow was bathed in moonlight as she trudged alongside the hill and pulled him to his knees in the snow. He rested his head on the warped, bloated beams of the outer wall, only half-visible beneath frozen earth as Kate shoved her heavy skirts aside and straddled him.

The snow around them melted, and Luca's cheeks flashed a bright pink at the dual pressures of the bitter cold and the heat of their rabid lovemaking. A guttural moan caught in his throat as Kate withdrew and bent over his lap to swallow him, raking her teeth along his flesh, taking sweat and blood into her mouth. He cried out in a blend of surprise and pain and bliss. When her ravenous tongue left him, his skin healed as fast as she had torn it. He clutched desperately at her cheeks, roving his hands through her hair with abandon. His voice came out raspy, needy.

"I love you wild," he purred, baring his teeth and sinking them into her throat just below her ear. She gripped his shoulder as he pushed into her with all his might, destroying her. She waxed euphoric.

~

A pale, hostile light crashed through Dracula's mind like a flash of lightning before a small, dimly lit space came into view. His eyelids had peeled back without provocation, revealing the world to him through thin slits. The heavy wooden door groaned on its hinges as it swung closed behind his son and his bride. Their cheeks were flushed, their breathing labored. Luca's fingers brushed her lips, pulling them back just enough to reveal the sharpened point of an exaggerated canine. Furtive smiles passed between them, and Luca lifted his knuckles to his wife's cheek. He brushed at the pale skin turned bright pink, barely touching her as his eyes gleamed.

"You grow more beautiful each day," he crooned.

Indeed, the resurrected vampire mused, his son's bride *was* beautiful. His fractured mind struggled and failed to recall one so fair. He watched them for a time, and as fatigue pulled his gaze downward, he spied the rounded edges of Kate's belly.

A knot coiled tightly in the dark lord's gut, and he imagined a frown forming at the sight of such marital joy, the love and appreciation plain on his son's face. He felt moments away from acknowledging his sullen agitation for what it was, but his thoughts were interrupted. Kate's gaze was on him. Their eyes met. He remained frozen in place as she moved toward him. As she came closer, she reached out her hand.

The vampire flinched. Her arm retracted a moment, surprised by his reaction but at the same time, not. She said nothing as she reached out again, pulling away a blanket Dracula had been oblivious to. He appeared to be wholly reconstituted.

Luca swiftly closed the gap between himself and his wife as she addressed his father, who, for the first time since she had incinerated him, simply blinked.

"Can you sit up?" she asked. Her eyes were as determined as they were when Dracula had seen them last, when she had proclaimed his death sentence. But he saw no malice there, only a slight, somewhat disconnected concern. Too long a delay heralded the end of her non-threatening demeanor.

Muscles and tendons stretched and snapped, heeding a thinly issued command to rise. When his torso was upright, he pressed his hands onto the bed, bracing himself for the bending of his knees. Dracula twisted his hips and hung his legs over the side of the bed, and faced his executioner. Luca fixed his father with a cold stare. As Dracula returned his gaze with a blank expression, the hard set of Luca's jaw drew tighter, furrowing from anger to confusion.

Kate turned her back to him, reaching behind to fill a bowl from the pot suspended above the fire. She laid the serving of steaming liquid in Dracula's lap. He tapped his long index finger along the length of the bowl, collecting his thoughts. After a long stretch of silence, Dracula felt enough like himself to speak.

"I have no use for this." His voice was cool, even, and haughty as ever.

Luca huffed, incredulous.

Ungrateful, arrogant son of a—

Dracula raised a rueful eyebrow, surprised that his son would be so careless with his thoughts, sending them out for all to hear. He readied himself to push back a retort, then stopped. It was obvious—the boy didn't know any better. And why should he? He closed his mouth at the realization. His son was unaware that his thoughts could be heard and should be shielded from prying minds. The vampire was disinclined to correct him.

He felt the pathways open up between the couple, but what passed between them had not been crystalized into words. Emotions, without being channeled into language, were imperceptible to those outside the blood-bond. But it was strong enough for him to know it was there.

Kate appeared to respond to Luca in kind, with an ease that suggested familiarity—suggested practice. That, and the exaggerated canine he had seen poking from her lips as Luca caressed her face, made the corner of his mouth twitch upward. His son, the man who alone had hurried more of his kin to their graves than all other hunters combined, was a hypocrite.

Kate nudged the bowl in his lap again, insistent.

"I think you'll find your bloodlust is less demanding. *Drink*."

Slowly, Dracula brought the bowl to his lips. The warmth on his face and fingers was welcome as a fierce wind bellowed beyond the walls. The broth had a woodsy aroma. He smelled wild mushrooms, heady nuts, and salted pork. His stomach grumbled, eager for the meal at his fingertips. Small, tentative swallows turned quickly to mouthfuls as the soup thawed his belly and reached his arms and legs, all the way down to his toes. He returned the bowl to Kate and nodded with restrained gratitude. She nodded back.

"Your predicament must be serious, for you to seek *my* help," Dracula observed.

"It is," Kate replied. "You can still change your mind now, if you wish. But tomorrow I will hold you to your promise. Your death will be swift and peaceful, as agreed." She took a deep breath. "Will you help us?"

Dracula looked at Katelyn, then at Luca. He knew that his refusal might simply hasten him to the end he craved, *had* craved, but there was no guarantee. His new daughter-in-law had incinerated him with ease. He shuddered at the alternative possibility, should she attack him with ice. And so far, they hadn't lost his interest.

"I suppose," he said carelessly, "if you'll take only my word for it."

"The word of a Transylvanian is his honor, is it not?" she countered.

Dracula snorted. "What do you know of Transylvania?" he asked, allowing the name of his homeland to roll thickly off his Wallachian tongue.

"Enough. I am a Londoner by birth."

This caused Dracula's eyebrows to rise into his hairline.

"In the year of our Lord, 1884."

What are you doing! Luca hissed at his wife.

Having a conversation.

He's a murderer!

So am I.

Dracula hid a smirk at the exchange. The tone of her thoughts was straightforward, confident. She was more at ease than Luca. Surely, he surmised, his son had expressed his deepest hatred. How could he not, with the strength of the bond he'd forged with her? Though he could not penetrate its barrier. The sheer force of their psychic intimacy rivaled anything Dracula had ever witnessed. Indeed, his own bonds to those he had sired were far distant by comparison. The weight of Luca's rage fell full upon her, he knew, yet she spoke and acted without malice, because it suited her purpose. He couldn't help but admire her pragmatism.

More flowed between them that he could not decipher, but as Kate's attention turned back to him, the dark lord saw his son's ire soothed.

He took in the look of her, and tilted his head.

"No," he said, causing her and Luca to furrow their brows.

"Your coloring," Dracula explained. "That speaks more of a Scot than an Englishman."

For a moment, Kate's eyes softened, and she nodded in acknowledgement.

"Perhaps" was her only answer. She waited, but only silence followed.

When Dracula refrained from questioning them further, she excused herself and stepped out to relieve the urge that pressed her with unrelenting frequency as the child she harbored settled against her bladder.

"She is *much* better than the copy," he observed, thinking of the creature he'd spent so long growing, only to be frozen by it. "She's more powerful, but she doesn't make a show of it. I like that."

Luca cast a hateful glance at his father.

"You touch my wife, and you'll spend eternity in pieces."

Dracula exhaled loudly. "I am *congratulating* you. Is that so hard for you to comprehend?"

Luca said nothing, causing his father to exhale again, louder.

"You might learn something, if only you would ask the right questions."

Luca's anger got the better of him. "There's nothing you could teach that I wish to learn."

Dracula puckered his lips. Luca looked imploringly at Kate the moment she returned.

Don't leave me alone with him again.

Katelyn did not reply, but her eyes twinkled with amusement as she seated herself.

Her eyes flicked quickly to Dracula's. For a moment, he suspected he was found out. He returned her stare with a blank, expectant expression. She sent out an inquisitive thought and met a wall. When she retracted, Dracula was unsure whether she had felt nothing in response to her query, or if she knew she had been rebuffed. Either way, she said nothing, and the vampire sensed in her an innate talent that did not derive from her relations with his son. Perhaps they were related to her control over the elements, he pondered, but not entirely. Perhaps she was simply hypersensitive.

"There is a woman, Haydee," Kate started, "who is unleashing shadow magic across the world. Her history and motivations are unimportant, but, as we were combating her in one place, Luca pursued her into the world of shadows, and saw her splitting her efforts between our kingdom, and the one to the southwest. Icarya is allied with Likhan, but I can't fight her on two fronts. Not without the two of you."

The vampire drummed his fingers on his knee, deliberating on whether or not to share what he knew. But withholding it might keep him from his aim, he knew, and he was under no illusions about the threat Kate posed to him.

"Is she a wielder, or a traveler?"

Kate was taken aback by his question. If it surprised Luca, he didn't show it.

"What?" Kate asked.

"Does she control the shadow, or is she simply a vessel?"

Kate stared at him curiously. "Where did you hear that?"

"I had started quite the collection in Cathair. That is, until your husband decided to burn it to the ground," Dracula spat, his tone bitter.

"What were you looking for?" Kate asked. Suddenly she realized the prying nature of her query, and added, "I'm just curious."

Dracula licked his lips. "I found more than I bargained for."

"We all did," Kate said grimly.

Luca shifted in his seat but held his tongue. It took every fiber of his being not to pounce on his father's every word. Knowing that his refusal to be goaded out of his silence agitated his father to no end steeled his resolve.

Kate continued. "When I first encountered her in Likhan, just being in her vicinity gave me a sharp reaction to the darkness surrounding her."

"You saw *into* the shadow realm?" Luca asked.

Kate nodded. "I think so, yes. But when I fought the hound—or whatever it was—I didn't see *her*, only—"

"How big was it?" Dracula interrupted.

"It's hard to say. Its shape kept shifting. It rose higher than the lintel of an open plaza, and was nearly the same in length. Does that matter?"

"It may," Dracula responded cryptically. He offered no further information, and posed no more queries, so Kate went on.

"I only saw the shadow, but Alaric said," she paused, closing her eyes to remember as exactly as possible, "Alaric said he saw her, that my binding spell flared on her as it did on her creature, and that when I set it on fire, she burned also."

"Both methods were effective," Luca observed, referring to the dual magics Kate had employed—blood and elemental.

Kate nodded again. "But it wasn't enough to kill her. While her monster turned to ash, she escaped."

"The second time," Luca began, "night had already fallen. The shadows were more expansive, creating spatial tears and spilling forth lesser monsters. I followed her through, but she moved quickly."

"You let her escape?" Dracula prodded his son, his tone snide.

Luca inhaled deeply to maintain his composure. "It was that or lose my way. That's when I saw her split herself between here and Likhan, though she has yet to manifest here. It's been a little more than a week."

"You may have missed your one opportunity to end her easily," Dracula said, addressing Kate. "You failed to give chase as well."

Kate's eyes narrowed to accusing slits. "I was slightly preoccupied."

Dracula pulled his gaze from hers awkwardly and turned instead to Luca. "Was she dead, in the traditional sense?"

"She was in the shadow realm for longer than any mortal could be. She drew strength from it, rather than the other way around."

"Then she's a traveler," Dracula said definitively.

"What more can you tell us?" Katelyn asked. "All my regular sources have come up empty."

"A wielder can manipulate shadows in exchange for her life," Dracula answered, calling forth all that he had gleaned on the subject. "She may be able to form shapes, though amorphous ones, or flit quickly through the shadows for a limited time. Was the beast you slayed more, or less distinct?"

"Less, I would say," Kate answered.

"Given the size you mentioned, it's likely that was a challenge for her to conjure. It would explain its inability to stay solid."

"It was solid enough to destroy the plaza," she quipped.

"But was that entirely of its own volition?"

The question caught her by surprise. "I—I'm not sure."

"It sounds like a woman stretching her abilities. If she'd been stronger, she would not have fled. But even that would have taken a lifetime to achieve. Many don't, it seems, from my understanding. They're swallowed up obtaining even *that* measure of control."

THERE WASN'T MUCH TO ARGUE WITH IN HIS LOGIC. INWARDLY, KATE kicked herself for fighting conservatively. But, she remembered, Luca had called for her. *Needed* her. She couldn't regret answering him.

"THE MONSTERS WE FOUGHT IN LIKHAN WERE CLEVER," LUCA SAID, AS HIS reassurance and sympathy wrapped itself around Kate's waist and shoulders. "They were coordinated, and there were scores of them. As for the woman herself, it was as if she was *made* of shadow. It was a natural extension."

"That is what all practitioners aspire to—*becoming* shadow. But the literature suggested it was speculation akin to a mystery cult, to become a vessel for the deity, or in this case, shadow."

"Can she be killed?" Kate asked.

"Of course." Dracula smiled wryly. "*We* may have an advantage," he said, indicating himself and his progeny, "but you already know the way."

"Will killing her break the darkness's hold on *this* world?" Luca pressed.

His father shrugged. "There is no account of the shadow realm being expanded or manipulated in this manner. Without the mind of its new master, it *may* dissolve, or it may become an inchoate force—a mindless void."

"Then what?" Kate asked.

No one had an answer for that.

The worry that had subsided at discovering Dracula's usefulness crept back into her soul. Knowing her fears would know no bounds if left unchecked, Luca channeled the conversation toward something productive.

"We'll leave at first light for Lowenherz—the castle," Luca said, checking himself when he realized his father's ignorance of Icarya's geography. "I'll remain there while Kate escorts you to Likhan. You'll be joining Hercules, who—"

"*The* Hercules?" Dracula interrupted, his voice betraying his surprise.

"Apparently," Luca answered, agitated by the disruption. "He's already defending the city. He knows you're coming, and you're to take orders from him."

"Orders?" Dracula asked, incredulous.

"If you disobey him, cause trouble in any way, or try to flee," Luca warned, "he'll snap you in half."

"I don't doubt it. However, you've sought my help, *my* insight—haven't I at least proven I can work within my own discretion?"

Luca's laugh was hard and cruel. The suggestion was just too absurd to him. Dracula took great offense.

"You trust me to travel alone, with your wife, but not to do what you brought me here for?"

Luca faced his father, staring him straight in the eye. "You're afraid of her," he said, seeing the truth of it in his father's usually calculating expression. "You should be. Still, touch one hair on her head—"

"I would never," Dracula retorted.

Luca's eyes widened. "Has your mind turned to rot?! You—"

"That was before."

"Before *what?*"

Kate shifted in her chair, uncomfortable at the conversation's turn.

Dracula looked at Kate, his attention drifting down from her eyes to her stomach. "What she carries now is more precious than any treasure."

Kate and Luca exchanged confused glances. Neither knew how to respond. Kate's mind wandered back to the day on the beach, and Dracula was able to sense her remorse. Killing someone, even scores of men, she was used to. As was he. But what she had done went beyond that. Destroying a thing down to the very nature of its being—that was an entirely different thing. The extent of the power she had exerted over him scared her. Dracula himself was terrified, though he masked it well. Still, it was an intensity that they had shared, and he couldn't help but be sympathetic to the way it jarred her conscience.

"That power could easily be turned on you," Dracula warned, but Luca smiled widely, baring his teeth.

The memory of Kate's fire and brimstone assault made the blood in his veins run cold. Dracula sought to change the subject.

"Why wait for morning? The night is ideal for travelling. Especially for us."

Luca shook his head. "She needs rest."

"Rest is for after your enemies lay dead at your feet."

"I *won't* risk her health."

"You're doing exactly that by failing to make haste."

As father and son bickered, a storm raged outside. But behind the shrill whistling of the wind, and the snow pounding against the hillside, Katelyn became aware of something else. It wasn't precisely a sound—more of a feeling. A sense of swift, hurried movement. The air blowing into the cabin through aged window frames crackled with urgency. Something flooded Kate's nose with burnt cloves. She fixed her eyes on an indeterminate point, seemingly staring into the night beyond the door.

"Do either of you hear that?" she asked.

The seriousness of her tone turned the men's attention toward her, and they grew quiet.

"I don't hear anything," Luca murmured.

"Shhh—listen," Kate insisted. "You don't hear that?"

Neither Luca nor his father heard, smelled, or saw anything out of the ordinary. But Luca knew his wife was not prone to fantasy. In response to Kate's words, the hairs on the back of Dracula's neck stood on end.

"It's—"

Kate stopped again, unsure of the words that would carry the proper weight for what she felt. The toasted spiciness in the air grew stronger, carried on the wind. A dark shape began to form in her mind's eye. Her skin prickled, and she stood up. She gestured in the direction from which whatever it was was hurtling toward them.

Luca drew his sword from over his shoulder, and Katelyn reached for the short swords at her belt. Dracula looked expectantly to Luca.

"You'll manage," Luca said in a gruff tone, not bothering to look at him as the trio fanned out, angling toward the edges of the cottage.

Luca neared the front door and pressed his ear to the chilled wood. Only the sounds of the blizzard greeted him. He put his hand against the door to open it and immediately felt pressure from the other side.

Kate turned her head in that direction as Luca stepped back and silently raised his sword high as the door pushed open. In the split second before Luca brought his sword down, Katelyn had seen the interloper's face.

"No!" she screamed, her cry reverberating between Luca's temples with such force that he nearly dropped his weapon and stumbled to plant his feet firmly on the floor again.

Rather than raise his hands defensively, the shape at the door had disappeared, dissolving into the winter wind at his back and reappearing before Kate as the gust blew through the cottage. As the man materialized, the wind retreated, pulling the door closed and leaving Katelyn, Luca, and Dracula alone in the room facing the stranger.

Katelyn stared, stunned by the presence of the man before her.

The man kept his focus on her, soft and contrite.

"I'm sorry. I dinna mean to scare ye. I jus' 'ad to catch ye now—ye'd have been gone in the morning."

Dracula raised an eyebrow. "A Scot," he mused. "How interesting."

"Who *are* you?" Luca asked, his blade still in his hand.

Kate turned to face her husband, dumbfounded.

"My name is William. I'm—" He paused, coming to stand beside Kate, and eyeing her sideways. "I'm Katelyn's father."

At this, Luca's eyebrows lifted as well. "Kate?"

She looked at William, her eyes still wide with shock. She gulped in breaths.

"You look…just the same," she said.

"Aye. I dare say yoo've grown a bit, though."

William turned to her and opened his mouth to ask a question. But then he saw—a patch of plaid, a pattern of sapphire threaded with gold, tucked beneath her winter dress, was pushing at her neck. His fingers trembled as they chanced to touch the ancient cloth, to feel its fibers between his fingers once more.

"You kept it," he said, his voice barely a whisper. He swallowed hard and pushed back the tears welling in his eyes.

Kate dipped her head ever so slightly in affirmation. Then, to Luca, she said, "He is."

William wavered on his feet, like he would hug his daughter. He searched her eyes, but only found his own uncertainty there. He swallowed his pain, and refrained. William moved toward Luca and timidly extended his hand.

Luca's eyes shifted back to Kate, but she was still numbed by the sheer surprise of it. Absent a reason not to, Luca shook the man's hand. When Dracula wasn't offered the same greeting, his skin bristled.

"I'm *his* father," he said, jerking his head toward Luca, his usual cockiness on full display. "Vlad Dracula."

"I ken who *you* are," William responded coldly.

The prince folded his arms like a petulant child. "I see."

Vlad? Luca wondered silently. Dracula caught the confusion in his son's thoughts, but they were quickly pushed away.

Kate blinked several times, trying to order her own thoughts, pushing herself to focus on the pertinent and drive the rest of her questions away.

"What are you doing here?" she asked.

"It's time for you to harness your power. Ye should 'ave learned a long time ago. I'm here now to teach ye."

Kate's expression turned incredulous.

"I've got more pressing problems than *that* right now."

"Aye, ye do. But you *willna* stop Haydee without it."

None spoke, so William continued. "She is infesting this place with darkness, changing the very fabric of the world. Ye did good," he said, gesturing to her husband and father-in-law, "bringin' 'em here, but 'tis *ye* Icarya needs."

"Me?" Katelyn replied. "You expect me to, what? Remake the world?"

"*Aye!*" he shouted, growing breathless. "Ye've got *so* much power Katelyn. So much more than me, or my mother, and it's jus' been growin' and growin' inside ye, and ye can barely control it! Do you no' have any idea what ye can truly do?"

"I *saw* what I can do!" Kate shouted back. In that moment, her emotions bled out of her. Luca was flooded with images, memories of destruction wrought in ice and fire. Kate shuddered as her thoughts rushed in on her, and said in a subdued, determined voice, "I will not be Icarya's end."

Luca reached out for her fingers, and she clasped at him desperately.

William pressed his lips together in a thin line.

"Aye." He nodded. "The power to destroy is yours. So too, can you create. I saw what ye did in Likhan."

Kate huffed. "Killed a demon?" she quipped.

"The grove, Katie. I saw the grove."

KATE PRESSED HER EYES CLOSED, WISHING FOR THE PURITY, THE OTHER worldliness she'd experience as the ground grew beneath her, the serenity that overtook her when her heart beat in tandem with the glade as she lay at its center. She longed for its euphoria, its transcendence. The lingering wisps of that sense were all but gone from her now, and she felt burdened, weighed down by the fire that had burned in Likhan without end, the flames that had consumed Dracula and turned him to ash. They weighed on her spirit like a mountain.

"I don't know how that happened," she said, her anguish at the thought of its lightness eluding her barely beneath the surface.

William reached for his daughter's hand. "I can't imagine what it's been like, having to live with a part of yerself that ye never understood, that was kept hidden from ye—"

At this, Kate's black stare shot upward to face him.

"Yes," he answered, "I know Drigory's been keepin' secrets. I know they think this is a mistake, my comin' to ye now, but—" his eyes pleaded with her, pleaded for forgiveness. "I'm done wi'that. I think you need me, as much as I need you."

Kate sat on the bed beckoning at the back of her knees and covered her face, trying to take it all in.

"I ken. I ken this is the last thing ye wanted right now. And I'm sorry. But I'm here now. I can show ye the way."

Kate took a deep breath and said, "Okay."

William couldn't suppress the smile that spread on his face, despite the dire nature that had brought his daughter finally back to him.

"Okay," he said. "Then we need to leave. Now." He held out his hand to Kate.

Luca took a hasty step forward. "To where?"

William turned. "I need to take her someplace. Someplace secret. So she can understand her power and tap into it."

"No." Luca's retort came out more a growl than a word. "She's not going anywhere."

"I'm sorry, but it *is* necessary. She'll be safe, I assure ye."

Luca remained unconvinced.

"What, then?" William asked. "Do ye honestly expect to stop this on yer own?"

"You *really* don't know me, do you?" Luca shot back.

Behind him, Dracula smirked.

"Come on, Kate," Luca said, stepping nearer to her. "We already have a plan. You can deal with this later."

Kate paused to consider both of them in turn. Her heart was crushed by the choice before her. Her unborn child chose that particular moment to flip over on its side, forcing Kate to shift her weight. It was as strong a sign to her as any.

"We can't afford to be wrong," she said to Luca. He tilted his gaze to the winter sky above them while her warm voice seeped into his brain.

He's right, Luca. It's going to come down to me. I can feel it.

I'm not *leaving you. Especially not now,* he thought back, his gaze lowering to her swollen belly.

I'll be alright. But I need to do this. For Icarya. For Charlotte. And for me. I can't live like this anymore.

He felt the chaos of her soul grating on her. His shoulders slumped, and he ground his teeth in resignation.

At the same time, she felt her chaos become his at the prospect of being separated from her yet again, and at so delicate a time.

"When she is needed, she will return," William said. "I promise ye."

Luca frowned. "How do we do this, then?" he asked, inclining his head toward his father. Dracula was rooted in place with his arms folded.

"You'll have to take him to Likhan," she answered. "The rest will be as we agreed."

Will you be alright just you and him? she queried.

The corner of Luca's mouth quirked upward. *I'll live. And the only reason I'm okay with any of this is because*—his chest heaved—*because I know* you'll *live too.*

Kate returned his warm smile.

"I'll give ye a minute," William said, and stepped out of the cottage. Dracula moved to do the same, but Luca caught him by the wrist. The vampire lifted his gaze to his son. Luca was surprised by the sincerity he found there.

"I won't run. Take the moment with your wife."

Luca's grip on his father's arm loosened, and the vampire followed William out the door.

THE SCOTSMAN STOOD FACING THE FOREST, HIS NOSE TO THE HOWLING wind. He paid no mind to the vampire who came to stand beside him.

Dracula upturned the collar of his coat, batting away the snow that blasted at his neck. He folded his hands behind his back.

"That's my grandchild you're taking with you," the dark lord said in a crisp tone.

"And mine," William answered.

"If anything should happen to it or its mother, you'll have *me* to deal with. Trust me when I say…you don't want that."

"Mother and child will be safe," William said. "Safer than they are with you."

Dracula nodded, ignoring the jibe and having the decorum to turn his ears away from the farewells exchanged behind him.

LUCA TOOK HOLD OF HIS WIFE WITH TEARS IN HIS EYES, HOLDING HER BY the hips as she clutched at his shoulders.

"If you need me, for *anything*, call me. I will come."

"I will. You're their king now. Protect them, Luca."

He brushed her hair behind her ear. "The whole world could fade away, as long as you're still with me."

She nestled herself under his chin. "Promise me the world won't fade today. Not on your watch."

"I promise."

They kissed—just once, because that was all either of them could bear, then emerged the cottage hand-in-hand. As she neared her father, she whispered in Dracula's ear.

"Touch one hair on his head, and what I did to you before will feel like a dream."

He simply nodded.

Katelyn squeezed Luca's hands a final time then released him and moved to stand beside her father.

"Ready, lass?"

She looked back to Luca, a lump forming in her throat.

Go, my love, he insisted. *The sooner you do, the sooner you'll come back to me.*

The wind hastened through the trees. In the blink of an eye, Katelyn and her father were gone, carried away through the storm.

~

Luca's anguish coiled around his stomach. He thought he might vomit. His promise to Kate, and to her kingdom—*their* kingdom, rang in his ears as he buried his agony.

~

Luca's heavy breathing was impossible to ignore. After waiting for what he thought was an appropriate amount of time, Dracula broke the silence between them. "I suppose now there's no reason for us not to travel this night as well?"

As soon as he had opened his mouth, Luca's agony turned to wrath.

"*She* may have been willing to talk with you, and be civil," he said, in a voice colder than ice. "She is my better, for that and so much more. *I* don't want to even hear your voice."

21

Arjuna adjusted the pillows behind her mother's back. If she could prop her up a bit more, her lungs wouldn't be so taxed. But Sufie was more concerned about the dour expression on her daughter's face.

"Why are you counting *yourself* out?" The Seht certainly hasn't, smart man that he is."

"Maman, please. Darien—"

"It's *Darien* now, is it?" Her mother raised an eyebrow.

Arjuna groaned into her lap as she bent her head down again to the tending of her mother. "The Seht has many responsibilities. More now than ever. He needs someone who can help *him*, not the other way around."

In every corner of the Council House, people huddled together with family and people of their own ilk—their own class. Grumbles of discontent rose from every side. And Darien—he was working so hard to ease everyone's fears that Arjuna hadn't seen him with a moment to himself for hours. She wondered how he didn't get dizzy, walking back and forth and every which way, trying to keep everyone happy.

It would have been impossible for Sufie to miss the concern etched onto Arjuna's face, even if she hadn't been staring.

"I'm sorry I didn't help you to see all you have to offer," she said at last.

Sufie's words stole Arjuna's attention. She clasped her mother by the hand and shared a sad smile.

"They will blame him for this," Arjuna said. He was a new seht. The threat of shadow had stretched itself over the city the very day of his succession.

Sufie was in agreement.

"They will say he invited it when he allied himself with Icarya."

"But they *saved* us. We'd all be dead if it weren't for them!"

"And some will argue that none would have died, had they not come."

Neither Darien, not the Icaryan queen, nor anyone else had any control over Haydee's movements, or her dark minions. They were damn lucky that the denizens of Icarya had been able to fight back at all.

But it wasn't enough, not when it was still night though it should be day, and Haydee's shadow settled like a funeral gauze over the city, its people in perpetual mourning.

To still their restless tongues, Arjuna approached the instruments that lay abandoned in a corner. All eyes were on her as she took up the harp. She hesitated as her fingers came to the strings. None of the traditional songs she knew were appropriate. The jubilation of the previous day was gone, but so was the chaotic torment of the last night. All was calm, but sad. She couldn't play anything else with sincerity. But such feelings were not those of songmakers, not even if one counted the funeral songs.

She thought of the faun, and how they had played together with no songs at all.

She started slow. The notes were long, drawn out, but beautiful. Once she had found that familiar place inside the melody, she let it carry her away, lost to time until she dared to open her eyes. The tenor of the room had changed. It was no longer despondent, but more settled. Comforted. Her gaze caught Darien's. He was staring openly, his expression one of admiration, and deep gratitude. She smiled, pleased to have pleased him, and returned to her music.

DARIEN COULDN'T CONCENTRATE ON ANY OF THE CONVERSATIONS HE HAD attempted to have. Once Arjuna started playing, it was the only thing he could focus on. That included Jisel, who hadn't left his side since the music began. She feared what Darien had already decided—that he would never choose her as a bride. He might have chosen Jisel once, but his heart was not moved by her. Arjuna was kind, generous, humble, talented, brave...and absolutely beautiful. As he spoke to Jisel, and countless other Likhanni, he only ever felt a tugging, a longing to be nearer to Arjuna, to gaze into her amber eyes and to alternately stoke and cool that fire that sparked in her cheeks whenever she looked at him. When he had seen her stand and go to the harp, her boldness had surprised him. And that melody—if his heart, his *soul* had a sound, she had plucked it out with her strings and sent it echoing into the world.

The thread binding them whenever their eyes met was powerful. It felt like she played for him, and for him alone. That she did it to help him. He hadn't been alone with her since she'd sewn up his hand. He rubbed at it just then, not because of any pain—she had taken care of him well—he wished to be with her. But his duties lay elsewhere. Though he was willing to forget everything else, for just a moment, and heap yet another responsibility onto himself as her protector. Especially in this uncertain future, for both her and Likhan, as none of the people who had disappeared had returned.

Darien had tried more than once to get some information out of Hercules. Though he had blown the Horn of Telmar and had come back with a man who glowed as if he were the sun itself, the two of them had done nothing but argue from the moment they had arrived. Who the brilliant man was or how he was meant to help was a mystery. But until Kate or Luca returned, they were all the protection Likhan had. But neither Hercules nor his brother (that was the only thing Darien *could* get him to say) seemed to be doing anything in the way of help.

There was no use getting angry, so there was nothing for him—for any of them—to do, but wait.

THIS TIME, APOLLO IGNORED HIM COMPLETELY. AS YET ANOTHER conversation with the pair led to nothing but a churning headache, Darien's mind wandered—rather naturally, he noticed—back to Arjuna. How long had it been since she had begun to play? Was it an hour? Or two? For however long it continued, her playing had a soothing effect. Most of the people taking refuge had fallen asleep or conversed quietly. Her melody was just as beautiful, just as fine, as when it had begun, but she herself had grown weary. He could tell in the longer silences, and the stretched, resonating notes. Her eyes were closed to all around her as he approached, ascending the stairs of the stage where she alone had quieted the Likhanni. He knelt beside her, waited for her chord to be strummed to completion, then curled his left hand around hers, being careful not to touch the strings or disrupt their sweet, melancholy vibrations. She turned and opened her eyes to him.

He felt all eyes draw to him, pulled out of their slumber, and still, he was senseless to all except his heart's flutter.

That blush he had begun to relish returned in all its fervor as Arjuna moved to withdraw her fingers from the harp, and from Darien's grasp. He held her, firm but gentle.

"Thank you, Arjuna, for your exquisite music. You have calmed *all* our hearts. But now you too must rest."

She looked at their fingers, still folded together as they came away from the harp. She looked up at him, frightened, but also hopeful. She tried to tear herself away from him, from his crystalline eyes and his sure and steady grip, but with every move she made, he held her a little tighter. He sought to reassure her.

"My Seht. Please. People are looking," she whispered, desperate to be free of the heat that radiated off her cheeks as more eyes fell on her, and on her hands, clasped by the seht's. His reply came clear and calm, and it melted the last vestiges of her fear.

"Let them look. The only one I see is you."

Without saying a word, Darien dared her to hold his gaze, without pushing her chin upward to lift her eyes as he normally did. The longer she gazed at him, admiring his green and blue eyes, the more alive his expression became, alight with a smile that barely touched the right corner of his lips. She reveled in it and prayed that the Council House, and all within it, would fade away, leaving her alone with her idol. Alas, all sweet things come to an end, and the spell cast over them for a fleeting moment was broken. He pulled her to her feet and escorted her down the stairs, back to her mother. He spoke softly in her ear as they walked, his velvet voice causing her knees to buckle.

"All of Likhan requires my utmost attention now, but I wish it were different. In the coming days or weeks, even, if I seem distracted or distant, or neglectful, know that I'm thinking of you, and that I am always looking for a time when we might be free to talk."

His words, full of caring and a true respect for his position, were why she had fallen in love with him in the first place. That and his outward charms, his irresistible smile.

"You bear a great weight on your shoulders. I have no desire to distract you from it, for without you, we all would be lost," Arjuna said.

"I am grateful for the trust you place in me. I will strive to be worthy of it."

"Darien, with all that you have done, you already are."

Apollo was completely at ease, laid out with his long slender legs crossed at the ankle, eyes closed, the sunbeam glow surrounding him pulsing strong then soft again in time with the music.

"Are you even listening to me?" Hercules cried.

As Arjuna's playing ended, Apollo opened his eyes, triumphant. "Now *she's* one of mine."

Apollo rose and approached her with a frustrated Hercules in tow as Darien escorted her to her mother's side.

"That was an excellent composition. Moving, full of soul, perfectly executed."

Arjuna bowed. "Thank you most kindly."

Apollo grinned in satisfaction. "You honor me. I would make a boon to you of my gratitude for such talent. What would you have of me?"

Arjuna looked to her mother, confused. Apollo's gaze passed knowingly from Arjuna to her parent, then back again.

"Of course."

His incandescence grew blinding at that moment, and Arjuna and her mother were bathed in a ball of light.

"Arjuna!" Darien cried.

Hercules held him back with a gentle pull on his forearm. "It's all right," he said. "Just wait."

Darien looked back and saw that the sunburst had faded, and Apollo had returned to his normal luminescent self.

Sufie was breathing heavily, staring at Apollo in disbelief. He extended his hand. She shifted on her mat and got to her feet.

"Maman? *Maman!*" Arjuna gasped.

Apollo smiled and spun Sufie around. The deep wrinkles in her face faded away, undoing the premature aging of her ailments.

"Health without youth is a waste, is it not?" Apollo said.

Arjuna stretched tentative fingers to reach for her mother's face.

"Maman..."

"My dear girl." Sufie squeezed her daughter in a tight embrace. Then she turned to thank the god, pressing her forehead to Apollo's hands.

"Thank you, my lord. A thousand times, thank you!"

Apollo gave a subtle nod. "Your daughter's music is the greater gift."

Arjuna's mother smiled and embraced her again.

Darien grinned at mother and daughter, his smile wide and full of wonder. To Apollo, he said, "You have my gratitude as well. Any aid to a citizen of Likhan is an aid to me."

Hercules stormed after him. "Careful," he said, his voice snide. "You might wear yourself out at this rate."

"I thought you wanted me to ease their suffering," Apollo replied, cool as always.

"I do. But what about the *rest* of them?"

"We shall see, Brother. We shall see."

At Apollo's departure, Darien spoke again to Arjuna. "You've done more for Likhan today than I have, and fortified all our spirits."

"That's all I could ever hope to do, Great Seht," she replied.

His heart struggled to keep pace as he tried his luck. "It's more than any seht, any man could hope to find."

Her eyes sparkled, but still she trembled with uncertainty.

"Till next our paths cross," he said in parting.

It took Jisel only a matter of minutes to corner him. It was inevitable, he supposed, that he would be confronted by those who believed they had a claim to him. He owed them nothing. But what he would give them was honesty. There was not much to confess. No arrangement had yet been made, nor promises broken, so when she questioned him as to his intentions, he said very little.

She moved closer to him, and undid the first tie on her bodice. With lowered voice and hooded lids, she asked, "Is there any way I might change your mind?"

Darien didn't bother to look down. His expression hardened. The cloying voice, the promise of pleasure—these were familiar to him, as were the machinations underneath. But he only realized it as such now that he was confronted with it.

"No," he growled. "There isn't." He tore himself from her, leaving her half-dressed in the corridor and scrambling to refasten her clothes.

22

Kate and her father traveled on the back of the wind until they came to a place in the forest that seemed familiar to her, in the sense of having visited it in a dream, but she could not recall clearly.

When she and William materialized again, Kate looked to her father with confusion. He cocked his head to the left.

"Do ye know the way?"

Her instinct led her through the first two passes into the grove, but then she found herself in a place where she had just been. She had the strongest urge to go right again.

"*No*," William corrected.

Against all her inclinations, she followed her father and took the opening to the left. William took her hand, and though they carried on at a gentle pace, she felt as if she were being dragged against her will, against her very nature. But she put her trust in her father's kind eyes, like a mirror reflection staring back at her.

The deeper they traveled, the more lost she became.

Their destination was tucked away and out of sight at the base of a tree. The bark served only as a gateway, which opened up to a wider space beyond, paneled in glass. Sunshine danced over the greenery of the forest and filtered through to the spacious rooms in which they stood, hewn from wood.

Meryn and Drigory stood in the great room, a wide-open space that felt more outside than in. William's brows shot up to his hairline at the sight of them.

"We want to help," his mother said, stepping forward.

Drigory was rooted in place, his hands firmly folded across his chest. "Took you long enough to get here," he said. "I'm surprised you could find the place at all."

Kate's gut roiled like a volcano.

"If you're concerned about wasted time, perhaps you'd like to examine your lifetime of lies more closely. If we're too late, it's on your hands."

He scowled and turned his face from her. William crossed the room to join his mother. Fragrant blossoms of every color greeted her with a cool breeze, full with the promise of life.

"It seems spring is coming early here," Kate said.

William responded, "It's *always* spring here."

Meryn's eyes grew round at the size of Kate's swollen belly.

"I didn't realize you were so far along already."

Kate shrugged. Standing off against the three of them gave her an uneasy feeling.

"What is this, some kind of coup?" she asked.

William rushed toward her again, arms outstretched. "No, no, that's not what—"

"Because that isn't happening. Icarya thrives because of my sweat, my blood and tears. Meanwhile, you and Meryn have done nothing to lay claim to the throne. *I* am the Queen of Icarya, Empress of the Far Islands, Master of the Great Sea. You'll not find a single Icaryan soul to say otherwise. Even this old troll can't argue you're more worthy of it."

"You are indeed the queen, Katelyn," Meryn said. "No one here's disputing that." She eyed Drigory, standing still as a statue that had been served a sour lemon. "*No one*," she repeated.

"Then why am I here?" Kate asked. "The time for this little reunion could be better."

"Look," Meryn answered, "you were right to send Hercules and Luca to combat the shadows. But their help will only go so far. If Haydee succeeded in becoming shadow, the world will be permanently tainted."

William nodded. "Ye cannae destroy something tha' doesnae really exist anymore but is everywhere at the same time."

Kate recalled the fantastical solution her father had suggested back at the hut. She tried the words out on her tongue. Speaking them aloud didn't make them any less ridiculous.

"The world must be made over."

"Aye. And only the Goddess can do that."

Something hitched. Kate's brows furrowed together.

"What about the Great Magician, the one who *made* the world?" She had always known, of course, that this was the creation story Icaryans held to. She was not and never had been in a position to question it. But she knew equally well that Icaryans worshipped a goddess of the forest. It had never occurred to her before now that, taken together, these two deeply held beliefs were at loggerheads with one another. She'd never had a reason to examine the contradiction, or to even realize it was there at all. She had simply accepted both, as all Icaryans did, without question.

"The Great Magician only *thought* he created the world and everything in it," Meryn said. "But he discovered something that was already there, something *he* didn't create, that had the power to give life or take it."

Kate nodded. "The Golden One."

Meryn dipped her head in return. "The bloodline of the Goddess survives in the royal family, in the legend you well know. The knowledge of *this* place, a place the Goddess holds dear, has been kept by our ancestors. They believed that, in a time of great need, they could return to this place and beseech Her."

Kate blinked. "Okay, so? Certainly you don't need me to pray. And to be honest, I have no use for gods. Being able to manipulate the forces of nature makes a god a rather unnecessary distraction. I'd never openly disrespect what Icaryans believe to their core, but..." She turned to her father. "Hasn't it done the same to you?"

"But that's the point," William said. "I can move through the air. But *only* air. I can't make fire, or ice, or melt into the earth…"

Kate shifted uncomfortably on her feet.

"My son William is even stronger than I," Meryn said. "I can't control any elements, but—"

"You can see into the future," Kate provided.

"*Sense* the future might be more appropriate. My faculty is not as strong as Drigory's. Or yours."

"I'm not related to the troll too, am I?"

Drigory sneered. Kate sneered back.

William held their attention, trying to get things back on track. "The *point* is, we've tried, Katelyn. We've tried praying. She won't speak to us."

Kate raised an eyebrow. "Did you consider the possibility that she doesn't exist?"

Drigory tugged at his beard. "I *told* you she was stubborn."

"You prayed to a god who didn't answer, now you want me to try, and *I'm* the stubborn one? You're wasting my time," Kate replied.

Meryn pleaded with her. "It's our only hope. We think, with your closeness to the Goddess, with so many of her gifts, that you'll get her attention."

William recognized the opening his mother had created and leaned into it. "When I saw you had summoned earth in Likhan, had created *life* out of a dead stump…" He shook his head in incredulity.

"And you saw that as praying to the goddess, did you?" Kate asked, her impatience heavy in her tone.

"Didn't *you*?" Meryn shot back.

Kate blinked. At that moment, everything in her field of vision, including them, was cast in shadow. Color drained from them like ashen ghouls. That same foul, disorienting smell Haydee had generated in Likhan invaded her senses. So sudden and unbidden, her insides turned over, and she grabbed the nearest basket to wretch into.

"Sit, sit," William urged, guiding her into a thickly upholstered chair.

Kate gulped for breath. The urgency was unmistakable.

"If I do this, and it fails, I will have wasted precious time. The consequences could be severe."

"What will they be if I'm right?" Meryn asked.

Still reeling, Kate hesitated to look Meryn in the face, for fear of what she might see there. When she did finally look up, all she saw was the strength of her conviction. Meryn took the seat opposite her and curled her fingers around her armrest. A nervous habit, Kate observed.

"There's something else," Meryn continued. "Was fire the first element you conjured?"

Kate shrugged.

"No," William interjected. "The opposite."

"I've never summoned ice purposely," Kate said.

"No, but ye did it before you set yer first foot on Icaryan soil."

"I beg your pardon?"

"That day, in front of yer flat. Ye turned the rain to snow."

"It was snowing."

"Nae, it *wasn't*."

Kate ignored the chill that ran down her spine. "What difference does it make?"

Kate was getting tired of seeing Drigory shake his head out of the corner of her eye.

"As elements go, fire and ice are seen as extreme. They signal volatility, over-strong emotions," Meryn answered.

Kate had heard this chorus before. It wasn't as if it had been something she could control. How could she have, caught as she was in the web of their secrets? Did they not *see* that this was, at least in part, a problem of their own making?

She said nothing in reply.

"Reorienting your talents should help you *gain* that control," William said. "By essentially 'unlearning' yer reliance on fire as yer primary ability, and shifting it to something more centralized—"

"Like air?" Kate asked.

"Earth would be better."

"Why?"

"All things stem from it." He lifted one of the many books from the low table at the center of their little gathering and turned one of its illustrations in her direction. It looked to her for all the world like an anatomical drawing. It rather reminded her of DaVinci's *Vitruvian Man*, only this image depicted the roots of a tree at the figure's feet, water as the heart and the sky above. Flames coiled on the right hand, shards of ice on the left.

So water was centering. That made sense to her. In Likhan, her eternal fire had only gone out when Alaric doused her. He'd seen it before, too. The first time she had encountered Haydee's shadows, when her thirst couldn't be quenched with all the water in the world. He had figured it out before she did.

Her skin shivered at the memory of the deluge he had inflicted on her. It was an intense shock, but after, all was calm.

"Water cancels out the others," Kate murmured.

William nodded. "That's what we want to do. And try to get your earth powers to take primacy. We hope that will get the Goddess's attention."

"How long is this supposed to take? I'm not exactly a woman of leisure," Kate said.

The trio exchanged glances, but no one answered her.

"There might be nothing left by then!" she cried.

"We can't predict this, Katelyn. It's never been done before," Meryn replied.

"What makes you think it's even possible?"

"My great-great-grandfather tried, once. In a time of great need, as now," Meryn said.

"How long did it take him?"

All at once their gazes sought the floor.

"Better ye don't know," William mumbled.

"Oh, that's wonderful."

Meryn interceded. "We shouldn't allow ourselves to be hung up on our ancestor's circumstances. This could be entirely different."

"Of course it is." Kate pressed her hands against the sides of her stomach. "Is it safe?"

No one said anything for a long time.

"I won't risk this child," Kate said. Her voice echoed off the glass with great force.

William stood and put a hand to her shoulder. "No one's asking you to do that. It's a lot to take in. Why not sleep on it, and, if you feel it's necessary, you can leave in the morning."

Kate expected the others to say something. She didn't know what, but nothing came. William led her into a small room with a comfortable bed, a vanity, and a modest bookshelf. She sat on the edge of the bed as he took his leave. He lingered in the doorway, his hand pressed to the frame.

"Despite the circumstances, I'm glad you're here. I guess what I'm tryin' to say is, if there's time, there is much to say." At that, he left her alone with her thoughts.

KATE HAD BEEN AWARE OF LUCA CREEPING AT THE EDGE OF HER MIND ever since she had left his side. He had contained himself for so long, allowing her to focus on what was right in front of her, but now that she was alone, he couldn't stand it any longer.

Are you all right? Where are you?

I'm fine, for now, Kate answered. *Somewhere in the forest, though I'm not sure which one.* She probed his mind for an update, and saw for herself that for the time being, Icarya was safe, if on edge, and Dracula was cooperating. Although that included driving his son mad by degrees.

Did you learn anything? he asked.

They want to help me harness my powers. To talk to a god.

It's what you wanted, isn't it? Learning control? he asked.

Now's not the time.

When, then? I'll always want to be close to you, but I'm glad you're far from danger. Do what you must, and come back to me.

I will, Kate promised.

Sweet dreams, love.

Luca faded to the background of her mind, just a warm glow.

She still hadn't told him that Dracula could read minds. That he was in all probability reading his. Kate didn't want to keep such a secret, but what good would warning Luca do, if even that would be overheard? If

Dracula remained unaware that she knew, then she could use it to her advantage just as well as he. She tried to find a comfortable position on the bed, one that didn't involve the baby sitting on any major organs, and attempted to settle her mind enough to sleep. That's when she noticed the books.

A mytho-religious tract of the beginning of the world, of the work of the goddess and the Great Magician, a history of the ancestor Meryn had mentioned, King Augur, and the journals of the man himself sat neatly stacked on the small table to the left of her bed. She picked up the tome of Icarya's birth. She was surprised that the work began by explaining, in great detail, all that the authors did *not* know. Long had scholars tried, the preface claimed, to determine the origins of the Great Magician himself. From where had he come? Why had he created Icarya, and by what means, what power? Had he been author to *other* worlds, before or since? It had been a call, perhaps, for others to take up the mantle where other researchers had failed, to seek answers to questions that were likely unanswerable.

The text began in earnest at the beginning, keeping a faithful record of all they had learned, all the stories they had been told. That their entire world had come into existence with the growth of a single tree.

Kate looked through the open door to her right, across the great room and past the glass walls to the forest beyond. She shut out the dizziness that frayed the edges of her vision at her newfound ability to see across great distances. Her mind adjusted, seeing the very tree at the center of the world in vivid, startling clarity. Her gaze tracked the grooves in its bark, followed the path up from the roots that wove themselves into the moss-laden ground up to the highest branches, stretching out their limbs in a desperate attempt to touch the moonlight. Its leaves uncurled with a sigh into the night, joining the birds who had quitted their nests and together began their nightly song. Insects buzzed and chirped in harmony, the beating of their wings adding sweet, high notes to the melody.

Kate could breathe the chill in the air. She filled her lungs with it, and tasted the coming frost on her tongue. She turned back to her book again to all she could see and hear wrought into words, of birds, grasses, meadows and mountains rising up to meet the sky.

~

The Great Magician stretched out his magic, breathed and created clouds that rained and formed rivers, lakes, and creeks, pouring into the Great Sea and giving the ground life. The waters became populated with fishes, winged animals soared through the air. He gave all breathing things the gift of speech, and forbade the eating of any creature. The forest was abundant in food enough for all things without the need for killing.

He walked in the meadow, enjoying his creation—the warm sunlight, the sweet air, the lush verdant grass, the fresh fruit of the forest. He leant on a hill, topped by a tree looking out to the river leading up to the mountain's peaks.

Kate shuddered. Something itched at her memory. But it was too far away for her to have any claim on it.

She paused and looked up from the page. What she had pictured in her mind as her eyes passed over the words before her was a place she knew well. *The* place, the one she called home. The one she longed for whenever she stayed away too long. The realization disturbed her, for she did not understand. When she looked down again, the story the book told did not come as a surprise. Something inside her already knew.

~

Across the river, the Great Magician spied a creature he did NOT *make —a golden hind with the horns of a stag and a glittering, golden mane. A creature he had not made, he could not ever have imagined or dreamed, stepped out of the ether into the realm he had forged himself. He moved not a muscle, not daring to startle the creature. They simply stared at each other from across the river. There was something quizzical and mischievous about her expression. She knew she was not meant to be there. In the heart of his supreme act of creation, her very presence challenged him. She watched him curiously. When he made, slowly, to stand up, the creature bounded away into the mountain pass. He raced after her, but he splashed clumsily into the stream and through the mountains as the golden one flitted about the rocks, appearing and disappearing. He heard laugher, a childlike sound, but without the innocence, mocking him in the wind that whistled past his ears.*

The frenzied flight of his quarry disoriented him. He was battered by the wind and ran headlong into a crag, cutting a deep gash in his head.

Seething with the anger of embarrassment, he trudged back across the river to wash his wound. The gash threatened one eye, swollen closed with blood. It is said he never opened that eye again.

He cursed the creature for its malice, and imagined he could still hear her taunts on the night wind as the skies gave way to the stars.

He slept fitfully.

When he awoke, he wasn't sure if he had dreamed the hind, and he'd simply run after a phantom in his sleep and cut his head open like a fool. He asked the birds, the squirrels, the deer, but no one said they had seen or heard of the golden creature. So he chided himself for a fool and soon forgot about what he had seen by the river. Then one night, he was woken by the swell of music and revelry. He came out of his castle made of stone and followed the sound. The laughter and music led him deeper and deeper into the forest, until he saw the warm golden glow of a fire. He came upon a clearing that held all his creations of the forest—horses, deer, squirrels, sparrows, mice, badgers, all dancing and singing joyfully in a circle, in a language he couldn't understand and hadn't taught them to speak. Wreaths of flowers were braided into their tails and manes, and hung from their necks. Frolicking and singing among them was a golden child, her pale-yellow hair dancing as wildly as her bare feet, her pale skin warmed by the glow of the bonfire.

The Great Magician became enraged. He screamed and hurled himself toward the circle. The noise he made crashing through the forest in the direction of the dancers broke their harmony and caught their attention. They stared at him like he was a stranger, an interloper in a foreign land, and it hardened his heart against them. He headed straight for the child, who glared at him with a wicked smile on her lips, but when he reached the clearing, there was nothing where she had stood but thin air.

He spun round, but there was no sign of the child, or any golden creature, no sign that something had rushed into hiding. He turned his ire to the creatures who remained, silent as stone.

"Who is she?"

Not a creature moved or spoke in response.

His fury only grew, and he shouted at them again. "Who is she?!"

Again, they remained mute, until the bright red fury staining his cheeks darkened to a deep purple.

"Ingrates! I teach you to speak, yet you will not answer me? For your disloyalty, you shall not speak again. I will bring men into the forest, men who will hunt you down and devour you like the common animal, for they will not know you were once something more."

With a hand gesture and words, he struck the animals in the glen dumb, and they and their offspring never regained the power of speech.

KATE DROPPED THE BOOK ONTO HER CHEST AND RUBBED HER HAND OVER her face. She was too drowsy to continue, and the child in her belly was silent now, still and peaceful enough to allow her mother the rest she craved.

She slept soundly, and dreamt of her home in springtime, and the urgent rush of the sea at its base. Luca sat to her right. He smiled at her, and took her in his arms, holding her close as they sat in the surf, as they had done every day on Oʻloa, where they had been able to ignore the distractions of her crown, and the world was not on the brink of peril, if even for a season. She longed for the return of summer. Luca's head turned toward the sea, and she felt a sharp pang in her stomach. She laid her head on the beach, wracked with labor pains. Luca spoke sweet, comforting words to her, but she couldn't hear them. His voice was barely a whisper above the roaring of the surf, and his face turned a dull gray, as if he were fading out of the world. Kate's heart pounded and her abdomen throbbed as she watched dark clouds rage across the blackening sky, and the surf thrashed mere feet from where she lay, unable to retreat, and shrinking from Luca's aid. A final wrench in her gut brought forth a primal howl, and her daughter came into the world. When Luca held up the child for her to see, sheer, unbridled terror robbed her of her screams and curdled her blood. In Luca's pale hands lay a tangled shadow, a dark amorphous cloud. From the smoky tendrils, a small face appeared. Two small, beady eyes were stark white against the face of ash. Its mouth gaped open, spewing forth more shadows. Kate turned to Luca in horror, but his face was also ash. The sea raged upon them, crumbling her family to dust and washing them away as the waves crashed over them.

KATE SHOT UP IN BED WITH A START.

"Fuck."

She rolled over on her side, sweeping her hair out of her face. She grabbed for the reassuring weight of her stomach and swallowed long draughts of air to calm herself. The baby shifted in its place, snuggling up close to one of Kate's ribs, causing her to grimace. She stood to stretch her muscles, and shuffled to the table, where she poured water from a stone pitcher into a wooden-hewn cup and downed it in one swallow. Her mind felt strained from the frenzy of the dream, and she struggled to achieve a sense of calm. Her breasts were swollen and sore, her legs ached, and neither sitting nor standing nor laying down made her comfortable in her own skin.

Her weary eyes were perpetually drawn to the moonlight that filtered through the window set high up in the wall. Kate reached her hand up to the pane to feel its coolness. Her tight dress strained her belly, and she scratched at the thick fabric. She longed for the chill of the night. She grabbed the blanket at the edge of the bed and wrapped it around her shoulders as she climbed up out of her room, through the common area, and up the stairs which let out into the forest. The great oak stood before her. She pondered its grooves and weaves as she exhaled the cold night air, tracing the twists and knots of the trunk with her fingertips. It felt full and supple at her touch, and the split of the roots where her feet now stood invited her to sit. She draped the blanket around herself and rested her head against the tree. Its bulges and knots massaged her back, and her eyelids grew heavy, her breathing calm.

~

Kate felt her aches and worries lift from her like fog. Through fluttering eyelids, she saw a light flicker and move in the distance. She blinked, trying not to nod off, when the light danced closer and closer to her and assumed a more definitive shape. Wavy bands of light radiated from the center, becoming arms and legs as it scampered closer to her.

It was a girl that approached her, with skin the color of moonlight, and hair just as pale, with only the softest whisper of the sun. Her eyes were clear and colorless as crystal. She wore no shoes on her feet, and was blissfully ignorant to the mud accumulating between her toes. A dress woven with fallen autumn leaves that looked infinitely older than the imp wearing them. She wore a strand of simple string tied around her neck, knotted with dried mushrooms, rocks, and what might have been bones. They made no sound as she approached on hands and feet like a young gorilla, only rising to her feet as she walked up on Kate's legs, coming to stand on her thighs.

"You've come to the First Place."

Her expression of deathly intensity broke into a giggle. "Wrong tree, wrong tree!" She hopped off Kate's legs, now standing on the roots of the tree. She pressed her petite hands and face to the trunk just to the right of Kate's head, and whispered, "Our secret."

The tree seemed to tremble at Kate's back, sending a shiver down her spine as the tree laughed in return. The girl looked at Kate, then offered her hand.

Kate's head felt light and dreamy, barely able to absorb what was happening. The air seemed still. Every movement, every sound of the forest seemed drawn out, deliberate. Kate didn't speak, but took the girl's hand and allowed herself to be led back into the wooded labyrinth through which she'd come. Kate felt that same tug as when her father had pulled her through by the hand, slicing against every instinct in her being.

Without warning, the girl leapt up onto her back, clinging to her neck and shoulders like a monkey. She tied a blindfold of supple black fabric over her eyes.

"Your feet know the way," she said, her voice light and quick like chimes twinkling in the wind. She bounded down from Kate's neck and pulled at the boots Kate had left unlaced on her feet, tossing them aside.

"Such a nuisance! A nuisance!"

Kate put her nose to the wind, like drinking from a cool pool. She felt the crunch of the earth and velvety mosses and grass beneath her feet. Her skin tingled, the small hairs on her neck and arms prickled as she pointed her feet to the right. She could hear the girl's small feet, frolicking, barely touching the forest floor as she leapt about, trying to confuse Kate, although they both knew that was useless.

Guided by instincts, Kate wove through the forest, laughing along with the little creature as her fingers brushed past the same trees two and three times, all of it feeling right as they inched, slowly but surely, into deeper, hidden paths. As her legs stilled their playful movement, Kate's eyelids felt the warm glow of the morning. She removed the blindfold, and reached out to touch the majestic oak to her left. Light glittered in its leaves. A flurry of insects chirped and buzzed a welcome. The grooves felt familiar in her palm, like a long-forgotten dream.

"Hello again," she whispered, half to herself. The tree twisted in reply, a slow noise that rose from its base. Kate smiled, remembering a conversation long since passed, the meaning of which she couldn't decipher. She turned her back to the tree and seated herself between two sturdy, moss-covered roots woven into the ground. Near her face, a wide, felt-like leaf offered her a drink of the morning dew. It slid down the stem of the leaf into Kate's throat with a sweet, refreshing satisfaction.

Kate closed her eyes and breathed deep of the crisp, clean air, feeling more rested than she had all night. On all fours, the golden child crawled up Kate's legs again, hovering over her swollen belly and pressing her ear to it.

"She is singing," the child said. Kate smiled. The girl turned her head and kissed the apex of Kate's curve.

"Charlotte is a good name. I always pick good ones." The child sat beside Katelyn, plucking a patch of hair from her scalp and weaving it into her own pale hair, braiding it into pale and copper twists. She tied off the end with the tendrils of wildflowers. Then she did the same to Kate, weaving a length of her pale tresses into Katelyn's.

"No one will separate us again."

Kate smiled at the cherubic face gleaming back at her.

The child laid her hands on either side of Kate's head. Kate complied, laying her head in the girl's lap as she stroked her hair. The girl sang—of the sacred forest, of the feasts of old where even the trees danced for joy, and how surprisingly graceful trees are. The song lulled her to sleep again, basking in the laziness of the morning and the glory of the sun. Kate's thoughts grew heavy.

"I'm sorry," Kate said heavily. "About Vehlen."

The girl continued to stroke her hair. "Life and death, death and life. Fire gives both, *is* both. To create, you must destroy, and when you destroy, you also create. It is natural."

"It still hurts. I don't want to destroy."

"Something will be destroyed. It is for us to choose."

This soothed Kate little.

"We are good at hard decisions," the child added.

Something in the air changed without warning, and Kate snapped awake. The back of her head thudded against the tree just beyond the door to her room. She rubbed the back of her skull, and craned her neck downward. She caught sight of her feet, filthy, and tucked them instinctively under the hem of her nightdress.

23

Luca and his father traveled through the night without a word between them. It was insulting. Luca didn't care one iota about his heritage. He didn't ask a single question.

Dracula was still sulking when they arrived at the castle.

Lowenherz was bursting at the seams with people and creatures. Even some here continued to surprise him. Though Dracula had been in Cathair for weeks, it seemed that there was yet more of the world to amaze and shock him.

They ascended the complex with determined steps. At last, his son deigned to speak with him.

"I need to check in, then I'll take you on to Likhan."

"You say Hercules is already there?" the vampire lord asked.

"Yes, with his brother."

Dracula stopped dead. "Which one?"

"Apollo."

Dracula was crestfallen. "Oh. I was rather hoping for the other one. Anyway, if Likhan already has two capable guardians, and is not even your home city, might I not be of better use—"

"No."

Dracula scoffed. "You always appeared to be above such things."

"What things?" Luca asked.

"Personal obstructions of judgement."

Luca grabbed him by the coat collar and didn't give a damn who saw. "I'd rather be anywhere else right now. But I don't care who's standing beside me. My concern is who's standing beside *you*."

"I'm not a threat to these people. Not while our bargain is in place," Dracula said.

"You'll forgive me if I call bullshit."

Dracula sighed, straightened his coat, and continued on. Women and men gawked at father and son, mirror images of each other. They peered at Dracula with a mix of fear and awe. It seemed his reputation had once again preceded him.

Corbin caught up with them in the great hall, which for the moment had been repurposed into a grand workroom.

"Your Highness—"

"That's not necessary," Luca said.

"Yes it is."

"Is that how you would address your queen?" Luca asked.

Corbin cocked his head. "Fair enough."

Dracula saw his opening, and seized it. "My—"

"Shut it."

Dracula snarled, and bit the inside of his lip.

Corbin waited, watching to see how things would play out. When both men were silent, he continued. "Another hundred lanterns just went out. We're holding some back, of course, and have been fitting them to the outer walls. All Castelmor is shuttered. The guest rooms are already full, so we're putting people in the armory again. We're moving the cannons up to the turrets so more people will fit more comfortably this time, at least. We're not *quite* full up, but we're getting there."

Dracula opened his mouth to ask a question, but he didn't get that far. Luca turned to him, eyes ablaze.

"I thought I told you not to speak."

Dracula was *really* indignant now. "I am *not* your lackey. You asked for *my* help, because I know more than you and I am more than an undead soldier. Stop being childish."

"Childish?"

Corbin raised his voice. "I've made additional precautions in the meantime, if you care to know the particulars."

Luca knew what he was trying to do. And he was right. He had to focus. And to do that, he had to get his father out of his hair as soon as possible.

"Walk me through it," Luca said.

Corbin nodded and summarized, as succinctly as he could, that the plan to defend Lowenherz relied on long-range weapons that could be set ablaze to keep the shadows at bay, and keeping the castle brightly lit both inside and out. The trio walked the hallway as Corbin spoke, surveying all the preparations already underway. A mountain cat rolling a cannonball past them caught Dracula's attention.

"May I see that, please? That is, with your permission, Lord Sire."

Luca seethed. But with all eyes on him, he would look like a pigheaded fool if he refused such a "polite" request. He said nothing, and simply tolerated his father's actions as his blood rose to a boil.

Dracula crouched before the ammunition, rotating the heavy metal orb as if it were made of nothing more than cotton. He sprawled his hands over it, trying to approximate its circumference. He scratched the surface with a long fingernail, and rubbed the debris between the pads of his fingers. Standing up, he surveyed the people bustling around him.

"I need a large...ah!" He found what he was looking for and strode over to a young man studying a map.

"Would you be so kind, thank you," Dracula said, not pausing to wait for a response as he took the map out of the lad's hands and began to fold it over the cannonball. The youth came over in confusion, and not a little bit annoyed, just in time for Dracula to lift a pencil from the crook of the boy's ear and begin making small sharp markings on the back of the parchment.

Luca leaned over him, saying nothing as his father concentrated on his work.

"Do you mind? You're blocking the light," Dracula said without bothering to look up.

When Dracula felt the fumes rising off his son, emanating from his pores, the vampire's mouth puckered into a wicked smile. But he remained undeterred from his work, only standing again when the parchment was covered almost entirely in markings. The back of the map appeared more black than ivory.

The boy's expression was equally dark and crinkled to see his work so used, but his ire went unnoticed by all, and he remained still, clenching silent fists at his sides.

"Here," Dracula said, and passed the map to Corbin. "These wards will cut more effectively though the darkness. Have them all marked that way."

Corbin hesitated. "We planned on covering them in tar and lighting them. Light seems to be the shadow sorcerer's fiercest enemy."

"These will not hinder that, nor will they *be* hindered if they are chiseled into the metal."

Corbin considered, then looked to his king.

Luca looked hard at his father, uncomfortable having people wield a magic he couldn't understand from the one creature he trusted least. It would be his fault if loosed canons turned back on those who fired.

Kate would know.

He opened his mind and was about to reach out, then he stopped. Would he do this every time a decision had to be made? What good was his presence here then? His role as king, and his promise to protect them? How much more would he add to her burden by relying on her for everything?

"Luca?" Corbin asked.

It had been her idea to summon his father. Luca didn't need to ask her what she would do. He already knew.

He gave Corbin a curt nod.

"Uh—" Dracula took the map back and folded the whole thing in a peculiar fashion, its edges and seams meeting perfectly into a pyramidal shape. "This way for arrowheads."

Corbin nodded back and scampered off down the hallway with a map four times his size rolled up over his shoulder.

The lad whose map it was clenched his fists tighter as all his work disappeared down the hallway.

ALLISTAIR WAS HARD AT WORK, TRYING TO MAKE THE ELECTRIC TORCHES both effective and efficient. The dining table serving as his workstation was piled high with panes of glass, filaments, iron frameworks, and gunpowder. With his head down, intent on whatever it was he held in his hands, Luca was careful not to startle him.

A gentle hand on his shoulder caused Allistair to look up.

"Oh—"

Allistair flipped up the shield obscuring his face and stood, discarding his gloves and apron. He looked quickly from Luca to his father.

"Where's my sister?"

Luca should have anticipated his question. He wasn't sure what to say, what Allistair knew of his parents or their mysterious origins. He didn't want to divulge by accident anything that Kate had meant to keep private.

"She...she's working on another strategy."

It was much too vague. Luca knew that. But what else *could* he say when Allistair, having none of it, put his hands on his hips and said:

"But *where* is she?"

"I can't tell you that."

With a heavy sigh, Allistair dropped it. He didn't really have much of a choice.

Kaspar materialized from behind his father, wearing similar protective gear in miniature. He stopped short right in front of Luca and his charge.

"There are *two* of you? Wow!"

Dracula looked down at Kaspar with a vicious gleam that made the boy leap two steps back. Both Luca and Allistair stepped forward, caging Kaspar between them.

"Who's this?" Dracula asked.

Allistair dug his fingers into Kaspar's shoulder. "Back to your post, man, on the double!"

"Oh now *he's* English," Dracula said.

"I beg your pardon?" Allistair asked as Kaspar scampered back to his workbench beside his mother.

"Just as I said."

Allistair ignored him and said to Luca: "I sent aid out to Likhan as soon as I received Kate's message. I hope the latest batch gets there before another night falls, although I don't even know what difference that makes now. If any."

"It *is* helping," Luca said.

"Is it?" Allistair wiped the sweat from his forehead with an oily rag, then pinched the bridge of his nose between his fingers. "My kid sister and baby brother are out there. I'm supposed to—"

"You are," Luca repeated. "You are. And you and I both know your sister can take care of herself."

"Right. Sorry. What do you need from me again?"

Allistair tried to explain what he was working on, but even attempting to articulate his ideas had him stumped. "I'm trying to get them to explode if they should be broken, given them a little extra oomph to repel the enemy, you know, but without having them explode the moment they are lit."

"Did you try separating the fuse?" Dracula asked.

Allistair knit his brows together. "What?"

The vampire stepped forward, taking the lantern lying open on the table in his hands. "If you put the ignition here," he said, pointing to the slim space between the bulb and the glass pane of the lantern door, "then it will only activate if the filament bursts first."

Allistair took it back from him and tried it out for himself with a minimal amount of power. It lit, no problem. When he stepped back and dropped the lantern at his feet, it burst into flames.

"Hah!" He stomped the little explosion out, grinning in triumph as he scribbled down a fast note and passed the new orders down the line.

"It doesn't excuse any of the terrible things you've done, but thank you."

Dracula was surprised at the man's open-mindedness. He bowed his head in acknowledgement.

"I'd rather have you on our side than not," Allistair said.

Luca interrupted him in short order. "I'm taking him to Likhan. Do you think you can hold it together here a little bit longer, just until I get back?"

Allistair eyed the both of them carefully. "You're going to send him to Likhan. With Hercules and Apollo already there?"

"Yes," Luca answered.

Allistair bit his lip. "Might I have a moment?" he asked, gesturing to a far corner of the room.

Luca sighed and said, "There's nowhere far enough."

Allistair shifted on his feet. His hands were back on his hips again, a show of confidence.

"He's more use to us here," Allistair said.

Dracula couldn't help himself. "You don't say."

Allistair fired back and made the vampire snort. "Yeah I can see why you *wouldn't* want that. But Likhan already has Hercules, and *he* will have his hands full soon enough with his own kin. We'd be left with only one guardian, while they'd have three."

Luca remained silent, as his gut twisted in wretched acknowledgment. His stare bore a hole in Allistair that would have turned the spine of any other man to mush. Allistair pushed forward.

"Better the devil you know..."

Dracula weighed whether or not it would be better for him to intercede. He knew anything he said came unbidden to his son's ears, yet he could not hold his tongue.

"He—"

"Enough!" Luca cried, then just as quickly collected himself. He looked to Allistair, softer, grateful for the sound advice, and his stalwart delivery of it. "Put the new lanterns on the outer walls, and send any extras to Likhan when you can."

Allistair got back to work. Luca had nothing more to say—to his father or anyone else. All he could do was wait. He turned to the tall window to his right and looked out at Likhan in the distance. The city was shrouded in shadow, with a few faint, blinking lights. Over the wide expanse of desert was an impenetrable blanket of darkness. He tilted his vision upward to the clouds above the castle. Dusk was falling, but there was nothing in the air or the clouds that looked, smelled, or felt out of the ordinary.

He was just so tired. Kate's expectations for herself were impossibly high. How could anyone, even him, ever live up to them?

Dracula's gaze followed his son's. "Perhaps even if Haydee has become a traveler, she may not be as powerful as you fear. She may not have the ability to stretch her influence beyond the borders of Likhan."

Luca answered in a grim voice. "I know what I saw."

Dracula nodded, hands clasped behind his back.

"It's a lot to carry. The lives of all these people, resting on your shoulders." His gaze passed over the people scurrying about as he spoke, preparing for the worst. "It is the heaviest weight to bear, the lives of others. I haven't shouldered that burden since I was alive." He shrugged. "My first life, anyway."

Luca didn't respond. But he hadn't silenced him yet, either. His mind reeled from the profoundness of his son's inner silence. "It's how I became what I am," Dracula continued, "in defense of—" he scowled terribly, the thought passing unbidden across his mind. Such things were unthinkable, and only invited the sharpest of pains. He corrected his thinking, redirected it toward the object of his ancient wrath. "To exterminate the heathen hordes."

"So, you created a race of monsters to combat your enemies," Luca said without intonation.

Dracula snorted. "What rubbish! That rot about vampire as a superior race is all stuff and nonsense, perpetuated by a select few who were never satisfied with what they had. Vampirism is a human condition, with gifts and afflictions like any other. A vampire is no more or less human than someone with arthritis, or rheumatism. I would have thought you would be above such drivel."

Luca's reaction pealed sharply across his brain.

How could I be?

That one simple word, "dhampir," had marked him for life—neither here nor there, its pronouncement was a death sentence.

Dracula pressed his lips into a thin line, becoming more conscious of the weight of his ring as he worried it around his finger. "You're a king now, a title you've earned in marriage and deed. But, you should never forget," he said, taking the ring off his finger and presenting it to Luca, "you've been a prince since the day you were born. A Dracul—hailed from dragons."

Luca's gaze lilted downward, studying the ring Dracula offered him. A blood-red gem, gleaming in a band of gold coiled into a giant winged serpent, teeth and talons bared.

The tension grew thick as Luca's attention rested stoically upon it, then was gone in a moment, his attention turned back to the night before them. Dracula swallowed hard as he returned the ring to his finger. Luca felt how this cut his father to the core. It made his skin prickle. But Dracula was unable to mask the dejection emanating from him.

Good, Luca thought. *Let him feel my pain.* He pushed harder, wanting it to hurt.

"A prince without a name. How unorthodox."

Dracula scowled as he pushed the ring back into place.

"You *forsook* your name. I did not withhold it."

Luca looked at him with earnest, inquisitive eyes, then quickly averted his face. He pushed away the query that bubbled up in his throat.

But Dracula caught his reaction. His eyes grew round as saucers. "You don't r—"

Georg hurried past carrying a pot of stew, filling empty bowls as fast as he could before the next wave of hungry mouths could be seated. Luca was grateful for the interruption. He cast a sideways glance at his father, surrounded by a cloud of confusion. He corrected himself just as quickly, turning his attention back to Georg.

"If you expect to eat tonight, you'd best see to it now," the chef wheezed. He mopped his forehead with a rag, wiping away the sweat from a hot kitchen stretched to its limit. "Merciful Goddess, there'll be nothing left of me by the time this is through." His face was a bright, shining red. The rotund man elbowed his raucous patrons and gestured for Luca and his father to fill the gap.

Luca stepped forward, but felt his father's solid grip on his forearm.

"Mircea. For my brother. But I usually called you Miru."

The memory struck Luca like lightning. He closed his eyes. The sound of his father's pronouncement sent his mind reeling back to his boyhood, exploring the woods around his house. Dried leaves snapped crisply under his small, clumsy feet as he ran, weaving in and out among the trees. Running, searching. Searching for…a shadow among the trees. A deep voice called to him, taunting, teasing, tempting.

Miru...Miru...

"Come, come!"

Luca snapped out of his reverie, pulled down hard onto the wooden bench as Georg served him.

He was shaken. Not sure how to feel, Luca buried it all in the bowl before him.

Dracula split his attention between his meal and his surroundings. He pointed to the ceiling. "Fascinating design. The craftsmanship and aesthetic are familiar, yet foreign. It's simple, yet at the same time opulent. Like a Germanic hunting lodge built on a Roman cathedral. It's a marvel."

Luca put his utensil down.

"Can you be silent, just for one minute?"

He clenched his jaw so hard it nearly shattered. He balled his hands into fists on the table.

There was an awkward pause while Luca waited to see if his father would comply. When quiet finally reigned, he picked up his spoon and finished his meal.

Their bowls were cleared, and a more awkward silence ensued with nothing to fill their mouths. Dracula's expression turned rueful.

"May I speak?"

Luca could refuse. He was king, after all. Though that didn't quite fit him right, yet, and he struggled to discern what he did out of true caution, and what was spiteful. He thought of Kate. She'd been willing to converse with him, comfortable as ever in her own skin, never doubting for a second her control of the situation, of herself. And he *was* cooperating. There was no sign he meant to betray Kate's bargain. Yet. Luca inhaled deeply and resigned himself to it.

Luca's deep breath was all the cue Dracula needed to know his son was listening.

"I'd like to inspect the lower levels. I cannot offer a proper strategy without knowing the lay of the field. With your permission."

Luca stood, and to his father's surprise, extended his arm and gestured toward an inner door.

24

The first wave of lantern bearers fanned out in concentric circles from the Council House to the higher houses, being closest to the city center. Lanterns from Icarya were sent to the corners of homes and businesses and over streets and alleyways to beat back the darkest shadows. More torches lit their interiors.

"We're using up a lot of the torches even in this first step, but without it no one will feel safe," Darien said.

Alaric agreed. "At this rate, we'll only be able to retake a fraction of the city, and maybe not even all the well-to-do neighborhoods."

"That's just as well. With the outer wall in disrepair, there's nothing that could render those areas abutting the desert safe, short of a ring of fire," Darien replied.

Ted reappeared with another wagonload full of lanterns just as they had used up the last batch. Darien was surprised, and somewhat relieved, that Ted had come himself.

"She may have sent me away," Ted said, "but she can't keep me there. Especially in absentia."

Darien furrowed his brow. "What do you mean? The queen didn't send you herself?" he asked.

Ted shook his head. "Luca came back to Lowenherz with his father, but *without* her. Said she had gone where she needed to. That's it—no explanation, no anything."

Darien could see the frustration and worry his father wore plain on his face.

"Luca also told me to tell you not to eat any food that's been left out in the darkness. It could be deadly."

Darien's heart raced. That would amount to total crop failure, even for the meager things that did grow in Likhan's uninviting climate. Harvest time wasn't supposed to happen for another few weeks. And with additional farming out of the question for the foreseeable future…

It took a long time for Darien to form intelligible words. "But h-how—"

Ted gestured behind him to crates of food airlifted by a fleet of winged creatures. Dark, hard loaves of bread, aged cheese, loads of meat, smoked and packed in salt, jars of pickled and preserved fruits. They kept coming, one overstuffed crate after another.

"That will feed the entire city for a month," Darien mused.

"We hope it won't be needed for nearly that long," Ted said.

Darien scanned the food again, this time his thoughts drifting elsewhere. "All the aid that Icarya has given, its queen and king, its warriors, and now, its food. It's too much to be given without receiving something in return."

"I'm sure my sister would agree with you," Ted replied.

Darien didn't know what to say, what to think. What did he have to give that would be fair compensation for saving, and now *feeding* the entire city? Whatever she demanded, it would be impossible to refuse.

Ted put a reassuring hand on his son's shoulder and interrupted his train of thought. "Let's take things one at a time, shall we?"

Darien nodded. "I'm really glad you're here."

Ted's face brightened.

Alaric approached. "Are we to take our orders from you now, Your Highness?" he asked.

"Nope," Ted answered. "I'm not a king anymore. I'm just here as a fa..riend," he said, correcting himself. "A friend and a concerned neighbor."

Ted moved away from his son to give him space to go about his business. He stepped closer to Gideon, who had unloaded the last of the chests that were his burden to carry. He ruffled the golden coat on the gryphon's neck.

"I wouldn't leave you behind either, old friend. Not for the world. But you must go, for your own safety."

Gideon leaned into the nuzzle. "The feeling is mutual, Sire. I would not leave you here, even on my own accord. But I have my orders."

Ted paused. "Which are?"

Gideon's reply was soft, a gust above purring before a long nap. "If the city should fall, I'm to bring you and a select few to safety."

"Would that list include the seht?"

"It would."

Ted breathed again, and patted Gideon's mane.

"I'll be nearby," Gideon said.

Ted smiled. "I'd be hard-pressed to lose you in this crowd."

"Indeed. Where will you be?"

"I have no reason to stray far from the seht," Ted said, his voice noncommittal.

Gideon's tone deepened. "I understand."

Ted looked into his friend's eyes and saw the truth reflected there. His voice wavered. "Is it that obvious?"

Gideon shook his mane. "Only to one who knows you so well."

ALL CHATTER CEASED AS DARIEN ASCENDED THE STAGE. "THE FIRST RING is completed. People in the Plaza District may return safely to their homes. You're not to eat anything you may have left out, but we'll be distributing food to those who are leaving, the kind of fare that will last."

Someone in the crowd very politely, but very pointedly, asked: "What about the rest of the city? When will it be safe?"

As Darien tried to formulate an answer, his gaze darted across the room. No one he would normally turn to for counsel was looking at him. Alaric and Christine were not to be found. Hercules was arguing with his brother, as usual. Only Arjuna was looking up at him. But there was nothing but concern on her face—no answers to be found.

Movement at the corner of the room drew his attention. The widow Solimani was urging her sons to stand up. The taller of the two spoke.

"We have six spare bedrooms, and three common rooms that are cool and comfortable. House Solimani would be glad to host as many families as we can until the darkness passes. About thirty people will fit comfortably. Fifty if we squeeze."

Encouraging nods lifted the mood of the room, and one family after another in the Plaza District opened up their homes to the public. Darien bowed in the Solimani's direction.

Inwardly, he heaved a sigh of relief.

Darien oversaw the first round of citizens preparing to leave. Even the decision of what food was to go to which household was an ordeal.

"We need the lighter bread. My husband's digestion wouldn't stand it."

"That bushel of berries is fresher."

"Why are they getting *three* casks of wine?"

"There's *two* casks of wine here, same as you!"

Naturally, the utopian cooperation that came in those life-or-death hours had faded. With even a modicum of normalcy came the petty bickering. Darien was waiting for some diplomatic revelation to come to him before he opened his mouth, when he noticed that Arjuna was there, kneeling over the crates. As the feuding parties stared in open-mouthed outrage, she switched things out rapidly between their baskets. They were mesmerized by the swift movements of her hands as she seemingly catered to all their whims. What they failed to notice, and what brought a warm, wry smile to Darien's lips, was that by the time Arjuna had ceased rearranging the foodstuffs, everything was back in its original place. The opposing households looked over their bundles, and the bundles of their neighbor, and nodded in approval. Arjuna dipped her head, keeping her smile to herself. Then she turned her head and caught Darien smiling at her. She knew he had seen what she'd done. It was a secret acknowledgement, a shared moment of mirth. She gloried in it.

The taller of the brothers Solimani came to stand beside her. "Are you and your mother all set?"

Darien's heartbeat tripped over itself. "You're leaving?"

"I must, I feel."

"No. I cannot let you—"

Arjuna did not give him the room to finish. "It is safe, great Seht. You, yourself, have said so."

His eyes blazed at her. Damn it all. If he contradicted her now, here, if he insisted that the risk was too great for those he cared about most, it was all over.

His hands balled into fists at his side. The next words out of his mouth stuck in his throat.

"Safe journey to you then. And to you all." He swept his gaze over the first party, ready to depart, sparing an extra second on Arjuna's sweet, forlorn face before turning away.

~

ALARIC AND CHRISTINE WORKED DOGGEDLY UNTIL THEY REACHED THE very outer edges of light. They had just enough to illuminate one more house, and then their job was done. At least for now.

Since their almost-kiss, Alaric had been taciturn, and had not sought opportunities for them to be alone. Answers to any questions she posed were short and to the point, if he answered her at all. Christine was left wondering what she'd done wrong. When she was absolutely *sure* he wasn't looking, she snuck glances at him. She admired his broad, muscled body, his sculpted features, his simultaneously rough and easy manner that was really an addictive quality. Without those jibes, compliments, and offhand offers to go to bed with him, she was left feeling rather neglected, just as she was starting to appreciate his attention. Despite her best efforts, sometimes he *did* catch her staring. But the cocky remarks that she expected never came. That worried her more than anything.

The last house was owned by one of the families they'd been surveilling, one of the patriarchs that Kate had slain in the arena and had exacted their revenge with brutal force. They ascended the stairs, affixing the last of the lanterns into a corner of the master bedroom.

"Hey. I just had an idea," she said.

Alaric cocked an eyebrow. "I'd love to sweetheart, but I haven't got the time."

Behind Alaric's back, Christine smiled. It was the first inappropriate thing he'd said to her all day. Maybe there was hope yet.

"Believe it or not, I wasn't thinking of *you*," she lied. "I was thinking we could take a look around a bit. See if there's anything useful."

Alaric came into the room then, his voice earnest. "What are we looking for?"

"I don't know," she answered, pulling open a set of drawers. "We'll know when we see it I guess."

Swiftly and silently, they rifled through House Fahrad's possessions, finding no more cash than would be expected given their stature, no more correspondence than what pertained to their business.

"C'mon, let's go," Alaric whispered. "We'll be missed if we stay any longer."

Unsatisfied, Christine came around the far side of the bed with a grunt. Halfway past the footboard her foot snagged and she careened headlong into Alaric's back on the way out the door. The crashing sound their bodies produced was deafening in the otherwise quiet house. Christine scrambled quickly to her feet as Alaric, stuck beneath her, struggled to get his bearings.

"Listen love, you don't have to—"

"Shut up, you idiot," Christine hissed. "I tripped."

Still tangled, they both looked down at their feet, and saw a dark wooden floorboard yanked out of place.

"Oh shit." Christine crawled toward the upended plank, looking for a way to restore it to its place. Before she could, she caught a glimpse of what lay beneath.

"Alaric."

He hunched over her, the metal cache secreted away glinting in his eyes.

"There must be over three dozen swords here," she said. Not enough for an army, but—"

"But it's a start," Alaric said darkly.

Christine turned her head to him, realizing for the first time how close their faces were. She hoped the shadows that remained in the room were enough to hide the flush that colored her cheeks.

If Alaric noticed, he hid it well. Christine felt stupid for being so awkward in the first place. It was her habit to play it cool in every situation. For some reason, Alaric got under her skin. She felt stupid for blushing, though she couldn't control it, and felt equally stupid for being upset that Alaric hadn't found her out, which would have only resulted in relentless teasing. She ripped her gaze from his, refocusing on what they had found. So far, no one had called after then, even with the ruckus they made. But their luck wouldn't hold forever.

"What do you think?" she asked.

Alaric took a moment, then said, "If we put them on the underside of the wagon, no one will notice. We can't take them all, though. That *will* attract attention."

"How are we going to get them out of the house?"

Alaric eyed her narrowly, his gaze falling to her cloak. Lightning streaked across his eyes as he ripped it off her back.

"What are you doing?!"

"Get down on the floor," he said. "On your belly."

"What?"

"Will you shut up and do it already?" he spat, pushing her head down to the floor as close as he could without smashing her nose into the wood. Before she could protest, Alaric was laying the swords onto her back, one next to the other, layer after layer. He laid them end to end, to stop the hilts from bulging at her shoulders. The growing weight threatened to crush her.

"I can't take much more," she grunted.

From behind her, she heard Alaric unbuckle his belt. He slid the leather between her stomach and the floor, and pressed his knee into her back at the center of her spine, squeezing out of her lungs what little air she had left.

"Get off," she wheezed.

"Sorry, love. Gotta make it tight." He pulled the worn leather as taut as he could before splitting it and knotted the lengthy cord carefully around Christine's back. "That should hold. Can you stand?"

Christine tried to push herself up by the arms, but her muscles screamed in protest. When she tried to tuck her knees in and go that way, she nearly speared herself in the ass.

"No," she growled.

Alaric snorted. He reset the floorboard, refastened the cloak around her neck, and shifted the dust around the floor to cover their activity, then put his open palms underneath her.

"Here. Roll into me."

Sweat gathered at Christine's temples as she put all her weight into her arms again, enough for her to flop over into Alaric's arms. He grunted, then stood with what Christine thought was amazingly little effort, considering what he carried.

"Easy now," he said. "Don't overdo it." He left the bedroom and descended the stairs, craning his neck to whisper.

"Lean in, you're straining my back trying to sit up like that."

"I can't. I'll cut myself."

"You *won't*. Trust me."

"Why the hell should I?!"

Alaric stopped short on the stairs and stared at her.

She shriveled under his intense gaze, instinctively leaning closer to the blades at her back, if only to get further away from his relentless, inscrutable stare. His expression was stony, and the only thought Christine had was to escape it.

After an interminable pause, Alaric continued his descent. "It'll be over soon."

Christine flinched, stung by his gruff words as they emerged from the building.

"Everything okay?"

The man standing outside the next house over hovered near them with his hands on his hips. His eyes glimmered in the light shining directly above him, wild with the possibility that some unspeakable horror had re-emerged and caused them injury.

"Yeah," Alaric said in a casual tone, his aloof yet friendly mask settled firmly back into place. "Just tripped on the stairs. Twisted her ankle is all."

"Ah," the neighbor said, visibly relieved. "Lucky you were here then."

"You bet."

Alaric laid Christine down easy inside the cart, leaning close enough to undo the knot at her back as he did so.

"Slip them between the slats to the bracers as we go," he said into her ear. "I'll drive slow. Here."

He reached inside his cloak and pulled out a wineskin. She drank very little before handing it back to him. He took several gulps before replacing it and setting about the work of bandaging Christine's ankle. For her part, Christine was preoccupied with watching the muscles bulge in his strong neck as he swallowed. It made her very thirsty indeed.

She pulled back when he reached for her left shoe, but at his reproachful stare, she quickly stretched out her leg again. He threw the boot to the side and inspected her foot, as if deciding whether or not to twist it himself for appearance's sake. She ground her teeth in anticipation, and tried to grab hold of the sides of the wagon to brace herself.

"Hey," Alaric shouted to the man to his right, "got any clean rags with you?"

"Right here," the man replied. Alaric took the bandages from him and wrapped Christine's ankle with as much care and tenderness as if she had broken it.

"I'm sorry," she whispered. He looked up at her. He wasn't smiling, but he wasn't scowling either. "I didn't mean—"

"Come on, let's get back," he shouted, before walking around to the front of the cart and taking the reins.

Christine had just tucked the last of the blades away on the undercarriage of the wagon as they pulled in front of the Council House. Darien came out to meet them.

"Everything alright?" he asked, seeing Christine laid up in the back of the wagon.

"Oh yeah," Alaric answered. "Christine, tell him what we found will ya? I'm starved."

He walked off in search of food without saying another word to anyone.

25

FROM THE TOWER LIBRARY TO THE ROOT CELLAR, DRACULA SURVEYED THE grounds of Castle Lowenherz with Luca close on his heels. He inspected every pathway, every major artery from one end of the castle complex to the other. Twilight approached as they traversed the outer environs, starting at the jagged cliff on which the castle was perched, down to the westward-facing corner that led out into the forest. The lush grasses underfoot were kept wild.

Luca adjusted his steps to avoid the path of a rather large snail, its iridescent shell turning luminous in the moonlight. Though it no longer heralded the end of a day full of torture under the sun's searing gaze, the coming of night still had a soothing effect. Luca and Dracula both felt it; the long silence between them, at first taut as a razor's edge, had taken on the patina of comfortable content as they descended the gentle slope. Crickets and nightbirds filled the quiet with their song, and when his father posed a question, Luca wasn't immediately overcome with the urge to rip his head off.

"Are there any private entrances or exits?" Dracula asked.

"Not that I know of," Luca picked his way through the meadow on the side of the castle that led away from Castelmor. "We don't stay here that often."

Dracula's eyes drank in the light; his lips curled into a curious smile. "It's your castle, and you say you don't stay here that often?"

"The demands of my wife's crown are many."

Dracula didn't respond, for his attention had been captured by the thickening of vines crawling along the castle's foundations. Luca came closer to him as his father felt along the foliage, then caught a glimpse of bright red leaves beneath with sharpened tendrils. Without concern for the poisonous barbs, Dracula felt underneath, closing his eyes to better discern the material to which the vines clung and grew.

"Let's see," he murmured, turning to face his son and brace his back against the vines. He rammed against it with his back, and heard the cracking of wood. He gave it another quick hard shove, and it gave way with a snap. "Yeah."

Luca couldn't help but be impressed. But he masked his surprise as they crossed the threshold, sweeping overgrowth and cobwebs out of their faces. Both men coughed from the must in the air. The dust settled to reveal a tight, dark space, with a bed tucked into the corner. The sheets were rumpled.

"I'll take it you and your wife have not explored this room," Dracula observed, his grin wry.

Luca shot him a look of pure venom.

"Never mind. Someone did though. Someone who wouldn't let the sheets grow mold." He pulled a deep red blanket off the foot of the bed. Rubbing the worn fibers between his fingers, he guessed its age to far surpass that of his son's presence in Icarya, or even his wife's reign for that matter. He tossed it back on the bed without care. It was curious, but ultimately unimportant.

"How did they get in?" he asked.

Luca didn't understand the question. "Through the door…" He jerked his thumb back to the way they had just come.

"No. That door was meant to be hidden, always," Dracula said. He looked down and scanned the floor quickly. "There." He crouched down and lifted a loosened floor tile, then another with ease. The earthen tunnel hidden in the floor led them back to the barracks where the few soldiers there were in the standing army slept beside families that had been moved from the outskirts of Castelmor to the lower levels for safety. They lifted themselves up out of the passageway and exited to the nearest hallway.

"There are more like that, I imagine," Dracula said. "But such paths are not made to move many people quickly. They will be of no use to us."

"I was never planning on moving people," Luca replied. "They were only just moved here."

"That was a mistake."

Luca shot him a warning look. Their conversation had been civil, tolerable even, but there were limits. "We possess a fortified position. I'm not—"

"Fortified positions fall," Dracula interrupted. "With surprising frequency. You must secure a means of escape."

Luca scoffed.

"So that if the castle falls," Dracula persisted, growing irritated, "*you* and *your people* survive."

Luca crossed his arms over his chest, without meaning to do it. "I won't let her get that far."

"Is there *anywhere* that shadow does not touch?" Dracula replied.

Luca's grip on himself tightened.

"How many times have you withstood a siege?" the vampire asked.

Luca gave no answer.

"*How* many?" his father pushed. "Do you mean, never have you *ever…*"

"All right," Luca growled. He conceded the point. But he could not bring himself to say it.

"By all means," Dracula said, "defend the castle. As long as you can. The wards I've provided to your archers and artillery men should help. But be prepared to fail."

Luca shifted on his feet, uncomfortable with how easily the word rolled off his father's tongue. But the lord of shadows was insistent. "What you do in those crucial moments will make all the difference. Lives will hang in the balance."

The matter was settled—as well as it could be, for the time being.

There was nothing to be done that day but to rest, and see what dawn would bring. If it would dawn at all. Luca led Dracula down a tight winding corridor to the stone dungeon built into the very bowels of the castle's center and gestured to the straw-laden bed in the cell at the end of the hall.

"Am I a prisoner?" Dracula asked.

"You're not a free man."

"What are you doing?" Dracula grew suddenly alarmed as Luca locked him in a cell then pulled a bench out of the cell next door and laid it parallel to the doorway.

Luca lay flat on his back and said nothing.

Dracula gripped the bars of his cage in protest. "You're no prisoner."

"Aren't I?" Luca's voice was heavy as he settled in to the grime-ridden bench and faced the ceiling.

Dracula began to pace. "You can't stay here. It isn't right. You're their king."

Luca remained silent, shifting to make himself as comfortable as possible on the hard, unforgiving surface.

"You murdered two Icaryans," he said. "You're not here as a guest, and I will *not* harbor you in the rooms I share with my wife."

"That's not why you hate me, for murdering two Icaryans. It's because of your mother. Because I murdered *her*."

Luca didn't actually know how he felt about that. He was not entirely sure what he was supposed to feel. But he kept his uncertainty locked up tight as Dracula stepped back from the edge of his cage and took a seat on the bench meant to be his bed.

"Many, many moons ago, I had a daughter. Ophelia. I loved her dearly, and kept her near me always. She grew to do everything I could, and more. She was terrifyingly beautiful, and always challenging me, challenging the boundaries of her own power."

Dracula licked his lips. His breath came long and deep as he fell into his reverie. "Think what you will of me, but that creature…she did things that made *my* stomach turn. And for sport. Her cruelty refused to be restrained, and I was forced…I had to put her down."

Saved me the trouble.

Luca's remark, made thoughtlessly but in earnest, sliced into the heart of the vampire.

"There's never been a day that I haven't thought about her. That I haven't regretted what I've done, though I was right to do it. I regret *having* to do it," he clarified after a moment's pause. "Having fashioned her in my image. I didn't want to put *you* down, too. What I didn't count on was your mother. If I had known what she would do, what she would become..."

Dracula's voice trailed off.

Luca closed his eyes. He remembered the day his mother threw him in the river, the day a dark shadow possessed of a deep voice shouted to him from the depths and dragged him ashore, giving him life again. That same voice spoke now.

"I believed she would care for you the way I could not. I chose poorly, and I accept my fault. I did what I had to, Mircea. For you."

That his son had not corrected him with some cutting remark was encouraging. "Mircea?"

Dracula stood up and peered through the bars. His son's chest rose and fell in a steady rhythm.

Luca was fast asleep.

THEY RESTED THROUGH WHAT LITTLE REMAINED OF THE NIGHT AND INTO the morning, until Luca was shocked awake. He shot up, his back rigid and eyes wide in fear.

"Kate!"

26

Kate's father rushed to her. Drigory and Meryn stood in the doorway. Kate hunched, hugging her knees, shaking away an uncertain feeling.

"I thought…for a moment I thought you'd left without telling us," William said, breathless.

Kate hugged her knees tighter. Her voice was muted. "No."

William's eyes narrowed. "Are ye all right?"

Kate blinked, unsure how to answer. When she remained silent, William extended his hands to help her to her feet.

"Come and have some breakfast with us," he offered.

She nodded. Her father reached out to touch the hair falling from her temple. "Was this there, before? I didn't notice it." The braid he held in his hand was a pure, gleaming white, but when the sun shone upon it, it reflected a pale gold. Kate tucked the hair behind her ear.

Meryn interceded. "Pregnancy will do that, William. Come." Sensing Kate's unease, she pulled her son back and led the way back down into the wood-hewn complex. The great room, spacious and with all four walls made of glass, gave the illusion of being outside when in fact you were not.

"Why bother with the glass?" Kate wondered aloud.

"To protect from the elements, of course," Drigory grumbled.

William whispered in her ear. "Wide open spaces make him a wee nervous."

"Good to know."

A long teak table was already set. Meryn promptly poured Kate tea as she took her seat. The breakfast was not a humble one, with eggs cooked in their shells, warm bread, smooth buttery cheese, an abundance of fruits, cold chicken, and a breakfast sausage.

"Venison?" William asked. "Or pheasant?"

Kate stared at the cooked meats on the table, and her stomach churned.

"Just bread, please, and maybe an egg." She speared the egg with the crusted edge of her bread, soaking up the golden energy as it spread on her plate. As Kate ate, sopping up the yolk with a second slice of bread and picking at the elderberries atop a breakfast pudding, she caught increasing glances from the company that stared at her but never dared catch her eye, and furtive glances exchanged quickly between the trio. As her appetite subsided she leaned against the back of her chair and folded her hands calmly in her lap. She suppressed a smirk as the tension in the room swelled to a fever pitch. The glances grew more frantic until Kate finally spoke.

"What is it you want me to do?"

The room breathed a sigh of relief.

"You'll stay?" Meryn asked.

Kate nodded.

Drigory snorted.

She turned to him. "*You're* free to leave."

Drigory's eyes flashed with indignance. He opened his mouth to say something, but Kate spoke over him.

"You had all the time in the world to help me. I sought *you* out, and still, you did nothing. Your pig-headedness could cost the lives of countless Icaryans, and I'm not even thinking of those lost in Likhan. I have no use for you."

Drigory's face turned a fiery red, and eyes gleamed with tears of fury. He pressed his hat down on his head and stormed out of the room without another word.

Meryn shifted in her seat, considering whether to get up and follow Drigory out. Her eyes shifted to Kate's. Kate held her look. Her lips were pursed, but Kate's eyes did not betray any hint of annoyance or expectation. She simply waited for Meryn to decide.

Meryn weighed her options, and, with a heavy sigh, settled again into her seat. Her son cast a sympathetic glance in her direction. Meryn pressed her lips together into a thin line. She gestured for William to finally answer Kate's query. William cleared his throat.

"Augur believed that, if done properly, he could conjure all the elements in their successive order, and that *that* would allow him to summon the goddess. We're hoping that—"

"Back up," Kate said, "and start at the beginning. Who is this Augur?"

"An Icaryan king many generations past," Meryn said.

"And you're related to him—*I'm* related to him?"

"Yes, the royal bloodline is a continuation of the Goddess who fell in love with a man. Just like the play."

"I *am* aware of the legend," Kate said, letting condescension seep into her voice.

In reply, Meryn grew doubly serious. "And you're aware most Icaryans hold that as sacred truth."

Kate nodded, her face earnest.

Meryn tried to summarize their ancestor's life, the circumstances of dangers, of his needing to summon the goddess.

"Why did he think that would work?" Kate asked.

"What do you mean?" William asked.

"Did he read about it somewhere, or hear it in a story…?"

"We don't really know. He was a student of the goddess, and he kept a journal during his experiments. In it, he makes references to things—books and such, that are lost to us."

Kate contemplated. "Are you sure?"

Their eyes furrowed, confused.

"Are you sure they're lost, and not holed up somewhere in a certain troll's secret stash?"

"He wouldn't deliberately hide vital information," Meryn said. "Not at a time like this."

"If you believed that, you wouldn't be sitting here," Kate replied.

Meryn shifted again, and bit her tongue. Kate didn't so much as twitch. Her ability to stay aloof, to use her intuition and mental acumen to give her an advantage in this situation, was an impenetrable shield.

William, ever eager to heal the rift that Kate's standoffishness threatened, continued.

"There was a fire in the old library in the Eastern Tower, where such things were kept. We believe they were lost at that time, along with other things."

Kate pulled the library to the forefront of her memory. Her mind's eye passed over the scorched corners of dark cobblestones, refitted now into a public repository for books gathered from across the universe. Signs of fire were indeed there.

"Do you have the journal?"

"It's on the shelf back there," William said, pointing to the far wall. "You don't need to worry yourself with that now."

"I've read it cover to cover many times. I can tell you what's important," Meryn said.

"How would you know?"

That ruffled her feathers.

Kate softened her tone, but persisted. "You may have missed something, not realizing its importance. If you want my help, I need to know what you know."

Meryn clearly disliked being told, albeit more politely, that she was also quickly becoming useless. But she conceded the point, and William rose from his chair to retrieve the journal from the floor-to-ceiling stacks on the far wall, and left the women temporarily alone.

Meryn tried to resist looking directly at Kate, but her blank stare, half-expecting something, half-not, was relentless.

"It's a lot, I know. You seem to be taking it well," she said.

"Do I have a choice?"

"No," Meryn sighed. "William was right to approach you. Before, and now."

"Did you know—" Kate paused, unsure of herself. "Did you know who I was, when you first met me? Who I was to you?"

Meryn answered with reluctance. "Yes."

"Why didn't you—"

She closed her mouth as her father resumed his seat. She tongued the inside of her cheek, but no more.

Meryn's fingers curled up again on the armrests of her chair.

William saw he had interrupted, and folded his hands and the book on his lap quietly as he said down. Something inside Meryn nudged her to answer the question Kate never voiced.

"I didn't want to interfere. To cast a shadow over you. I thought it was for the best. And," she finished, looking at her son, "I had other concerns as well."

"You were pregnant."

Even now, the admission of it seemed to embarrass Meryn, as her cheeks grew rosy. "I needed to protect myself. And when I saw you—" Her eyes took on a faraway glint. "I knew you were meant to be the queen. I could *feel* it flowing through you like sunshine. I felt I had no choice then, but to leave you to it. So I left, and lived a mostly quiet, happy life."

Kate's eyes shifted to her father. "In Scotland."

Meryn nodded. "Meeting your granddaughter before you've even had a child is a strange experience. On top of everything else…" She sighed again. "Despite what you may think of me, I don't have all the answers."

But Katelyn did think that. She had thought that for so long, that all the answers she sought herself—who she was, who she was meant to be—were just out of reach. Seeing the looming specter of Meryn as the great arbiter of the world's secrets crumbled before her, and left her with a sinking, empty feeling in her stomach.

When neither his mother nor his daughter had anything more to say, William lifted the book he had retrieved from his lap to the table. It was bound in leather dyed an indigo blue, with a hand-sewn spine.

Kate turned it over in her hands. "It's a bit thin. What was his first element, did you say?"

"Water," Meryn answered.

"And he succeeded in shifting his center?"

An uncomfortable silence fell over the trio.

"What happened?" Kate prompted.

"He..." William stammered. "He...caught on fire."

Kate blinked. "He immolated himself. That's not very helpful." She moved to a new line of inquiry. "What was *your* first element?"

"Air, but...Katelyn, I am *only* able to conjure air, and my mother—"

"Foresight is all I have. I'm not able to commune with the elements."

Kate rubbed her eyebrow. The sinking feeling in her gut deepened. Now that she was here, she'd never felt further away from her own truth. The prospect of leaving reared its head.

William's shoulders shot up to his ears. "Are you doing that?"

"Doing what?" Kate asked.

"It just got ten degrees colder in here."

"Probably," she answered nonchalantly, the swirling worry of her thoughts uninterrupted.

"Can you stop it?" he asked after a pause. Kate couldn't tell if his halting tone was from concern, annoyance, or something else.

The air swung to sweltering.

"I thought that's what I came here to learn. And now you're telling me you don't know the first thing about how to help me."

"We do..."

"How?! How can you teach me to juggle when you've only got *one* ball?"

William's face grew long and determined. "*I* control the wind. It does not control me. It comes when I call, and *only* then. Can you say the same?"

Kate tapped her fingers forcefully down on the table, trying to stamp out the fury radiating off her skin.

"Take a deep breath."

She refused, but her father persisted.

"Breathe."

When her lungs stayed stubbornly empty, his eyes and his tone softened.

"Come lass, what harm can it do? Breathe."

Kate complied.

"Clear your head."

Kate snorted.

"Try," William urged. "Clear your mind." A million things raced, until she settled on one thing she could hold on to. A pair of eyes as clear blue as crystal, flaring to red.

"Good," William said. "Now let your breath go. All of it."

Air shuddered out of her, and she felt the absence of air as powerful in her lungs as she felt the absence of Luca in her arms. Her lips twitched, and fire burned at the rims of her eyes.

"Hold it," William warned.

Kate stopped her breath until the image of her mind turned fuzzy, and the child shifted inside her womb.

"Deep breath."

Kate complied, and felt relief, and a burst of clarity as oxygen washed over her brain. His eyes beckoned her to hold his gaze.

For a moment, Katelyn was still. She looked at her father, who remained silent. He challenged her to remain in that moment, without anger, or hope, fear, guilt, regret, longing—only waiting. She sat entirely focused on his face, awaiting the sound of his voice, the next instruction. Nothing came. Kate waited, alert, but at ease. The humidity of the room had long since dissipated, but now the air took on a thin clearness. Her awareness climbed, full of potential not yet realized. She felt the power building in the air, but it had not yet taken shape. Waiting to be given a form. A command.

The call came. "Heat up your right hand."

The palm of Kate's right hand did not visibly redden or flare with heat, but when William inched slowly nearer to her, reaching out his hand for his daughter's palm and placing it face up on the table, her skin burned like a child's virulent fever. He tested the other hand. He was surprised to find it also burning. He tried not to let his disconcertion show. He tapped the pads of his fingertips on her left palm, took a deep breath, and offered the challenge, not knowing what to expect.

"Freeze."

Kate twitched in concentration. "Not possible."

"Freeze," he repeated.

Both of her hands got progressively hotter as she concentrated. He sensed it was becoming a strain for her and pulled his hands away. The harder she tried, the hotter her hands became.

Katelyn's temperature returned to normal, then her hands retreated into her lap. Then, from somewhere inside her brain, something shifted.

"Here it comes."

He reached out to feel her hands, but she pulled back sharply. "It isn't safe."

"I was safe from the fire. Why would this be different?"

"I have no control over it. It just comes."

He watched her hands as traces of blue veins crawled along her fingers and a freezing mist gathered around her hands.

"Always after fire?" he asked.

She nodded, hanging her head.

"It's okay," he reassured her. "It takes time."

"I don't *have* time."

William offered her a sad smile. "Why don't we take a break? Just a short one. I need to think a bit about what do to next, what might help."

Kate reached for the book Meryn had left on the table as the others departed.

MERYN FOUND DRIGORY STOMPING ABOUT HIS ROOM, PREPARING TO leave. The slamming of his personal artifacts was punctuated by grumbles of indignation.

Meryn sat on the bed as he rushed back and forth across the whole room, grabbing things and smashing them into his pack.

"She's right," Meryn said.

He stopped and pivoted to stare at her, his eyes bulging out of his head. She continued calmly.

"You were not a very helpful teacher. No one asked you to keep secrets from her. Yet you did. She couldn't have learned what she was meant to know."

"She *wasn't* meant to know. She was a child, a stranger, given a crown she couldn't have possibly understood, set to rule a people she knew *nothing* about."

"You made that harder than it had to be. She wanted to know, tried to know. You stopped her."

"You're the one who didn't want to get involved."

Meryn shook her head. "I didn't want to be an influence. *You* kept her in the dark. Those are two different things."

"Why should I have divulged the secrets of the royal family? She is *not* my queen!"

"*Yes*, Drigory, she is!"

He slammed his pack shut.

"Why didn't you fight? You were so willing to abdicate, to flee. People looked up to her, saw hope for Icarya. "The whole *world* would have followed you. They were armed and ready. You were Icarya's great hope. What could have been more important than that?!"

"I fell in love!"

Tears came to Meryn's eyes. "He and William were what mattered. Nothing else. And I'd do it all again, just the same, just to have one more minute." The words nearly choked her. She clutched at the large dark pearl hanging around her neck, trying hard to tamp down her emotions.

Drigory wouldn't give up.

"It should have been you!"

"But it isn't." Meryn dragged a reluctant breath into her lungs. "I was never meant to be queen. Your personal loyalty to me clouded your duties to her."

He grumbled in reply. He wasn't ready to accept his guilt. His responsibility.

"I couldn't have done what she has done, protected Icarya the way she has. Icarya is flourishing. Because of her."

"So you're willing to forget all that she has done *wrong*? The destruction of other worlds?"

"It's not for me to forgive her. I'm not her judge. Her arrival was my salvation. With her on the throne, I knew I could leave. That Icarya would be in good hands. The *right* hands."

Meryn left the room, and the conversation, without a resolution.

KATE RECLINED AGAINST THE HEADBOARD IN HER ROOM, LISTENING TO their conversation. It wasn't that loud, but now she heard everything people said, even if they were whispering. She even heard critters and mice and birds nesting inside the walls. She didn't know how Luca tuned it all out, how he ever got a moment's peace.

Though she had just eaten, she was hungry again. This time for something salty. She settled for a full glass of water from the stone jug in her room, and a bowl of pumpkin seeds. She moved to an oversized wicker chair to read King Augur's notes.

THERE WAS A KNOCK AT THE OPEN DOORFRAME BEFORE SHE'D GOTTEN very far.

"Are you ready to try again?" William asked

She put the book down and followed him out beyond the glass to a seating area carved in stone. The bench and table were nearly overtaken by the verdant foliage that was allowed to run wild. From some hidden source came the sound of gently rolling water. Kate felt the pressure it produced on her bladder, but subdued it.

Her father set two small bowls of tepid water in front of her.

"You said that water neutralized you in Likhan, after a night's worth of fire?" he asked.

"Yes." She hesitated, but then decided that withholding anything did neither of them any good. "It came without my calling, but then I was able to fall into it. I don't know what else I could have done with it. I didn't try to shape it, or..."

She saw William furrow his brow in confusion.

"With fire," she explained, "it's flexible. I can make it do different things, and I can be creative in a fight to suit my needs. Just touching the shadow creatures with ice gave them the edge I needed to subdue it. It hardened their edges, giving me something I could thrash. I didn't *need* to adapt my strategy, so I didn't attempt to see what more I could do."

"And when it was defeated?"

Kate shrugged, not really recalling how or when it had faded. It just…powered down. "Darien was holding the flame."

William's eyebrows shot up at that.

"I had projected it onto him, so I felt…clear."

"Ye didna feel the presence of the fire?"

"Only at the very smallest corners of my mind. The parts that wouldn't remember unless you mentioned it."

"So, it's worth another try then, to see if you're capable of both in the same moment."

"We can try, but I'm not optimistic. Even if I can conjure ice, to do both feels like a physical impossibility. Like I'm thinking of an apple at the exact same time that I'm *not* thinking of an apple. I'm not quite sure I have the capability to pull my thoughts that far apart."

What Kate didn't say was that it reminded her of the shadow of herself, the thing with the face like hers and the empty eyes, that she'd killed by putting a knife through her own chest. The thing both familiar and foreign, that frightened her still, if she dared to think about it. The things she had done with flames still gave her nightmares, but at least it was the devil she knew, and it was of her own making.

Kate's ears were again filled with the sound of running water. She rubbed her thighs.

"Are ye all right?" William asked.

"Fine. I can control myself."

William nodded. "How are you feeling, then?"

"Sore. Tired." She quirked her mouth in up a smile. "Absolutely perfect."

"I never did say…congratulations."

"Thank you."

"Luca seems a good man." It came out with a sigh. There was nothing else to say.

"The best I know."

"I'm sorry, Katelyn. Sorry I wasna a bigger part o' yer life. I wanted to be."

Kate said nothing. She was willing to listen but unsure of how to respond. She let her mind wander to what Luca might be facing at this moment, about Dracula's reasons for staying away. If they were noble.

"I dinna want to cause trouble wi' yer mother. She—" He struggled for words, not sure what he should say. "Well. I suppose ye ken how she could be."

Kate's response was flat and cold.

"I don't want to talk about her."

"Aye, she said ye dinna get along. That's my fault too, perhaps. She saw too much of me there, I think."

"I did love her Katelyn," he said after a pause. "And you. I stayed away because she asked, and then, when my mother asked…"

You didn't ask what I *thought. What* I *wanted.*

Kate didn't say it aloud, didn't let it show on her face.

"I truly am sorry."

Kate thought about the one memory she had of him, on that day stranded out in the rain. Nothing could have made her happier in that moment.

"You gave me what I needed."

William lifted his eyes to her in a question.

"Hope," she said.

His cheeks flushed. "Let's hope this works then, eh?"

He gestured for her to put one hand in each bowl. She became instantly aware of the surface of the water rippling against her wrists, lapping softly against her skin as the water settled into place around them.

Without being told Kate closed her eyes, filling her lungs with deep breaths, emptying out again to the point of deprivation, then letting oxygen flood her brain for a sharpened clarity.

"Eventually, you should be able to achieve this focus without thinking about it. A second nature."

Kate nodded.

"Boil the water in the left bowl. Only the left."

Kate took her time. Small bubbles formed slowly at the bottom of the bowl. They rose and popped at the surface, brought to a rolling boil. William dipped his finger tentatively in the right bowl. The temperature remained as tepid as when he had poured it.

"Keep it going, but stop thinkin' about it."

William left his instructions hanging in the air long enough for the lines in Kate's face to ease.

"When you're ready, freeze the water in the right bowl."

Kate took a shuddering deep breath, but didn't voice an objection.

For a long time, William waited. Nothing appeared to be happening, and he couldn't tell if she hadn't yet tried, or if she was failing. He dared not ask. He dipped half his index finger in to test the water without her noticing. It was flashing shoots of warm water like a current.

He looked at Kate and saw her lips set in a hard line. She was trying to hold it back, but when she attempted to exert power, it was only coming out as heat.

"Stay calm," William suggested. "Focus on the water." The warm bursts petered out. Then without warning it flashed explosively hot. He yanked his hand back, blowing on it, sitting on it, tucking it under his armpit—anything to relieve the incredible pain. He cursed silently.

He saw how much she was straining, saw the creases on her face deepen with fatigue.

"All right, stop."

Kate brought her hands out of the water as she opened her eyes. Her frustration was obvious. "I told you I couldn't—"

She took in a deep breath and quickly pushed her fingers back onto the surface of the water, just long enough to make contact. The water froze instantly.

He looked from the bowls to her in a bit of shock.

"It's like a…a surge. A sort of tension builds and…and I have to release it."

"It's done now, then?"

Kate nodded. "It's usually quick and violent. It's always been that way. Only recently have I been able to sense its coming."

"That's something then, I guess."

"I guess."

"It takes time, Katelyn."

"You keep saying that."

He rubbed his fingers, trying to ignore the throbbing pain and think on what to try next. Even if he accepted that ice and fire would not neutralize each other the way he thought they might, the more pressing matter was to see if she could control earth, water, sky…*anything* as well as she did fire.

"Did I do that?"

Kate interrupted his thoughts. He caught her staring at his fingers.

"No. Well, not on purpose, you didn't."

Kate reached out her hand and closed her fingers over the offended digit.

"I'll be fine, I—" He stopped talking, and felt his finger cool. The agitated swelling shrunk away.

When she released his hand, his eyes went wide.

"You did it! You cooled my hand!"

"No," Kate said sadly. "I just quickened your own healing. Not with fire *or* ice."

"If not ice, what then?"

Kate smiled, feeling her eyes glow red with longing. And hunger. "Something different."

Meryn poked her head outside. "William?"

"Yes?" he asked.

"I'm sorry to disturb you. Lunch is ready."

"I'm not saying I'm not hungry, but we've only just had breakfast," Kate said.

William looked back at her, a curious smile on his lips. "You're really not used to meditation, are you?"

Kate raised an eyebrow, impatient but not understanding.

"We've been sitting here for hours. Look." He pointed to the sun, already past its zenith in a sloping position that suggested it was quite late into the afternoon.

"Oh. If you insist then." Kate pushed the thoughts of Luca creeping up her skin to the back of her mind. Thinking about something she craved but absolutely could not have in this moment was no way to stay calm. She felt the blood light circling her irises recede as she focused on the prospect of an appetite she could sate.

When he didn't leave, Kate turned back to her father. She saw him staring at her with a sad look in his eyes.

"So…you're like him now, then?"

"Yes."

"I saw, that day, what he—" William bowed his head, closing out the image of his daughter's life being drained. He told himself over and over that Luca had *saved* her that day, not killed her, but he could not sponge out from his mind what no father should see.

"Did he…did it hurt?

"Not half as much as it hurt being dead."

"Right. Of course. I'm…sorry."

Meryn grimaced and tried to extract her son from his daughter's awkward stare. "Come on, William," she said, taking him by the arm. "Let the girl eat."

When they sat down, Kate noticed that only three places were set. William shot Meryn and inquisitive glance, but Meryn dismissed it, and began serving a warm stew of wild mushrooms, beans, and cabbage with a hearty sour bread.

"Thank you," Kate said as her bowl was filled. She chose to say nothing about Drigory's absence. Meryn wasn't offering any excuses. Rather than eat in silence, she could contain her curiosity no longer.

"I'm not quite sure I understand. You're my grandmother."

"Yes," Meryn answered.

"My father's mother."

"Yes."

"But I met you before…I was born? Before *he* was born?" she asked, nodding her head toward William.

"Yes." Meryn smiled.

"And, you say you knew that at the time."

Meryn opened her mouth, but Kate continued. "At least, you had a sense that I was."

"A very *strong* sense."

"Right." She swirled her bread around her bowl, allowing its tender flesh to soak up the heady broth. "Sorry, how does that make any sense?"

"You've traveled between Earth and Icarya more times than I have. Did it ever make any sense to you, how time passed?"

"No..."

"You were locked in the dungeon for trespassing. I released you."

"Yes."

"Before parting, I gave you an amulet, one containing the greatest Icaryan treasure. The bloodstone."

"Yes."

Meryn nodded. "After leaving you, I left Icarya through a gate that led to your world. To Earth. In the year 1859. Later that year, William was born. Much later, in 1882, your brother was born, and you followed shortly after."

"'84," Kate added.

"You were nineteen when your stepfather died, and you left London for Edinburgh. When you took your first step in Icarya, you experienced the day that I had lived through many years before."

Kate scratched her head. "Time went backwards..."

"You arrived in what I would call the 'proper' time. It's happened to you before, hasn't it? First to cross paths with Hercules, and then—"

"Luca."

Meryn bowed her head in acknowledgement. "Things always find their proper place. And their proper time."

Kate accepted that, knowing there was not much more than Meryn could tell, and dug into her soup. She hadn't noticed how hungry she was until she began to swallow. The baby moved the same way it did every time Kate fed her mushrooms. Thinking about the growing baby made her happy, but those thoughts were quickly stifled by worry about what kind of world her daughter would be born into, and whether or not she'd have any time to enjoy her pregnancy before the baby rushed its way into the world.

"When did you come back? To Icarya, I mean," Kate asked.

"Not for many years," Meryn answered. "It took a long time for me to feel…safe…again, coming here." She shrugged. "Many I had known before were gone, so…" she breathed heavily, and Kate could see she was biting back tears.

"I came to be with my son. He's my only child, and…"

She swallowed hard and reached for her son's outstretched hand. "He grew up on stories of this place. When you came, he followed. After that, it became hard for me to stay away."

Kate was able to hear what she wasn't saying, what the pain in her voice expressed without words. She'd returned after William's father had died. Meryn seemed to sense that Kate's sympathetic smile was a knowing one. They stared at each other and, for a fleeting moment, they could read each other perfectly.

"I'm sorry," Kate whispered.

Meryn's head lilted to the side. "It happens to all of us."

Kate's gaze broke from Meryn's. Meryn bit her lip as she realized—death's maxim did not hold true for Luca, or for Kate. Meryn and her son had struggled to understand why Katelyn had allowed herself to be changed, to have her very existence altered. Now, with her husband in mind, it was perfectly plain.

Ever tactful, Meryn swallowed her grief and changed the subject.

"Have you made any progress?"

"No," Kate said.

"Yes, we have," William insisted. "We *have* Katelyn. It may not feel like it, but—"

"It doesn't. I'm sorry. I'm not trying to insult you, but none of this is going to help me fight Haydee. I did pretty well with blood magic, I just didn't finish the job. I was distracted."

"By what?" he asked, his tone one of feigned innocence.

Kate pushed her lips together.

William answered for her. "By yer own magic, ye say? Aye, well, if only there were a way of being able to *control* those impulses, then perhaps they wouldn't rule yer life."

Kate tongued the inside of her cheek and shot her dad a snide glare.

"I understand your point, and I'm not saying that I shouldn't learn, but—"

"But?"

"I don't have the time. Every minute I spend here is another minute *she* gets stronger."

"And what about you? Do ye feel more or less in control these days?"

"I've been dealing with this for a long time."

"You're lucky it hasn't caught up with you."

"Oh, it caught up with me alright. But I handled it then, and I can handle it now."

"But the baby," Meryn interjected.

"The baby's fine. I'm fine."

"How can you be sure?"

"I've got one more fight in me," Kate ground out.

"Don't push yourself," William warned.

"Don't *push* myself? That's all I've ever done! Lives depend on it. I didn't get to be the most powerful creature in the whole goddamned world by not *pushing* myself."

"Katelyn," William said in a low voice. "Calm. Down."

Katelyn inhaled, deep and quick. "I can do this *my* way."

"You know what your problem is?" Meryn said. "You're still thinking like a warrior."

"I *am* a warrior."

Meryn upturned her nose at her. "You're something much more, now. You're a mother."

Kate pressed her lips firmly together.

"You may be right. You may fight Haydee and you may win. But at what cost?"

Meryn sensed Kate's growing unease. She latched onto that thought and dug deep, dredging up the fears that Kate herself would never voice.

"What did your own husband tell you? That if you stay too long under the shadow, the *child will die*."

Kate shifted at the words. Meryn pushed harder, echoing the doubt racing across Kate's mind.

"How will you know? How long is too long? What will you do if you can't get out in time? And then what? An hour goes by, and she doesn't jab you in the ribs. Then a day, then a week? How long will it take for you to know? To realize what can't be undone—what can never be undone—"

"Stop!"

Kate's chest heaved, her eyes burned with anguish. "Stop."

Meryn had hit her mark. "You've risked *your* life before. Are you willing to risk hers?"

Kate turned her head to the side as tears fell down her cheeks.

William started up out of his chair as Kate's skin began to emit a pale vapor that circled tightly around her like a winter wind.

"Kate—you're!"

"I know."

William stretched out his fingers toward her, but she stopped him.

"Please don't. I don't want to hurt you."

"How is this any more dangerous than fire?"

"That's what it does. It's what it always does." Kate closed her eyes again, and her eyelids were flooded with the sight of Vehlen, of the boy in pieces on the ground. The soup turned sour in her stomach, and she turned a sickly green.

Meryn felt awful. She'd pushed too far. She knew it was a terrible thing for any mother to hear. Especially for someone who was still so vulnerable to the pull of her emotions.

"I said too much, Katelyn. I didn't mean—"

"Yes you did."

Meryn grimaced. It would be hard convincing her of the untruth of things born from within in her own mind. It's what made Meryn's extra sight such a useful tool, but even the best practitioners were guilty of misusing their gifts from time to time. This moved them further away from their goal, and Meryn cursed herself for it.

"It's going to be alright, Katelyn," William said. "Really, it will. You don't have to do this anymore, without wanting to. I promise. Let's relax now, Katelyn. Just relax..."

Katelyn understood what he was saying without saying it. He wanted her to clear her mind so she could stop emitting the freezing mist that shrouded her. She closed her eyes and stretched her mind out.

Luca...

He responded in less than a heartbeat.

What's wrong?

The baby...I don't want to hurt the baby.

I can sense her as I sense you. She's fine, Kate. Why wouldn't she be?

She breathed deeply, savoring Luca's velvet voice soaking into her head. It was a salve on her overwrought nerves.

Whatever you need, love. I'm here.

I know. That alone was enough.

Kate opened her eyes, feeling as calm as she could be under the circumstances. Just as she expected, the billowing clouds of frost no longer surround her.

"I really am sorry, Kate, truly," Meryn said.

Kate shook her head. "You said what needed saying. Let's just get back to it, okay?"

William scrunched up his face. "You're feeling a bit raw, now, I gather. I think it'd be best if you rested for a while."

Kate took a deep breath, preparing to protest. She was still formulating a polite response when William spoke again.

"Part of this process is achieving a neutral state, one without distractions."

"You...know that's impossible for me, right?"

William smiled back. "Difficult, but not impossible. Go on. Catch forty winks. One way or another, you will need to find at least a small sense of peace."

~

KATE WAS TOO UNCOMFORTABLE TO SLEEP, SO INSTEAD SHE WENT OUT again to the garden, dressed only in a simple dress of flowing white silk she had found tucked into her wardrobe. She stepped past the stone courtyard where she'd unwittingly spent most of the day, and slid into the lake that lay further into the wilds of wherever they were. Surrounded on all sides by the forest, the surface was painted in springtime colors from the fresh blossoms that fell and floated down to the surface, drifting about and bathing in the stark sunlight as it poked through the canopy.

The water was cold as melted ice. Kate inhaled sharply as she submerged herself up to her neck and stretched her mind out again toward Luca.

How are you *doing?* she asked.

Oh I'm just having the best time, came the reply.

Kate laughed out loud. *It's really that bad, huh?*

Luca's mood shifted. She felt his growing confusion.

He's cooperating, but...I don't know. He...keeps trying to talk to me. To tell me things. It's weird. Like he doesn't remember killing Rene, or Carla, or you. *He's not what I expected.*

What did you expect?

I don't know. An enemy, I guess.

Are you saying he isn't? Kate asked.

Luca had no ready answer.

Will the two of you be alright? she pressed.

We can handle it. And I can handle him. The world is in safe hands, Luca replied.

Okay.

Even though those hands are not yours.

Okay, she answered. She tried her utmost to mean it.

All right. Go on, now. Get some sleep.

~

KATE LET HER CONNECTION TO LUCA FADE INTO THE BACKGROUND, AND focused her attention on the soft, furtive symphony of the forest. Most small creatures were still asleep, but she could hear them rustling to wakefulness. Something furry readjusted a bed of feathers. A bird replaced a fraying twig in its house with a stronger one. Another chirped greeting to its mate. She listened mostly to the whistling of the wind as it moved through the trees, the crackling and dancing of leaves, and the hum of the trunks as they swayed in their moorings. There was a stillness to all this noise, a contentment. Just a quiet, unassuming existence. A pureness of only living for the present, a slumbering life that needed only what the forest provided. Sun, air, water. Kate's limbs no longer prickled at the chill. Her dress floated out around her, soaking up the water to a thin paperiness, making it almost impossible to tell where Kate's dress ended and the water began. Thoughts and worries beckoned but weakly at her door. Luca's firm voice had been a great comfort, and allowed her to feel that she could take this time, and the world wouldn't be overturned as she slept.

She slipped further into the surface, first her ears, then to the line of her hair. She let herself drift further away from the edge and into deeper waters, keeping her eyes on the dazzling light of the sun as it bounced off dewy treetops. Her pupils dilated, drinking in the light. Her mind floated back to Likhan, now, laying as she had on the tree stump at the battle's end. The sky had seemed to swallow up the world, then. As it did now. It stretched before her, the sky and the lake became all she knew. Her breaths came long and freely, even after she allowed her body to sink lower, submerging her mouth, her nose and her eyes, and watching the sun glimmer and dance about the shifting surface of the water. The lake's surface softened the sun's harsh light, bending it and blending the warm oranges and pinks of the coming sunset together with the cooler whites and yellows of the water's surface. She lost track of time as she lay submerged, and even the sun seemed to have slowed in its descent. She fell deeper and deeper into the simple act of existing in that moment, until she felt something brush against her left ear. She felt the cuff that allowed her to breathe underwater fall away. She blinked, and slowly made to turn around to spy its whereabouts and retrieve it, but before she could, the pale child edged in gold filled her vision. She pressed her bare feet against Kate's thighs, pinning her down. She stood on top of her, a watery image wavering and flickering in the light of the lake's ever-changing surface. Her owlish expression turned mischievous as she held up her hand, turning the cuff she had pinched in her fingers.

Kate bucked her legs to oust the child from her stance, but the weight of her stare was as two stone pillars, refusing to let her rise. She thrashed her arms about, but there was nothing to lean on, no solid rock or handhold to push against. She could not sit up. Her belly had grown too large, and she could not straighten with her abdomen alone.

Kate's lungs burned. She conserved what little energy she had left, and stared up at the child, her eyes pleading for release.

She was immovable.

Kate was running out of air. Her head was spinning, and the sun, which had hung lazily in the sky, for hours on end, turned black as ash.

The imp bent down, submerging her face into the water and coming within a hairsbreadth of Kate's nose. Her round eyes captivated Kate's. She spoke into the water, her voice clear and crisp as a spring day.

"Breathe."

Kate trusted the golden irises that dominated her vision, and opened her mouth. Water rushed in, and with it a surge of relief. Of air. It was not like wearing the cuff, for that only allowed for breathing in water. This was more complete—the edges of her body felt blurred, less finite, allowing water to pass freely through her, now just another part of the lake.

The girl giggled, and Kate felt the weight on her thighs disappear. The child drifted downward, descending upright as she came face to face with Kate. The two stood suspended in the dead center of the lake.

The girl held the cuff out to Kate.

"Useless. But, beautiful."

Kate took it and returned it to its customary place on her ear.

They floated down together, the lake getting darker and colder, far deeper than Kate thought the lake could be. They moved in silence. Kate's body had become less tangible, inconstant as the cold current that passed through her as they floated down, down, down.

The darkness that surrounded them was complete, and yet Kate was not blinded. Luca had tried and failed to explain when she simply could not understand, that it was different from seeing in daylight. Her eyes did not conjure light were there was none. But she could still see through it. She could see the lines and features of the girl sinking beside her, despite the absence of light. The darkness undulated in waves of progressing night, but the lake was barren. There were no plants swaying in the frigid current, no fish or aquatic lizards skittered into view.

When they had traveled so far that Kate began to wonder if they had floated to the end of the world, she saw a soft yellow glow beneath her feet. The light grew as they descended toward it, and Kate became increasingly aware of the light's warmth, radiating upward.

As they approached the light, Kate and the girl surfaced in the new place head first. Kate stepped out of the lake and onto feathery grass. The new place was thickly forested, with wide open grassy spaces between ancient trees, that all seemed to twist and bow in their mooring as the golden girl surfaced.

Kate's robe was as dry as it had been when she'd first donned it. Not even a drop of water remained in her hair to trickle down and splash back into the pool at her feet as a silent farewell. She felt the full weight of her form again.

Plants of deep reds and violets and blues stretched up from the ground and clung to the trees, as did pale, translucent fungi that lit up as Kate touched them. The girl gave a warning as she saw Kate sniff, and nearly nibble.

"Careful. Not even I could save you then."

The forest was drenched as if by heavy rains and the ground at every few feet was spotted with unfathomable puddles, like the one from which they had emerged. Some were larger, some smaller, and as Kate walked gingerly around them, attempting to follow the sprite, who pranced with confidence through the glade, she saw that all were just as fathomless and inscrutable.

As Kate fought to catch glimpses of the girl's back and keep up without falling into an unfamiliar abyss, a distant part of her mind became aware of the nature of her company. She was mindful of what her purpose was to be in seeking this entity out, but here, in this place, it felt wrong to ask her to rid the world of shadows. Somehow, the end of the world here felt small, insignificant, and to speak of it felt like a rude incursion. And yet she felt the urge to speak, to converse with her.

"What is this place?"

"It is not a place. It is between places." The girl finally stopped in her sprint and knelt beside a very small spot, a deceptive little puddle barely big enough for the child to submerge her face in its surface. Rising again, she beckoned to Kate, who knelt beside her, and with some hesitation, did the same. She could see all the world, from one edge to the other. Her vision travelled much faster through the puddle, following the light to its edges, even seeing the whole thing, she could spy the quiet, everyday life of a small farm as its inhabitants rose before the violet dawn, walking to milk beasts that moved strangely and stood heavily on six legs.

"This one I like. And this. And this."

Kate was shown one world after another. Some she had become familiar with, having ridden the wind and flown through the stars astride Philip to distant worlds. Some she had never seen nor heard the like of before.

"They all see something different. A girl, a man, a fawn, or even a lion." This made the child laugh, as if it were a game.

Through all their traveling, and though each puddle looked much like the next except perhaps for its size, Kate's head turned instinctively back to where, beyond the trees that she could not see, lay the one that led to a lake somewhere in the hidden heart of a forest.

"Home," the child said. "Always home." Moving to the tree beside the pool leading to Icarya, the girl ran around to the other side, and Kate saw the intricate carvings there, ones she knew very well. She traced the curves and lines with her fingers, that had made the vines and roots of trees intertwining into a continuous braiding loop without end that had been part of her medallion. The one she had shattered on the Ancestor's Mound on the day she had died. Where the blood stone had been in the medallion, on the tree there was a darkened knot. Kate had the feeling that the shapes spelled Icarya. Not with letters or words, but the whole world, its nature and creatures, carved in magic.

The girl came to stand with her back to the tree with her palms pressed to the thick trunk. She smiled, and then was gone.

Kate started, and spun around, but the girl was nowhere. She turned again to the tree, but it gave no clues as to where the golden child had slipped away to.

She heard a low groan, and then turned back again to the tree. It shivered with mirth. The lines of the tree trembled and curled, protruding outward from the trunk until their color lightened, the bark softened, and the child stood before her once again.

Before Kate could blink, the child grabbed hold of her hand and pulled her through the tree. No—*into* the tree. Everything moved more slowly, and she felt stiff and strong, and of a clear purpose.

As they sank down into the roots of the tree, she heard the child's voice again.

"Do you remember?"

A question began to form in Kate's mind, but the effort felt gargantuan, and what felt like centuries had passed before the germ of the thought had been formed, then considered, then shaped into a well-wrought question.

Just as the question began to settle on the humanly recognizable sound of "Remember what?" the darkness paled, and Kate saw trees she recognized, standing in the path that led north to the river, and then on to the mountains. The midday sun shone brightly, glistening off the leaves and the supple grasses on the forest floor.

There was a fair-haired boy. He was beautiful, happy, graceful in the sunlight, with a smile like sunshine. A familiar pain throbbed in Kate's heart at the sight of him, but she remained still as the boy was oblivious, dancing in the wind. A golden faun approached slowly. She observed his mirth. It was contagious. The faun inched closer and closer, drawn in by the beautiful face and his boyish happiness. Spinning around, he spotted the faun, and they stared at each other for a long time. The faun was curious, and could not turn herself away from the face of the innocent. He spoke to it.

"I have heard of creatures who could speak. Surely you must be one of those."

The faun laughed, but said nothing. He picked up a lute, and played a beautiful, happy song on the strings. "Will you sing for me?" The song drew her inexplicably in.

He began to play and sing a song, a song Kate knew very well. It was played every year at the harvest festival, to commemorate the love that blossomed between the boy and the golden faun.

And indeed, it blossomed. Kate watched as the faun returned to the river every day, where the boy would meet it, play his lute, and sing of love of the forest and the joys of summer, always with hope in his heart that the beast would join him in his song. After many days, the faun began to notice a change in the boy. He no longer smiled. His face was darkened by shadows, and when he played, his strings sang of a broken heart.

The faun's heart was breaking too, for the beautiful, happy boy who drew her to him every day was fading from the world. But she could not sing for him, could not love him the way he wished. Not as she was. For her heart was full of the world, and all the other worlds, and she could not empty it to love only the boy as he deserved.

On the last day, she came to see him, not wanting to hear a sad song, but still being drawn to him. He sat with his knees folded up by the river, his lute beside him. The faun folded her legs and nestled close, but he refused to play.

"You don't love me," the boy lamented. "I have given you all of myself, and now I will die here by this river without your love." He closed his eyes to the faun as tears wetted his cheeks.

Seeing the boy's heart break, and knowing herself to be the cause of it, filled her with anguish. She had destroyed what she had cherished, and drained the light from the beautiful boy's eyes with her silence. Unable to bear the pain of it, she wished herself into a girl.

She sang for him. Of sorrow, of love, of broken-heartedness and of joy. When he opened his eyes, he saw for the first time a youthful goddess, her plain dress, hair, and even her skin a pale shimmering gold.

But the faun was still there, retreated to the shelter of the trees. The girl knew what she was, but her form was heavy and hard—human—and remembered what she had been as one remembers walking thickly through a dream. Without the whole world in her head, she was free to love the boy with all her heart.

The girl and boy found bliss in each other's arms, but the goddess grew terribly unhappy. She was anguished for the loss of her human form to the boy. She loved the girl more than she had ever loved the boy, for she was a part of herself, and her heart broke to be separated from her. The goddess no longer felt whole. She still loved the boy, and reveled in his happiness, but only as much as she loved every tree, every fish, every badger and gryphon in the world.

As the girl grew to a maid, and the boy into a man, the goddess began to resent the boy for causing her this pain, this loss, though she knew it was what her heart had wanted, what she had wished for with all her being.

When the young man asked the maid to marry him, the girl answered that she would be the happiest bride in all the world.

The boy smiled. "I must have your name, then."

The maid hesitated, for she knew no name for herself that was not also the name of the goddess, and that name could not be made with only the use of the clumsy human tongue, but needed all of the sky, the trees, and the water that raced in the rivers to speak it.

"I would be your husband and love you until the end of your days," he pressed. "Am I not worthy of it?"

The maid had nothing to answer. The object of her love pressed her every day for a name, so they might be wed. Each day that she did not give one, he grew sullen and withdrew his affections. The maid's heart ached for him, and so at last, she gave him a name. One she had chosen just for herself.

No.

Kate tried to warn the girl. She knew how the love story went. Or thought she did. But this sickly turn felt familiar too, in the way you try and fail to remember a nightmare to banish it, but it revisits you when you are alone.

It was no use. The maid was not aware of her, and what was to be had already been.

Once she had spoken the name aloud, and had allowed the young man to hear it, that's what she became. She forgot about the other part of herself—the golden one in the forest. She no longer dreamed of breathing in the wind or rushing with the river down the side of the North Mountain. She was no better able to remember her true name than she was to speak it.

The maid and the man were wed in a shaded forest glen, with only the trees and the birds for company. The golden faun stood hidden in the shadow of a tall oak. The boy no longer saw the faun. He had found his love requited in the girl, and no longer needed or even remembered her.

As the ceremony ended and the man led his bride deeper into the woods to claim her, the faun curled up on the ground, tucked its delicate nose underneath its front legs, and wept bitterly, for she would never be whole again.

Time passed slowly in the goddess's sorrow, and as her thoughts were lost in bitter anguish, something terrible happened. A searing pain exploded on her left shoulder and knocked her onto her side. Out of her collarbone rose the shaft of an arrow. The goddess bled a warm crimson, soaking her magnificent golden coat. She scrambled quickly to her feet, but the pain shook in her limbs like thunder, and she collapsed again. As she laid panting in the grass, she felt the magic burned onto the tip creep into her body, rendering her still.

Dark laughter echoed through the forest. The goddess blinked and grimaced as the bowman appeared. She recognized him from long ago, when she had shown herself to him on the bank of a river, and mocked him for believing himself to be the Lord Creator of the world.

"You may be clever," he snarled as he approached, kneeling beside the goddess, "but I have been patient, and now I have you."

He gripped the arrow piercing her shoulder and ripped it free, causing her blood to rush forth, staining the grass, and even the fine clothes covering his knees. He let the blood puddle in his hands, guiding it into a glass bottle that he withdrew from the inner seams of his cloak. He kicked her hard in the ribs as he rose to his feet and disappeared again into the woods.

The man who fancied himself the Great Magician left the goddess for dead. But he was a fool to underestimate the rage he had instilled in the ancient goddess's breast. As her blood fed the grass, she realized the weight of the magician's words, and she accepted it, pouring herself forth onto the dirt until the golden faun was one with the soil. She raced across the roots of the grass, the trees, the flowers, tracking the path the magician had trod through the forest.

~

"Where did you go?" the maid asked when her bridegroom returned. After leading her to the home he had built for them, he had left without an explanation. She had sat alone, unsure of herself and anxious for her husband's return.

He said nothing, only smiled at her in a way she found unfamiliar. He approached her, slipping the dress from her tender shoulders and hefting her onto the bed.

All his affection disappeared. As he mounted her, all she felt was a cold, hard lust. His grip was unshakeable, digging into her legs, and neck. She squirmed in his grasp, but it only made him press himself harder and harder into her, bruising her fair skin.

He grunted like a bear, and was off her in an instant. He pulled his robes closed again, never having taken the care to defrock himself. The girl's crushed body writhed with pain, and tears welled in her eyes. He laughed, and she covered her face, ashamed of her nakedness before him. When she finally gathered the courage to look up at her husband, her eyes bulged in terror. The face of the boy she had fallen in love with contorted, revealing the hard, sinister expression underneath.

"Who are you?!" she screamed, pulling desperately at the bedclothes to cover herself.

The man's smile widened to a wolfish gleam, and the woman saw a flash of metal as he reached inside his robes.

The ground beneath them thundered, and the magician dropped his knife, fumbling to regain his balance. Out from the ground sprang a horde of golden stags, bursting through the wooden floor and charging the magician. He was trampled, gored by countless golden hooves. The shattering of nose, the smashing of teeth, and the splintering of bones was drowned out by the thunderous sound of the unending herd. The stags soaked their legs up to their knees in his blood, pulverizing his body until there was not even enough left of him to stain the dirt.

The girl on the bed screamed and fainted. When all went silent, the stampede had gone, and only a small golden child remained. She shuffled her bare feet in the dirt and unearthed a small gleaming red stone. She picked it up and felt it pulsing with her own life, her own magic, between her fingers. She pressed it into the palm of the sleeping woman, kissing her fingertips and cleaning her wounds with her tears.

The woman began to dream—of running through the forest in the hours before dawn, of dancing in the spring wind, of sliding down the peak of snow-capped mountains. When she opened her eyes, they were met by the child's.

"I know you," the woman said. "Don't I?"

"Yes," the child answered. "You do."

The woman who had been crowned queen of the forest, spent much of her time with the child, who told her of things she didn't remember and could barely understand. She was amazed to find she could bend the forest to her will. Trees would bow and dance at her call, flowers bloomed in defiance of winter, and the world hummed with life. The goddess fashioned a gold necklace for the queen, scratching onto its surface the same markings on the tree that stood at the pool at the bottom of the world. She fired the stone into the center, so that its power would never again leave their hands.

But if ever the woman thought of the magician, of how she had been deceived and abused, her wrath burned like a white-hot flame. And when she thought of the boy she loved, the one who had never existed at all, her heart wept and turned itself to icy stone.

The queen lived and reigned for many years, loved by all the creatures of the forest. Those who couldn't speak, as well as those who could, all recognized her as their sovereign, and worshipped her as a goddess. But the goddess lived still in the hidden heart of the forest, where the first trees had sprouted, and where the sun shone on the first Icaryan day. She showed herself much to the woman, who tried, but who could not truly remember what she had been. She went to her grave with only fractured dreams and memories. Except…except…

Kate's vision once again filled with the pale child's face, her golden eyes swallowing her up. There was an urgent intensity there Katelyn couldn't escape.

"Say our name." The whisper crackled like thunder in her head.

Kate? Kate!!

"Kate!"

"Katelyn!"

Kate heard her name shouted over and over again, a cacophony of voices shouting at her, none louder than the one between her temples.

The goddess closed her all-consuming eyes and turned her head away, fading back into the darkness.

"Kate!"

Kate! Kate!!

"What?!" she shouted finally. "What!"

She felt a tugging pressure on her arm, and blinked furiously as her father pulled her from the lake and dragged her back against the water's edge. A cold evening wind chilled her, and she became aware again of her soaked clothes.

"What happened?!" her father cried, at the same time that she heard Luca calling frantically to her in her head.

She held her hands out in front of her, stilling the tongues of her father and grandmother.

Luca. What's wrong?

Kate, where are you? Are you all right? The panic in his thoughts put the hair on her neck on end.

I'm fine. I haven't gone anywhere, Kate said.

No, you were—the thread of his thoughts paused as he tried to find a way to express them. *You weren't. It was like you disappeared. I couldn't sense you at all.*

Kate was at a loss for words.

You've been gone for hours. Where did you go?

I was sleeping.

Do you want me to come get you? You're scaring me. I don't want to lose you. Not ever.

No. I'm fine. Really.

Luca was silent. He was unconvinced, but Kate could tell that something else weighed on him.

Luca?

There are storm clouds, gathering off the coast. They'll be here by nightfall.

A stark terror raced down Kate's spine.

I'm here, love. And...my father's here. The castle is safe. Just, don't...don't scare me like that again. I can't think of anything else.

27

Christine pulled Darien aside, told him what they had discovered, and asked him what, if anything, he wanted her to do about it.

He wasn't quick to answer.

"Your orders don't come from me," he said at last.

"While we're here, we're *your* agents. Your word is law for the Likhanni."

Darien new full well he needed to be strong to earn their respect. But that didn't preclude him from being merciful. The way Christine looked at Darien was puzzling. She expected an answer, but there was no hoped-for solution written clearly on her face. It was a relief, he supposed, a marked contrast from the looks of people who knew exactly what they wanted from the seht, and who would withdraw their support if they didn't get it. But that knowledge didn't give him any great insight or inspiration either, didn't make the decision before him any less difficult. It was hard to think of consequences in the long term, when all he, or anyone else, for that matter, could see was an unending darkness on the horizon. That required his utmost attention, even if his hands would not be the ones to beat back the darkness, how he led Likhan through the crisis that cut through every class would make or break his rule. Of that much he was painfully aware.

"For now," Darien started, "let's maintain some surveillance, as much as we can under the current circumstances. No hands have yet been raised against me, so I have no just reason to punish the ownership of such weapons. And it would be hard enough to report them missing. In the meantime, let's hope we can get through this with minimal loss of life. That just might be enough to change people's minds about me."

Christine left the seht alone with his thoughts. She debated whether to give Alaric space, or to approach him with an apology. Her instincts told her that if she stayed too far away, he might lose interest. If in fact he had ever been interested in the first place. She thought of what she would want *him* to do if she'd been the one insulted, and made her way back to the main area of the Council House.

WHENEVER ALARIC ALLOWED HIMSELF TO THINK OF HIS WIFE, IT ALWAYS inclined him to drink. He was settling into his second jug of huchera, made from a hard desert plant. It had an awful taste, but it had the benefit of getting men drunk fast. This time, it was the realization that he no longer remembered his wife's face. Not while she was alive, anyway. Not when she wasn't bloated and swaying slightly, the way the rest of the room soon would if he could only get the wretched liquor down his throat fast enough. When Christine appeared before him, he looked up at her with mild amusement. It was a rare opportunity for her to be towering over him.

"I have a habit of saying whatever comes into my head, even if I don't mean it," she said. The seriousness of her expression tickled him, but he couldn't bring himself to laugh. He wasn't nearly drunk enough yet.

He touched the floor next to him, beckoning her to sit down. She leaned against the column holding Alaric up without sitting too close. She wasn't all that far away, either.

She took the wineskin from between his legs and downed several mouthfuls before handing it back.

After Alaric didn't talk for a while, she said, "I don't think I could have said anything to put you in this kind of a state."

He shook his head, more with a fluttering of the eyelids than any actual movement of his neck.

"I was thinking of my wife."

Christine shifted on the floor, and her breathing grew audible.

"You have a wife?"

"Had. Dead now. Killed—by my lies."

Christine didn't know what to say. "I'm sorry" was trite and meaningless. As the instinct toward platitudes faded, she blurted: "What did you lie about?"

"To protect her. I thought it was better than telling her the truth."

"What truth?"

Alaric took the jug back from her and downed another long swallow.

"Your secrets are yours, but it's hurting you to keep them. And telling someone who won't ever share all *her* secrets is hardly better."

Alaric shot her a sharp look. Or what passed for one given his condition. She returned it with a sad smile.

"I know that look because I *own* that look. Kate will lend an ear to whatever you say. But she's terrible at sharing."

"The more I know, the more I don't want to know," Alaric said.

Christine shrugged. "It's who she is. Look, if you need to get something off your chest, it's safe with me. Whatever it is can't be that terrible, for her to think so much of you."

Alaric raised a curious eyebrow.

"If I'd ever asked her to hand me the reins to something as big as this, she wouldn't even look me in the face."

"I didn't ask for this," Alaric said.

The revelation cut deep. "How nice. I don't know what I did wrong. Just when I thought my skills were improving, and we were getting close, she sent me off to the ends of the world on a bunch of dead-end jobs."

Alaric cocked his head. "She was protecting you."

"I didn't *need* protecting." Christine scowled. "I can protect myself. What I *needed* was a challenge."

"She knows. But…it's who she is. She cares."

Christine shook her head, unconvinced. "Meanwhile, she sent *you* here. In *my* body. Like I couldn't handle it myself."

"I'm sure she doesn't think that."

"How could she not? She's stronger, faster, smarter, prettier—"

Alaric grabbed her by the chin and whipped her around to face him. "Don't ever think that."

Christine glared at him, daring him. "Isn't she?"

Alaric shook his head, keeping his eyes firmly on hers. "No." The corner of his mouth quirked. "You are eminently fuckable."

His smile turned wry as she jerked her head away.

"Don't live your life in her shadow," Alaric warned.

"Like you, huh?"

Alaric pursed his lips. After a pause, he said, "I didn't tell my wife, and I didn't want to tell you, because I didn't want to hurt anyone. I *don't* want to hurt anyone. Not anymore."

Christine became so very aware of how close their legs were stretched out before them, how near Alaric's hand was to her own. The rapid pace of her heartbeat was at the choking point.

"You'd be trying something different, at least. Your secrets can't hurt me, Alaric."

"Can't they? You wouldn't be sitting here if you knew who I am." He put his hand over hers, arching his palm and tracking her fingers with his own. The gesture sent a jolt of electricity down her spine.

"Who are you?" she asked, her voice wavering as if in a dream, her vision locked on their interlaced hands, terrified to look up.

Alaric inched his shoulders closer to her, and his lips flitted on her neck as he spoke.

"A murderer."

Christine hunched up her shoulders, senseless to the entire Council House as she wished to be even closer to him than she was already.

"You were, or you are?"

Alaric's voice was quiet, but firm. "Were."

Christine finally got up the nerve to look into his eyes. Their piercing intensity threatened to swallow her whole, and her voice felt small when it issued forth again from her lips. "Then I don't care."

Alaric swallowed hard. "That's quite a thing not to care about."

Christine shook her head. "What I mean is, I already knew that..."

Alaric started back, caught entirely off-guard.

She quirked her mouth upward.

"Of course you are. You're one of Kate's. Although I admit I've never met a Spider before."

"What do spiders have to do with anything?"

Christine straightened. "Nothing. Never mind."

"No no. What the hell are you talking about?"

Christine cleared her throat. There was no way out now. "Her den of spiders...?"

He had no fucking clue what she was talking about. He kept his voice for her ears alone. "I'm not a spider, whatever the hell that is. I'm a murderer. *For hire.*"

"I heard you." Christine licked her lips. "She told me once that the only thing worse than murdering someone was making someone else do it. She has an extreme aversion to causing people to shed blood in her name."

In that moment, Alaric remembered the guard Kate had dispatched without a thought in Mehmnet's courtyard. Her firm grip on his shoulder before she stepped into the area. Her halting order before being attacked by a small army. He pressed his palm to his forehead.

"By the gods. She accepted the challenge herself because...because she knew I didn't want to do it anymore. She killed them...so I wouldn't have to."

Christine's lips pressed together. She nodded.

Alaric took another drink as he took it all in. "And still you look at me like that?" he asked, his heart unsteady at the glimmer in her eyes.

"Alaric?" She stopped, and brought the jug back to her lips again. His eyes darted to hers. "Me too. Not directly," she said, "but by proxy."

A curious eyebrow lifted.

"Rumor has it, that one of my little mixtures did in the Phantom himself."

She felt his body jolt at that name. Christine laughed under her breath. "Uh-huh. I thought as much."

Alaric couldn't help but grimace at the memory.

"Where did a sweet little thing like you learn to make such nasty stuff?"

"My father was an alchemist. I grew up around dangerous substances, and have a resistance to things that have felled much bigger men than me."

"Well. We make a fine pair, don't we?"

Christine's voice assumed a sultry quality. "Too soon to say."

28

"Is everything all right?" Dracula asked.

Luca wiped the sheen of cold sweat that had gathered on his face. He tried, hard, to steady his breathing.

"Mircea."

"*Don't* call me that," Luca spat.

Some hidden part of him, not as small as he'd like to admit, regretted the rebuke the moment he'd said it.

"Luca. *Is* everything all right?" Dracula asked again.

He'd wanted a name for so long; hated that he hadn't been given one. This one was his. Why was he so eager to throw it away?

"Come on," Luca said. "We have work to do."

His father just shrugged and shook his head. "Yes, Sire. Whatever you say." He groaned as he stood and stretched his back. Something somewhere made an audible crack.

"These boards are hellish on the spine."

"It's a prison. It's not supposed to be comfortable," Luca said.

"You may have a point there."

The psychic walls father and son had been so careful to build were showing signs of crumbling. Today, they were simply too tired to care.

The sky was overcast when they reached the parapet of the Western

Tower, where a darker, more menacing storm loomed in the distance. It creeped ever closer.

Luca folded his hands together in front of him and closed his eyes. He summoned the winds, and brought all their force to bear on the creeping shadow. Pressing his eyelids more tightly shut, Luca pushed harder and harder, battering the shadows with terrifying force and speed. But no matter how hard he tried, the shadow only curled into itself, growing tighter, thicker, denser. He could not penetrate it, could not grasp it by even the tiniest of holds and begin to disperse it. It endured his assault, and advanced.

Luca scowled.

Without a word, Dracula walked briskly to the ledge and stepped off into the air, spreading the leathery wings of a bat as he approached the darkening clouds and roiling sea beneath.

Luca didn't have time to object. His nerves increased by degrees as he watched his father flit around the cloud, keeping away from the edges. At one point he dove right in and came out again at another angle.

Luca was anxious to learn of what his father had seen. More importantly, he wasn't at all sure he could take his father's word for it. If ever there had been an opportunity for Dracula to cross him, this was it. And Luca was helpless to stop it.

The broad flapping wings once again became the fabric of his father's coat as he stretched out to his usual self.

"It is as you said," Dracula said. "Shadow filled with beasts. They are growing."

Luca crossed his arms. "And yet, they live. *She* lives."

Dracula raised a single eyebrow. "A single bat is no match for a pack of wild demons. Although I appreciate the compliment." Turning serious, he added, "If Haydee was once a woman, she is no longer. Only her will remains."

Luca was silent. Dracula gestured to the storm cloud with a broad sweep of his arm. "See for yourself, then."

The vampire lord sensed his son's hesitation—his embarrassment. "You've never flown before?"

Luca shifted on his feet and unfolded his arms. "It never seemed worth the effort."

"Being airborne can be quite useful. I could teach you, if you weren't being so pigheaded."

Luca huffed. "We need to prepare. We can't begin to guess how long it will take for the storm to reach us, or how big it will have grown by then." They climbed back down the tower to the main hall, crossing through Kate and Luca's bedroom.

Luca felt his father's head turning every which way, his overwhelming wonder, over his shoulder.

"Don't," he warned.

Dracula's voice was breathless. "I didn't say a word."

No matter which way he turned, Julian couldn't get comfortable.

But it wasn't the pillow or the mattress that was the problem. It was that Lilla would not stop pestering him.

"Julian?"

"What, Lilla?" He didn't even bother rolling over this time.

"She'll come if she needs to, won't she? I mean, if Luca can't…"

He turned over then, and cupped her cheek in his hand. He could read the fear in her eyes as plain as day, even though the sun had long since set, and the lanterns were kept on low, just enough to stop those moving about from stumbling blindly.

"She's always protected us before. And she always will."

"But she isn't here," Lilla protested. "She left Luca in charge."

His name grated whenever Julian heard it, but that was beyond the point now.

"That's right, she did," he answered. "Do you think she would do that unless she knew he could handle what's coming our way?"

He felt the tension in her muscles ease as she sank more fully into the mattress, and into his arms.

"I hadn't thought about it like that. Thank you."

"All right. Go to sleep now."

She smiled and turned over, pressing her back to his. He kissed the back of her head, and looked forward to being able to close his eyes.

ALLISTAIR SAW, JUST AS PLAIN AS ANYONE ELSE, THAT THE SHADOWS WOULD be upon them come nightfall. He wrestled with his armor, making sure it was secured correctly, though he knew from his sister's communications that a buckle or strap, whether out of place or just right, would do very little against the enemy he now prepared to face.

Cyrene's protests filled the room once again.

"I just got you back, and you're going to risk your life?"

He stopped what he was doing and took gentle hold of her with both hands. She needed to know that his attention was undivided. And she needed to hear him.

"I must. *All* our people's lives are on the line. They, and I, must risk our lives to defend our families. Our homes. We've been given a great gift. But you and I both must accept that death comes to us all. And this, *this* is worth dying for."

He kissed the tears that fell from his wife's cheeks as she nodded her assent.

"I know, love. I know." He rested his chin on her head, cradling her stomach, when he heard the clanking of metal on the other side of the room. He lifted his head to find his son fiddling with a sword almost as tall as himself, trying to figure how the scabbard was meant to be secured across his back.

Allistair crossed the room and pulled the weapon, leather, steel, and all, away.

"I'm big enough!" Kaspar cried. "It's my home too!"

Allistair smiled and ruffled the boy's hair. He *was* growing up, whether he wanted to admit it or not.

"Your day will come, my son. Now, your job is to look after your mother." Allistair crouched down and whispered, nose to nose, "And your little brother or sister too. They're counting on you."

That was enough. Kaspar stood at attention.

"There's my good lad."

Allistair swallowed hard. It had been just him and Kaspar for a long time. They'd survived tragedy already, and done it together. Allistair realized, then, that he would fall apart, completely and irreparably, without him.

'Sire?"

Corbin stood at the very bottom of the door, entering silently through the smallest of cracks.

Allistair stood, and pushed down the pain and fear in his heart. "Yes, Corbin?"

"Final checks, sir. It's time."

29

Luca's voice trailed off in her head, and Kate became keenly aware of her father's harried face bending down toward her.

"*What* is all the commotion about?" she asked. "Am I not allowed to take a nap?"

William's eyes bulged. "Take a—Katelyn, where the hell have you been?"

"Right here. I came out for a swim; I must've dozed off."

"In the middle of the lake?" Meryn cried. "That's a good way to drown!"

Katelyn flicked at the cuff atop her ear. "Maybe for you," she retorted. "I've slept underwater before. It's relaxing. *Usually.*"

"No. No you weren't here before," her father interjected. "I checked."

Kate shrugged, not knowing how to answer him.

"We thought you'd left, at first," Meryn explained. "But your room was undisturbed, so…"

"We looked *everywhere,*" William insisted. "You weren't here. And then you just appeared, out of nowhere, drifting like a…like a—" William stopped his sentence short.

"Did it ever occur to you that I was *in* the lake?" Kate asked.

Meryn started. "What did you say?"

Kate turned to her, but as she did, the thought that was on her tongue a moment before left her.

"What?" She scrunched up her face as if she'd been presented with a riddle she couldn't solve.

Meryn pressed her. "What did you mean, you were *in* the lake?"

Kate's scowl deepened but still she had no response. "Beneath the surface…" Kate felt again instinctively for the cuff at her ear, relieved to find it there. For a moment, she had the strongest feeling that she'd lost it.

"I don't know. What does it matter?"

William shook himself alert and helped Kate to her feet, draping his burgundy cloak over her shoulders. "Come on, let's get you dry."

Meryn lingered for a moment longer, turning a wary gaze toward the lake. She leaned over to peer through its crystalline depths, so dark now at this late hour, that she could not see the bottom. The thought crossed her mind that the lake had no end. She blinked, shook the idea loose, and joined her son inside.

William was feeding logs into a freshly sparked fire.

"I don't like this," he mumbled. He kept his eyes trained on his task as he spoke. "She *wasn't* there before. You know she wasn't. And then she just—"

"I know."

"What can it mean?" he asked.

"There's something she's not telling us."

William turned to his mother. "What reason does she have to lie to us?" Satisfied with the strength of the flames, he took the open seat beside his mother in a plush upholstered chaise.

"She's not lying," Meryn answered. "It…may be something she herself is unaware of."

"What in the hell does that mean?" he asked.

Kate re-entered the room in dry clothing, taking the seat nearest her, which kept both William and his mother at a fair distance. She drummed her fingers on the armrest of the heavy chair expectantly. She'd heard their exchange, of course. There was no way she couldn't, no matter how much they lowered their voices. They could have been whispering on a nearby mountaintop towering in the distance, and still she would have heard them. But that wasn't what bothered her. Though she had been cavalier in the face of their pointed alarm, she suspected that Meryn was right. Something at the back of her mind nagged, and it made her uneasy.

The silence filled the room until there was little space left for the hissing and crackling of the fire warming Kate's toes. She spoke first.

"I couldn't sleep, so I went back to the garden. I thought a dip in the lake would calm my nerves."

Meryn passed a scrutinizing gaze over her, causing Kate to raise an eyebrow when Meryn kept her silence. The wooden legs of Meryn's chair creaked as she shifted in her seat, cupping her fists under her chin. Finally, she asked:

"Did you dream?"

Kate shuddered at the words, feeling an unseen wind crawling down her spine. Her eyes shifted to the fire. For a moment, she felt its impatience with her, the flicking flames upward, pushing her, urging her to see what lay beyond the veil of her waking mind. Just as quickly, the impression was gone. Kate answered in the plainest way she could.

"I don't remember."

Something sighed in the distance. Kate couldn't discern the source. Her family, however, remained silent.

"I'm...sorry," she said in a subdued tone, although it wasn't them she felt like she was disappointing. "I *am* trying."

"We know," William said. "We're asking a lot of you. Something we couldn't accomplish ourselves."

Meryn rose out of her chair. "I'm going to make some tea," she said, and left father and daughter alone.

William warmed his hands by the fire, wringing them, as if he could squeeze out of them something to say.

"I was worried about you," he said finally. "I know you don't believe that, and why should you? I never showed my concern before. Never looked out for you the way a father should. I'm nothing but a shadow. And it's my own fault."

What could Kate say? What he said was true. The specter of him had haunted her from childhood—a passing phantom that pointed the way, only to point to darkness. It was better than nothing, or the alternative, the drunken, lustful father who daily wiped his boots on her. But she had been left in shadow, led to a world she inherited, only to be abandoned again amongst its secrets. She wasn't angry. Not exactly. Still, she wouldn't offer false sympathy. Instead, she turned her mind to the present.

"I didn't leave the lake," she insisted, "but Luca sensed something was amiss as well." William looked up from the fire to his daughter's child's face.

"What do you mean?"

"He said I…disappeared," she said, unable to hide her discomfort. "That he couldn't sense me."

William narrowed his eyes, scrutinizing her. "Luca's not here, Katelyn. He's at the castle." He sounded nervous, not sure of how to respond, not wanting to upset her.

She was amused by the delicate way in which he chose his words.

"And we converse nevertheless."

Realization followed by embarrassment swept over his face. "Ah. Did he say anything else?"

"No. But I don't feel right."

William raised his eyebrows, just as his gaze dropped to her stomach.

"No, no, she's fine. But all the same, ever since I got here, I've felt off-kilter. I just…can't put my finger on it." She squinted. "Everything here is so familiar. It's like I should remember it. But I don't."

"We're not blind to the amount of pressure on you," William offered.

"Indeed not," Meryn said, re-entering the room with a silver service in her hands. "I don't envy you." Meryn set the tray down on the wide, smooth stump acting as a table, poured Kate a generous cup of dark-colored tea, and passed it to her.

Kate took the cup in both hands, warming her fingers and inhaling the woodsy aroma.

"Arrowroot?" she surmised, separating the aggressive scent from the subtle, more expected tones.

Meryn nodded. "To help you remember your dreams."

The bitter smell was like a ward to Kate's nose. She sipped timidly, not wanting to be rude, but when the acrid, moldy taste hit the back of her throat, she gagged, and had to bite back her nausea.

"It's terrible, I know," Meryn acknowledged, "but it really should help."

Kate nodded in gratitude. After a small, hard swallow, Kate posed a solemn query.

"What will we do if it doesn't work?"

Meryn shrugged. "There are other roots I can try, or maybe brew a more potent—"

"Not the tea."

Meryn and her son exchanged looks. From the solemnity of their faces, Kate already knew what their answer would be. William spoke first.

"We don't have any other ideas. We're not sorcerers, or necromancers. Our abilities are so limited compared to yours. Drigory is always telling us that your powers know no bounds. We thought—well, we hoped that if we guided you in the right direction, told you things Drigory never did, that it would be enough."

THEY SHARED A LATE SUPPER IN SILENCE. WHEN THE BOWLS WERE CLEARED and their bellies full, William tried again.

"I've been thinking about what you said. About my ignorance of the nature of your other gifts. I thought maybe if we can come to some kind of an understanding with the one gift we share, then you could apply it to the others, better than I can."

Kate took her time in answering. After some deliberation, and with a great deal of tact, she said, "I'd rather not."

William tried to remain unaffected, but his disappointment shone clear on his face.

"It's important that we have an alternative," Kate said. "And it's something I have to think on for a while."

Reluctantly, William nodded and left the room. Kate waited for the small but growing child to settle comfortably in her place before she stood, walking over to the stacks of books encompassing the left side of the parlor. Her eyes scoured the titles, searching for grimoires, particularly those inclined to necromancy.

Her choices were slim. Drigory kept the best, most powerful books in his own collection, she knew. She wished for them now. She was still angry, still hurt by his chronic refusal to provide her with the knowledge she had always sought. But still. He had come through when it mattered, on the Ancestor's Mound. She hadn't thanked him for that. And secretive though he was, his mind was a more practical one. Something she couldn't say for her present company, who pinned all their hopes on Kate's ability to have her prayers answered. She wondered, then, how he had felt about this plan. He hadn't said. His counsel may have been of help now.

She took what tomes she could find, a copy of a spellbook she knew well, and another on the dangers of necromancy. She reasoned that a well-versed critic of blood magic might serve as a useful back door to spells and practices beyond her repertoire.

She retreated to her room, opening the spellbook first. More than two-thirds of the book she knew by rote. The rest was unhelpful. Not unless she could bind the entire world. The idea of replicating herself appealed for a moment, until she realized they would be equally uncontrollable. An army of the dead, with naught to lose, might be a better defense against shadow demons, but that only scratched the surface of the problem. Nothing she read held a glimmer of hope for destroying Haydee, if she *could* be destroyed, or for undoing the effects of the shadows she cast.

What she really needed was a book of shadows, dangerous as it might be. She'd never seen a copy of the tome such practitioners held sacred. They were exceedingly rare, their writings more so. Luca's father had alluded to a copy he'd acquired, but it had been destroyed in the mad chase to hunt him down.

Kate swallowed against the stabbing pain in her chest at the thought of Luca's reaction as she slowly, stealthily, let her mind stretch toward

Dracula. She caught a sense of him, but he rebuffed her, feigning ignorance of her presence. She pushed past the barrier like it was nothing.

I know you can hear me, she pressed, her voice in his head sharp.

Kate sensed his amusement, mixed with approval. *What do you want then?* He inquired.

You mentioned reading about shadow magic before.

Yes.

Did it say anything about their weaknesses?

They're as vulnerable to bodily harm as any human, he replied, *if in fact they remain that way.*

Kate absorbed the information, disappointed. Though no one had solid proof that Haydee had permanently dematerialized, it seemed likely given the state of things in Likhan.

It's not wise to keep anything from me, she warned.

Kate felt his earnest agreement and knew he had no more to share.

You have good instincts. Trust them.

With that, Katelyn retreated from his mind. She began perusing through the second book, but it failed to hold her interest. Her mind wandered instead back to the Ancestor's journal, which she'd left untouched for longer than she meant to. She put the hefty volume in her lap on the desk and swapped it with the journal, finding her place easily. She tried to drink tea but could not get it down, and left it to turn cold in her cup.

30

Alaric couldn't sleep. All he could think of as he lay on his bed, stripped down to his waist, was Christine. His was one of the few rooms left, reserved because of his relationship to Darien and the closeness necessary to protect him. But the privacy did nothing to stifle the heat. Restless, he got up and leaned out the window. Nothing was better, nothing worse. It was all he needed for his mind to be made up. When he opened the door, she was already standing there, her hand raised, ready to knock. The spike in his body temperature set his skin on edge.

"Get in here already." He pulled her through the door and hoisted her up by her hips. Christine ran her hands through his wild hair. His usually nimble fingers got tangled in the satin ties of her bodice as their mouths collided, teeth and tongues and all fury. His only focus was on her ravenous mouth. Fed up, he grabbed the fabric on either side and pulled it apart, releasing her breasts with brute force. They were even better than he remembered. He crushed her between the wall and his body when his mouth wandered to her nipples. Her moans hardened him in a second's time.

"Give me what I want," she growled, and dug her nails into his belt, freeing his cock. She screamed as he crashed into her, her skirts lifted up by his forearms as he kept her pinned to the wall. She squeezed her eyes shut as his forceful thrusts nearly undid her. But he kept coming, again and again, until he was grinding his teeth together so hard he winced. Seeing the look on her face, he withdrew and held her in his arms with his back curved forward, their foreheads touching. He felt her whole weight in his hands like it was nothing.

"You're so small," he panted, his mouth coming to rest on the curve between her neck and her shoulder.

When she opened her eyes, they were blazing with a lust that knew no bounds. She tugged hard on the hair at the back of his skull, pulling his face to meet hers.

"I'm not made of glass," she hissed through her teeth.

Alaric tightened his grip and threw her halfway across the room, where she landed on an unmade bed. He pounced on her, ripping her skirts to shreds until his mouth could reach between her legs. She writhed and moaned until Alaric came up for air and pushed into her with a force that made his head spin. He was eager to comply when she pleaded for more, and more.

His whole body trembled. Alaric had to crane his neck to see Christine's minute form beneath him. Her head only came halfway up to his chest. She stretched up and rifled his hair with one hand. He untangled his fingers from her dark curls and reached for her throat. When she opened her eyes to face him, his fingers drew instinctively back. Instead, he caressed her bottom lip with his thumb before bringing his mouth to meet hers. He swallowed her screams as she climaxed. It was all he needed to push himself over the edge. Before collapsing, he twisted his hips to the side, spooning her rather than landing on top of her in a heap.

Christine nuzzled herself under his chin and fell right to sleep. That was it—no great reckoning, nothing to say.

Alaric bit his lip and laughed to himself. "Greedy little thing." He kissed her hair and followed her lead.

He woke up sometime later to the feel of her thighs grinding against him. He opened his eyes to a lovely sight of Christine astride him, her firm breasts needy and waiting to be squeezed. His hands went first to the round ass swaying on top of him, diggings his fingers into her soft, inviting curves.

"You've got great hips," he said.

"Thank you," she replied, feeling the rise of his flesh beneath her. He gripped her more firmly, moving his hips to her rhythm, but she tensed her muscles, keeping a miniscule distance between them.

Alaric caught a glint of fire in her eyes, and wasn't sure what to expect. He pursed his lips in wolfish anticipation.

"If we're going to do this again, we should have some ground rules," she said.

Alaric tempted her, jutting forward and bringing his right hand up to cup her breast, thumbing her nipple. A moan escaped her lips, and she laid her hand over his in an attempt to remove it, but he was implacable. Her resolve was melting into a puddle on the floor.

"I'm listening," he challenged.

Christine struggled to form coherent thoughts, and only with great difficulty did she remember what she'd meant to say.

"No other women."

Alaric's brows lifted. "You're hardly giving me the chance to think of anyone else right now."

Christine relaxed into his hands, putting herself at his mercy. He squeezed her hips and brought her down hard. How had she lost control of this situation so quickly? Oh, but he felt entirely too good for her to be astonished.

"I mean it, Alaric. I'm not good at sharing."

"No women?" Alaric repeated, attentive now.

"And no lies."

Alaric hummed, feigning deep consideration as his fingers traced lazy circular patterns on her skin and he slid, oh so slowly, not stopping until he was nudging at the edge of her core. Everything inside her clenched at his absence. Christine bit her lip to stop herself from begging as she waited. Alaric opened his mouth to reply when it occurred to him.

"What about you?"

"What?"

"Are *you* allowed to be with other women?" he asked.

"That's different."

"The hell it is!" Alaric laughed. "You're a selfish little imp, aren't you?"

By way of reply, she pressed her hands to his abdomen and took what she needed, driving him deep.

His breath hitched, and his eyes narrowed to slits.

Alaric took a deep breath and tried to think.

"What if *I* don't want to share?" His right hand moved from her breast to her cheek.

Christine managed to blush. Her smile turned devilish.

"You can watch," she offered.

Alaric's ears perked up, but just as quickly, he flexed his muscles, sitting up while keeping them joined. She gripped his thighs, and breathed heavier as his lips approached hers.

"Watch, but not play? That's cruel." Licking her chin. "How about when you're feeling so inclined, you tell me first." She craned her neck backward as he drew his mouth to it, brushing his lips along her flesh. She shuddered at the warm feel of his hand as it sprawled across her back.

"I can live with that," she panted, her voice a ramble.

"Good," Alaric replied in a deep, demanding voice. "Can you fuck me now? *Please?*"

Christine's eyes flashed. "Since you asked so nicely…" She shoved him onto his back again and settled in.

~

ALARIC'S HEART WAS ON THE VERGE OF EXPLODING WHEN HE FINALLY answered the incessant pounding at the door. He opened it without giving Darien time to speak.

"Water," he begged. He slumped in the doorway. Breath came hard and irregular, his skin was slick with sweat.

"What happened?" Darien asked at a fever pitch.

Alaric tried hard to smile, but he had no energy left. "What didn't?"

"I—" Darien shut his eyes and maintained his focus. "It's getting dark outside."

Alaric sobered up. He stood upright, at least, though his knees were not happy about it.

"What happened?"

"I don't know. I think some of the lanterns are going out. There are people in the city," Darien said.

Alaric looked down to see him wringing his hands.

"Arjuna's out there," Darien said.

Alaric shook his head to clear it of the haze. "Right." He called over his shoulder. "Babe come on, we gotta go." He turned back to Darien. "Two minutes."

Darien stepped back from the doorway. "I'll wait."

"THERE HAVE BEEN NO SIGHTINGS OF MONSTERS YET, BUT WHY WAIT AND give them a chance?" Darien asked as he, Alaric and Christine walked down the corridor leading back to the central hall of the Council House.

"Right. Stay here," Alaric said.

Darien stopped in his tracks, and balled his hands into fists at his side. "No!" He shouted.

Alaric and Christine stopped and turned to look at him.

"What good am I if I can't protect the city, or even the people I care about? I'm coming with you," Darien said.

Christine tried to reason with him. "You're no good to anyone dead."

"What difference does it make?"

"What?" Alaric asked, incredulous.

"What good am I, as seht, in a world shaped by magicians and warriors?" Darien asked.

Alaric took a step closer to Darien. "It doesn't have to be. Not when there's men like you."

Darien didn't know what to say.

"You've given the city hope, and a future. You and I know Haydee would have done this one way or the other, and it's because of *you* that any of us were here to stop it."

"Can you? Can *she*?" Kate was still nowhere to be seen, and Apollo, aside from healing Arjuna's mother, hadn't done a damn thing. Kate was their only hope.

"You and I saw what she can do," Alaric said. "And those two downstairs, they have not *begun* to fight. Let me do this for you," he pleaded. "I can't protect you and Arjuna both."

Darien absorbed what he said, and his higher purpose prevailed. "Bring her back."

Alaric nodded and put a reassuring hand on Darien's shoulder before they dashed off.

He turned to Christine. "The same goes for you."

"Excuse me?" she said.

"I can't rescue someone else if I'm thinking about you. The lot of you —stay close to Hercules."

She pulled on his forearms, drawing him nearer. "I'm not nearly done with you yet."

"That's what scares me the most. I'll be back."

She was on him in a second. "No. We stay together."

31

The storm clouds raced in, menacingly close. Luca and Corbin rushed down the line of battlements to reach the Western Tower, Dracula close on their heels. They didn't want to waste any of their firepower until the shadow was well and truly within range. The Western Tower had the best vantage point.

Dracula finally dropped the pretense, and opened his mind to Luca.

Luca's eyes flashed in rage when his father flooded his consciousness, and he realized Dracula had been privy to his thoughts all this time. Dracula brushed it aside.

That doesn't matter now. A vampire's ability to communicate by mind is his greatest weapon. Embrace it.

His father's words threw Luca's mind back to Cathair, when Luca had feared that his nature would lead to Kate's death, and her ultimate betrayal. Dracula's admonition had been cold. Calculating. And exactly the same.

Luca stopped himself from drowning in his own fear. He didn't loathe what he was. Not anymore. Kate had taught him that—to push beyond his insecurity, and turn his talents into a weapon. And she had charged him with the defense of her home. Their home.

The shadow tucked low as it approached, casting a veil of darkness over the town below. That was all it needed to spread itself aground. In its deepest pockets, beasts big and small disappeared. Even small birds in flight were not fast enough to escape its grasp. Their brightly colored wings grayed and stiffened like aged paper before they too crumbled to ash, carried on the winds of Haydee's relentless storm.

The larger canons were fired first. The fireballs soared in the air, illuminating the yawning nothingness where Icarya had vanished as they arced through the sky. The volley hit its mark, ripping a flaming tunnel through the center of the cloud. The darkness split in two. A wave of cheers rose up as Icaryans looked anxiously on, but Luca's intense concentration silenced them.

The two halves of the cloud stretched to fill the void in no time at all, billowing ever darker.

"It's like a hydra," Dracula said. "The more you attack it, the more dangerous it becomes. Do not give it a chance to regroup."

At Luca's command, archers sent a rapid-fire volley of flaming arrows to meet the storm. Each arrowhead bit into the darkness, dispersing it into smaller tufts before its efforts to resolidify could gain traction. Bits of shadow dropped out of the sky, leaving the main cloud headed toward the castle a fraction of its former size.

"You'll run out of ammunition sooner rather than later," Dracula observed.

Luca heard, but his attention was on the fragments of shadow that fell from the sky like weeping rain. They were slithering together, gathering themselves into things with arms and legs, snouts and tails, and racing toward the castle gates.

The remaining cloud crouched low, and raged toward the castle like a violent wave. Thunder cracked as it collided with the stone walls of the ground floor, rushing through them like a shock wave, soaking everything in shadow from the bottom up and causing it to sink. People caught in its wake ran amok, not sure if safety could be found by racing up the nearest flight of stairs or out into the forest. But the forest seemed to have disappeared to those trapped inside looking out; the entire level was awash in sinister fog. Those who chanced it were spirited up into the cloud above, only to fall screaming to their deaths.

Those huddled in the armory beneath heard the cries over their heads, and were left staring up at a ceiling that was no longer there. A starless sky sprawled above them, hovering like death. At first, the shadow's energy was focused on the floors above, then slowly the darkness slid down the walls and pooled onto the floor, opening up into a gaping pit.

Luca raced from one end of the tower to the other, his muscles screaming under the strain to keep him upright as the ground shifted beneath him. The surge had gone right through, leaching its way into mortar and stone.

Dracula's next suggestion sent shock waves of its own down his spine.

"Set the forest on fire."

"That's the heart of Icarya," Luca raged. Kate's heart. She would be devastated if he destroyed it.

Dracula's voice in his ear was brisk and impatient. "The shadow will spread too far to contain. We need to keep the fight targeted, and limit the damage."

"No, I said!"

"They can rebuild. You must do this. *Now.*"

Luca ran from his father, from his terrible suggestion. He only made it about halfway before he stopped and turned again. Then he howled and slammed his fists into the walls on either side of him, causing them to crack.

"Do it, Corbin!"

Corbin shouted down the line. Every archer turned to face north, into the Indigo Forest.

"Take your aim!" the rat cried.

It was half-hearted, at first. Only some of them did what they were told.

"Come on!" Corbin shouted. The company ground its teeth and set their sights on the forest. On their homes.

Corbin scratched behind his right ear. His nose twitched, and he turned his face away.

"Fire!"

The flames from their arrowheads created a ring around the northern wall. The forest was cold and brittle. The fire bit into its bared limbs quickly. The blaze did its job, crawling down the length of eons-old trunks and keeping the shadows at bay. Luca only let the fire stretch so far until he ordered a stone barrier to be dropped into place from above and constrain the flames from consuming the entire forest. It was a small band, the most Luca was willing to sacrifice.

"Those trees won't burn forever," Dracula said.

"They don't have to."

Luca snatched a bow from the nearest archer and leapt down the slim balcony from an upper bedroom. He leaned out into the air and took aim at the line of newly outfitted lanterns across the face of the castle. He waited, while the castle teetered on its now porous moorings. When he shot came, he took it. He fired straight through the metal rings fastening the lanterns along the stone wall. The hooks acted like grenade pins—once the lanterns came loose from their tethers, they dropped to the ground and exploded, creating a mote of fire shielding the front walls of the castle.

The darkness recoiled, its grip loosened. Tendrils of shadow from the castle's ripped interior withdrew.

~

"Oh shit!"

Julian cowered as the dark fingers stretched out above their heads retreated, and was replaced by nothing but empty air.

Gravity caught up with them, and the ground floor, now left *without* a floor, came tumbling down on top of them.

There was a hailstorm of bric-a-brac as paintings came off their hooks, bookshelves emptied and toppled over, and glass cabinets shattered. Lilla screamed, and threw her hands above her head to protect her face. The palms of her hands were cut to ribbons.

Julian pulled her off the upper bed to the space beneath. All around him, Icaryans were scrambling to overturn the bunks to use as shields against the onslaught of rubble, but all Julian could do was focus on

Lilla's bloodied hands, how they trembled as he tore the sheets off the bed and bound them up in strips of linen.

"We can't stay here," he said. The castle dipped sharply to the right as the shadow reeled back from where the burst lanterns had made the most immediate impact.

Lilla's head turned to take in the chaos. "But where are we going to go?"

ANOTHER BALCONY GAVE WAY, AND SHOOK KASPAR OUT OF HIS MOTHER'S grasp.

"Kaspar!" she screamed, but the tilt of the tower was too steep. Even Allistair wasn't fast enough or tall enough to reach him before he slid out of the window and into the night. Their wails tore the night air apart.

KASPAR STARED AT HIS MOTHER'S HORRIFIED FACE UNTIL THE WORLD turned upside down. He was plummeting headfirst, and flailed about for a handhold, anything to stop him from falling. Fear clawed at his limbs, his screams swallowed up by the thin air until he felt the cold darkness cradle him in its arms. Kaspar was brokenhearted. He had waited all that time to be reunited with his mother, only to be separated from her again. He reached out to what he thought was a dream of her, and gave in to the dark bosom of death. But she jerked him quickly to herself. She was warm and alive, as was he, and he clung to her. He heard a great flapping of wings. He turned to see the shadow behind him retreating, but not before he saw Dracula's face.

ALLISTAIR'S SHOCK BARELY REGISTERED BEFORE DRACULA DISSOLVED INTO a cloud of smoke, crawling down the castle wall and filling in the gap where the ground floor used to be. Dracula spread himself out thin, creating a film between the upper and lower levels of the castle. He called out to Luca.

Get them out!

An image took shape in Luca's mind, of the underground pathway to the lover's nest. It might still be open to them.

Corbin led the way, his rat brigade carrying lanterns strapped to their backs to guide people out and under the castle, beyond the burning strip of forest and to the safety of the woods beyond. Those in flight carried what they could. It wasn't much. Blankets were easiest, ripped right off the beds set up in the armory and slung over the shoulder. Cookware was heavier and unwieldy, but necessary, which made the journey through dark passageways of frozen mud all the more difficult. What was left of the kitchen staff grabbed any food they could, but the larder had been hit hard. The cooks and servers who overturned the kitchen shelves to barricade the door saw their hard work disappear in a bellow of dark smoke, and many of them along with it.

But the night was far from over. Once enough Icaryans had made it through to the other side, they got to work, pitching tents, lighting fires, and covering the frozen ground enough to keep people warm. These people were terrified, traumatized, some of them wounded, all of them grieving. They didn't need to be freezing too. Those who still had limbs and their wits about them worked furiously to protect the rest coming through from bitter winds.

Dracula shifted the weight of the castle on his vaporous shoulders and tilted it, ever so slowly, to ease the way between the upper levels and the towers to the tunnels below. The castle groaned from the stress. It could not take much more. When Luca finally gave him the signal that it was all clear, he let the castle down. The ragged edges where the shadow had cut through crashed together like gnashing teeth. Smoke and rubble covered everything in the haze of a palace long abandoned. Dracula stood on two legs once more, his calves tensing to maintain his perch on the Western Tower, leaning sharply forward.

Making his way up the ruined tower, Luca caught a glimpse of his and Kate's bedroom. Everything was in shambles. A pang resounded in his heart. Not for the room, for the whole castle. For what he, Kate, and so many others had called home for so long. By the time he joined his father, Luca was seething. There was no animosity between them now, no obstinate embarrassment about his father's plan being the right one and no question about whose side he was on. All Luca's fury was directed outward.

They did not surveil the damage, not yet, but looked to where the shadows still remained. He tossed his father a sword.

Dracula caught it with ease. He admired its craftmanship before returning his attention to the ground below.

The cover of true night had fallen. Nothing that lurked in the shadows shrouded the castle. Luca's skillful blow had effectively ended that. The ground behind the castle leading to the camp was clear, the fire still burning trees, holding it at bay. But the ground before the castle, going out to the sea, was writhing.

The wind caught in Dracula's hair, blowing it behind him in long graceful curls. He flashed a wicked smile.

"A head start is best." He gestured to a lower level that led to a wide area, with enough room to run.

Luca understood his intention. He stopped fighting his father's psychic bond, fell into sync with him easily. The connection ran so deep it was overwhelming. The bonding of sameness, of blood. It was so different from all the time he had spent treating vampires as other, trying to understand them and himself only to become more effective at killing them, and yet all the while hating himself for his own nature, decrying it at the same time that it gave him power over them. His life with Kate had changed all that. With her unending kindness, he had finally accepted his dual nature, and embraced it. And now, he felt something he never had with any vampire before—belonging. His mind thrummed with newfound confidence as they raced toward the edge. He welcomed his father's crisp command between his ears as his feet met the air.

Now!

Words were not enough to describe it. It was more of a sensation, an urgent imperative, as they took flight. Understanding was fluid as he assumed control of wings. He spread them out, testing their span as he sliced through the air.

Their descent was swift. Luca landed upright on human feet. Beside him, his father was a flock of bats, all screeching and curling around themselves as he resumed a human form with practiced ease and a sinister grace. At Luca's raised eyebrow, Dracula simply smiled. The name that instilled fear in every heart was not just an account of his powers or skill. It was how they were displayed.

Without any words spoken between them, they drew their swords and descended upon the horde.

32

Shadow billowed up from the ground like fog. By now, everyone knew that if someone got stuck in its darkest tendrils, that person might never see the light again. That didn't stop people from running panicked into the streets as the lights burning throughout the city dimmed. But their only source of protection was left abandoned on account of their intractable fear.

"Damned fools," Christine cursed, but the weight of her words left her in a great "whoosh" as Alaric scooped her up to stop a shadow from coiling itself around her ankle, and forced her onto a rickety ladder that led up to the rooftops. They were ready to leap to the next rooftop when it started to wobble. Alaric hooked Christine around her middle to stop her momentum before she was swallowed up too. The ground began to churn and sink underneath them like quicksand. They steadied themselves by holding on to each other.

Alaric pulled her by the chin to meet his gaze. "If we die tonight, in this darkness, I want to die with you knowing that I was thinking only of you." He kissed her, hard. When they parted, Christine's eyes went wide, tracking a path to something over his shoulder.

"Alaric. Look." Behind them was the house that they sought. Shadow creeped its way up the sides of the tall, narrow column of stone, ready to engulf the entire building.

"How to get there?" Christine asked.

Alaric stepped forward to get a closer look and tripped on a wire. A paper lantern had come loose from its mooring and fallen to the ground.

"Come on!"

Using the lines that once hung for the festival, they zipped across the gap. Their bodies slammed together into the adobe walls with a hard clap, but there was no time to feel pain or wonder how any of them would make it out as they scrambled into the open window below.

~

PANIC REIGNED INSIDE THE HOUSE, WHICH DEVOLVED INTO FIGHTING about what to do. The brothers Solimani seemed content to blame their situation on the fact that the lamps that had arrived from Icarya were not as strong as Kate's eternal fire. But their bickering gave Arjuna an idea.

"She's not the only one who can make fire." She grabbed the oil pots piled in the corner and poured their contents out the windows. "I need a match!" she cried. The woman of the house rushed to hand her what she needed, and in a flash Arjuna lit up the house from the outside. The stone exterior itself wouldn't burn, but the fire would keep the shadow at bay, at least for as long as it took for the fire to consume the oil. The widow Solimani breathed a sigh of relief.

"You're a resourceful one, aren't you?"

~

ANOTHER SECOND AND ALARIC'S HAIR WOULD HAVE CAUGHT ON FIRE AS HE and Christine tumbled through the window.

"That was a little too close for my liking," Alaric grumbled as he rose to his feet.

Arjuna's hands rushed to cover her mouth. "Oh! I am so sorry, I didn't see you there!"

"How could you see anything?" Christine coughed. Between the shadows and, now, the smoke furling into the windows, staying put was not an option. "Do you have anything else?" Christine asked. "How about the larder?"

"What for?" Sufie asked. "The house is already burning."

"But we can't stay here," Alaric answer. "If we could lay down a path to the Council House, it might stop the ground from disappearing under us."

"Got it!" The two brothers re-entered the room, each carrying a jug of kitchen grease.

"That'll do it," Alaric said.

The siblings exchanged a glance. "Race you."

They ran as straight a line as they could back to the Council House. At least, that was their original intention. But when they reached the Queen's Garden, they stopped. Everything there was bright, and green, and as undisturbed as it had ever been. It was a safe haven from the chaos creeping up from behind and unfolding just ahead of them.

~

The marble of the Council House was cracking and shifting beneath them as if it were in the path of an earthquake. People everywhere were losing their footing, sliding into broken walls and columns. The unluckiest ones slid right into nothingness as the shadow seeped in.

Ted grabbed his son by the wrist. "Right, okay, we're leaving."

He pulled Darien down the Council House steps and whistled to Gideon, who was already airborne and headed his way.

Darien struggled to pull his wrist free.

"I can't leave these people to die!"

Ted shouted back, "I left once to save your life. I won't leave you again just so you can end it. You can rebuild, but now we have to leave!"

Darien grabbed hold of his father as the top of a column came hurtling toward them. From out of nowhere, Hercules raced forward to catch it, tossing it aside with just enough time to catch another.

"Go!" he cried.

Ted hoisted Darien up onto Gideon, who took off again as the base of the column to their right gave way. The column swung wildly about from being suddenly unmoored, but Gideon dodged it with ease and soared away from the crumbling structure.

Darien gaped in wonder at Gideon's broad wingspan and his incredible speed. Before they had reached any significant height, he saw a crowd of people waving and shouting from the Queen's Garden.

"Down there!" he cried, and pointed to the bright spot of green.

A voice that sounded like heaven reached his ears as they landed. "Darien!"

Arjuna ran to him. She threw her arms around him, all sense of propriety gone. He clasped her face and kissed her. "I thought I lost you," he said.

"You almost did."

"I'm never letting you out of my sight again."

"I'm surprised you ever did in the first place," Alaric said. "Now can we get out of here?"

Using a length of rope to secure people to Gideon's sides, the gryphon carried the small party up into the air across the desert. Darkening sands rose up to meet the sky. Gideon soared, weaving as he went to avoid dark spots. With several miles behind them, but with Icarya many more ahead, he let out a pained squawk, and landed on a large outcropping of rock. The powerful flapping of wings did nothing to soften the rough landing that nearly sent his passengers tumbling, if they had not been tied to him so tightly.

It was too dark, and too far.

Gideon put his head down and rested his head between his paws.

Ted tugged on the gryphon to assess the situation. "What's the matter? Gideon!"

"I'm dying, that's all." His golden coat began to gray.

“No. You can’t.” Tears fell down Ted’s sand-beaten cheeks. He ran his hands through Gideon’s proud mane. The creature sighed, and stretched out his wings to either side. Lightning flashed, and cracks of thunder pealed in the distance, over the city. They didn’t know which was more dangerous—the shadows, or the storm.

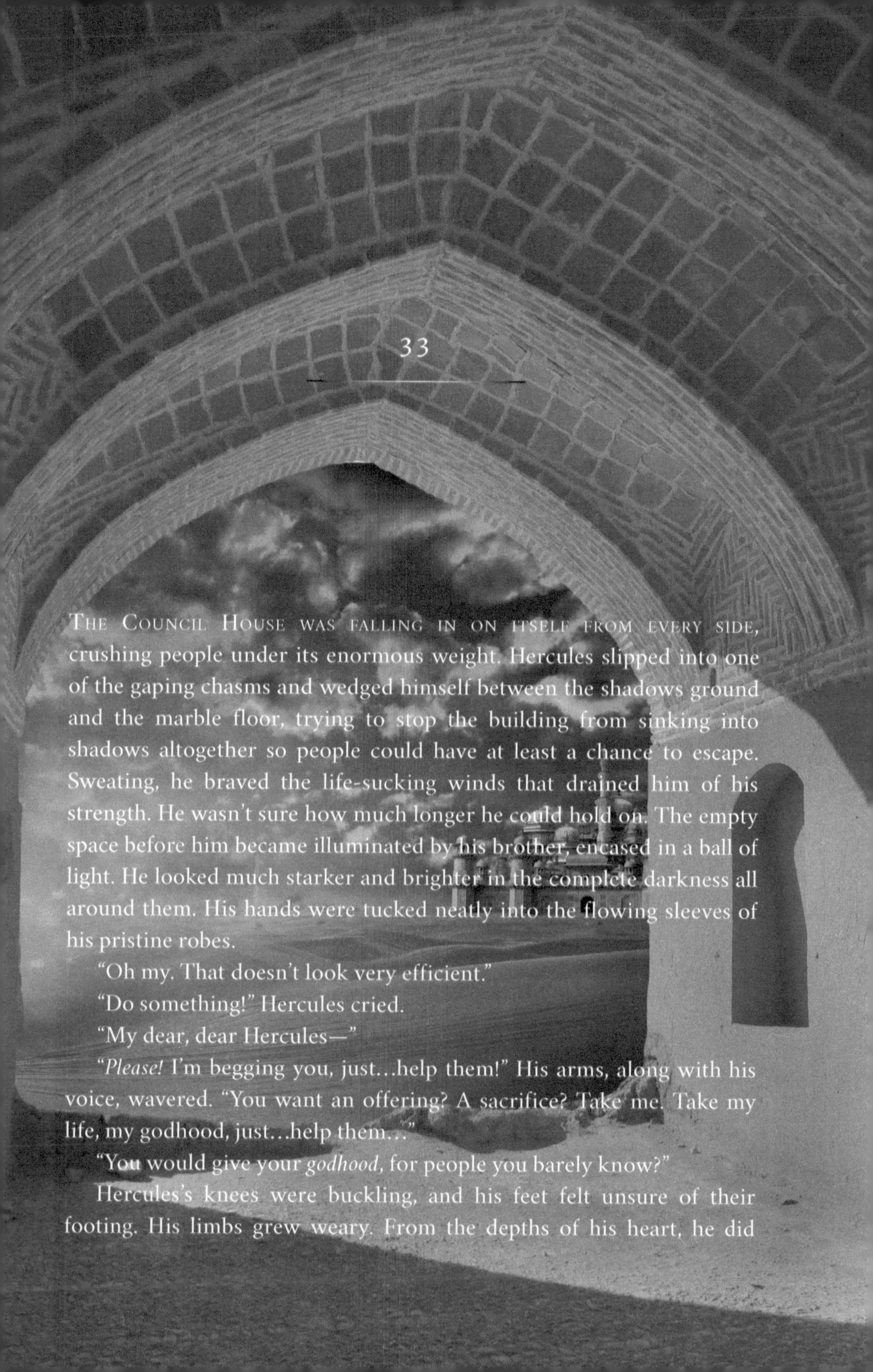

33

The Council House was falling in on itself from every side, crushing people under its enormous weight. Hercules slipped into one of the gaping chasms and wedged himself between the shadows ground and the marble floor, trying to stop the building from sinking into shadows altogether so people could have at least a chance to escape. Sweating, he braved the life-sucking winds that drained him of his strength. He wasn't sure how much longer he could hold on. The empty space before him became illuminated by his brother, encased in a ball of light. He looked much starker and brighter in the complete darkness all around them. His hands were tucked neatly into the flowing sleeves of his pristine robes.

"Oh my. That doesn't look very efficient."

"Do something!" Hercules cried.

"My dear, dear Hercules—"

"*Please!* I'm begging you, just…help them!" His arms, along with his voice, wavered. "You want an offering? A sacrifice? Take me. Take my life, my godhood, just…help them…"

"You would give your *godhood,* for people you barely know?"

Hercules's knees were buckling, and his feet felt unsure of their footing. His limbs grew weary. From the depths of his heart, he did something he never had before, not since he was a little boy who didn't know any better. He prayed.

"I'm nothing if I can't help them."

Apollo closed his eyes and bowed his head. Thunder rumbled in the distance. In an instant, Hercules was aboveground again.

He couldn't believe what he was seeing.

Shadows swirled away from the lightning that split the darkness with terrific force and illuminated the night. Each bolt pierced through the shadow like a javelin. The darkness curled up on itself in retreat. Hercules looked for his brother, but he was nowhere to be found. The sun dawned at last, beating down upon the city as if drawn in from the cosmos. Lightning bolts blasted the ground and shrank the shadows into the world's corners and then, all was quiet. The terror of the night had come to an end.

Hercules looked to the sun, grateful. Apollo's voice hummed softly in his head.

Farewell, brother. But beware—for as surely as day follows the night, wherever there is light, so must there be shadow.

34

THEY ATTACKED SWIFTLY AND WITHOUT MERCY. TRUE TO HIS NATURAL tendency, Dracula impaled a fair number of the hound-like beasts, though they didn't stay aloft for long. The shadows simply broke apart, withering away into the clean night air. In less time than it takes to blink, he shifted to suit his position and gain advantage over his opponent. The change between mist, wolf, and human was almost constant.

Luca remained in his true form and bullied his way through. Minute twists of his body and flicks of his wrist were all that were visible as he cut into those that descended upon him, piling atop him like a plague of rats. The charred dust that remained smeared his cheeks and dirtied his hands.

In a matter of seconds, the night was once again still. Dracula bared his teeth in a broad smile, swallowing invigorating gulps of night air. His eyes gleamed. Luca felt his father's heart race at having fought "the good fight," defending those who deserved it. It had been so long since he had done that. He felt the deep sense of fulfillment Dracula had at fighting alongside him.

Luca was in awe of what they had accomplished. And they were only two. He remembered how difficult it had been to take on two, three, or even four vampires at a time, how he'd only barely come out of those fights. It was unthinkable to imagine facing an army of vampires, as humans had tried and failed to do. They'd never had a chance. Vampires shared a powerful connection that was impossible to fathom, living and hunting as a clan with a hive mind, all drawn to a cool, calculating, charismatic sire.

He had never desired it before. Only after turning Kate had he understood the depth of that bond, how essential it was to his own well-being. Instead of it something to exploit, isolated and cut off from that connection, he felt the loss of what might have been. What he had destroyed. So that humans might live. Even though the human's he'd known had been no better than thieves, liars, and murderers. For the worst vampire, there was a human counterpart in equal measure.

With the battle finished, Luca and Dracula made their way to the forest where Icaryans had built their makeshift camp. In order to reach the others, they had to pass through the wall of fire protecting them.

Dracula paused at the threshold. His daughter-in-law's capacity to destroy him still haunted him.

Luca turned his gaze on him, not understanding. The elder vampire's hesitation lasted only a moment, and together with his son they passed through the barrier.

The camp came into view as the smoke cleared. The length of the perimeter spanned five lanterns high, interlocked in a tight pattern. They were fastened to all kinds of things: tent flaps, wooden boards, tree trunks, upended furniture. People left in such a rush, they were lucky to get out with what they did.

Corbin sought them out first. His eyes met Luca's in a solemn expression. Things were much worse than they had anticipated. All the same, Luca nodded his approval at Corbin's attempts to secure their encampment. The little creature dipped his head in acknowledgement. Then he handed Luca a rolled-up piece of paper. It seemed so small.

"I've been trying to account for everyone. The missing, the..."

Corbin cleared his throat and moved on, his message clear without having to spell it out. "There's not enough food. Also, I have rotating patrols across the perimeter. So far, we haven't seen any creatures or untoward movements in the darkness. I was in the process of gathering food, though with it being winter, I'm not sure how useful that will be. There are already people searching for nuts and berries that are inside the camp."

"I'll go," Luca said.

"But...you just got here. After all you've done..."

"There's more to do," Luca replied coolly. Corbin didn't bother arguing with that.

Luca's eyes shifted to his father.

Dracula was confident that his son's thoughts were not meant for hm, but it was so big a feeling that Luca couldn't contain it. It seeped out of his pores like a plea. He wanted to be alone. To avoid facing the people in the camp for as long as he could. The faces of those who had lost their families, everything they owned, and their questioning expressions, demanding why he was unable to protect them the way Kate might have, were too much. The signs of his failure as their protector, their king, surrounded him.

Dracula said nothing in response. He knew that feeling well, and knew there were no words in all the world to comfort his son. He only let Luca know that he could venture out into the forest, that those left with him would be safe. That, if they should need it, he would protect them in his absence. To his surprise, there was no mental pushback, no snide remark or narrowing of eyes. Luca took him at his word, and ambled into the forest alone.

LUCA DIDN'T WALK THROUGH THE FOREST. HE WANDERED, LEANING HIS hands more and more heavily on each tree as he passed them, blind and deaf to any potential food source lingering in the frozen wood. He dreaded the camp, and the scores of the brokenhearted. The bereft. He dreaded Kate's face when she became aware of his failure, the pain of it rending his soul in two. He kept it bottled up for now, giving her one more night of peace. But she would know come morning. He dreaded the dawn.

His inadequacy choked him, and he clutched the tree nearest him, digging his nails into the bark for support. He turned his nose high into the air to fill his lungs, and saw the crumbling castle, sloping downward to the right. In a day or so's time, the weight of it would carry it downward into the sea.

Luca's footsteps carried him to the foot of the castle. He traversed the wreckage, finding his way into the kitchen. Everything was in disarray, but the food was salvageable. He exited again, scanning the debris, until he found a toppled over roof. Any shingles that weren't missing entirely were badly cracked, held together by luck alone. Luca flipped it over, forcing the shingles to relinquish their hold. Using the upended wood beneath as a sledge, he ferried smoked and roasted meat, bread, cheese, and wine back to the camp. Atop his cache he laid coverlets, rigs, window dressings, anything he could find that could be a source of warmth. Fastened to his chest with thick rope, once a servant's bell pull, he carried the lot. He trudged through the forest back to the camp, digging in his heels as the sledge behind him scored deep tracks in the snow-covered dirt.

DRACULA SAT ALONE ON AN ERRANT TREE TRUNK THAT HAD LONG AGO fallen over. Allistair approached him with a bowl of hazelnut broth in hand. Dracula thanked him for it as Allistair took a seat to his right. The combination of heady herbs was warming and calming at the same time.

"Thank you," Allistair said.

It took a minute for him to get the words out, but when they came, it was all in a rush. "Thank you for saving my son's life. I'm in your debt."

"It was my pleasure."

Dracula had noticed the change in Corbin too. His demeanor toward him had softened. No one had forgotten what he had done to Rene, or Carla, or the threat he had posed to all of them as he unleashed the icy shadow of their queen into the world, but they did not deny the aid he had given them this night, that he had saved countless lives.

His ears pricked at the sound of something coming closer,

something sliding along the forest floor. He stood as his son reappeared with a sledge full of supplies.

The camp breathed a collective sigh of relief.

"Thank the Goddess for him," Corbin said. "I don't know what we'd do without him." True to his nature, Corbin was shrewd. The divergent paths of father and son were never far from his mind. To Dracula, Corbin said, "You should be proud of him."

Dracula was so proud words could not truly express it.

~

THE FACES THAT GREETED LUCA UPON HIS RETURN WERE BRIMMING WITH relief, not anger, when he arrived. No one looked at him sideways, no one asked any uncomfortable questions. Not one showed a hint of disapproval, or betrayal. Icaryans were sad, shaken, but they did not lay blame at his feet.

Luca was so relieved himself that he felt faint. He chided himself, fearing people who had never done anything but love and support him. Those fears lay only within himself, and it was time for him to join in their sorrows, for he was one of them.

Luca sat as Allistair rose, ceding his place on a fallen tree to him.

"Can I bring you some food?" Allistair asked.

Luca shook his head, and kept his gaze trained on the ground in front of him.

At a volume only Luca could hear, Dracula said, "You must eat. And keep your chin up. They'll take their cues from you."

Luca blinked, then lifted his chin, face pointed straight ahead, staring out a nothing in particular. Until Corbin returned. Luca could see the bunched muscles between his shoulder blades.

"What is it, Corbin?"

Corbin handed Luca the list he had been working on. It was not yet complete but at the bottom, Julian and Lilla were listed among the lost. Luca drew in a sharp breath.

"I heard...she fell," Corbin said. "And he wouldn't leave her."

Luca's hands trembled as he rolled the paper back up and handed it to Corbin.

The dam broke.

Luca's frame shuddered. He could no longer keep the tears in his eyes from falling. He felt his father's hand press on his shoulder. "Mircea…"

"Get your hands off me," he spat.

Dracula squeezed his shoulder harder, stood silent, and let his son cry.

35

Kate lay on her side, awake. Her eyes burned as tears welled up. She sobbed. She had seen, through Lucas's eyes, watched all through the night, as the castle tumbled into the sea, and lives were lost. She couldn't save them. Wasn't *there* to save them. She dragged herself out of her room and into the great room. The somber looks on her relations' faces told her there were more bad tidings.

They stared helplessly at her as she sat, the words too painful to speak aloud. The ticking of the grandfather clock on the wall struck the hour, calling itself violently to Kate's attention. It tolled nine—and yet it was as dark as midnight. The room was illuminated only by small lamps dotting the room's many nooks, and moonlight that was actually the sun, strong in this grove, and standing tall against the darkness.

Kate broke the heavy silence.

"Lowenherz has fallen."

The sleepless hollows in the eyes of father and grandmother deepened, their sorrow increased tenfold. Kate hung her head. She'd failed in her ultimate duty to protect Icarya from harm. All her magic, all her strength and courage, had not been enough to save them. She longed for the medallion that had for so long hung at her neck, and yearned for its power to make the world over. She began to doubt if she had too soon destroyed it to conquer one enemy, just to face another more powerful still.

"We've run out of time," her father said, his voice barely a whisper. She could sense that he felt the failure as his own.

Kate had taken their request seriously. She'd tried everything they had suggested in the hope of summoning the goddess and begging for her intervention. She was no closer to reaching the deity than she had been before she'd ever set foot in this hallowed place.

No one spoke for a while.

Movement at the corner of her vision caught Kate's attention. She rose from her seat. The grand tree just beyond the door caught her eye. It might have been a trick of the faux moonlight, or the howling of wind, but the tree looked like it was trembling.

Kate walked toward it, her gaze soaking in with wonder that it was not the wind that moved through the leaves, but rather that the violent shaking of the tree, trunk and all, *came from within*. Kate's eyelids began to feel heavy, and her limbs swayed in response to the tree's shuddering. She was senseless to her family, standing mute behind her.

Kate's skin tingled in the cold morning air. Her mind cleared like a fog bank that had been lifted, and her mind felt light, airy, unmoored. The rustling of the leaves, the stretching of the roots beneath her feet, flooded her head. Her eyes narrowed in confusion.

"What are you saying?" she whispered. She heard the tree's cry, its voice unnatural as it rushed to be heard.

Kate reached a tentative hand out to the trunk, to calm its shrieking. But its cries only thrummed against her palm and between her temples all the louder.

"What..."

Kate closed her eyes and listened.

~

Her family stood by with rapt attention as Kate spoke to the unmoving oak, not knowing what to expect, what Kate could possibly have expected.

KATE OPENED HER EYES, PULLING HER HEAVY LIDS OPEN AS OF WAKING from a dream.

"Wrong tree," she translated softly, "wrong tree."

She drew in a sharp, cold breath and her irises stretched open. She set her sights behind her, and sped headlong into the forest.

"Kate!"

Her father called after her, but she was too fast.

Kate raced through the wood like a wild thing, weaving maniacally between trees at such a pace that it was impossible for him to keep up.

She ripped the boots off her feet and discarded them as she came nearer to the forest's dark heart. The undergrowth barely rustled under Kate's feet as she flew through the wood, heedless only to the mindless pull that drew her further and further in.

Suddenly, she stopped. Before her stood a wizened tree. Beside it, a young girl, her hair and eyes soaking in all the light that shined from the late morning sky above her. The shadows bellowed and nipped at her heels, but could not conquer her.

The golden one's eyes were sad, and weary.

"Say our name," she pleaded.

Kate drew in long breaths. Her cheeks grew wet with tears.

"I can't leave him," she said, her voice trembling.

The goddess blinked, but said nothing. She didn't have to. Kate felt the weight of the golden one's stare, the weight of her choice. Luca, or the world.

Kate pressed her eyes closed, and stretched her spirit, beyond herself and bent the howling of the wind, the rushing of water, the crackling of ice and fire, and the dancing of the trees into harmony, for she was all these things, and the life they held. She came back to herself, and opened her eyes.

The golden one extended her hand. Kate reached out to grasp it. A blinding light enveloped them, and spread outward across the forest.

36

The forest dwellers of Castelmor took turns keeping watch and trying, as much as they could, to get some rest. Luca's sleep was interrupted by the sound of animals deeper in the forest. He rose, and followed the movement to a small gathering of creatures. There were none that he recognized. The furtive circle whispered a secret song. Luca's eyes went wide when he saw a figure, pale as a ghost, dancing and carrying on, leading them from the center.

Their ears pricked and they scattered. The forest was silent, as if they'd never been there at all. Dracula stood close behind him, peering at the scene from over Luca's shoulder.

Luca found his voice at last. "You saw that?"

He felt, rather than saw, his father nod behind him.

"In the middle. What did you see?"

"A child," Dracula answered. "A female child. Why?"

Luca shook his head. "I would swear…I saw my wife."

37

"Come now," Gideon said, "come close to me. I can still protect you, for a while at least." He flicked the tips of his feathers, and gestured for them to take shelter beneath them.

"*No,*" Ted insisted. "You're not giving up now. I need you."

"I'm sorry, Your Highness. But I'm afraid I must."

"I'm not a king, I told you."

Gideon's eyes shined with sadness, slowly overtaken with shadow. His golden coat dulled, and seemed to be fading away. "You'll always be a king to me."

"Gideon—" Ted devolved into sobbing, pushing his tear-streaked face into the gryphon's darkening mane.

Darien, Arjuna, and the rest huddled under the protection of the dying beast.

His wings fluttered as he breathed his last.

Thunder settled over them. Then the world ended with a deafening crack and a flash of blinding white as lightning struck.

38

Luca and his father led a scouting party to look for survivors trapped under castle rubble, or to retrieve further resources. They tried, and failed, to see any possible way to salvage the structure torn asunder.

"The night is free of monsters," Dracula said, "but the sun will not rise today, I think. We've done all we can. Your wife will decide the day."

"How will she?" Luca asked, overturning a bit of tower wall and finding nothing underneath. "What more can she do?"

A wry smile spread over the elder vampire's lips. "You must feel it."

"Feel what?"

"The power that runs through her veins."

Luca turned his head away. It was too personal, too intimate.

"Do you not see?" Dracula pressed. "Insects chatter and sing as she nears. Blades of grass, the branches of trees, bend in supplication. The wind howls and bows before her."

Luca shut out his words. "She has an attractive personality. It draws people to her."

Dracula shook his head. "It is more than that. She is the soul of this place. She *is* Icarya."

Luca tried to deny it. Yes, she had unspeakable power, and magic that filled him with as much wonder as dread, and yet, he felt that power tingle and slide down his throat to the ends of his hair as he drank lustily of her. But she wasn't just the center of the universe. She was the center of *his* universe. She was witty, and generous, and playful, perfectly flawed. Thinking of her sharpened his yearning, his fear of having to face her pain.

"I'm sorry. About your mother."

To Luca, it came out of nowhere. Dracula's words dragged him down one dark and bottomless rabbit hole to the next.

I'm not sure I am.

Then, from feeling rather than telling, Luca understood that his father was not sorry he had killed her. He was sorry he had *chosen* her.

"You deserved better. Better than I could give. The one who should have been your mother wouldn't have me. She didn't want this. Didn't want...what I am. I laid her bones in the ground eons ago. She loved the idea of you with all her soul." Dracula exhaled a ragged breath. "Hold dear to your wife, Mircea. If I'd have had a woman like her walking beside me, I might have been a man like you."

Something hard formed in Luca's throat, and filled his chest. It was several moments before he realized that the anguish that washed over him was not his own. When he looked to face his father, who turned and quit his side, he saw that his father's eyes were rimmed in red.

~

THERE WAS A CHANGE IN THE AIR—THE WAY THE WIND MOVED THROUGH the trees, and across the surface of the sea. Luca sensed Kate all around him, though she was nowhere to be seen.

"Something's happening," he whispered.

Others began to notice too. People's gazes shifted from one side to the other, searching for the cause of it all, their ears and noses, their very skin keen to the shift, but not its source. Animals without the power of speech began to squall and make a fuss, the way animals did when they sensed something coming. Every Icaryan, from the deer to the fauns to the squirrels and the birds knelt and touched their heads to the rubble and inhaled a deep breath as the world went white.

A bright whiteness was enveloping the world far in the distance. There was a panic, but it came on them faster than they could do anything about it. As the sudden whiteness washed over them, the world and all its creatures were swallowed up in it, holding their collective breath.

Luca was unfazed—he needed no breath to live. He existed alone in the whiteness, but felt his fear rise as Kate's essence faded again from his mind, spirited away from the world. Dracula gripped Luca's shoulder to steady himself. He was doubled over in pain. Without thinking, Luca clasped him, and their eyes met. His earnest concern was a surprise to both of them.

Luca was unable to help his father. Shadows—all the vampire's powers of the dark—were being ripped from him.

Luca sensed movement in the whiteness, but saw nothing ahead of him. The world was no more. He closed his eyes, searching for Kate through the void. In his mind's eye, he saw a pale pair of hands drawing all the world's shadows to itself, stripping the world bare until the world existed no more. The shadows shrank and shrank, coiled into a dense cloud as the hands began to press together, stamping the shadows out of existence. The last remnants flailed and thrashed violently, but the creature made of shadow could not withstand the pressure. The hands flipped over themselves in a crushing grip, the shadow between them snuffed out.

All was still. Then, Luca felt the warmth of the sun on his face. He looked down, and saw the pale shadow he cast grow long at his feet. The world breathed again. Lush grass rustled in the gentle breeze. He heard the scraping of stone against stone behind him, and spun round to see Lowenherz raising itself anew, the creamy bricks and indigo tiles of the roof glistening in the sun.

The call of gryphons filled the air on a distant hill. Luca caught sight a woman whose robes, skin, and even her hair shone a pale gold, except for a thick braid of familiar red on the left side of her head. Her stomach was flat.

Before Luca could rush to her, she was upon him.

Luca stared in terror at the sight of his wife's face, her features drained of their color even as she glowed with golden vivacity. The smile across her face was alien.

She did not recognize him.

His heart and mind searched frantically for Kate. She wasn't there. She didn't exist. It was as if she had never really existed at all. He sought the mind of the woman before him, but he could not penetrate the unspeakable power flowing from her.

Luca's knees failed him, and he sank to the ground.

"Wh-where is my wife?" he stammered, unable to stop his tears. He felt his father's hands pressed against his shoulder, and began to sob.

THE GOLDEN ONE FELT A DISTINCT, SEPARATE PRESENCE SLAMMING ON THE hidden doors of her mind. It was insistent, desperate in its pleading. Her greatest pain was fighting to live, to be. To remember.

Katelyn! My name is Katelyn! Katelyn! Katelyn! Katelyn! Katelyn! You promised *me!*

"PLEASE," LUCA IMPLORED, LOOKING UP AT THE GODDESS. "DON'T TAKE her away from me."

The goddess tilted her head, but did not answer him.

He hung his head, unconsolable in his grief. The air was filled with it. Then he felt a warm, soft hand on his cheek, beckoning him to look up. He did. Through tear-filled eyes, he saw Kate smiling down at him.

He was on his feet again in an instant, cradling his bride's face in his hands.

Luca's eyes wandered to the braid of golden hair hanging near the left side of her face. He fingered it gingerly. It was supple and luminous, just as the rest. He swallowed hard.

Are you a...a god?

Yes. Not now. Not anymore.

Luca blinked. He nodded even though he didn't understand.

"I am *yours*," she said, curling into his arms. "Forever yours."

They came together swiftly, wrapped in a tight, passionate embrace. They remained close together, even as their mouths parted. Luca's heart trilled at the sound of the smaller heartbeat echoing his own, warm inside Kate's protruding belly.

When they parted, her eyes flickered to Dracula.

He stared at her wide-eyed. His voice, when it came, was meek.

"What did you do to me?"

"You wished for your mortality," she said. "And so you have it."

Dracula looked down at himself, cowed by the truth of it. "I'm… human?"

"Did you ever stop being that?"

His eyes shifted to an indeterminate focus as he reflected on his long life, on the power he had gained, and the terrible deeds that had robbed him of his respect for life.

He turned his head to the side, taking in the sight of the castle made new behind him.

"You made some improvements," he observed.

Kate shook her head. "I always saw it like that." She smiled, and just then a small, pale child leapt brazenly up onto Kate's shoulders, wrapping her arms around her neck and kissing her cheek.

Luca and Dracula drew back at the sudden appearance of the golden child, her hair laced with a braid of Kate's brilliant red. Woman and child smiled at each other with the same wide, bright smile, before the girl hopped off Kate's back, scampering between her legs and then across the wide field before them on an invisible plane in the air, headed toward the Likhanni shore. She turned back to Kate.

Kate's chin jerked quickly in that direction, bidding her go. There were no words between them, only the music of the world as it thrummed back to life. The girl giggled, and ran, disappearing from sight across the horizon.

39

The lightning had stopped. Having lived his whole life in a desert, Darien had never seen the skies rage before. It was more terrifying than he could have imagined, even without the torrential downpour that usually went hand in hand with thunder. Those claps of fury shook the world. It had sucked the very air out of them, blanketing them in white as his little group inhaled a collective breath. That last bolt seemed to strike right at the heart of him. He didn't think lightning had the power to do that. When he was finally able to breathe again, he opened his eyes to a world no longer robed in shadow.

The world was quiet. The sun had returned, but it had not brought joy. Darien, along with his father, Arjuna, Alaric and Christine, the brothers Solimani and their mother, were stranded in the middle of the desert. They had no food, no water, And Gideon was dead.

Darien leaned against the ribs of the grand gryphon. His golden coat had turned dull and, one by one, his broad feathers came loose from their moorings. They scattered around the little promontory on which the group huddled, and were carried away by the whirling sands.

His father caught one. He had sprung up to snatch it before it drifted too far out of his reach. Now, in the blistering sunshine, it hinted at its former glory if he turned it in the light just the right way. Another tear fell down his father's cheek. But Ted didn't cry; he didn't make a sound.

None of them did, for there was nothing to say. The day had dawned, but the night's destruction remained.

A light, silvery sound rose Darien out of his solemn stupor. He jolted upright when he caught sight of a trail of impossibly small footprints heading their way.

"What..."

He clasped Arjuna's hand in his as he leaned forward, dislodging her head from his shoulder, where it had been lying for the last few hours.

Like a mirage in searing heat, one minute the golden child wasn't there, and then she was. Everywhere her feet touched, a puddle formed, so that by the time she was right in front of him, her toes were caked in mud.

They could all see her now, but no one said a word. There *were* no words, in the face of the little golden creature's intense state.

Darien squinted and tried to place her familiar features that were clearly defined and yet, at the same time impossible to grasp. But there was no mistaking his aunt's silhouette—the sharp lines of her nose, the high cheeks—and there was no way anyone could miss the streak of red woven through a braid at the child's left temple.

The impish girl seemed to have no interest in conversing with them. Everyone to a man shifted to the side as she approached, parting before her, eager to get out of her way.

She went straight to Gideon and fell upon his stiffened neck.

A small tinkling noise escaped her lips, like the frantic call of a bird in its death throes. Darien felt her pain in the very core of his being.

The child rose up, wiped the tears from her eyes, and pressed a kiss onto Gideon's beak.

"Oh!"

Ted's face brightened with joy as Gideon rose on his haunches. He shook the dust off his mane and flapped his broad, powerful wings, blasting them with a great gale, and sending Ted's tears far, far away.

"Oh Gideon, Gideon!" Darien's father laughed and buried his face in the winged creature's mane.

Gideon returned the affection, then turned his attention outward to the goddess whose kiss had once again given him life. He made a noise, deep within his throat. Only the girl seemed to understand, and she replied in kind.

She turned her gaze again to Darien. He swallowed hard as her limitless gaze ensnared him.

"You have forgotten me. *Remember*."

Then she was gone, a sprite on the wind.

"Darien?"

"Hmm?"

He heard his father calling, but had not yet regained the power of speech.

"Was that my—"

"Mmhmm," Darien answered.

"I…I don't understand."

Darien didn't either, but in his gut, he could feel it.

"She did it. It's over."

Arjuna collapsed in his arms. "Thank the gods."

The Solimani family fervently agreed and touched their heads in gratitude.

"*Goddess*," Darien corrected. But there would be time for that.

"Well, I don't know about the rest of you," Gideon said, "but I'm starving. And I feel like stretching my wings. Shall we go, and see what's left of Likhan?"

Darien nodded, but he didn't need to see. He already knew.

All of it.

40

Kate's face puckered. She doubled over and gripped Luca's shirt hard.

"Oh bugger me, never a moment's rest."

"What?" he cried, bracing her and clasping at her stomach.

"I think my water broke," she answered. Or tried to answer, before a groan swallowed it up. Luca swept Kate off her feet and raced back into the castle, shouting to crowds of stunned people that he needed help. That the baby was coming. Kate's family drew near to her as he rushed her to their chambers and laid her down on the bed. Sweat had already begun to collect on her brow.

He parted from her to usher in a parade of female servants, bringing in stacks of clean linens and water.

Kate growled.

"She's in good hands," one of the women said, shooing Luca out.

Her short, stertorous breaths devolved into a wail. "He stays!"

"I wasn't going anywhere," Luca soothed. He felt a hard grip on his arm yanking him out of the room and turned to face his father. He looked deathly serious.

"*Don't* go in there," he warned.

Kate's screams almost took the doors off their hinges. "Do I have to hypnotize myself?!"

Luca shook himself loose and rejoined his wife, shutting the doors behind him.

Dracula stood staring after him, mouth agape. Allistair came to stand beside him and did the same.

"He's dead," Allistair said.

"Uh-huh."

Luca was met with a tight scowl.

He centered all his focus on her and sliced through her pain. He saw the calm settle over her, and she exhaled, her expression one of pure bliss mixed with gratitude.

"I love you," she said.

"Nice to see you again too." He smirked.

Kate smiled up at him as he wiped her forehead. Then he took her head in his hands and pressed their foreheads together.

Meryn put herself in charge and brooked no argument. "Okay Katelyn, this baby's coming fast. When I say…push!"

Charlotte was born with a head of beautiful dark ringlets pasted to her head. She was the most perfect thing that Luca had ever seen. And she was all his. Meryn wrapped her up and handed her to him as she tended to Kate. The little princess opened her big blue eyes at him, and he could feel a rush of all her emotions, too big for her tiny, perfect little body. She was cold, and wet, and hungry, and scared and confused. He simply held her, staring into the starry depths of her eyes, and he felt her little mind sync with his. They were bound, forever. She was safe and warm and loved in his arms. Loved more than any child ever was. She smiled. Luca's heart was full.

"Kate," he croaked. "Katelyn." He passed their daughter to her, and saw the same wonder pass over her eyes as his girls—*his* girls—made the same connection. He knelt by the bed, holding his family in his arms, and wept with joy.

41

Darien clasped Hercules firmly with both hands.

"From the bottom of our hearts, we thank you. We will honor your brother for aiding us in our hour of greatest need."

"Don't," Hercules said sternly. "There'll be no more living with him."

Tsk. Why do you always feel the need to intervene? Can't you leave well enough alone?

42

Cyrene held the door open to let in those who had been waiting outside to see the queen and their new princess. Allistar cried and kissed his sister on the forehead.

Kaspar was the first to ask. “Can I hold her?”

Luca dropped to his knees and passed her to her cousin.

“When you get bigger, I’ll show you all the best hiding places,” Kaspar said. “We’re going to have such great fun together.” He looked up at Luca. “What’s her name?”

“Charlotte.”

“That’s real pretty. Kind of long, though.” He looked back down at her. “I’ll call you Charlie, for short.”

Luca smiled. “I think she’ll like that.” He took her back into his arms and stood up to see his father looking at him with glistening eyes. Luca had never seen the greatest vampire, lord of all shadows, so unsure of himself.

“Can I…” Dracula cleared his throat, and swallowed hard. “I never got to hold either of my children.”

Luca’s first reaction was to refuse him outright. Be he knew his father had no power. And he saw the honest eagerness, the mixture of joy and pain in his eyes. He passed her to him, and in an instant, she curled her finger around his slender pinky finger. Dracula smiled, and cooed to her in Romanian. He savored the moment, then returned the child to her mother.

"She's beautiful," he said.

"Thank you," Kate replied.

The moment she was out of his hands, Luca gripped him by the shoulder and yanked him out of the room.

"Wait!" Dracula cried.

But it was fruitless.

Luca dragged him down to a lonely corner of the dungeon, forced him on his knees.

"Our bargain is concluded," Luca said. His voice was ice.

Dracula forced back tears. "I was ready, for so so long. And now..."

Luca drew his sword. Dracula kept his eyes on the blade, and knew his son would show no mercy. There was no sign of forgiveness in his son's eyes.

He stretched his hands up in front of him in supplication. "Will you tell her that I love her? Tell her I wish I'd been a better man, that I wish I could have earned the right to watch her grow? Tell her—tell her that her grandfather gave his life, and his soul, for a god I'll never meet." Tears stained the ground before him. He sobbed, then moved his hands shakily, in the only way he could think to do, in the only way that mattered, touching his head, his heart, then his shoulders, left to right before bringing his palms together again.

Dracula bowed his head and bared his neck. "Strike me from her life, Luca, the way I struck myself from yours. I may be a demon, and I've made an eternity of mistakes, but I know at least I got that right."

A hard lump formed in Luca's chest, squeezing his throat and refusing to relinquish its grip. His hand trembled.

Luca...

Kate's calm, plaintive voice soaked into his head.

What would you have me do? The pause was short, and the answer firm.

What do you want to do?

~

DRACULA WAITED FOR THE COLD STING OF LUCA'S BLADE ON HIS NECK. But it didn't come.

"Dad?"

Dracula looked up, and saw his son standing over him, sword sheathed, hand outstretched.

His eyes shone in disbelief. He took the hand Luca offered him and got to his feet.

"*Fiul meu.* My son," he said, clasping his shoulders and pulling him into a tearful embrace. He kissed one cheek, then the other. "My little Miru."

He clapped his hand on the back of Luca's neck, and pressed their foreheads together.

All the tension that had built in Luca's veins since the first day he'd been left alone with his mother—all the confusion, the loneliness, the sadness, and the anger—all melted away in his father's embrace. He'd come back for him. He had finally come home.

~

LUCA AND HIS FATHER RETURNED TO WHERE KATE LAY RESTING WITH THE baby asleep on her chest. She smiled at them as they walked side by side.

Cyrene sighed, exhausted, and leaned back in her chair at the edge of the bed. "This family keeps getting bigger and bigger."

"Darien should be with us too," Allistair said.

"He will be," Kate answered. "All of Likhan will. We came through the night together. One Icarya. One family."

Allistair looked to his sister, and nodded. "One Icarya."

Meryn, moved to tears, put her heart to her chest, looking around her, at her grandchildren. "I wish your grandfather was here."

"Me too," Kate said.

"I wish I'd met him," Allistair said.

Meryn smiled. "You did. A long, long time ago."

Kate smiled. "I *knew* it!"

Meryn blushed in acknowledgement. "We got so used to keeping our love a secret, it became a way of life. One that was never really undone. Maybe it's time," she said. "Time our story was told."

EPILOGUE

Late into the night, Luca watched Kate and Charlotte sleeping nose to nose. He sat and stared, etching the image onto his eternal memory. After a long while, he lay down beside them, and wrapped his arms around them both. Kate opened her eyes. She worried that they wouldn't have many moments like this, just the three of them. There were always too many people around, vying for their attention. A thought passed between them, neither one of them sure who thought it first. They smiled. Luca got up again and packed some clothes, and some blankets. Together they snuck into the kitchen. Luca grabbed bread, fruit, cheese, and slung the lot over his shoulder. They were caught out by Georg.

Kate flushed as she clutched Charlotte's sweet little head to her neck. Georg did not need an explanation.

"Take a little treat, for the little queen." He kissed Charlotte on the head, then Kate, and went back to bed. When they reached the shore, Luca pulled the boat sideways to allow Kate to get in as she clutched Charlotte to her breast. The baby started to rustle, and let out a little whimper.

"No, no, my love, don't cry." Kate lowered the left side of her dress down past her shoulder. Charlotte settled again against her mother's warm skin and fed. Luca slipped the satchel into the middle of the boat and shoved off, grabbing the oars and pointing their boat toward O'loa.

Thank you for reading! Did you enjoy? Please add your review because nothing helps an author more and encourages readers to take a chance on a book than a review.

And don't miss more from Kathryn Troy with THE SHADOW OF THERON available now. Turn the page for a sneak peek!

Also be sure to sign up for the City Owl Press newsletter to receive notice of all book releases!

SNEAK PEEK OF THE SHADOW OF THERON

It would have been a pleasant day, if not for the hanging.

The sun glistened off the newly constructed gallows—it was not often Lighura had a public execution—and people greeted each other in the square, staking out spots with a good view as they consumed their sweet buns and boiled eggs.

Lysandro was not hungry. He couldn't see how good people could be content to stuff themselves before a man was set to die, before the stench of a man expiring in his own piss filled their nostrils. He could smell it already.

Kato brushed against his elbow.

"You'll be able to see better from here, Don de Castel."

"I can see all I care to from here, thank you."

The innkeeper nodded. "As you say, Signor. But if you change your mind—"

Lysandro nodded and planted his feet on the ground, fists clenched at his side.

The crowd snapped to attention as the door to the magistrate's office opened. Lysandro's stomach soured at the sight of Marek. He exuded a sense of utter disinterest in the events of which he himself was the director. But Lysandro saw the glint of malice in Marek's eyes that he was unable to hide. He relished the power over the life and death of the wretch behind him, his broad chest inflated with self-importance. In short, Lysandro loathed him.

His attention turned to the bound man following the magistrate. Two of Marek's officers stood beside him and another behind, forming a diamond around the condemned. It was clear this man would not go easily to his death.

He writhed and twisted his body to get away from the men holding him, one at each elbow, kicking and flailing his legs out in a childlike tantrum. He was so focused on trying to escape their grip that only inchoate groans passed his lips. When they ascended the steps to the platform, the man's struggling became more desperate, more violent. The crowd gasped when the man wrangled one arm free, and it looked like he might escape. But he fell to the ground as two of Marek's men fumbled after him, fighting to keep him in their grip. They forced him to his feet again.

Without saying a word, Marek turned to face his underlings. They redoubled their efforts, squeezing the prisoner tight between them until his feet barely touched the ground. The man's struggling didn't cease, but his range of motion was now severely restricted. The captive's eyes went wide in fear, showing the whites of them like a man held in the throes of a hysterical fit.

Drop back, Lysandro thought. He couldn't stop his mind from racing through all the ways the man might free himself. If he could just loosen their hold on him again, he could run. But he'd never make it. Not without help.

When Marek turned his face to the crowd, his eyes had narrowed to murderous slits, and his jaw was tightly clenched to preserve the façade of a smile that he wore there. He lifted his chin and addressed those who had gathered:

"People of Lighura—Jair Oreyo is guilty of killing Don Aldo Carras, who caught him stealing silver. His crime was discovered by his widow, Doña Sofia Carras, who tripped over her husband's body when responding to his screams."

Lysandro heard the gasps of those around him as Marek recounted the grisly details. Marek was either too stupid or too cruel to show more consideration for Carras's family. They stood huddled together in a tight circle, their faces pointed at the ground, while Marek expounded on the way Don Aldo's brains had been bashed against the stairway of their own home and turned the entryway slippery with blood. The women and children who congregated in the square turned their heads away from the platform as if to shut out Marek's words and shield themselves from the nightmares such lurid descriptions were bound to produce.

Lysandro could feel his face flushing hot. A good man's guts were being strewn about with words. That he couldn't stifle them turned him livid.

Seemingly sated by his talk of violence, Marek shifted to patting himself on the back for a job well done. He turned to his officers and beckoned with a small gesture for the prisoner to be brought forward. His men accomplished it, but with great difficulty.

"Any last words?" he asked in a cool, collected tone.

Jair was foaming at the mouth. Lysandro could see the veins on his neck bulge as his face went purple with rage, and he lunged at Marek.

"Liar!"

Lysandro's ears pricked up. Alarm bells rang in his head like the one in the temple tower—a full-throated clang that deepened his suspicion.

"Murderer!" Jair shouted. "You're just as guilty as me!"

He pled with his captors, who rammed the noose around his neck. "Don't listen to him, he's a liar! *Stop,* or he'll do the same thing to you!"

The knife tucked up Lysandro's sleeve prodded him at the wrist. He calculated the distance and the force it would take to sever the rope swinging from the beam.

He could do it. Avoiding notice, though—that would be another matter entirely. But something else stopped him from sliding the hidden blade into his hand.

You're just as guilty as me.

Jair was a murderer; he just wasn't alone.

The corner of Lysandro's mouth twitched as the officers tightened the noose around Jair's throat, but his fingers remained loose at his side.

~

The blood in Lothan Marek's veins hissed in fury as his brothers dragged Jairo, kicking and screaming, toward the noose. He was being ridiculous. It was one thing to steal from the poor, and another to murder a pillar of the community and think no one would notice. Lothan had no choice but to act. And Jair had the gall to call him out in front of the whole village.

His behavior worked in Lothan's favor. He was acting like a lunatic with his hair on fire, and Lothan expected people to discount his exclamations as the ravings of an almost dead man. Jair's outrage was Lothan's shield, so long as he kept the anger from his face.

Jair had been effective at his job; his taste for brutality had served him well on occasion. He was perhaps the strongest among them, excepting Lothan himself, and it was a bitter shame to kill him. Almost.

All those who shared his blood were a greedy, groveling, worthless waste of a power that should have been his alone. Today brought him one step closer to the magic scattered across their veins being made whole.

Lothan quashed his annoyance as Jair squealed and squirmed to the last minute, wriggling like a worm until the floor gave way beneath him and silence reigned over the square, heralded by a definitive, satisfying crack. Jair's latent power shivered up Lothan's spine. The surge of energy buzzed through him like a current, crackling at his fingertips and the ends of his hair. It was delicious. But not nearly enough.

Lysandro was grateful for the silence; it was infinitely better than a roar of cheers would have been. The Carras family remained clustered together as the knot of onlookers unfurled itself, and people returned to their routines to try to forget what they'd seen. Lysandro made his way toward them. Marek approached at the same time, holding a large wooden box in his hands.

"Doña Carras," he said, presenting her with the recovered silverware.

He looked so pleased with himself.

Don Aldo's widow stared at him, then took the box into her hands with a dumb expression on her face.

Lothan furrowed his brows. "This *is* your stolen silver, is it not? I imagined its return would bring you some comfort." He had to fight to keep the bite out of his voice.

Lysandro could hold his tongue no longer.

"Perhaps she'd be more grateful if you'd preserved her husband's dignity, rather than turn his final moments into a spectacle."

Marek looked up at him, his eyes bright with challenge.

"Or perhaps they'd have been grateful if you had arrested Jair weeks ago, after he'd already been accused of thievery by the blacksmith. Granted, his family's possessions are humbler than this fine collection," Lysandro continued, gesturing at the box of silver, "but had your justice been swifter—"

The widow sobbed, and Lysandro let his accusation hang in the air.

"The blacksmith's account was not reliable. He was not as—"

"Worthy of your attention?" Lysandro offered. His mouth set into a hard line. "I shouldn't need to remind you that the office of magistrate is bound to protect *all* of Lighura, not just its wealthier citizens."

Lothan scowled.

"What did you lie about?" Lysandro asked.

"Excuse me?"

The abrupt turn took Marek by surprise. Lysandro lifted his gaze over Marek's shoulder to the hanged man. "With his last breath, he called you a liar. What did you lie about?"

Marek huffed through his nose and shifted on his feet like a bull in a pen.

"He called me a murderer too. Do you also accuse me of that?"

Marek fixed him with a venomous stare. Doña Sofia's hand flew to her mouth, and her younger children hid their faces in her voluminous black skirts.

Lysandro didn't flinch.

He waited for an answer with feigned curiosity. Marek had walked into the trap himself. Lysandro wasn't about to help him out of it.

Marek's gaze slid to the widow. "I did my duty here today. No one can say I didn't." He turned his back on them both and left.

Doña Sofia let out a sigh of relief. "Thank you."

"Someone had to say something."

She looked down again and brushed her fingers against the grain of the box Marek had given her as her children came out of hiding. Lysandro smiled at them and ruffled the younger boy's hair before turning his gaze back to their mother.

"Is there anything you need?" he asked.

"We'll be all right. Thank you again."

Lysandro nodded and looked to her eldest son. "Take good care of them."

The young don was a strapping teenager, who tried to act older than he was by appearing to be unmoved by the whole affair. He was managing it badly. The boy's eyes darted from one end of the square to the other, not finding an answer to the question forming on his lips.

"There's so much to go through. So many papers. I don't even—"

"There's nothing that can't wait a few days' time," Lysandro interrupted. "I'll come see you soon, help you get everything sorted. Let's see if we can't make any sense of it."

"Thank you."

"It's my pleasure," he replied. "Take care."

Before departing from the square himself, Lysandro spared one last look at the hanged man, cast in silhouette by the sun's rays as Marek's officers worked to cut him down. Lysandro wondered at all he might have inquired of the dead man—all the questions he could never ask.

The cheerful weather was wasted on the somber mood that hung over the dusty little village until nightfall. Lysandro called on his father for a late supper, having finally found his appetite after a full day's abstinence. He greeted the doorman genially.

"Good evening, Diego."

"Good evening, Don Lysandro. You'll find him in the dining hall this evening."

"The dining hall?" Lysandro asked. "Does he have guests?"

"No, Signor. He simply said he longed for some formality."

Lysandro raised an amused eyebrow. He thanked the man and headed through the familiar hallways of the house in which he had grown up and found his way to his father. Don de Castel the elder was already seated at the head of a long wooden table in an elegantly papered room of cream and burgundy. Cheeses, warm bread, and a stiff fortified wine lay fanned out before him.

"Standing on ceremony today, Father?" Lysandro asked, seating himself at his father's right hand and pouring himself a drink.

"Indeed," Elias answered, not looking up from his plate as he tore off a piece of bread from a larger loaf and soaked it in a spiced olive oil.

"In your dressing gown?" Lysandro asked.

Elias grunted in the affirmative. "It's my best one."

Lysandro smiled and took in the image of his father. His robe was one of fine fabric, luxurious and warm against the chill in the air coming off the sea. The wine-colored gown was elevated by an intricately embroidered scroll pattern, with golden threads woven into the cuffs and collar. His father's face was thin, but sharp, and marked by an imposing chin and a well-kept, respectable beard of silver to match the hair smoothed back on his head. Yes, Lysandro thought, his father looked every ounce a don.

"Marek hung Carrass's murderer today," Lysandro said.

"Mm."

"How *he* got to be magistrate I'll never know."

"That's easy. You didn't try for it."

Lysandro sipped at his wine. "Surely there are other able men in this village."

"There's so much influence you could wield, if only you would. There's no one sitting on the Andran Council now for Lighura."

"I doubt the Council would take kindly to my views."

"You still think you should give up all your land, and have it owned by the peasants who live there?" Elias asked.

"I clearly can't manage it on my own. Why *shouldn't* they own the fruit of their labors?"

"Without their rents you would be impoverished."

"I've known many men poorer than I who lead much happier lives."

Elias reclined in his high-backed seat and studied his son's reserved expression. "The social season starts in a few days. Will you attend the opening ball?"

Lysandro's heart constricted at the mention of it. He tried to dodge the question by digging into the slice of pork loin on his plate, but his father's expectant stare was unwavering.

"Why?" Lysandro asked, swallowing. "So I can mix with ladies almost ten years my junior and talk about the latest fashions?" Women saw his wealth and his title, and little else.

"That problem will get worse the older *you* get without choosing a bride. You're almost thirty."

"I seem to have exhausted my prospects."

"You only need to choose one."

If only there was *one*, Lysandro thought. *Just one*.

"You ask too much," Elias said.

"I just want what you had with Mother. Is *that* too much?"

Elias's eyes softened. "No. Maybe some travel would be in order. You've always longed to see Mirêne for yourself."

"Perhaps." Though Mirêne was more attuned to the Goddess's loving and more artful face, and better reflected Lysandro's own inclinations, he couldn't leave Lighura now—not after what had happened. There was a tension in the air, a sense of trouble brewing into something darker. More sinister.

He returned home and descended into the cavernous rooms carved out from underneath his estate. The space was sparsely furnished, with only a small dresser and a low bed covered in soft, dark furs. Wax puddled at the bases of the wrought-iron candelabras that flanked the corners of the room and lent it their dim light.

Lysandro considered what his father had said. He might find more in common with the people of Mirêne, but his heart belonged to Lighura too. Lysandro couldn't leave the fate of its people in the hands of Marek. Lysandro's belief that he was a thief and a murderer was stronger than ever. But he needed proof to remove him. Proof that might finally be within reach.

The trading ship that had quit the port yesterday had left heading north, rather than back the way they'd come. It would be easy for them to round to the other side of the coast unseen, rather than out to sea.

He stripped down to his skin and donned much simpler attire, dyed black to blend with the coming night. The worn fabric often felt more familiar and reassuring to him than the fine clothes he wore in the daytime. Too fancy an outfit would give him away and would more than likely get in his way. He didn't wear any metal or ornamentation that might glint in the moonlight; he had to be able to weave in and out of the darkness unseen. He completed his ensemble with a broad hat, leather gloves, and a sword honed to a fine point. He wrapped a strip of black cloth tightly around his face, revealing only his eyes, and tucked his long hair, kept in an older, more distinctive style, inside his shirt.

Lysandro abhorred violence. In the full light of day, it went against the example of kindness he worked so hard to set. But the edge of a sword carried a certain sense of rightness. So he sought justice from the shadows.

~

Lighura's coast was too small to be a true harbor. It could only manage two ships at once, three in an emergency. Tonight, as most nights, the port was empty, leaving the water to creep slowly up the narrow beach without disruption. The only sounds for miles were the breaking of the surf and the call of gulls. But Lighura had pride of place in Andras. Aside from its beautiful coast, it was reputed to be the birthplace of the hero Theron, though exactly *where* he had lived had been lost to the passage of time.

As Lothan made his way down the sloping path to the shore, past the grass-covered dunes and toward the thin strip of sand, he spied the merchant vessel he sought approaching from a distance. They were still too far away for Lothan to tell if they carried any genuine relics aboard. If they truly possessed what they claimed, he would know—just as the work of Argoss sang in his veins, the lingering sense of the goddess sent his skin crawling. The only thing he felt in that moment was the blade pulsing against his abdomen. Under his coat blossomed the scent of fresh blood—a river's worth of it.

The drums of the broken metal shard's magic beat furiously between his ears. It was perhaps the only proof in the whole world that the goddess had failed—Argoss may have lost his life, but his sorcery was beyond her ability to destroy. A hot determination overcame Lothan as he brushed his fingers against the makeshift handle at his belt, drenching them in gore. What the goddess's whores insisted did not exist was his birthright, to bend and shape to his will. It had eluded him until now, with no clean or clever way to adhere the bleeding metal to the handle of his cheap knife, no symmetrical point or edge to pull them neatly together. But Jair's energy had come to roost in him, and he willed the broken fragment to cling to the grip. This time, it had obeyed.

The flow of blood racing along its jagged edge made him sticky, lapping at his skin like a wonton lover. It turned his blood feverish, and made his mouth run dry. He licked his lips as a distraction.

The sense of triumph he had first experienced when the shard had come into his possession had waned. What good did it do him if he couldn't find a way to salvage what remained of the once-mighty Blood Sword? It was so small. And he was not a blacksmith or a sorcerer. At least, not in the true sense of the word. He'd managed to find its location, and had it transported from the farthest edges of Andras without raising suspicion, but that had been accomplished through instinct and sheer luck. The "why" of it eluded him. It was a constant source of frustration. When Lothan jabbed it through the air for the first time to test it, blood didn't fly off the edge in a venomous spray, which was a bit of a disappointment. But this was only one piece—Lothan consoled himself with the prospect of finding more, and one day wielding the full blade without squandering its power as Argoss had.

He had half a mind to slay his brothers right where they stood and take back from them what was his. But he was tied to his post, and much of what he craved lay beyond his grasp. He needed them. Although at this particular moment, the furtive glow of the lanterns on the beach was infuriatingly stationary. Lothan quickened his steps, and almost barreled into Jenner.

"What are you doing just standing there like an idiot? Spread out! Who do you have on the cliff?"

"That was Jair's job, Lord Lothan."

Lothan stared at him, and the man's legs nearly buckled as he spun on his heel and hurried to do the job himself.

They scattered at his command, taking up their positions as the ship made land.

Lothan was incensed by the illicit goods as they received the smugglers. They had only trinkets to offer— illustrated pages and "blessed" bits of junk, useless things that allowed deluded fanatics to feel nearer to the goddess and their hero—but nothing that bore the mark of Argoss. They had promised him more. They had promised him the Cerulean Key. Lothan did not take kindly to being lied to.

He turned to the man standing at his left and whispered in his ear.

"Get Gorin down here."

His brother retreated up the cliff face to recall the lookout. The more of them Lothan had nearby, the quicker he could dispatch the two-faced captain and his crew.

Lothan was still waiting for the pair of them to come back down when Jenner handed the captain his money. The captain in turn handed it to his second, who scurried up onto the boat. Lothan shot a piercing look to the cliffs, but neither man was anywhere in sight. He'd just about lost his patience when a single head popped into view.

"He's gone!"

"What do you mean, gone?"

"Like he's just vanished into thin air."

Lothan's skin prickled. Then he heard a scream, and a splash. That's when he knew they were not alone.

The sailors aboard the ship drew their swords, but it was useless against an invisible enemy. One man came flying in their direction and landed face-first in the mud. Another two, from Lothan's vantage point, seemed to disappear entirely, as if the floor had opened up from under them. Pandemonium erupted on the small vessel, but no one could discern the cause.

"It's him!"

"It's the Shadow of Theron!"

Marek's men watched but made no move to help, their eyes round in the lantern light. They grew skittish, wavering in place like horses ready to bolt.

He screamed at his men —better they fear him than some impostor who styled himself after a ridiculous excuse for a god. But his raging was drowned out by another voice that echoed across the sea.

"Ho, there! Looking for this?"

The Shadow of Theron appeared out of the darkness. He stood balanced on the thin outcropping of the ship's prow, with the sack of coins Jenner had just given over to the captain dangling from his hand.

The realization that he'd snuck past the lot of them without so much as a ripple out of place seized Lothan with a fit of rage. For too long, the Shadow had plagued him. Whenever he had come close to achieving even the smallest of his aims, Theron's Impostor had been there; he always knew the precise moment to strike, and always came away laughing—leaving Lothan chasing after him like an empty-headed fool. He reached for the bleeding dagger at his belt.

Not this night.

"Get him!" the captain shouted.

Jenner lunged for the chest, but the captain kicked the lid shut with his boot and caught him by the hand.

"No money, no trade!" The captain scooped up the ill-gotten treasure and sped back to the ship. The sailors seemed to have the Shadow cornered, stuck as he was on the thin bowsprit poking out over the water, but he batted their swords away with ease, their seething violence no more than a child's game to him. He pretended to lose his balance and flung the coins far out to sea.

A blood vessel in Lothan's neck threatened to burst; the smugglers howled in indignation. But when they charged him, he cut one of the lines connected to the foremast and used it to sail clear across the water to the stern. He bounded off the ship and landed on the beachhead with the grace of a jungle cat. He turned his back on Lothan, not showing a care in the world, and waved the ship off.

"Safe journey! Be careful of those rocks, they're trickier than they look!" Then he returned his gaze to the men on the beach, and grinned.

All Lothan needed was to get close enough to deliver one small slice.

But the Shadow was untouchable. He dodged Marek and his men with nimble steps at every turn, cutting through their number as he stayed always just a hair's breadth out of reach.

In a matter of minutes, Lothan's lieutenants lay sprawled flat in the sand, bloodied and unconscious. Lothan slowly worked to close the circle tighter and tighter as the Shadow danced around him. He was close enough now that the Shadow could see what it was that Lothan held; the broken blade shimmered brilliantly in the moonlight. The Shadow grew more careful, pushing Lothan to the brink of his endurance.

Lothan shot him a grim smile and tried to knock him off his balance.

"Was Theron himself such a coward in the face of great magic, or is that just you?"

But the Shadow was relentless, and deftly avoided his blows.

Lothan was rewarded for his patience. He thrust straight ahead, causing the Shadow to twist away to the side. But instead of righting himself, Lothan stepped into the dodge, leaving himself exposed, and retracted his arm back at rapid speed.

It was a shallow cut on the upper arm, nothing more. But Lothan felt the edge of the blade bite through the Shadow's sleeve, and the soft release as it rent open his flesh. The tang of blood filled the air as the tiny droplets joined the flood along the enchanted metal. The Shadow staggered backward, his chest heaving.

Lothan shivered in triumph. But he didn't stop. He struck again, aiming high for the head. The Shadow of Theron deflected the blow with more force than Lothan thought possible. But the power that pulsed at his fingertips didn't lie. Lothan stood grinning in the moonlight as the Shadow turned and ran for his life, although he was somewhat perturbed by the Shadow's speed. He shouldn't have been able to run at all.

The others were rising from the ground as his enemy shrank back into the shadows.

"Where did he go?"

"Should we go after him?"

"Let him be," Lothan said, a devilish grin on his face. Lothan was giddy, drunk with victory. "I cut him. With this." He held out the vermillion remnant of the Blood Sword of Argoss. His brothers gaped and dropped again to their knees, pressing their heads back into the sand.

"It may not be what it was. But if it has even a fraction of its old force...he won't live through the night."

Don't miss more from Kathryn Troy with THE SHADOW OF THERON available now and discover all the books at kathryntroy.blogspot.com

The powers of old are fading. A new Age is dawning.

Holy relics are all that remain of Theron's sacred legend.

Now those relics, the enchanted weapons forged by the Three-Faced Goddess to help Theron defeat the wicked Sorcerer Argoss, are disappearing.

Lysandro knows the village magistrate Marek is responsible, and he searches for proof disguised as the masked protector the Shadow of Theron.

But when Marek wounds him with an accursed sword that shouldn't exist, Lysandro must find a way to stop Marek from gaining any more artifacts created by the Goddess or her nemesis.

The arrival of the beautiful newcomer Seraphine, with secrets of her own, only escalates their rivalry.

As the feud between Lysandro and Marek throws Lighura into chaos, a pair of priestesses seeks to recover the relics and return them to safekeeping. But the stones warn that Argoss is returning, and they must race to retrieve Theron's most powerful weapon.

While they risk their lives for a legend, only one thing is certain. The three temples to the Goddess have been keeping secrets: not just from the faithful, but from each other.

Please sign up for the City Owl Press newsletter for chances to win special subscriber-only contests and giveaways as well as receiving information on upcoming releases and special excerpts.

All reviews are **welcome** and **appreciated**. Please consider leaving one on your favorite social media and book buying sites.

For books in the world of romance and speculative fiction that embody Innovation, Creativity, and Affordability, check out City Owl Press at www.cityowlpress.com.

ACKNOWLEDGMENTS

Thank you to all the folks at City Owl Press that helped this book, and this series, become a reality. A heartfelt thank you to all my readers for their support and their patience as I completed this series. Sam, Robin: you are my rockstars. Your support got me to the finish line. From the bottom of my soul, thank you for everything.

ABOUT THE AUTHOR

KATHRYN TROY is a historian by day, author by night. She lives on Long Island with her two kids and an army of rats. She likes to write what she reads —fantasy, romance, gothic fiction, historical fiction, horror, and weird fiction. When she's not writing or reading or teaching, she's either playing a board game, watching a horror movie, traveling, making croissants, or adding some new weird creepy cool thing to her art collection.

kathryntroy.blogspot.com

ABOUT THE PUBLISHER

City Owl Press is a cutting edge indie publishing company, bringing the world of romance and speculative fiction to discerning readers.

Escape Your World. Get Lost in Ours!

www.cityowlpress.com

facebook.com/YourCityOwlPress
x.com/cityowlpress
instagram.com/cityowlbooks
pinterest.com/cityowlpress

www.ingramcontent.com/pod-product-compliance
Lightning Source LLC
Chambersburg PA
CBHW030020060826
49398CB00031B/157